Writing on the Wall

CINDY RAS
A ROMANTIC COMEDY

This is a work of fiction. Names, characters, places, and incidents either are the product of the author's imagination or are used fictitiously. Any resemblance to actual persons, living or dead, events, or locales is entirely coincidental.

Copyright © 2024 by Cindy Ras

All rights reserved.

No part of this book may be reproduced in any form or by any electronic or mechanical means, including information storage and retrieval systems, without written permission from the author, except for the use of brief quotations in a book review.

Book Cover by Cindy Ras

Editing by Katie Savoie

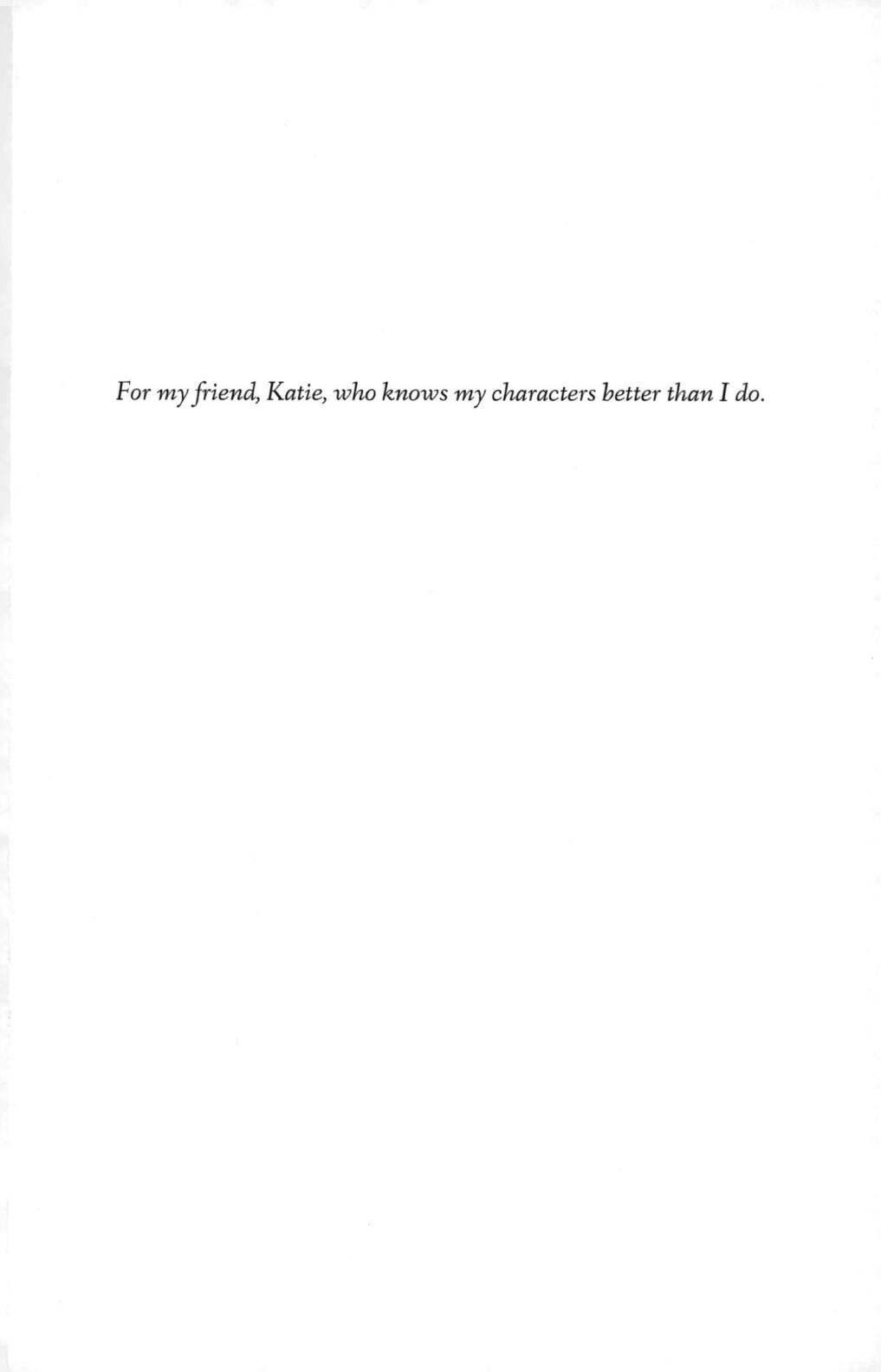

For my friend, Katie, who knows my characters better than I do.

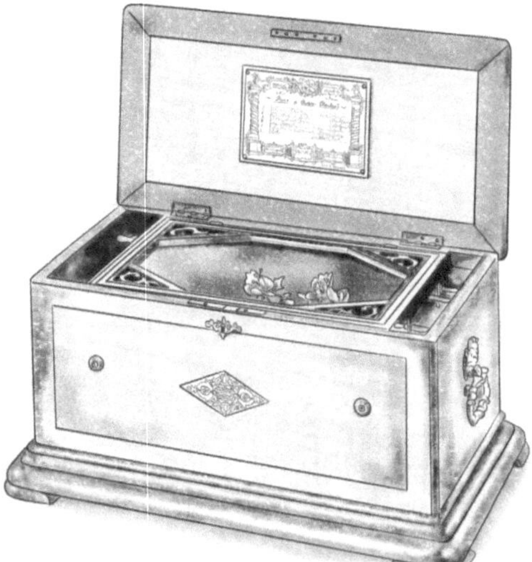

CHAPTER ONE

IVY

"Come on, Ross. Pick up, pick up, pick up!"

I lean on the bare kitchen counter with one hand, hating the echo of my voice within the empty room. I fix my eyes on the moving boxes scattered across the living room as I wait for Ross to answer my call.

A guttural growl escapes after I hang up. I can't believe my brother left me in this position.

The doorbell rings, making my shoulders drop, but I refuse to let defeat drape its heavy cloak over me. *Everything will be okay.*

I roll my shoulders back, forcing my chin up as I swing the door open with a tight smile. "Hey, Carl," I greet the man at my doorstep, and he removes his hat as he takes a tentative step inside.

"We still..." He motions sheepishly to the boxes with his hat in hand.

"Yup."

"Right." He takes a step into the hall to signal someone

with a nod. A string bean of a man joins us, tightening one of those back support belts around his waist.

"Mornin', Miss Ivy. We'll take good care of your things till you're ready for 'em. Don't you worry."

"Appreciate it." I smile back, dragging a hand over the box with my *The Lord Of The Rings* DVD's inside. Why am I still hanging on to these? Everything is digital now. "I've gotta get to work. Thank you, Carl. You can leave the door key on the counter on your way out. And remember, don't say anything to Gran."

I'm taking a huge risk by getting the man who works as a security guard at Gran's retirement village to put all my things in storage. But he owes me a favor, and I'm officially desperate enough to cash it in. Still, I'll have to be careful. The last thing I need is Gran catching wind of my current situation.

"You gonna be okay getting the small things to your friend's house?"

"Oh, uh...yup. I'll manage. This is a huge help, Carl. Thank you again." I shoot him another smile as I offer a quick side hug.

My left heel bounces as I drive to the school where I teach second grade. I fear the sudden change in my life will be glaringly obvious to my coworkers, and my stomach knots from the combination of hunger and anxiety as I park in the teachers' lot. I skipped breakfast and spent the morning stuffing things into my car, so I guess it's the mystery basket in the teachers' lounge for me today.

When I step into the lounge with an exhale, I find my work husband Toby in his usual spot by the table near the window.

"Hey Bee," I greet him with a wave. He lifts his head, a warm smile on his classically handsome face and his trademark bow tie on display. His thick hair holds a slight curl, and I imagine most women would love running their hands through it. He's mastered the preppy hipster vibe, having owned the style long before it was cool. All this, and he's innocently unaware of his nerd-appeal.

I fish out the least suspicious bag of oatmeal then pull out a large mug and empty the contents inside.

"You have a good weekend?" Toby asks, pushing off the counter to open the fridge and retrieve the milk before handing it to me.

"Oh, um, yeah. It was okay" I nod, filling up the kettle. "How was dinner with your parents?"

"More of the usual." He shrugs. "My mother comparing me to my brother. Dad trying to ignite a sudden love for football." His self-deprecating chuckle makes me grimace. Toby is one of the smartest, most caring people I know. Unfortunately, his passion for inspiring young minds goes unnoticed by his family because they've never been able to accept that he's not the next Patrick Mahomes.

"I'm sorry, Bee."

"You're committed to that nickname?" He winces.

"It's that or *Toblerone*. But you'll have to fill out an application for a status change. We take these things very seriously. *Rollin' with my bro Toblerone*."

"I think I'll stick with Bee, then," he deadpans.

With my wedge heels on, I'm only a few inches shorter than Toby. Most people tower over my five-foot-half-inch stature (yes, I'm fighting for that half-inch), but Toby is on the shorter side, too, and I appreciate that he doesn't tease me about my height. Maybe it's because he's had to contend with his own share of short jokes over the years.

"Is there anything I can do to help?" I ask, tossing a pinch of salt into the mug.

"I don't think so."

"What you need is a fake girlfriend to appease them." I point toward him with my spoon.

"You offering yourself as tribute?" He arches a brow with a smile.

The idea simmers in my mind as I add hot water and stir. It wouldn't cost me anything to go along with the ruse, and if it helps Toby, I'm happy to oblige. Besides, there's no risk of feelings getting in the way, since Toby and I see each other as siblings. No fake dating turning into love here—no tropes in my world. The blind dates I went on last year were all dull enough to put me off dating for the foreseeable future. My life is already a mess, and adding romance to the mix would only make things worse.

He silently shakes his head while he sips his coffee. I know he's only half-serious about taking me up on my offer, but I'd never pass up an opportunity to help a good friend.

"I'd do it, you know."

"Pretend to be my girlfriend?"

"If it helps you, yeah." I shrug, adding honey and milk to my oatmeal then lifting the mug. I blow into it while Toby washes his coffee cup in the sink. He finishes, leaning against the counter while he rubs his chin. "That might actually work."

I'm about to interject more of my bright ideas when the door swings open.

C.J. Crowley—Aster Elementary's principal—struts in, her hair meticulously styled and her classic stiletto heels and fifties pencil dress on point. She's tall with a brow that raises at the perfect arch for making kids spill their secrets. She's fiercely protective of her clan, and I'm desperately trying to solidify my place in it. I feel like I'm almost there.

"Staff meeting in five," she informs in her authoritative voice while laying a tray of muffins down.

"Can we chat about it this afternoon?" Toby whispers.

"You got it, Bee." I wink. "Hey, C.J. Can I carry those for you?" I slide the tray into my arms while she hurriedly brews a cup of coffee.

"Oh, thank you, Darlin'. You can bring them next door. I'll be there in a minute."

"Yes ma'am."

We take our usual seats, and I'm probably the only one who wouldn't stand out if the students filed in and sat down. Heels do nothing for one's height when sitting.

C.J. click-clacks into the room as the rest of the staff greet one other and settle into the remaining chairs.

"Happy Monday, team! I'll get straight to it. Just a few things to take note of. I know it's only February, but spring is upon us and you know how the spring winds make these kids crazy, so be warned. Have your *'poop just hit the fan'* strategies and contingencies in place."

C.J. preps us every year like we're gearing down for some kind of alien invasion. She's convinced the spring winds change the frequency in the air, making all the kids more wild than usual. I'm not a conspiracy theorist, but I *have* noticed a correlation and it helps to have a plan in place when the students decide to impersonate everything besides humans for the day.

"And lastly, you'll notice a few gentlemen at the playground after school this week," C.J. says.

"We renting out the swings, now?" Toby chimes in, eliciting a chuckle from the staff.

"As much as I'd like to see that show, Toby, they'll be here to install the shade covering over the play structure. I have no other announcements, so that concludes this morning's proceedings."

We shuffle out and disperse to different classrooms, but Toby nudges my arm before we part. "I'll catch you before you leave this afternoon?"

"Sure thing, Bae."

His chin scrunches while his lips puff out. "I can't decide if that's better or worse than *Bee*."

"You've leveled up. It's better."

He pivots after an eye roll.

When I reach my office, I check my phone one more time before stuffing it in my desk drawer. Still no word from Ross. But I can't keep covering for him like this. For so long, I've hoped that showering him with unconditional love and understanding would encourage him to join me on the right path—the path of hard work and an honest income, that is. But I'm not so sure my approach has been working.

I inhale and release a slow breath, and it feels like trying to breathe with an X-ray vest draped over my chest. All I can do is take things one day at a time.

The first thing I do each morning is ensure the projector is working. I'm in big trouble if that device fails. Then I prepare anything that I could possibly need to write on the whiteboard by typing it on my computer instead. For information that needs to stay up all week, I enlist students with neat handwriting to help transcribe it onto the board. Sometimes we turn it into a game called "Catch Miss Marsh's Spelling Mistake," which the students enjoy. This not only instills a sense of responsibility in the kids, but also saves me a lot of stress.

Ten minutes later, my students are lining up in the hall, and the craziness is about to begin. I give my hair bow a tug, tightening it before pasting on a giant smile. By the time I greet the first student with a fist bump, I'm already feeling my anxiety melt away. Most people would find this situation stress inducing, but being with kids who are open to learning and free to make mistakes is my happy place. There's no pressure here. We're equals, learning together.

Second graders and senior citizens are my favorite age

group to be around. Things tend to even out in some ways on both ends of that age range. These thoughts bring with them an uninvited reminder of a dream to follow that passion and pursue furthering my education. These thoughts of studying more periodically flicker in my peripheral, blinking like a tiny flashing light I keep trying to ignore.

But it's Monday, so I have a morning routine to get through. And certainly no time for dwelling on silly, unrealistic dreams.

Just before snack time, I turn on my teacher-voice, capturing the class's attention. "Okay friends! Listen up! It's Katie's birthday today." I smile, opening my arms for Katie to come stand beside me. "We'll sing, then she'll help hand out cupcakes. Jace, honey, pencil out of your ear please, thank you."

Boys are a different species. That's all I'm saying.

The class is abuzz with excitement as they huddle closer, and Katie sidles up next to me.

"Miss Marsh," she tugs on my arm, whispering in my ear. "What are you supposed to do while people sing happy birthday to you?"

This kid's throwing out the big guns. My nostrils flare as I stifle a laugh, not wanting her to feel embarrassed for asking one of life's greatest questions. I bend a little, putting an arm around her and she snuggles closer.

"Well, I'm still trying to figure that one out myself. But I think if you just smile politely and think about cake, you'll get through it."

She nods, accepting my plan. Kids are the best.

We make it through the out-of-tune happy birthday serenade, and before I know it, it's 3 PM, and my classroom is empty. I'm going over tomorrow's lesson plans when a text comes through over my phone.

> ROSS:
> I'm sorry, Vee, can't talk. I'll swing by your place tonight.

Well, I guess he'll figure things out when he arrives at my empty apartment.

CHAPTER TWO

IVY

Nobody likes showering at the gym. You never know what jiggly bits might assault your eyes while people with flushed, post-workout cheeks parade around naked in the locker room. But beggars can't be choosers, and a girl's gotta get clean.

I wave guiltily at the receptionist after swiping my membership card, heading straight for the locker room. I give the fitness machines a cursory glance as I pass them. It's been a while since I nearly killed myself on a treadmill. My annual *'I'm going to get fit'* resolution only lasts two days for a reason. Those contraptions weren't made for the accident prone, like myself. I hate how much I resemble Bella Swan in this shortcoming. But regardless of my lack of fitness, my morning has begun, and I still have to complete the slightly degrading task of showering before school. My car might be able to serve as a makeshift bedroom, but it can't replace running water.

I'm enveloped in the humid aroma of chlorine and generic body wash as I walk into the locker room, clutching my bag. I round the corner to the showers, coming face-to-face with the first pair of senior citizen dangly parts for the day. That's the downside to arriving before 7 AM—the bits that hang and swing around the locker room mostly belong to an advanced generation. Now, I'm not saying there's anything wrong with aging and being proud of what ya mama gave ya—it's just a lot of pruney skin for 6:30 in the morning.

The first thing I do is brush my teeth, then I remove my shoes and shuffle into a pair of flip-flops before picking an empty shower and making sure the curtain is well and truly closed. I don't quite share my fellow locker roommates' affinity for nudity. Before I turn the water on, I hang up my clothes in the hopes that the steam from the shower might smooth out some of the wrinkles.

There's still no response from Ross when I check my phone one last time before stripping down. My brother has been MIA, leaving me in a pile of trouble. He sends the odd text, like yesterday, telling me he can't talk but never answers any questions or picks up the phone when I call.

I think I shed a few tears under the spray of the water, but one can never be sure when crying in the shower. Am I just silently making ugly faces in an attempt to process the crap storm that is my life? It's a little less cathartic when you can't feel the salty drops on your cheeks. I give myself sixty seconds. That's all. Sixty seconds to cry (probably) and let out my frustrations.

That's all I have time for, and it's as much as I can allow myself to feel at the moment. If I were to try and face everything that's happening at once, I'm not sure I'd be able to hide my desolation very well. The puffy eyes would be a dead giveaway, not to mention the fact that I'd be reduced to a pile of emotions, curled up on the floor. Because I need a place to live, and I can't see any way of making that happen if Ross doesn't pay me back.

So sixty seconds is all you get, Ivy June.

I twist my blonde hair into a neat bun, not wanting any visible evidence of being out of my element. A silky teal ribbon finishes the look. I chose it to match my teal wedges—perfect height extenders for the vertically challenged.

As I leave, the check-in lady's eyes narrow my way, tracking my exit, and the shuffling of my heels quickens.

"I swear I'll work out next time!" I grimace, timing my words so that I'm out the door before she can reply. There's nothing in my gym contract that says I have to step foot in the workout zone.

I amble through five minutes of traffic, preparing to slip into my professional persona—Happy Ivy—carefree and committed to helping everyone, despite the extra hours of work that sometimes lands me.

It's not hard to smile throughout the day when you get to spend it with a bunch of eager eight-year-olds. We're currently learning about countries and cultures around the world, which feels like a delightful little escape on its own.

The school bell rings, signaling the end of the day and causing my shoulders to slump as I survey my empty classroom. There's a sudden longing for the noise that I use to drown out the chaos of my personal life. I linger there as long as I can, delaying the inevitable for a while longer before finally getting into my car and stopping at the nearest grocery store for the day's discounted hot meal.

When I'm done eating, I park on a side street within eyesight of Carl's security booth at Crystal Retirement Village. That small fragment of familiarity and just knowing someone kind is near makes things feel a little less dangerous.

There's a theory that the human psyche can survive anything—the harshest conditions, imprisonment, capture, extreme poverty, and trauma—when routine exists. The simple act of waking up and choosing to repeat the same order of mundane tasks each day and having the same place to store important things creates a sense of stability for the brain and allows it to find a semblance of normality amidst chaos.

Knowing that my sanity is hanging by a thread, I've quickly established my own routine. For instance, I ensure I have a full bottle of water by refilling it at the last place I visit. This is my final normal act before slipping into my alternate life.

My little routine is simple, but I know it's important for my state of mind.

I wait until sunset to sort through the clothes I plan to wear tomorrow and lay them on the seat behind me, next to my wedges. I retrieve my toiletry bag from the glove compartment and use travel supplies to clean my face and brush my teeth. This is where the water comes in handy. After checking the road for lurkers, I do a quick swish and spit onto the sidewalk. It probably looks gross, I know, but this isn't a long-term thing—so don't judge me.

Next, I recline my seat as far as it'll go, grabbing my pillow and blanket from underneath the piles of things behind me. Pro tip: When living in your car, the actual sleeping accessories are the most important things to hide—they're a dead giveaway and raise too many questions. Not that I want anybody to ever end up in this situation.

I get through the night relatively well. It's not comfortable, but again, I don't plan on doing it much longer, so I muster through because Ross said he'll have my money soon.

Waking up is another thing. The level of *where the hell am I?* in those first few seconds is unmatched.

There's a chill in the car this morning, even though the temperatures don't usually drop too drastically in this part of Texas. I start the engine, holding my hands over the vents to warm them. But the thing I miss the most about having my own apartment isn't a warm bed or a hot shower. Nope. It's having a place to pee at 5 AM in the morning. Even in the most primitive form of camping, you can find a bush to squat behind. But when you're parked on a quiet suburban street, those kinds of things are frowned upon.

I reach for my stash of breath mints in a cup holder and suck one while driving the two minutes it takes me to get to the nearest Starbucks. This is my pee stop. As much as my veins crave a caffeinated fix, I'd be less than broke too quickly if I added daily coffee purchases to my routine.

After Starbucks is a ten minute drive to the gym for a shower, and then the transformation from my night-life to my day-life is complete.

At the end of the school day when I'm alone in my classroom again, Toby walks in, holding two cups of coffee.

"Oh my word, you're an angel!" I sing, practically snatching one out of his hand.

"Those could have both been for me, you know."

"Uh-uh" I mumble over a sip, the steam fogging my glasses. "That would be weird. That's good coffee. Where'd you get this?"

"I may have put my own machine in the utility closet in my classroom."

A burst of laughter wants to erupt, and I barely avoid a spit-take. "You did not."

"I swear. The coffee here sucks. It's a matter of survival."

"Who else knows about this?"

"Just you." He grins over his cup.

"You're my supplier now. I can't go back to the bad stuff."

"A wonderful sentence for a second-grade teacher to be saying."

"We can call it a girlfriend perk." I slump back, tilting my head wistfully. "It really is a pity I don't find you wildly attractive."

"Stop, you'll make me blush."

"You know what I mean."

"I do. It would be convenient if I didn't already think of you as a sister. It's too bad you're not my type, either."

"I'm not sure I'm anyone's type," I grumble with only a tinge of sarcasm. That statement is a little too on-the-nose.

"Vee—"

"This isn't about me," I swat his words away, shifting onto a desk, and Toby scoots beside me. "Let's talk fake relationship. How're we doing this thing?"

"I'm thinking a few dinners, maybe some photos of us together to sell it? I'll tell my parents it's just casual and new. My mom will love you, though, which will momentarily distract her from my other shortcomings."

"They're only shortcomings to her, Bee. You're a catch." I sip, swinging my legs as they hang off the desk. "How long are we doing this thing for, anyway?"

"Till my brother moves back in two months? By then, mom will have a new grandbaby to focus on."

"Cool." I nod. "Should we take a photo now so you can have it ready to send the next time she bugs you?"

"Yeah, but it can't look like we're at school. She doesn't need a reason to think I'm making all this up."

Toby pulls out his phone, and we giggle through the awkwardness of pretending to be an item. And through it all, I find myself wishing I had someone to do this with for real. I want there to be one part of my life I don't have to pretend or fake. I want a genuine relationship with someone I could confide in. But that would mean relying on another person and making myself vulnerable, and facing all the scary parts of giving my heart away.

Instead, I'll be leaving school alone to go to sleep in my car.

It's still way less risky than trusting someone with my heart.

CHAPTER THREE

ETHAN

"Hey Marco, grab the demarcation poles and tape. I'm gonna head inside and chat with the principal." I spin my hat around backward before wiping my hands on my thighs. They're not dirty, but I feel like it prepares me mentally for walking into the school I attended as a child.

"Hey, Mrs. Crawley," I say to my old principal with a smile, the woman whose office chair I warmed more times than I can count as a kid. It still feels strange to interact with her as an adult.

"Mr. King," she croons, extending a hand to me. Even after all these years, she's still as classy as ever.

"Ma'am," I answer her with a tip of my head.

"We're so grateful you're doing this for us. With summer approaching, the kids will be glad not to get third degree burns on the playground."

I chuckle, recalling the memory of sweaty recesses and roasted elbows. "I bet they will."

"I'm assuming you'll need to rope off the playground for a few days?"

"Nah, we'll mark off the poles while the concrete dries. The kids can still use the play structure as long as they stay clear of the taped-off area. It should be ready by the end of next week."

"Oh, that's perfect! Is there anything you needed from me?"

"No, ma'am, just letting you know we're getting started."

"Well, it's a good thing you're starting after school. Some of our younger teachers might have gotten a bit too distracted during school hours. Especially with your face bein' on TV, and you gettin' all famous on us now." She winks.

I chuckle, unfazed by the so-called fame I've encountered since my appearance on a morning show for my brother's business over Christmas. Apparently, my face went a bit viral—or so I'm told. I don't pay much attention to social media, aside from following a few extreme sports personalities. Still, it did bring some exposure to my home renovation business and even sparked an opportunity for me to earn a role on one of those house-flipping reality shows.

"I wouldn't wanna cause a stir." I smile.

"I think that's exactly what you've always liked doing, Ethan," she laughs back. "I'll be here if you need anything."

My head tips in another nod, and I make my way through the hallway back toward the playground. My steps slow as I pass one of my old classrooms, the corners of my mouth curling up nostalgically.

The sound of laughter from a nearby classroom draws me closer. But I freeze when another loud cackle erupts, because I immediately recognize that voice. It belongs to a tiny but lethal package—One I'd rather not interact with any more than necessary.

I peek carefully around the doorway, and my stomach does a quick flip—a phantom reaction, like the urge to hurl when you catch a whiff of something that once made you sick. And the few altercations I've had with the woman now cozying up for a selfie with another man have certainly left me feeling queasy. Anyone with a mouth as sharp as hers and a gaze as antagonistic as the one that habitually pierces mine would provoke this kind of reaction.

Her companion curls an arm around her and presses his cheek to hers for another photo. That siren-call laugh bubbles out of her again, eliciting another stomach swirl. My hand goes to my middle as I take a step back, planning to execute a casual walk-by, but my movement alerts the tiny blonde.

"*You.*"

That one word is coated in so much disdain I have to fight a shiver.

I know we got off on the wrong foot the first time we met. By that, I mean I saw a woman in my brother's fiancé's office doing something reckless and may have unintentionally insulted her while simultaneously saving her from a small accident. But it came from a place of wanting to protect a stranger from harm.

Who stands on a rickety bench in heels and *twirls*, anyway? Talk about lack of common sense.

Yeah, okay, the delivery of my concern could have been better. But I still caught the woman and saved her from injury, and I stand by my act of chivalry, even if she *did not* interpret the interaction in the same way.

Regardless of my heroic intentions, I lit a fuse between us that day. If she'd had a weapon, I'm not sure I'd be standing here now.

Her husky throat clearing brings me back. "Ethan. Lurking much?"

"Ivy." My eyes flick to her canoodle partner. "Flirt much?"

"Excuse me?" She laughs, but there's zero humor in it. Not

that I expected any. I'm pushing her buttons again, but it just comes naturally with her. "What is that supposed to mean?"

"Nothin'," My eyes move lazily around the classroom. It's colorful and welcoming with printed words and pictures. I glance back at the couple, the muscle in my jaw pulsing at the clear display of familiarity and intimacy between them. I'm not sure why witnessing Ivy Marsh getting cozy with a man has me so riled up. Maybe I just pity him and want to save him from this woman's wrath. "Have a good day, you two," I reply dryly before I salute and turn to leave.

"What are you doing here, anyway?" she calls toward my back.

My thumbs hang loosely in my pockets while I pivot to face her again. She's closer now, those big green eyes framed by gold-rimmed glasses and a sharp scowl. I take in the man beside her. His preppy look—sweater vest with a bowtie—causes a tug of my mouth. Figures she'd go for a man like this. I bet he's no better than a little puppy dog, happy to be ordered around.

"I'm workin' on the playground, Marsh. That okay with you?" My eyes flicker to her windows and the view of the structure outside. "You'll even get to stare daggers at me from inside the comfort of your lovely classroom." I flash a teasing grin—the one that seems to ruffle her feathers.

She exhales sharply, and it's a marvel that her glasses don't fog up with the effort.

"Careful, Marsh. The steam coming out your ears might cause those things to rust." My eyes trace the rim of her frames, noting how they hover just above the freckles on her cheeks.

She lets out a growl, and her boyfriend steps closer, grinning like a cheesy bobblehead doll.

He hangs a pale hand over Ivy's shoulder and holds the other one out in front of me. "I'm Toby."

I try to ignore it, but my gaze is still drawn to the spot

where his hand rests on the bare skin of her arm. I tear my eyes away, but I'm equally annoyed by how easily they meet those giant green orbs with the big V-shaped crease between them. I sense the need to end this conversation as quickly as possible, because I'm not sure what the hell is going on here. I shake Toby's hand without breaking Ivy's stare. It's unnerving having this much feisty energy zeroed in on me, like she's peering into my soul and garnering all the intel she needs to make a voodoo doll so she can torture me later.

Ivy folds her arms, shifting slightly nearer to Toby. "Well don't do anything *dumb* out there."

A short puff of air comes out with my laugh. I roll my lips over my teeth, trying to hide my amusement. Yeah, I deserve that one. I may have insinuated that her choices weren't the smartest on the day we first met. If she'd stop biting my head off every time we see each other, I'd try and apologize.

Toby is still smiling like a puppy awaiting a treat. I frown, taking him in again from head to toe. The man is wearing loafers, for goodness sake. I turn, still scowling about her boyfriend's fashion choices as I look at Ivy. As usual, she takes my expression personally. And I realize it's time to extricate myself from the ticking time bomb glaring at me.

"See you around, Marsh." I tip my head before leaving the room.

Another feminine growl echoes down the hall, making me shake my head. That woman is scary as hell.

I head outside to meet Marco. He's leaning on the posthole digger as he waits on me, our supplies laid out beside him.

"What's that scowl for?" He squints at my face.

"Nothin'. Let's get started," I deflect, unclipping a measuring tape from my belt. I survey the area, pulling out the blueprints for the updated playground.

"You found a woman to piss off, didn't you?" Marco strolls

behind while I pretend like that skirmish with Ivy didn't just make me feel alive for the first time since—*dang*—since the last time I saw Ivy two weeks ago. We'd both been invited to meet my brother and his fiancée, Ember, for drinks. Since Ivy is Ember's best friend, it made sense that she was asked to be the maid of honor when Colton asked me to be his best man.

"Why do you assume I go around looking for women to irritate?" I pause from looking at my plans to question Marco.

"Maybe it's the angry blonde who looks like she wants to put your face on a dartboard." He says, nodding toward the parking lot behind me.

Sure enough, when I turn, there she is, wearing an expression that says she'd enjoy watching me get eaten by sharks.

With a shake of my head, I fold the plans and stuff them in my back pocket, then I hoist a bag of cement over my shoulder. "I may have pushed a few of her buttons, but she started it."

Marco chuckles but lets it go, and we dig the six holes for the posts while I force myself to forget about the blonde spitfire in question. It might prove difficult, considering my brother and her best friend are engaged, but I know the less time Ivy and I spend together, the better. Because that woman has complicated written all over her.

CHAPTER FOUR

IVY

Toby slams the trunk of his car shut, his gaze darting between me and Ethan across the field. "You sure there aren't any sparks there?" he asks, leaning back with his arms folded.

"The only sparks are the ones I'd like to light under his butt." I smile, imagining that delightful scenario. "He's an egotistical nerf-herder."

"Remind me why you hate each other again?"

"I told you about the day I met him, didn't I?" Toby just shrugs, so I take it as his permission to unload the full story while he organizes files and boxes in his car. "Ember was at work, and I stopped by to show her the *cutest* hiking boots. I mean, you should have seen these boots! For a thrift store find, they were in pristine condition—" My eyes flicker to Toby's bored face, making me pause. "You don't care about the boots, do you?"

"Not even a little bit."

"Okay, so I'm showing Ember the boots, and I climb onto a step to give her a better angle, and in storms Mr. Grouchy pants. Doesn't say a word, either, just manhandles me off the bench I was standing on then insults me *and* my choice of footwear!"

"And that sealed your fate as mortal enemies?"

"Well, obviously. You know how I feel about both of those things."

"I'm sorry, Vee." He smiles softly. "I'll kick his butt if he insults you again. After all, it's my fake boyfriend duty."

"My hero." I let out a short laugh, picturing Toby trying to take on Ethan. He sure has the muscles to pummel Toby in seconds. *Stop thinking about Ethan's muscles.*

He shuts the door to his car. "Of course. I'll see you tomorrow. Want me to text you those photos later?"

"Yeah, thanks." I whisper as Toby pulls me in for a tight hug. I get a lot of hugs from eight-year-olds who squish me around my waist. But Toby's slight height advantage means I get an over the shoulder squeeze that momentarily fills some of the voids.

I get lost in thought on the way to my own car, reflecting on how nice it would be to get some kind of affection on the regular. If Toby's hug makes me go, *that was great, I needed that*, I can't imagine what the strong, protective embrace of a man who saw me as more than a sister might feel like.

My eyes catch Ethan's form once again, and I snigger, pitying his poor dates and what they must suffer through. The douchery that spews out of his mouth can't be worth a hug from his admittedly ripped arms.

"Ivy! Wait up!"

"Hey Stef." I wave to one of my co teachers, turning back toward her to avoid any questions about the state of my car. But I'm too slow. She's jogging, reaching me in seconds with her long, giraffe legs. She's probably around five-foot-eight, but staring up at her with those extra seven-and-a-half inches still elicits a crick in my neck.

Stef's a first-grade teacher, but she and I are cool for the most part, having been hired within the same year. We've figured things out together, bonding over our mutual *what did I sign up for?* feeling.

Stef's eyes track Toby's car as it pulls away, a small furrow on her brow. He's finally out of sight and she turns her attention back to me. I bite my top lip when I catch her frowning at all the stuff in my Toyota.

"You moving?"

"Oh, um...no. Taking some stuff to Goodwill. What's up?"

Please don't ask more questions.

"Right, listen, I'm glad I caught you. Can you look at something real quick?" She opens the tote bag hanging from her shoulder, her head of dark curls almost disappearing while she digs around. The oversized tote is a teacher's best friend. In fact, I have everything I could possibly need to survive an apocalypse stuffed inside the one I'm currently carrying. Sure, I'd probably be zombified in the twenty minutes it'd take to dig up a weapon sharp enough to defeat the undead, and I can't carry a knife around at school, but I guarantee I have at least four things I could use to impale a zombie's brain in here. Destroy the brain, kill the zombie. It's a pity my second graders are too young for me to impart this knowledge.

Stef's taken a full two minutes to locate the paper she's now holding out for me.

"I wanted to run the field trip schedule by you before passing it along to C.J. I've planned out all the time slots and proposed activities, as well as the small group numbers for each. I was going to email it to you, but seeing as you're here, I thought I'd swing by and hand it to you. Can you see anything I've missed that should be on there?"

I reach for the paper, hoping it's not as number heavy as she's just eluded.

Yeah. Numbers. Numbers that jump out and hide all at the same time. My eyes bounce over the page, trying to catch a single category I can make sense of. It's like looking at an infographic a four-year-old made, except I know Stef's actually put together a very organized schedule.

I usually get Toby to help with these things. He must have caught on to my struggle over the years, but he's never asked. He's just become my unspoken support system who's willing to help me with all the things an adult should be able to do.

"Um..." I lift my wrist, pretending to glance at the time. "Can I get back to you? I'll text you my thoughts. I've gotta rush home."

"Oh, of course. And those are just suggestions. Feel free to shuffle things around. Thanks, Ivy. And good luck with your Goodwill dropoff. Looks like you've got a lot of stuff there." She smiles kindly before walking back to her car.

I wave like a dork as I watch her drive away. When I turn, Ethan is sauntering toward his truck—parked just two spaces from mine. He's carrying a contraption that looks like a giant pair of chopsticks. With a casual lift, he hoists it over the back of his truck, then he leans lazily against the tailgate as he eyes my overpacked car.

If the earth could temporarily swallow me up, I might actually sign up for that. Not a permanent end, just a temporary hidey-hole type thing, so I can be spared the result of the cogs about to turn in this man's pompous head.

I don't want him figuring *anything* out. From what Ember has told me, Ethan is the biggest snitch alive. I'm sure he'd just love the chance to pass along incriminating information to his brother, which means Ember will know I'm homeless, too. And I refuse to give my friend cause to worry or to risk a distraction during her beautiful wedding-planning season.

I'm still shuffling over to my car when Ethan has the

audacity to wipe his face with the collar of his shirt, flashing a sliver of tanned skin. I stop to unlock the door, and his eyes move over me slowly, starting at my shoes and continuing up to map every inch of me with a narrowed gaze. His brow lowers as he shifts to scan the contents of my backseat.

"Why's there so much stuff in your car?"

"Why's there so little stuff in your head?"

"You know, Marsh, it would help if you at least *tried* to be civil. Seein' as we're going to be spending more time together."

"Right." I nod, opening the door and immediately shifting clothes and shoes over so I can climb inside. It's very anti-climatic. "Let's try to keep that to a minimum, shall we?"

I feel the satisfying *clunk* once I finally slam my door shut and bug my eyes with a tight smile before driving away.

Gah! Aggravating man!

The first time I met him, he basically called me stupid for wearing heels, and now he has the nerve to question the state of my car?

I can't deal with Ethan's lack of human decency on top of the turmoil in my personal life. He and his ego need to float on out, because the last thing I need is a man telling me all the things I'm doing wrong.

CHAPTER FIVE

ETHAN

I increase the speed on the treadmill, aiming to raise my heart rate with a sprint before the end of my run. Sparring with Colton is usually my preferred form of cardio, but he's understandably busier than usual since getting engaged. My mouth curls with a smile as I think about how happy my brother is.

The machine's whirring slows after I hit stop, and I wipe the sweat from my face and neck as I catch my breath. Then I turn at the high-pitched whispers from two college-aged women nearby.

"See, I told you it's him!" I overhear as they cycle leisurely on their stationary bikes, unaware that I can see their reflections in the mirror. A series of arm swatting and elbowing ensues after they catch me glancing their way.

I guess I should get used to this happening more often if I plan on moving forward with the reality TV show thing. It's a weird feeling, though, being recognized by strangers. I'm wiping down my treadmill when they walk over, each of them nudging the other forward.

"Hi...I'm Layla, this is Chloe..." The taller one nods her head to her friend and clears her throat. "We were wondering... are you...that guy from the morning show? The one that went viral 'cause you made the hosts practically fall in love with you?"

I let out a small laugh, my chin dipping to my chest. But when I look up, ready to deliver my flirty response, I'm distracted by a flighty blonde speed walking into the gym. Layla and Chloe turn, noticing my attention has strayed, and Layla angles her body to block my view. "Is it true you might get your own show? You're really hot, so you'd be a hit." She smiles with a coy lift of her brow.

Yikes. Is this what's in store for me? Women coming on to me purely because of my looks? *That's what men do ninety-nine percent of the time, dumb ass.*

Right. I guess that's true. And kind of sad. I frown, pouting my lips as I stare off to the side. I may be guilty of the same thing. This is turning into a wonderful moment of self-reflection.

My eyes return to the restrooms where Ivy's disappeared. "Yup, that's me. I'm not sure on the TV show part, though. Sorry ladies, I've gotta make a call." I grimace, leaving Layla and Chloe looking a little confused. I'll need to figure out a smoother way to get out of these situations when all I want to do is get in a quiet workout.

I'd actually planned on weight training today, too, but I don't think I fancy working out with Ivy Marsh around, especially since it's only a matter of time before I find her staring and willing my head to spontaneously combust. It's best I steer clear of the sea witch, especially so early in the morning. And if the day goes well, I'll avoid seeing her at school, too. I've had enough communication mishaps at The Adventure Project this week, dealing with suppliers who don't speak the same language as I do. I don't need another round of that when Ivy inevitably chooses to misinterpret something I say.

The other problem is that even when a conversation starts off civil, I can't seem to help pushing her buttons.

I don't even want to explore the reason for that.

Like she said, it's best if Ivy and I keep our interactions to a minimum.

My phone rings as I'm preparing to walk out of the building, and I pause, only answering once I realize it's the agent from the TV network.

"Hey, Glenn."

"Ethan, you got a minute to chat?"

"Yeah, shoot."

"Great. So I've been putting my feelers out, and even though there are plenty of renovation shows with couples, single ladies, moms and daughters—that kind of thing, if you can present a unique angle, I think we've got a good chance of you being picked up. We've gotta pitch you as a single guy, dripping with all that Southern charm."

"Oh-kay..."

Glenn laughs at my hesitation. "Don't stress. It's not something you need to *come up with,* rather something that you've already got. We need to show everyone that charisma on the screen. I've seen it, and I think America is gonna love you."

He continues to rattle off terms I've never heard before, but he also promises to email everything he's telling me. By the time we hang up, I'm pinching the bridge of my nose, wondering if I even want to do this anymore.

You did want more adventure, I remind myself.

I'd pictured that being a three-day hike through the Texas panhandle. But even though the TV opportunity was unexpected, it's undoubtedly going to be an adventure.

I slide my phone into my pocket as I realize I've been staring at the ladies' restroom doors the whole time. It's been over ten minutes, and Ivy still hasn't emerged.

That's weird, right?

Go home, King. She's trouble.

Yeah, yeah. I'm going home.

With my mind made up, I toss my towel over my shoulder, just as Ivy steps out, now changed from the sweatpants and tank top she was wearing before. She doesn't see me as she hurries toward the exit, already dressed and ready for the day. But as I move toward the automatic door, she looks up and flinches, noticing me scowling at her.

"Why are you showering at the gym?"

"Good morning, Ethan. I'm just peachy, thanks for asking. How're you?" she retorts.

"Ivy." I'm unable to hold back the growl through my clenched jaw.

"You must not have heard, considering your pungent odor, but people actually shower here. I highly recommend it."

I huff, feeling the frustration percolating in my veins. "Don't be smart." My blood pressure goes up just being near this woman.

"Goodness, I'm flattered you think I'm even capable of such a thing," she flutters her eyelashes, pressing her lips into a flat smile. Then she rolls her eyes and shifts her bag up her arm as she walks past me. But for some reason, I can't let this go.

She's once again speed walking in those senseless wedges. I shake my head, my lips rolling in as she narrowly avoids tripping on the uneven gravel where she's parked. My legs are almost double the length of hers, so it doesn't take much effort to reach her car at the same time she does. The car that still looks like someone's living in it.

My eyes snap up, a deep groove forming between my brows

as I stare at her, piecing things together. The muscle in my jaw begins to ache.

"Wait... tell me you're not living in your car?"

She opens the door, plopping her duffle bag on top of...so many things, then she pivots, folding her arms with another tight smile. "Okay. I'm not living in my car."

"Ivy—for the love! Why?" I grunt, rubbing a hand roughly down my face. Her chest rises with a heavy sigh, arms still crossed while she looks off to the side. "Look, it's temporary, okay? I'm moving and...I'm between places while I'm waiting to get the keys to my new apartment." She turns to glare menacingly at me. "Please don't say anything to anyone. Seriously, Ethan. This isn't a big deal. I don't want Ember stressing over me. She has enough to worry about."

I purse my lips, narrowing my eyes as I consider her plea. She really shouldn't be living out of her car. Once again, this infuriating woman is putting herself in danger.

"Ethan..."

"Promise me you won't sleep in your car tonight, and I'll drop it." It seems like no matter how hard I try to get this little pixie off my radar, her obnoxiously bright light keeps blinking its way back across the screen, triggering alarms in my head every time.

"I'll crash with Opal and Gail if I have to. Are you happy?" she asks disdainfully.

"Elated."

There's a stretch of silence as we continue staring at one other, like this weird energy between us is somehow too intense to ignore. "But if you're still," I pause to motion to the catastrophe behind her, "between places by tomorrow, I'm telling Ember."

"Fine," she snaps, sinking into her car and slamming the

door. Then she rolls down the window to add, "And I hope the movie adaptation of your favorite book has a terrible cast."

She drives away after that, her sunshine yellow hair ribbon blowing in the wind. She's a beautiful disaster, this one, the most dangerous kind.

Yup. Going to steer very clear of this human tornado.

Starting tomorrow.

CHAPTER SIX

IVY

I come to a full stop at a traffic light, tapping my thumb on the steering wheel. I'm on my way to see Gran, but there's time to kill until she's done with her bingo game at five.

I told Ethan I'd crash with Opal and Gail, so I should at least pay them a visit, even if I don't plan on allowing my mess to spill into their lives. It helps that they live in the apartment complex opposite Gran's retirement village, and I know they'll feed me—that being one of their love languages.

I smile at the vibrant surge of color as my car glides into the parking lot in front of the charming apartments where I first met my best friend Ember's seventy-year-old neighbors. Pots and planter boxes overflow with flowers, as if a riot of colors has burst forth and refuses to be confined.

I lock my house-car, letting out a heavy sigh as I walk up the path to Gail and Opal's apartment.

"Knock knock!" I call through the open door.

"Ivy June?" I hear Opal's voice from inside the apartment.

"That's me!"

"We weren't expecting you today! Did you come to see Ember?" she smiles as she approaches.

"Oh, nah," I wave with a laugh. "I know she technically still lives next door, but she's definitely with Colton when she's not at work. How're you two doin', though?"

"Pretty good," she squints at something behind me. "But that Robin keeps crapping in my rain gauge."

I love it when old people cuss. Can I call "crapping" a cuss word?

"Ivy!" Gail claps triumphantly behind Opal. "You're just in time to try the top secret new cake recipe I've been working on." She scuttles off, and Opal turns to me with an eye roll.

"The secret is still rum," she grumbles before her veiny hand pats my shoulder affectionately. "Tea?"

"Yes, please."

"Gail! Put the kettle on!" she hollers. Then her eyes lock onto mine, like she's seen something, a crack in my mask. Those same kind eyes narrow, searching deeper, and I hold my breath.

"You're not sleeping well."

"Yup."

That small word is all I manage while we walk to the living room to sink into well-loved floral printed chairs. If I say more or attempt to deny anything, Opal's laser gaze will only sharpen and cause me to spill my guts. The whole ugly truth will be laid bare.

Unfortunately, I don't escape her scrutiny. "Brother or Gran?"

"Brother." My shoulders straighten while I inspect my nails on my lap.

"Hmph. That boy needs a good dose of tough love, Ivy June."

My head snaps up, and my jaw drops. My parents, bless their hearts, gave him the toughest love possible when they cut ties with him a year ago. But I keep thinking he needs a gentler approach this time. So help me God, I will see him on the right path.

"Ross is a good person. He just needs someone to believe in him."

"Honey, if you believe in him any more, he'll grow wings and start flying."

Thankfully, Gail shuffles in and saves me from further defending my brother.

"Oh, I'm so glad you stopped by. Tell me if you can guess the secret ingredient. No spoilers." She flares her eyes at Opal.

"Visiting your Gran after this?" Gail's face softens while she pours tea into three dainty teacups.

"Yup."

"We'll have to meet her someday."

Opal humphs, folding her hands in her lap. "Hopefully she hasn't been influenced by that old bat, Agnes. That woman is a menace."

"Hmm," I hum over a bite of cake, brushing over her last comment. "This is delicious, Gail."

"Oh good. I'll send some home with you."

Opal smacks her tongue, one eye narrowing. "A bit too heavy-handed on the rum, maybe."

"Oh nonsense, a little rum never killed anyone. Besides, you have to die of *something*."

"She's right." I look at Opal with a finger pointed toward Gail.

Another eye roll. That must be why she can peer into my soul. Her eyes have been training for marathons with all the cartwheels they do.

I soak in their banter along with the cozy atmosphere of their apartment, trying to store up warmth for the uncomfortable night I have ahead of me.

"This was perfect. Thanks for the booze cake, Gail. Never disappoints."

"My pleasure, sweetheart. Wait a minute so I can wrap some up for you."

Gail leaves us, and I'm once again the focus of Opal's eagle-eyed stare, her eyes glistening with concern. "You're hiding something, and I'm going to figure it out, young lady."

My throat tightens slightly as I try to come up with something that will convince her that everything is fine. Thankfully, I'm saved when Gail shuffles back, oblivious to my internalized panic.

"Here you go." Gail returns with a saran-wrapped slice of heaven. "You shouldn't need to put it in the fridge till tomorrow."

That won't be a problem seeing as I currently have no fridge.

I hug them goodbye before either of them can question me further. Their sassy, petite frames bracket the doorway after I rush out.

"Watch the st—"

But it's too late. I nearly faceplant after tripping on the step Gail was attempting to warn me about. By some miracle, my wedges only wobble, and I manage to right myself.

"I'm okay!" I wave back. Gail is hiding a laugh behind her hand while Opal's arms are folded, eyes still narrowed too perceptively.

"I'm leaving my car here. Don't let your robin poop on it!" I yell.

"I'll protect your car if you find that Agnes and tell her to quit stealing my azaleas!"

"You got it." I throw up a thumb but secretly vow to prevent that from happening at all costs.

I cross the road and stop by the security booth to sign in.

Carl smiles widely when I skip closer. I trade him the wrapped plate for a clipboard, and he hums with delight.

"Miss Ivy, marry me?"

"You're a few decades too late, Carl. But the nice lady who baked that cake is single."

He leans over to peer across the road behind me. "Single huh?"

"As single as they come," I confirm once I finish signing in.

"Ayep...that's how they getcha."

"With cake?"

"That's how it starts." He nods absently.

Definitely some wounds there.

"Hey, any luck with the—"

"Nope," I respond before he can remind me I'm still homeless.

"Well, you just let me know when you're ready."

"I will." I smile gratefully.

"Word is your Gran was on another one of her Bingo streaks."

"You sure she wasn't cheating again?"

"You never know with that one," he replies with amusement.

"Thanks, Carl." I laugh and return the clipboard.

Once I reach Gran's apartment, I shake my head at her name printed in swirling letters on her door.

Agnes Christine Marsh

Opal and Gail might actually bury me alive when they find out my Gran is the *"old bat"* who keeps stealing their flowers. I should talk to her about that.

She seemed unaware of her crimes when I last mentioned it, which makes me question whether she requires more extensive care. What if she's experiencing cognitive decline? My parents are off on their travels again, building clean water sources in Nepal or wherever they've ended up this time, while I'm left holding our family together—and not very well. I don't know if I have the strength to continue shouldering this much responsibility.

I'm clearly failing with Ross...and myself.

I knock and enter to find Gran reclining in a wingback chair and paging through a gardening magazine. A vase of azaleas rests on the table beside her.

"My Ivy!" she croons when she spots me. I smile at the familiar eyes that disappear when she laughs and the hairstyle that's remained unchanged since the seventies.

"Hey Gran. I missed you!"

"Oh, I missed you too, honey. So sweet of you and Ross to visit on the same day."

I blink. "Wh—uh—Ross visited you?"

"He brought me a picture. Oh, where did I put that thing now?" She rises and shuffles around the room, searching through various bits of clutter.

Frik. My fingers trace the edge of my lips. It's worse than I thought. She thinks Ross is still a child. I need to tell Mom and Dad. I can't be the only one dealing with this.

"It's okay, Gran, you can show me later. Why don't you sit, and I'll get us some water?"

She straightens, turning to me with a hand on her hip. "Ivy June. Don't patronize me just because I have to eat extra fiber every day."

She smiles softly and holds out a folded piece of paper, and I hesitate to take it.

"Why would Ross bring you a photo of this?" I frown, staring at the image of a music box—my favorite music box. The one I spent hours winding up and listening to as a child. I'd curl up next to the side table where it resided, watching in wonder while the mechanism turned and the little bird inside flapped its wings and sang along with the music.

"Oh, I imagine he's figured out it's valuable." She straightens some of the clutter before pausing for a few seconds, a small sigh making her chest rise and fall. Then her head snaps up sharply as something like hope sparks in her eyes. "You didn't find it, did you?"

I frown. "I haven't seen it in years. You don't know where it is?"

"Oh, it's a long story." She bats a hand dismissively. "But no, I don't know where it is. I've been hoping it'll show up somewhere. But don't you tell that brother of yours anything about it," she adds sternly. "That boy is up to no good."

I may be the lone member on *Team Ross* these days, but knowing he'd probably sell the heirloom makes me determined not to mention it. Even if I haven't thought about the music box in years, the happy memories it evokes make it priceless.

"Besides, if that box ever shows up, it'll belong to *you*," she whispers.

"Oh...wow. Thank you, Gran," I choke out, more relieved to hear her mind isn't stuck in the past than anything. Although some of her behavior is still concerning, it would be a much bigger problem if she were jumping around in time in her head.

"Lovely flowers." I tip my head to the vase.

"Oh, aren't they just stunning? Can you believe they grow across the road? I pick one every time I go for a stroll. Before you know it, I've got a bouquet."

I nod slowly as I stare at the vase. She's crafty, I'll give her that. Surely she knows what she's doing. At least, I hope she's intentionally being mischievous.

Part of me worries Gran may be blissfully unaware of the feud she's created between her and the feisty pair of green thumbs across the road.

"Now *you* sit down, and I'll get us a little treat."

She pats me softly on the shoulder, and I return a warm smile. "Thanks, Gran."

My head falls back as her pastel blue loveseat pulls me in. I close my eyes for a second before the vibrating in my pocket has me reaching for my phone.

A message pops up with two photos of my face squished against Toby's, followed by a text that has me giggling.

> TOBY:
>
> #couplegoals

My fingers pinch the screen, zooming in to make sure it doesn't look like we're in a classroom. Then I flinch and drop the phone at the high pitched shriek from behind me.

"You have a boyfriend? Ivy June! Let me see that handsome fella!"

My grandmother hastily sets down a tray of triangle-cut sandwiches to snatch the phone from my lap and scrutinize the photos.

"He's actually—"

"I'm so happy for you!" she interrupts me to declare, her glistening eyes blinking down at me. My hand fidgets with my shirt collar as I stand and brace myself to clear up this misunderstanding.

"Oh, this is so wonderful," she continues to gush at the photos. "I think you're finally ready for the house."

Say what, now?

"Gran, I can't take your cottage. You've got tenants, remember?"

"And they've finally moved out, with perfect timing! Oh, sweetheart, I'm so delighted," she says with a hand over her heart. "Please tell me you'll accept the house? You can get it ready now for when you and your young man get serious." There's so much joy in her eyes, saying no to her offer feels like denying a child their favorite candy.

"Oh...um...well...he's—"

"That little cottage is everything to me, and I wouldn't trust anyone else but you to restore it. My life is in those walls. It should go to someone who cares about it as much as I do. I want you to have it, Ivy, so you can make new memories there."

This situation is escalating pretty quickly. So why am I not objecting?

"You're giving me a house," I say, my eyes moving around the room as I process this gift.

She claps her palms together. "It'll need some TLC, now. I'm afraid my last tenants got creative in their liberties. But I've already got money set aside for renovations. Oh, my great-grandbabies will grow up in this house!" she mimes a squeal, then fans her face, puffing air out of her mouth.

I should interject, right? Correct this little misunderstanding?

On the other hand, her state of mind *could* still be fragile... and she seems so happy.

"It won't be too much will it? Taking all this on?"

I force an awkward smile. "No, um, of course not. Thank you, Gran."

The hope blooming in her expression quickly eclipses my remorse after allowing her to make those incorrect assumptions about my current relationship status. And it's actually kind of ideal, having a place to call home that also happens to be the setting of so many special memories. After all, Gran's house used to be my favorite escape when life got to be too much. It was the one place where I didn't have to keep pretending everything was perfect.

"I know it's a lot to take on, and you'll probably have to be frugal with the renovation budget. I'm not exactly sure how much work it needs or how far the funds will go. But it'll be such a fun project, I'm sure!"

She looks so delighted, I can't bring myself to dull the joy that seems to emanate from her entire being. And I feel even less guilty about accepting this gift when I remind myself that I'm the one who's been left to deal with Ross and his many screwups. He's always required so much attention and discipline that I had no choice but to be uncomplicated and unneedy.

A lifetime of wearing this mask and faking being okay coupled with the responsibilities I'm still shouldering have earned this. And accepting the house will solve some pretty big problems while allowing me to fulfill my sweet Gran's dreams at the same time.

I think I can make this work. I'll have to let Toby know our fake dating goes both ways now, but that shouldn't be a problem.

Gran's voice brings me back as she digs in a drawer and pulls out a file folder. "Yes, here it is." She looks up at me. "I'll phone my accountant in the morning. He'll get you sorted with the financial side of things. But here's a key to the front door, at least." She places the key in my palm, closing her hands over mine.

"Thank you for accepting this gift, Ivy. You're going to do such a great job."

CHAPTER SEVEN

IVY

I leave Gran's and head back across the road to find Opal and Gail peering into my car with their hands cupped against the glass like a pair of curious meerkats.

Dang it.

"Yup...I told ya, Gail. The girl's definitely living in her car."

As I approach, Opal turns to face me, one fist on her hip and the other resting against the side of my Toyota. Meanwhile, Gail continues inspecting the contents of my car, doubt etched on her brow as if she can't believe I'd do something so foolish. I wish I wasn't about to disappoint her.

"I'm not living in my car," I begin.

Opal says nothing, but the slits in her eyes narrow as she dials up the intensity in her stare. How do older people gain this skill?

Congratulations on reaching the age of sixty-five! Sneezing might throw your back, but it's not all bad—You've gained a superpower: when you stare at young people, they spill their guts!

"Not *anymore.*" I emphasize, folding my arms.

"Oh, sweetheart." Gail rounds the car to wrap her arms around me, enveloping me in her flowery scent. She's always the good cop. Opal, on the other hand, relishes her role as the intimidating bad cop. I know she's soft on the inside, but she'll make you work hard to reach that part of her.

We sink down onto the steps that are still bathed in evening sun, the bees buzzing in the oasis around us. I'm sandwiched between Opal and Gail, each with an arm looped through mine.

"Look, Opal," Gail squeaks, shaking the link of our arms. "It's our favorite mailman...mhmmm...the suspenders on that one. Makes me wanna just walk up to him and *snap 'em*."

"I'll be sure to bring you fresh underwear and soap when you're in jail. Now will you pipe down so the girl can tell us her story?"

"Right, sorry, Ivy." I catch her executing one more ogle at the poor mailman before she scoots closer.

"What's goin' on sugar?"

"You sure I can't ask that nice mailman to come over and do some push-ups?" I deflect.

"Gail!" Opal scolds when she catches her friend's eyes straying back to the mailman.

"Oh, I'll catch him tomorrow. Spill," Gail demands.

"Ugh! Fine." I wipe my hands down my face. "Ross has landed himself in a bit of trouble." Opal snorts but I continue. "He's trying, I swear. But his problems may have sorta spilled over into mine this time."

"You gave him money again, didn't you?" Opal accuses.

"He swore he only needed it for a few days."

"Oh, honey," Gail coos in a comforting voice, rubbing circles over my back.

"And last month, I found out that the owners of my complex were selling my unit, so I had to move. But I'd already given all my money to Ross and couldn't afford to pay a deposit on a new place. I hadn't planned to sleep in my car this long. It just sorta happened."

"Ivy June Marsh, did it not cross your mind to ask for help?"

"I honestly didn't think I *needed* help. Ross was supposed to repay me weeks ago. I've only spent a few nights in my car. That's like a road trip. It's no big deal."

"What about Ember? You don't think she'd want to know about this?"

"Uh-uh, you can *not* tell Ember. She has enough on her plate. I don't want her worrying about me. Swear you won't tell her, y'all, please?" I turn to each of them, unashamedly giving them my best puppy eyes.

"Fine, but you should've come to us. And you're sleeping here tonight." Gail nods.

"Thank you, but I actually have a solution to all of this, for now."

Opal lifts a chin to the retirement village. "You get hitched to one of the old geezers about to kick the bucket while you were over there?"

"Ew, no. Gran gave me a house," I say proudly.

"Well, excuse us! You're going to have to back way up, missy." Opal's eyes grow wide as she blinks at me.

I give them a recap, leaving out the faking-dating bits. It's just easier. Lord knows I'll screw up if I have to constantly remember who knows what, so I also tell them I'm currently in a very casual relationship with my coworker.

"I have the keys to my new home and a place to sleep. Problem solved."

I also skip over the part about my new home possibly being unlivable, because I've had enough vulnerability for one night.

I'll have a roof over my head and hopefully a working toilet. I can deal with the rest later.

I sigh. "Opal, your robin just pooped on my car."

"I swear they're spawn sent by that witch across the road. Speaking of Agnes, did you find her and tell her to stick it where the sun don't shine?"

"Stick what?" Gail chimes in.

"Anything'll do." Opal's bottom lip arches and she shrugs. "A shoe comes to mind."

She turns back to me, gaze sharp. "Well...did you find her?"

"That's a negative," I fib. "Also I'm not comfortable telling a complete stranger to suck it."

"Coward," Opal grunts, and Gail snickers while my head falls to her shoulder. It truly is a marvel how I've kept this secret from them for this long, although I'm still a little worried they'll murder me with hard stares and elbow pokes when they find out my beloved Gran is their sworn enemy.

CHAPTER EIGHT

ETHAN

My foot pushes against the floor, making my office chair swivel around for the third time. I may look bored, but my brain operates best when I'm on the move. That need to stay busy feels like an itch; my body doesn't tolerate stillness for too long.

My brother taps on my door as he enters and leans on a cabinet with his arms folded, watching me spin.

"Eth."

"What?" I pause my swiveling.

"Do you need more work? What is...this?" He gestures at my chair.

"My morning routine."

"Okay, then. I need a favor."

"*We* need a favor," Colton's fiancée, Ember, announces as she enters and goes over to mirror his stance.

"Shoot."

Ember glances at Colton before continuing, and the sneaky little look she gives him tells me I'm probably not going to like what's coming. "You're between house flips at the moment, right?"

"Yeah, the only job I've got outside of this one is the thing I'm doing at the school. Besides my own house, of course." I usually work on at least two houses at a time, in addition to the renovations I'm doing on my current fixer-upper. But I've found myself in a lull between house flips, and I don't know how to feel about it. The work I do to help Colton on the creative team for his adventure subscription box company is fun, but it's always left me looking for the next thing to come calling. I just don't know what that is yet.

"And you're bored?" Colton frowns.

"Who says I'm bored?"

He unfolds an arm to make a twirling motion with his finger, his eyes darting between me and my chair. I smile up at him before doing another rotation. "A spinning brain is a working brain."

Ember straightens things on my desk as she continues. "You haven't heard back from the network about your show yet?"

"I did. I'm just waiting for clarification on what they want from me."

"Well, that's perfect, then." She aims those big brown eyes at me, and I'm annoyed at myself for having developed a soft spot for my brother's fiancée. It means I get roped into things I'd normally avoid. "While you wait to find out if that major network wants to make you America's next reality TV star, I have something that'll keep you busy."

"Why do you look like you're about to send Frodo back to Mordor?" I ask, squinting at her.

"That's weirdly specific. Anyway, this is for you." She slides one of my favorite candy bars across the desk, along with a catalog from a place called *"Toolz Unlimited."*

"What game are you playing, Flames?"

She reaches over to open the catalog and tries to look

impressed with its contents. "So many shiny tools to construct with."

"You have no idea what any of those are for, do you?" I scoff, plucking it from her hands. I spend a minute perusing the inside while the two of them silently and creepily communicate with their eyes.

I open the candy bar and take a bite. "All right, I'm buttered up. What do you need?"

Ember sighs. "I need you to check in on Ivy."

"What happened to her?" I pause my chewing to blurt out. Then I catch myself straightening and trying to read their expressions, so I slouch back into my chair.

"She's fine. At least for now. But she's attempting to renovate the house she just moved into...by herself. I'm legitimately concerned for her safety."

I'd call Ember out for worrying over nothing, but I've witnessed Ivy's propensity for clumsiness. It's what got my hackles up the first time I saw her. I'm also slightly relieved to hear she's not living out of her car anymore, in a purely 'concerned for my fellow citizen' kind of way. All that aside, just because the woman has a bum house doesn't mean I want to step anywhere near it...or her. She'd probably use my offer to help as an opportunity to arrange for a rogue beam to fall on my head or something—the perfect *'accident'*.

I glare at Ember. "You know she hates me, right?"

"She doesn't *hate* you," she replies like the word *hate* is a tad too strong but still quite close.

Colton's eyes narrow. "What did you do *now?*"

"Nothing," I reply, standing to toss the candy wrapper in the trash. "I saw her at the school and we may have...*clashed*..."

"Oh, Ethan." Ember slumps, closing her eyes while she rubs her forehead. Her shoulders rise with a deep breath, then her imploring puppy eyes zero in on me, enlarging by the second. How does she do that? "Can't you just *try*? Please? I'm not saying the two of you have to become best friends. Just swing by, offer her some help, and *don't* let her refuse. It'll be easy."

I turn to Colton, gesturing a palm to Ember. "Make it make sense."

"Please, Eth? Ember can't focus on wedding stuff as long as she's worrying about Ivy. And this would mean a lot to both of us." He wraps an arm around her, pulling her close. My brow lowers and I look away. I don't like feeling like I'm missing out on something. It's literally my worst fear—I'm the poster child for FOMO. Usually, I'm just afraid of being excluded from the big things, like adventuring and traveling. But lately, I've started to feel a slight pang when I catch these moments between my brother and the woman who simultaneously lights him up and brings him a peace I've never seen in him before.

And I don't like that gnawing in my chest, the one that always appears when it starts to feel like something's missing from my life.

I've avoided long term relationships with women for a reason. I'm too easily distracted, and I can't bring myself to make a commitment knowing I'd inevitably get bored. I know it sounds like the douchiest thing ever, but I can't help the way I feel. I'd have to see the writing on the wall before I'd ever consider taking the plunge and getting serious with anyone.

I run a hand through my hair, realizing this isn't going to be limited to one small favor. Because if there's anything I know about Ivy Marsh, it's that she's a feisty, complicated package. I must be a sucker for punishment if I'm considering walking into an active war zone like this. But I'm struggling to say no with Ember's giant brown eyes peering down at me. It's highly inconvenient.

"Fine," I concede with a groan. "I can swing by over the

weekend. But if this ends poorly, I reserve the right to say I told you so."

"Noted. I'll try to warm her up to the idea when we're all together tomorrow night," Ember says with a wide smile.

"Remind me why we're doing that?"

Ember's arms fall to her side, and I catch Colton's grin as she stomps her foot. "Come on, Ethan, I told you this! We're going over some wedding plans. I need help coming up with a plot to simmer the parents down. The moms are taking things too far."

"Good luck with that," I tell her with a salute, making Colton laugh.

Then I sigh inwardly, because I suspect I just got the fuzzy end of that lollipop.

CHAPTER NINE

IVY

My routine is changing once again—this time for the better. After school on Friday, I bought the cheapest inflatable mattress I could find and set it up in the cottage. Then I collapsed into my squeaky new bed as the bone-tiring effects of the last week finally caught up to me. And it's a good thing I finally caught up on some of the sleep I've been missing, since the rest of my weekend was filled with wedding planning and made-of-honor duties.

I woke up this morning with the luxury of peeing in my own toilet and climbing back under the blankets. It was heaven. Well...almost heaven, since my air mattress is a bit noisy. But once I get my real furniture from Carl, I imagine it'll be pretty darn close.

The house has yet to be fully explored, but I plan to remedy that after school. First, I need to hurry my butt up if I plan to get to work on time.

My body feels sluggish with the aftereffects of all the changes I've been hit with over the past few weeks. I've had to vacuum pack each new stressor I've faced and shove them out of sight to be dealt with later. Now that the stakes don't seem quite so high, I can sense that seal breaking. Apparently, my body's way of dealing with all this is to catch up on sleep and ignore the many alarms I set for myself.

As much as I hate it, I'll have to forgo the shower this morning. I dig through the two duffel bags I have yet to unpack and pick out the least wrinkled clothes. The rest of my *stuff,* as Ethan called it, is still piled in my car. Again—I'm too exhausted to care whether my car looks like a troll has been living in it for one more day.

By the time I dump my teaching tote behind the desk in my classroom, I'm out of breath and hungry. I may have a house, but I haven't ventured to open the fridge since it probably needs disinfecting before I can fill it.

I grab one of the mystery bars from the staff lounge on my way to Toby's class. I take a cautious bite as I walk in to find Toby writing what looks like a quote from *The Lord of The Rings* on his whiteboard.

"Even the smallest person can change the course of the future," I read aloud. "Is that one just for me?" I point, grinning at my friend.

"For all the vertically challenged," he affirms proudly.

"This vertically challenged friend also has a favor to ask." I bat my eyelashes, trying for humor since asking for help feels so unnatural to me.

"Hit me with it."

I remove Stef's hieroglyphics chart from my pocket and hand it to Toby. "Can you help make sense of this?" I chew on my lip as Toby takes the paper, a sinking feeling settling in. It's just another reminder that my ambitions to further my education might just be unrealistic dreams. What's the point of aiming higher when something as simple as reading a chart feels like an insurmountable hurdle? How could I possibly handle more years of study?

Toby unfolds the paper, silently frowning in concentration. He doesn't ask why I can't understand the information on it for myself.

"It looks like Stef organized the groups of your field trip into time slots. She added a heart next to her name," He adds with a smile before clearing his throat and continuing. "Most of the groups are all together, but two require different groups to go to certain locations..." He continues verbally breaking down the schedule for me as I nod, committing as much of it to memory as possible.

"You want me to type this up with bullet points?" he asks, like it's no big deal. It isn't often that I need to ask for Toby's help like this. I don't encounter too many documents of this format—numbers and letters at war with each other, interspersed and trying to assume some form of order, but they won't stay still. And when I do, I usually get Ember to help if we're together.

But the way Toby offers to go above and beyond what I've asked him to do just to make my life easier threatens to crack a piece of my heart wide open. I desperately want to confide in him about my struggles. I don't fully know why I hold this particular battle so closely, like a shield. Maybe it's become a habit, or maybe it's my pride. I'm probably making things harder for myself, but lowering the guard you've held up your whole life is daunting. If I let go, I'm not sure I'll know what to hide behind or hold onto anymore.

Toby's kindness makes that shield feel a little heavy though. Without answering, I step forward and wrap my arms around him. He pulls me close, giving me the brotherly embrace I so desperately need.

Footsteps shuffle past Toby's door, and I let go of him,

casting a glance at the doorway as our koala hug ends and finding it empty. "Thank you, Bee," I say, dabbing at my eyes. "That would be amazing. I'll grab it from you after school." I offer him a watery smile before jogging back to class.

Then again, there's no need to tell anyone about this, right? Toby seems to understand. Besides, I'm managing just fine.

CHAPTER TEN

ETHAN

"I'm heading inside for a second." I turn to Marco, flipping my hat backwards. "Can you get the tarps laid out?"

"You got it. Try not to be too big of an ass to *Miss Marsh*."

"I'll do my best." I salute, trying to disguise my involuntary smile with sarcasm.

There's really no reason for me to enter the school. But I'm still a sucker for punishment, because I can't ignore the annoying urge to see her.

I'm just checking on her because Colton and Ember asked. That's all.

Today will be our last day working at the school. All that's left to do is attach the tarps to the poles. It'll take a few more hours before we're done, but I figured I may as well see how Miss Feisty Marsh is doing before I get all sweaty.

I peek my head into each classroom I pass, my steps faltering as I approach an open door bearing the name *Mr. Jenkins*. My jaw clenches, because *Mr. Toby Jenkins* has his scrawny arms wrapped around Ivy as she burrows cozily into his neck.

Well. Looks like I won't be poking any tiny bears this morning.

I stomp back through the corridors and march outside to meet Marco.

"Lucked out, did ya?" He grins smugly.

"What are you talking about?"

"You've got that *I didn't get to stir the pot and I'm sulking* look."

I scoff. "No way you can tell if someone's face has that kind of look."

"I've seen this one before." He sniffs like he's got me all figured out. "It's an obvious lead-in to a trope."

"What do you know about *tropes?*"

"Only what I've learned from Reese Witherspoon movies. So...everything."

"I don't know what to do with that." I blink at him, pursing my lips.

"I'm kidding. I only watched *Sweet Home Alabama*. The rest I learned from your books."

"My books," I repeat, unsure where he's heading with this.

"Yeah, the ones you always hide under your seat. I read 'em every now and again."

"I don't know what to do with that either."

"Don't worry," he says, picking up a tarp. "I won't tell anyone you're a giant book nerd who reads old-timey books."

I shrug. "Didn't you hear? Reading is cool now."

I've always been a reader, but that fact seems to throw people off. They never know how to connect the joking, good-time guy with someone who also loves books and staying home to read. My family doesn't even know how deeply my love of books runs.

Marco scratches his chin, looking thoughtful. "You got any more?"

I can't help the slow grin that splits across my face. "Yeah. I've got more."

Marco and I spend the next two hours securing tarps to poles, just in time for the kids's first recess. My shoulders and back ache with the satisfaction of honest, hard work.

I stretch my arm across my chest, loosening my muscles. As I turn, I catch sight of Ivy's small figure framed in her classroom window. I continue flexing, and even from this distance, I can feel the intensity of her molten stare—until she abruptly pivots and vanishes from view.

Marco and I go out to the parking lot to load the last of our supplies after that. But my eyes can't help drifting over to Ivy's car. The backseat is still piled with random stuff.

I wait for Marco to drive away, stalling in my truck before eventually deciding to torture myself. I climb out, lumbering back into the school. It's probably a good idea to let C.J. know we're all done. I mean, I told her we'd be finished soon when I spoke to her earlier, but it would be rude not to say goodbye to my old principal, right?

I purposely take the route that goes past Ivy's class, indulging in my self-inflicted torment. Then, she rushes out distractedly just as I approach her classroom door, a deep frown creasing her brow. She bumps into me, and her hands and forehead collide with my chest.

"Oof, sorry," she mumbles, her face buried in my shirt.

I catch her by the shoulders and steady her, ready to make a joke about her being too clumsy and ending up in my arms once again. But my flirty smile falters when I see the way she's avoiding eye contact. In all my interactions with her, she's never backed away from an opportunity to at least throw a few eyeball daggers my way.

"Hey, you okay?" I ask tentatively while the eyes in question dart back down to the paper she was reading before.

"Ethan? What are you—Oh, yeah. I'm...uh...I need to go." She chews on her bottom lip, barely even acknowledging me as she walks on. I watch her scurry away, her wedge heels moving in quick, short steps, and it requires more effort than I'm willing to admit to snap myself out of the trance she's just put me in.

"Where are your minions?" I jog to catch up with her, slightly shaken by the effect she's having on me.

"They're at recess." She continues ahead, her eyes burning a hole in the paper in her hand. Then she stops at a classroom and peaks her head inside, growling when she finds it empty.

Dang.

I blink away the fog of what that noise just did to me.

Whatever the effect it had on me, it evaporates when I realize whose class we've stopped at.

I'll admit, this whole exchange is bruising my ego the teensiest bit. I still don't even know what the heck I'm doing here in the first place. But I ignore my pride, because I'm still concerned about the visible distress in Ivy's eyes.

However, it's like I'm not even here as she whisks past me, catching another teacher as she's walking her class down the hall.

"Hey Stef. D'you know where Toby is?"

"Uh...I think his class is doing a science thing in the gym. You okay?" Stef looks slightly annoyed as she glances over me and back to Ivy.

I watch Ivy's hands tighten into fists. "Yup. Thanks."

I'm once again trailing after her while she rubs at her forehead, obviously still in distress. Her muttered "frik" has me frowning, too. She rushes into a new classroom and whirls around, pinning me with another furious glance.

"Why are you here? Can't you see I've got things to do?"

She's like a vicious snapping turtle. She's making me work

for every inch of civility, but I can tell that the stress in her clenched jaw is only disguising itself as anger.

"Gee, I dunno, Ivy," I lift my hands then let them fall against my side. "Maybe 'cause you clearly need help with something and I'm not a heartless monster?"

She leans against a desk while one dainty eyebrow slants with suspicion. "You want to *help* me?"

"I'm considering it. How bad do you need me?" I flash a cocky smile, trying to get a rise out of her. But the innuendo is lost on her as she glances back and forth between the sheet scrunched in her fist and the whiteboard hanging on the wall.

"Can you *please* help me?" she grinds the words out through slightly clenched teeth.

"That cost you, didn't it?"

She's back to avoiding eye contact as she ignores my question. She hands me the paper before stomping over to the whiteboard.

"I have to sub for a class in a minute while my students go to P.E. It was a last minute thing...anyway. Can you write those letters on the board, same as they are in the grids on the page?"

I hold onto the paper, but I'm still trying to catch her green eyes while she folds her arms, studying her shoes. Something about this specific task has her retreating. The evasive eye contact, lip gnawing, foot shuffling, hand hiding—I may not spend a lot of time with Ivy Marsh, but I have a feeling this is her majorly stressed out look.

I glance down at the page and find eight five-by-five grids with letters jumbled inside. It seems simple, but I don't dare say it to her.

"This is like Boggle or something?"

"Yeah. It's a game to test their spelling words. They're hidden in there. The uh...the other teacher prepped it. It's not something I'd plan." Her eyes meet mine for a second before she's studying the white-board. "So, will you do it?"

For some inexplicable reason, I want to scrutinize her more, to freeze this moment long enough to discover the secrets she's hiding. But she's obviously uncomfortable, and I don't think stretching this interaction out will help me thaw her icy exterior. The one that only seems to ice over around me.

"Sure," I say. Then I step closer, my gaze locked onto hers as I bend to pick up the marker beside her.

"Thanks," she whispers from behind me after I turn and start copying the grids onto the board.

"Your boyfriend usually helps you with this stuff?" I'm not exactly sure what *'this stuff'* is, but hell if I'm not desperate to find out.

"Uh..."

"Mr. Jenkins," I clarify dryly. "He's your boyfriend, right?"

I don't know why I think I need the verification, but saying the words makes my stomach roil.

Weird.

"Oh. Yes, yeah. He's my boyfriend. Yup," she says, emphasizing the pop at the end of the word.

Well, there it is.

She's officially off limits. Not that I care.

She watches in silence while I finish copying the grids. When I'm done, I turn to hand her the page. "Hope I got it all down right."

"I'm sure it's fine. Thanks."

I hate seeing the feeling of powerlessness etched on her face. This woman is a wild force of nature whose fire should never be dimmed. But because I'm an ass, I don't offer to build any bridges. No. Instead, I carry on with my new favorite thrill. I poke the bear.

My eyes flicker to her heels, then back to her eyes. Because

I need to see them light up with passion again. If getting mad at me ignites that spark, then poke, I will.

"Still wearing those death traps?"

Her eyes widen as the storm rolls in.

"You're a butthead, Ethan King."

There it is.

One side of my mouth turns up in a satisfied smirk, and we're back to our usual state of mutual disdain. "Guess you're having dinner with a butthead. See you tonight, Marsh."

CHAPTER ELEVEN

ETHAN

The sky is a deep purple, the stars beginning their show as I pull up outside the restaurant to meet Ember, Colton and Ivy. I blow out my cheeks, unsure of what I'm walking into.

Ticking Ivy off again wasn't the best idea. I know I should be playing nice for Ember and Colton's sake, but it's already getting exhausting, especially since it's proving impossible to avoid her altogether. Ivy and I are like oil and water, which makes it even more amusing when I shake things up just to get a reaction out of her. But I'll admit, it would make nights like tonight more bearable if we could tolerate each other's company for more than two minutes.

I walk into the restaurant and immediately find Ivy and Ember with their heads huddled over a magazine while Colton sits across the table, watching them with a soft smile. There's a faint tightening in my chest at seeing Ivy so at ease beside her friend. I slow my steps, trying to stretch the few seconds before I reach the table. It's a strange phenomenon, getting to observe her without her scowl directed at me. For some crazy reason, I wonder what it's like to be the person she's smiling at for once.

"*Fratello.*" I clap Colton on the shoulder, unable to prolong the moment any longer.

"Eth. Beer?" Colton asks, already flagging down a waitress.

"Yeah, sounds good. Hey, ladies." I nod, watching as their shared giggles fade, only to be replaced by Ivy's stiff smile. The stormy expression she wears contradicts the bright yellow ribbon glistening in her hair. I slide into the empty seat across from her, tapping the toe of her shoe with mine and earning a sharp glare.

"Boyfriend not joining us, Ivy?"

"*Boyfriend?*" Ember tilts her head, frowning at her friend.

"Oh...um...It's new. And no." She flashes those angry eyes in my direction. "Tonight is about Colton and Ember."

"Okay, but hold up!" Ember raises a palm with a slow blink. "When the heck did you get a boyfriend? And *who* is he?"

"Recently?" Ivy answers like it's a question. "And...it's Toby."

"You're dating *Toby?*"

"Mhmm." Her eyes jump to each of us then back to Ember.

"But I thought you said he's like—"

"The sweetest. I know, he's so sweet. Just...the sweetest."

I release a short puff of air with the roll of my eyes. *Gag.*

"He's sweet, you're sweet, we're all sweet. Can we order now?" There's a slight edginess in my tone, making my irritation evident. I realize I sound rude, but I'm irritated *about* being irritated...about the memory of seeing Ivy and Toby together. And I don't want to examine those feelings *at all*.

Colton catches my reaction, silently questioning me with a frown. I reply with a quick headshake, which he interprets using brotherly telepathy.

Ember's brows crease for a second. I don't look at Ivy. I don't want to see the effects of my poor attitude etched on her face, especially not after Colton glances at her and immediately turns back to aim his big-brother glare in my direction. And he's wielding the one when he doesn't blink and only shows the slightest hint of a scowl at full strength.

His brow lifts, silently scolding me for being a giant ass and telling me I better tighten it up this time.

God must be smiling on me or giving me an out, because my phone rings, breaking the tension. "Sorry, I've gotta take this," I announce, as I stand. "Get me the burger, Colt."

Ivy

"Someone woke up on the wrong side of the construction zone." Ember scowls as Ethan stomps out of the restaurant doors.

The guy's got something up his butt, that's for sure.

The waitress takes our food orders, and as soon as she leaves, Ember unleashes an onslaught of questions regarding Toby. She's so excited I can practically see the stars popping fireworks in her eyes.

"Em. I'm not marrying the man. We're just hanging out."

"But you *could* marry him." She arches one brow.

I roll my eyes, but instead of drifting back to Ember, my gaze settles on Ethan as he rejoins the table wearing the same scowl. What is it with this dude? And what have I done to annoy him this time? Is it my breathing? Maybe he had a traumatic experience with heels in his past. I bet an enraged ex threw one at his face, and that's why he's such a poopyhead about it.

"Phone call not go well?" Colton asks, clearly reading Mr. Grumpy Pants's face.

"It was great. The network wants me to fly to Frisco in a couple weeks to shoot a test episode."

"And that's not good?" Ember scrunches her nose.

"It's great."

Colton throws his hands up, letting them plop on the table as he shakes his head. "That makes perfect sense, since you look like someone just sat on your origami collection and all."

"Colt, Don't be the wigs from the *Twilight* movies. It's good news. I'm happy. Let's move on." Ethan smiles more genuinely, seemingly returning to his usual relaxed state. I don't know where the Kings get their weird analogies, but it's definitely a family trait.

Maybe that heel to the head did permanent damage.

"By the way, I saw you chatting with Sandra on your way out today," Colton pries. "She ask you out again?"

Ethan scratches the back of his neck with a sigh. "Yeah."

"Did you say yes?"

"I was on the phone. I told her I couldn't talk."

"Interesting," Colton replies.

"Can we stay on track?" Ember interrupts. "I need to give everyone their duties for the wedding day." Colton apologizes, and she continues. "Seriously, I want to make this as small of an event as possible. And with our moms running the opposite direction, maybe it'll end up being a regular-sized wedding." Her elbows rest on the table as she massages her temples with a groan. "Are you sure we can't elope?"

Colton shrugs. "I suggested that last week, baby. Just say the word."

"I'm not ruling it out at this point. Ugh...okay. Let's focus." She pops her eyes open, determination in her posture. "Vee," she hands me a pen and legal pad. "Can you take notes?"

I slowly slide the pad closer, my heart rate climbing as my palms begin sweating. Ember is one of the only people who know I struggled with dyslexia as a child. But I've only briefly mentioned the challenges I face with mentally processing numbers and letters. It's so much more than that, but it's my own fault for leaving my best friend unaware of the depths of my battle.

I fiddle with the pen in my hand. "Can I type them on my phone?" I'm praying nobody thinks twice about my sudden paper aversion. Numbers aren't my thing, but handwriting is another huge trigger. I can do it. It's just that my terrible spelling gives me extreme anxiety, because I know it'll end up looking like a note written by a five-year-old. At least I can blame the spelling errors on autocorrect when I use my phone.

There's a reason I chose to teach second grade. So much of their learning at that age is hands-on, and the methods I get to use to teach them are easier for the kids and for me. Plus, there's a teacher's aide in the room, so I can often get away with delegating tasks that seem too tricky for me.

The silence around the table stretches for a fraction too long. This is exactly what I dread most—sensing someone's confusion with my coping mechanisms and the tension that creates. Everyone is about to wonder why I'm being this weird about something so trivial, and these incidents usually lead to me overexplaining some lame reason as to why I'd rather not do the thing that should be so simple to do in the first place.

I'm about to pull a Michael Scott and start a sentence without knowing where it's going when Ethan jumps in, sliding the notepad out from under my palm. Then I'm overwhelmed by my senses for a moment, and the only thing my mind can process is the rough graze of his calloused hand over mine.

"I'll take notes," he offers, his eyes flickering to mine before he clicks the pen and waits for instructions.

"Oh...okay." Ember frowns at him for a second before she begins rattling off ideas and a very long to-do list consisting mostly of parental management/babysitting.

I bite my lip, trying to decipher the enigma of a man across from me. It's the second time today he's gone out of his way to help me like this. I can't figure out his angle, and it's nearly impossible to keep up with all his mood swings and the emotional whiplash they're giving me.

Thankfully, the evening continues without any more hiccups. I'm also grateful when Colton insists on paying for dinner since I'm still broke, not to mention the thought of figuring out a split bill is enough to make me barf. I have no problems using an app on my phone to calculate tips. But unless someone is willing to tally my order for me, I'm a mess.

Then, just when we're all walking out of the restaurant and I think I might escape peacefully, I hear Ethan assuring Ember that he'll see me to my car.

I scoff internally. What does that even mean? Does he actually think I'm at risk of getting lost or forgetting where I parked?

I ignore Ethan's hulking frame as he stomps behind me. But as soon as I unlock my car, he lunges over me to open the door and inspect the contents. I still haven't gotten around to unloading the rest of my belongings. It's been a busy day. I also discovered the water heater in my new house is a bust, so I had to live through the trauma of a cold shower this afternoon.

"Are you still living in your car?"

I step closer, squaring my shoulders, and the man is so freaking tall that it's like trying to peer over the top of the Eiffel Tower. Even with my wedges, I barely reach his chest.

"Listen here, King," I snarl at the giant. "You don't need to take notes for me, or concern yourself with my shoes or the state of my car. Ember and Colton aren't here, so we can stop pretending we actually get along." I plop down into my hoarder-mobile and grip the door handle. "Leave. Me. Alone," I say, ready to yank the door shut with dramatic effect. but Ethan puts a hand on the top, hindering me.

I'm fighting back a sob—the need to be alone is clawing at me. The vulnerability I'm feeling from whatever Ethan is beginning to figure out, whatever he saw that made him jump to my rescue at dinner—it's too much. I can't take all this exposure.

Then again, maybe it's not the need to be alone that has me retreating, but the opposite. Ethan's small acts of chivalry are shining a sudden, unwelcomed spotlight on my desire to be close to someone. I swallow hard, because if I'm being honest right now, I want nothing more than a hug. I want to have someone in my life that I can trust to pull me close and remind me that they'll always have my back.

But that's a fairytale. People let you down.

All of these thoughts spiral through my mind as Ethan steps closer, his nostrils flaring ever so slightly before he smiles.

"I don't think I can do that, Marsh. Who's gonna stop you from injuring yourself in those ridiculous shoes?"

And then he steps back with so much smugness as he shuts my door. I force myself not to glance back at him as I drive away, even though I desperately want to see him one more time.

CHAPTER TWELVE

IVY

The beeping of my alarm pulls me out of sleep. My air mattress squeaks as I roll off and stretch. I'm so glad Carl is bringing my furniture this afternoon. This thing wasn't made for long term use. I pick up the fuzzy cardigan that's puddled next to my makeshift bed and pull it on.

My toes squish into the stained, sun-weathered carpets. These will definitely need to go. I make a note on my phone to find a Youtube video on DIY carpet removal. Hopefully there's salvageable wood beneath.

I pad into the kitchen, noting the faded floral print that borders the trim. Nearly everything in this room looks the same as it did to my seven-year-old eyes, just a tad more faded. There's a bittersweet nostalgia in the twirl of the vines on the wallpaper and the light spilling through the window above the sink.

This house was my childhood refuge, the only place I could be myself without any pressure to perform. Not to mention, I got much more attention here than in my own home. My parents were usually more focused on their missionary work or busy dealing with Ross, and he was usually getting up to mischief with friends and uninterested in spending time with his quirky Gran. Meanwhile, I lavished having her all to myself.

Throughout all of the years I walked around with my stomach in knots, the only time I remember feeling it unclench is when I walked through these doors. None of the things I had to prove to my parents mattered here.

But today, standing in this kitchen seems to have dragged up a few of those insecurities from the past. Now that I'm older and my problems have only matured over time, this place no longer feels like the sanctuary it once was. But if Gran wants to see it restored, I'll give that to her.

Plus, homeless beggars can't be choosers.

My chest rises with a heavy inhale as I shuffle into the living room, only to find more work to be done. That to-do list in my head is growing by the second. I'm supposed to be meeting with Gran's lawyer this evening, and I'm praying her reno fund will be enough to cover everything, or at least enough to make the house livable.

Some of these walls will be coming down, that's for sure. My slight claustrophobia will throw a tantrum if I'm forced to keep the narrow kitchen separate from the living room. Give me all the open-plan spaces.

But to my unskilled eye, the bones of the house appear good. I'm hoping most of the repairs are surface level and therefore less expensive.

My cold shower may be on-trend, but I still scream when I step under the freezing spray. I'm *not* looking forward to hair-wash day, and I shiver again at the thought. I'll admit, I feel very alert and can even picture my endorphins putting on their party hats, but I won't be joining the cold-plunge evangelists any time soon. There's nothing like a hot shower.

During my drive to school I get lost in thought, daydreaming about the possibilities for restoring the cottage to its full glory. I have yet to explore all the nooks I remember as a little girl, but I can't wait to get into it all. My mental Pinterest boarding is interrupted by my phone ringing.

"Ross," I say after answering on speaker phone.

"Vee."

"What. The. Heck!"

He sighs heavily into the phone, and I can picture him rubbing his forehead. "I know. I'm really sorry."

"I love you, Ross. But you've gotta meet me halfway here. You left me in a really sucky position."

Understatement of the year.

"I know. I'm—ugh, I'm in a bit of trouble. I just need a little more time."

I lean forward, resting my forehead on the steering wheel when I stop at a light. Just once, I'd like to see my brother making the *right choice*.

"What kind of trouble?" I mumble through my curtain of hair.

"I had a bet go bad. It was supposed to be a sure thing. But I'm trying. I'll get your money soon, I promise."

"A bet is never a sure thing. That's why it's called a *bet*. Did you look into those community college classes I sent you?" I straighten, motioning with my hands even though he can't see me. "Electricians are in high demand in this area, and I think a career like that could be so good for you. I'll even help you pay for your classes. Just *please—*"

"So you have a little more you could give me?"

I pound my fist on the steering wheel. "Ross! Are you for real right now? I literally have *nothing* left to give you!"

I hear him grunt through the phone, like he's annoyed his

ATM is out of cash. "Okay. I'll fix this, Vee. I love you." And then he hangs up.

The loud blast of a car horn startles me, and I raise a hand in the rearview mirror in apology.

The rest of my drive to school is spent pushing back tears and berating myself for wasting my energy being so upset about something I should have expected. I know better. But he's my brother, and I just can't give up on him.

Toby is the only one in the teachers' lounge when I use my shoulder to push the door open. He's sipping his coffee calmy, like an old man cherishing his quiet morning, but this fake girlfriend is about to mess that up.

"Hey, Tobes. Can we talk?"

"Of course." He smiles, setting his coffee down. "I'm sorry you couldn't find me yesterday. Stef said you were looking for me?"

"Oh, that's okay."

"She also said that 'hunky playground dude' was with you. It seems all women want a tall man," He grimaces through his use of air quotes.

"Ugh." I roll my eyes, looking to the side. "Not all of us, trust me. Hey...um, by the way, my Gran sorta thinks we're dating. So I'm going to need you to return this fake-dating favor on occasion if that's okay."

Toby's head falls back with a burst of laughter and a loud clap.

I get it. Our storyline is getting more complicated than a plot on *Days Of Our Lives*. But unlike a soap opera, these tiny fibs and omissions of truth aren't hurting anybody. In fact, mine's more of an assumption I've yet to correct.

"Wow. Nice deflection from your grumpy construction man," he says, wiping a tear from his eye. "But, yeah, that's fine with me." He lets out a loud, slow exhale as he finishes laughing, then pushes off his chair. "I've got some things to prep in my class. I'll see you later." On his way out he pauses, turning to me with a hand on the door. "But next time, text me if you need my help. I've got your back, Vee."

A sudden ache forms in my chest, along with a giant lump in my throat. I manage a series of quick, short nods to avoid letting him hear my voice crack. I honestly don't know what I'd do without Toby, and that's scary.

What *would* I do if I didn't have someone with the intuition to fill in the gaps for all my shortcomings? Would I crack under the pressure or be forced to finally seek the help I know I need?

I bend to adjust the strap on my wedged heel before shuffling out of the lounge. Every now and then, I get the urge to wear flat shoes to school. But ultimately, I chicken out, afraid of having to hear someone compare my stature to my second graders'. Plus, parents tend to take me less seriously when I'm only a few inches taller than their eight-year-olds.

C.J. pops her head out her door, catching me on my way to my classroom. "Ivy. Can you step in here for a minute?"

"Sure." Even as an adult, being called to the principal's office is a new experience for me. As a child, I struggled to skate by and avoided any kind of reprimanding with every fiber of my being. Not letting my grades slip was a daily battle, and living in the shadow of my brother and his poor behavior was just as difficult.

You'd think that with such determination I'd have excelled and earned straight A's. But I was stuck in that invisible state between under- and over-performing. My dyslexia was never diagnosed because I hid the evidence of my handicap so well. I was so concerned with making sure I never caused my parents any trouble that I internalized it all and made do with whatever

I had. I guess it's too bad I'm breaking my principal's office streak today.

C.J. perches on the end of her desk chair at an angle, like she's the model under the green check mark that says "Do This" in a posing tutorial. She's all sleek lines at flattering degrees, while I'm the tiny slouch under the big red "What Not to Do" section.

"How's the prep going for your field trip with Stef?" She glances at me over the rim of her dainty half-glasses. They're the kind you'd call *spectacles* and then stick your pinky out while sipping tea. I'm getting etiquette lessons just watching her.

"They're going great," I say, leaning forward. "I've confirmed all the details with the exploratorium, and Stef is sending emails to the parents this week."

"Good." She smiles, taking a seat and flashing me her perfectly white teeth framed by her flawless red lips. She's like a living advertisement for graceful aging, and her fingers fly across her keyboard while she talks like she was born multitasking.

"Anything you want to tell me about you and Toby?" She peers at me briefly with a teasing smile, though her fingers don't rest for a second.

I open my mouth to deliver the same fib I've given to everyone else in my life so far, but I just can't bring myself to put on the fake-dating show for C.J. It feels like a 'don't poop where you eat' sort of thing. And now that I've allowed this white lie to seep into so many other facets of my life, I realize the need to protect the place I call a second home.

"Only that Toby's my favorite coworker and that he's like a brother to me."

Her dancing fingers pause their routine as she gives me one

of her gently appraising looks. One that lets me know I made the right choice telling her the truth.

"Okay. But if that changes, let me know." She turns back to her computer before her hand shoots up to stop me. "Oh, wait! While I have you here..." Then she lowers her spectacles over her nose as she squints at her screen. "Where's that email from Gil..." She intones the words as she searches, like she'll forget I'm here if she doesn't work to keep me entertained. "Here we are. As per Gil's words, 'We desperately need someone to head up the parent volunteers to paint backdrops and props for the end of year recital.'"

The glasses come off, and she holds them daintily in her hands as they rest together on her desk.

"I don't want to overload you, but I'm asking you first because, well, you're here. Do you have time to help with this?"

Nope.

"Absolutely." I dip my head in a nod.

Do I have any more room on my plate right now? Of course not. But I desperately want to please her. Heck, I might accidentally call her 'mom' if I'm not careful here.

"Wonderful!" She beams at me, warming my people-pleasing little heart.

Welp.

What's one more thing on my to-do list? This shouldn't backfire on me at all.

CHAPTER THIRTEEN

ETHAN

My Saturday mornings are usually slow, and that's how I like it. It's the one part of my life that holds a semblance of a routine. I'm a spur-of-the-moment guy in general, always ready to fly off to different locations or down for an adventure at the first suggestion. But Saturday is the only day of the week when I allow myself to act like a boring, old bachelor, spending my morning with a good book while I sip coffee in the rocking chair on my front porch.

I don't make any commitments for the first half of the day. The second half is reserved for running errands and working on my own home renovations.

And this house has been my favorite fixer-upper so far. It's the closest I've come to customizing everything to fit my tastes instead of what's easiest to sell and the closest I've come to calling a house *mine*, despite never seeing myself being able to settle down in one place. I've always been afraid of watching my sense of adventure mockingly wave goodbye as soon as I claim a piece of land as my own. But for some reason, I've been feeling oddly satisfied with my work on this reno. I keep waiting for that familiar sense of restlessness to kick in, but so far, it's been replaced by a fondness for things like front-porch coffee sipping and my weekend routine.

So my Saturdays have become mine, and my family knows not to expect me to be present unless absolutely necessary.

But not *this* Saturday. Today I'm tasked with offering my help to an alligator that hasn't been fed in too long. Although, I kind of feel like a hangry alligator, too, with my weekend being disrupted. I'd originally planned on checking in on Ivy and her house reno tomorrow, but the producers scheduled a conference call to go over some of the logistics for my pilot episode, and no telling how long that will take.

I squint as I try to make sense of the road names, leaning forward to peer under the visor at the house the GPS led me to. A mighty Spanish moss-draped live oak frames one side of the cottage-style home. The house is whimsically bathed in the yellows of morning light, and I feel a tug at my lips when I imagine a younger version of Ivy scaling the limbs of the ancient oak tree. I bet she was a menace as a child, stomping on hearts and bossing kids around like an angry little dragon.

I inhale deeply, trying to curb the last bit of my annoyance at having my Saturday hijacked. Because if my grumpy attitude were to meet the piranha-like fury of Ivy Marsh, I'm afraid we might leave a giant crater behind.

I'm careful not to shut my truck door too loudly so I can snoop out the condition of the house without alerting the ogre inside. Boxes litter the porch, and I stop to give the front-porch steps a good bounce, testing the integrity of the wood. The squeaky reply tells me that either the wood is dry or the boards haven't been nailed down securely.

I walk around the house next, scratching at the paint and finding that the slightest wind would be enough to flake it off. The entire exterior will need to be blasted and repainted.

I continue my inspection on the other side, and Ivy passes by the window at the same time I walk by. She does a double take and flinches, before she clutches the back of a chair and lets out a high-pitched screech. I stop and offer her a friendly wave, while her comically round eyes bug out and her hands fly up to cover her mouth. That scowl still manages to do something to me, though, and the way it makes my stomach dip is concerningly addictive.

"Ethan King," she bellows through the glass. "What. *The. Heck!*"

"Mornin', Ivy June," I reply calmly, attempting to contain my amusement.

Her stomps echo through the cottage, and the front door swings open.

The ground threatens to swallow me up as she glares, folding her arms over her light blue cropped T-shirt. She's a pastel paint sample with her cream sweatpants and baby pink hair ribbon. And, of course, the platform sneakers. They're not heels, but they're technically still safety hazards.

"Explain yourself," she demands through her teeth.

I lean casually against a tree, crossing my feet and my arms. "Well, let's see. Where to start? You already know my full name. Ah, yes. I'm twenty-nine-years old, and I was born in—"

"Ethan! *Why* are you being a creepy McCreeperson and stalking around my house?" she asks with wide eyes and a tiny headshake.

"I came to offer my help," I say simply.

"Ember put you up to this, didn't she?"

"Do you want to cause her more stress and have me tell her you refused help? Help which you *clearly* need." I gesture to the house with a wave of my hand.

Her brows pull down a fraction more, making her glasses slide lower on the bridge of her nose. She uncrosses an arm and reaches up to touch the corner of the frames. The movement reminds me of a fierce lioness pausing mid-roar to sneeze.

I run my eyes over her again. She just looks so damned cute and huggable, and I wonder whether she'd melt or explode if I stepped forward and wrapped my arms around her right now.

Whoa. We won't be doing any of that, King. You don't like each other, remember?

Her fingers tap against her arm while she contemplates her predicament. "Fine," she grunts after a while, turning back toward the house. I follow her inside, but before I make it through the door, she whirls around, that fire in her eyes lighting me up from less than a foot away.

"House rules, King: Don't tell me what to do, don't comment on my shoes, and *don't* be a butthead," she counts off on her dainty fingers, two of which are wrapped in Elsa and Grogu Band-Aids. Then she whips back around, barely scooting a chair out her path in time to stop herself from tripping.

"Am I even allowed to breathe?"

"If you can do it without being a butthead, sure." She tilts her head with a tight-lipped smile. If there was ever someone whose feathers I enjoyed ruffling, it's this woman staring at me like she'd relish the chance to watch me fall into a pit of lava.

"You forgot one rule," I say, resting an elbow on the kitchen counter and ignoring the state of the place since it looks like it was abandoned mid-demolition.

"Please, enlighten me," she adds with an eye roll.

"You're supposed to forbid me from falling in love with you."

She snorts out a sardonic laugh. "No chance of that, I assure you. Come on," she turns, leading me down a short passage. "Might as well put that height to good use."

I want to ask her why she's so sure I'm not in danger of

falling for her, besides the obvious fact that she's already dating that doofus, Toby. But my eye catches on a mattress lying on the floor in the first room we pass.

I stop at the open doorway, blinking in disbelief at what I presume is her bed. Ivy and her swishing blonde hair and pink ribbon continue for a few steps before she notices my absence.

"You can't sleep here. This house isn't habitable." I cross my arms as she takes determined steps toward me.

"That's a violation of rule number one," she announces with a tsk. "And I don't remember asking you for permission."

I groan, running my hand through my hair. "Seriously, Ivy, look at the ceiling!" I gesture with my palm.

"What about it?"

"There's a giant hole in it!" I yell incredulously.

She leans forward, peering into the gaping portal above us, then shrugs a shoulder. "The roof is still there."

"Unbelievable," I mutter under my breath. "Whatever you needed my height for can wait." My eyes scan over all the areas of concern, citing the red flags everywhere. "We need to write a list," I announce, pursing my lips.

Her head turns my way, eyes locking onto mine. There's a question swirling in her gaze. This woman is always armored up, on the defense, and the curiosity in her green eyes is the only sliver of vulnerability she's showing me.

She won't use words to reveal any of her weaknesses, but her expression tells me she's desperately trying to figure out if I mentioned "writing a list" on purpose. I didn't. I've picked up on the fact that, for whatever reason, she isn't comfortable writing things by hand. But realizing she believes I'd purposefully say something to make her feel bad is a sharp blow to the gut. She really does think I'm a giant ass.

My words come out with a gentle rasp. "*I'll* take notes."

She swallows hard and nods before she goes into a different room. "I'll get the paper," she mumbles over her shoulder.

My hands rest on my hips as I walk the space, busying myself with taking mental measurements. But it's either that or cataloging all the bits and pieces of the chaos around me that make up Ivy. I can't help noticing some of it anyway, like the unopened boxes with misspelled labels scrawled over the sides.

Before I know it, I've unintentionally made a list of all the things I've learned about this woman.

There's an attempt at order, but each area looks incomplete, like the next one distracted her before she could finish. The only flat soles in sight are the running shoes peeking out of a gym bag against the wall. Stacked boxes labeled "pots" and "kitchen utensils" await their unpacking, although I assume it's because Ivy wants to do something about the outdated cabinets before stocking them.

Where is that woman, anyway?

"Ivy?" I call out.

"Keep your panties on, King. I'm coming." She lets out an exaggerated sigh once she steps out from the room where she'd been bustling around, a fresh Olaf Band-Aid adorning her arm. How does she manage to go into a space for five minutes and come out with a new injury?

My jaw pulses as she nears. "What happened to you in there?"

"Rule. Three."

I groan in response. "Did you at least clean it properly?"

"Yes, Nurse Ethan. I managed to thoroughly clean my gaping wound before stitching and bandaging myself up." Another eye roll. She must practice those with Ember. "But I wasn't able to find any paper."

"No problem. Hang on to this." I unclip the measuring tape from my belt, holding it out to her. "You can take measurements in a minute." I dig a hand into my pocket, searching for my carpenter's pencil.

A few seconds pass before I realize she hasn't moved to take my offering. I look up, finding Ivy gnawing on her lip again, staring at the tape measure like it's a spider I've asked her to cuddle.

Then I notice the grooves etched on her brow. Just as I'm about to lower my hand, she reaches out slowly. Her fingers brush against mine, sending a tingle throughout me as she tentatively takes hold of the tape.

"I can—"

"It's fine." Her words are clipped, and she flashes a tight smile. "What now?"

The air grows thick with tension as she avoids my eyes. It feels like I'm tiptoeing across a fragile glass ceiling, every step threatening to shatter it. But I'm not alone—Ivy is there with me, and one wrong move puts us both at risk of getting hurt.

I'm learning there's a lot more to this woman than I thought. Yes—she's still a porcupine with complicated written all over her—but seeing what makes her so prickly makes me want to put on a thick coat and hold her closely so she doesn't fall through any ceilings—literally and metaphorically.

"Now, we make a plan." I grin and walk to the end of the living room. Various stains and sun-bleached patches decorate the bare walls. I write 'FIXIT LIST' in big, bold letters across the center of the twelve-foot-wide wall.

A gasp echoes behind me. "What are you doing?"

"Relax. We'll paint over it. This way we don't lose the list. I do it all the time."

Ivy inhales and releases a heavy sigh, like she's dealing with a child who's testing her patience to the limit.

This house is a huge project. But I think the bigger mission

—hopefully not an impossible one—will be getting through this without killing each other.

CHAPTER FOURTEEN

IVY

I'm unscrewing old light switch covers in my living room, wearing my earbuds and pretending to listen to music. I'm sure I'm convincing, even throwing in a fake hum now and then. But the truth is that I paused my Billy Joel playlist the moment Ethan's phone rang. I could hear the dejection in his voice as he answered, and I couldn't help but continue eavesdropping.

He's made two more calls since then, and now it looks like he's wrapping up the second one as he stands there all sweaty from climbing on the roof. I notice him throwing sneaky little glances my way, probably checking to see whether I'm listening.

Ha! Newsflash, Buster: I will absolutely intrude on others' conversations every chance I get.

"Hey, no worries man. I'll find someone to help me," he says with a soft laugh hanging up.

"*No worries*, man," I mimic his voice under my breath.

He turns sharply, aiming a scowl my way.

Shoot!

"Got something to say, Marsh?"

"Mmm...nope. Just singing." I smile, pointing to my sleeping earbuds. Ethan continues to frown at his phone, mumbling to himself.

"What's got your panties in a twist there, Tool Man?"

"Nothing," he grunts, grabbing the ladder and stomping outside. I watch carefully as he climbs back onto the roof, his forearms flexing as he pulls himself up each of the rungs and that frown still etched on his face. It's not that I'm being a perv—it's more like scrolling and stopping on a reel of a tree being cut down or a rug getting cleaned. It's universally fascinating.

Once he disappears past the gutters, I refocus my attention and manage to remove three more ugly light switch covers, adding them to a pile on the dining room table. And it just so happens that, like my involuntarily eavesdropping ears my eyes have a similar snooping problem. Let me be clear—there are no fingers involved in this curious streak, strictly eyes and ears only. I have a line I won't cross, but that line's looking a little blurry right now, and my gaze locks in on the message that just popped up on Ethan's phone screen.

> **COOPER**
> Sorry I can't help you, bro. I'm in Cleveland for...

I can't read the rest, though, because that would involve breaking my self-imposed sleuthing rules, specifically the one with the fingers.

So, that's why Mr. Grumpy Pants is in a mood, because he needs help and can't find it?

You should offer to help him, Ivy. He's gone out of his way to help you, after all.

Do what? I don't even know what he needs help with. What if it's something super annoying or gross?

Besides, Ethan is obnoxious and bossy, and we don't need

any more reasons to spend time together. Not to mention, he'd probably just twist my offer around and try to make it sound like I'm hitting on him or something like that. He can call one of his many previous flings if he's desperate. I may be nosy, but I have too much self-respect to let Ethan King set me up that way.

I flinch when I hear the door closing, so I back away from the phone. Then he saunters inside, wiping his forehead with the crook of his arm. The man never just *walks* anywhere. It's always a strut or a stomp or an overconfident waltz as he enters a room. It makes it so much harder to ignore him the way I really want to.

He strides over to the sink and pours himself a glass of water before gulping it down like a barbarian, letting some of it trickle down his chin and neck. I bite my lip and continue observing him. He picks up his phone, and I notice his shoulders deflate as he reads the text I'd examined earlier.

"I can help you. With your thing," I blurt out. "Or whatever it is you've been on the phone about all morning."

Hang it all, Ivy! You weakling.

He lowers the glass, twisting slightly to glance behind him. "*You're* offering to *help* me?"

"You have ten seconds to accept or the offer is rescinded."

That head of dark brown hair is thrown back, his Adam's apple bobbing with a throaty laugh. "You're somethin' else, Ivy June," he says, shaking his head. "But seeing as literally everyone else in my life is busy this weekend, I guess you'll do."

I scoff. "Rude!"

"Sorry," he cringes, rubbing his chin. "I meant, thank you. I could really use your help, if it won't kill you to be civil for an afternoon."

I glare at him, folding my arms. "Yeah, well, sometimes

exposure to pathogens is good for the immune system...in small doses."

Why did I sign up for this?

CHAPTER FIFTEEN

ETHAN

"Did you press record?" I ask, leaning against Ivy's kitchen counter.

"Well, now you're gonna need to edit this out, 'cause yes, I know how to press a red button, Ethan," Ivy retorts, heavy on the sass.

"You're a real peach, Marsh." I smile flatly. "Okay, walk with me," I motion with a tilt of my head, followed by a wink. She leans out from behind her phone, pretending to gag. I shake my head, turning on my charm as I address the camera directly and do my best to imagine Ivy's not the one filming me right now. I give a tour of the living room and kitchen, explaining what we plan to do to the rest of the house. Once we make it back to the kitchen, I signal for her to stop recording.

I'm feeling uncharacteristically self-conscious as I clear my throat. "How was that?"

"It was great. I'm not so confident in my camerawoman skills, though."

"I'm sure it's fine. And this isn't anything they'll actually use. It's more of a 'pre-sizzle' reel for Glenn to get a better idea of my persona in front of the camera. I'm flying to Frisco later to film the actual screen test."

"Look at you with the production jargon." She snorts. For some reason, she's still clinging to that giant D-bag image of me in her head. I don't know how or why we've trapped ourselves on this axis, stuck sharing the same orbit while unable to move away from seeing the worst in one another, but her response still ticks me off.

Yeah, okay, maybe I've been a tad crabbier than usual today, but she seems intent on keeping me in a very one-dimensional box, regardless of what I say or do.

And for the record, it actually took some in-depth Googling of all the terms Glenn's been throwing at me to understand half of what he says. Ask me about load-bearing walls or stock forecasting and I'm good to go. Or better yet, let me build something with my hands. That's the part of this show I'm excited about—having a large budget and a small timeline to make people's dream homes come to life.

I scratch my brow with my thumb, recognizing the need to step away before I end up snapping at Ivy in an attempt to defend myself. Not that it would do any good.

"Yeah. I, uh...I've gotta grab a pair of gloves from my truck before we film that mock demolition. It'll just be some B-roll, like a minute of pulling out one of the cabinets."

Ivy looks up from her job of rewatching footage on the phone. Her eyes sweep over me like she's trying to read my mood. "Okay...should we try it from a different angle? Switch it up?"

"Sure." I nod, breezing past her. As I walk down the porch steps I hear her sarcastic "Why, thank you, Ivy, how thoughtful of you," in her deep, faux-Ethan voice again, making the corners of my mouth curl up without permission.

I locate the pair of gloves in the back of my truck before I stall for a few minutes by quietly reorganizing a toolbox. I'm delaying going back inside, psyching myself up for whatever I'm going to do that will affirm my asshole status in Ivy's mind. Why am I so bothered by what she thinks of me anyway? That's half of my frustration—that I care in the first place.

Don't overthink it, King. Just get this over with.

I finally walk back into the kitchen, and I freeze, my jaw clenching as my nostrils flare to stifle a growl.

"*What* are you doing?" I grind out in a low voice.

Ivy stands with one heel-clad foot on a step stool, which is precariously placed on a rickety chair, and the other foot balancing on the counter. She glances up from the phone, her brows slightly furrowed.

"Waiting for you," she says matter-of-factly.

I keep my feet planted and my movements slow, because I'm legitimately afraid of what will happen if I cause her to react and turn this trapeze act into a worst-case scenario. "Ivy, were you by any chance a circus performer or a gymnast in your former life?"

Her nose scrunches up with a frown. "What are you talking about?"

I close my eyes, running a finger over my brows. "I'm trying to understand why you think this is a good idea." I gesture to her setup with my palm.

The corners of her lips dip down as she leans over to survey her location, and I instinctively jump forward.

"Woman! Would you *get down* from there?"

She wobbles for a moment, then straightens as if it's no big deal that she just nearly toppled off her Cat-in-the-Hat tower. "Ethan, you're being silly,' she reassures me with a smile. "This spot has the best lighting. I'm taking creative liberties. You'll thank me in editing."

"I don't *care* about the lighting, Ivy. You're not filming from up there!" I grind out.

"Would you take off your bossy pants for one minute? I'm already up here!"

"Not for long," I declare, stepping forward and wrapping my arm around her thighs. I lift her from her perch, and the tightness in my stomach eases once she's finally safe.

Everything she does feels like torment for me.

She lets out a small yelp of surprise as I pull her closer, her body pressing against mine as she clings to my shoulders. When her feet touch the ground, I release her, needing a break from the sizzling current between us. But I'm still unable to resist pushing her buttons, so I lean in with a cocky smile. "I'll just pretend you didn't ask me to take off my pants."

She scoffs in disgust. "Ugh! Figures that's the only part of that sentence you'd hear. And stop manhandling me!" She steps back to dust herself off before flexing her fingers.

"Stop testing the laws of physics, and I won't have to!"

"Can we just get on with this?" She forces a smile. It's one that says I'm still firmly in the asshole box and not likely to escape the label any time soon.

I have to work extra hard to turn on the charm once she starts recording again because I'm still thinking about how much she annoys me by doing something reckless every few minutes. But there's also that tiny niggle of self-consciousness making me hyperaware of her irritation with me.

I don't think I like this awareness.

CHAPTER SIXTEEN
IVY

C.J. is onto something with her theory about the weather turning kids into little gremlins. The wind was gusty and unrelenting this morning, and my kids were bonkers. The silence in my car is a stark contrast to the deafening chaos of my classroom today. I had my "weather contingencies" in place, but the kids walked in wild and ready to flip tables.

If only I had a water heater that worked, I could end my day with a nice soak in a hot bath and go to bed with relaxed muscles. Not to mention, it's freaking hair wash day tomorrow.

"Ugh," I groan aloud. I forgot to mention the broken water heater to Ethan when he made his fixit list the other day. I'm sure he'd have used it for more ammunition for his argument that I shouldn't be living here.

I near my driveway and release a whimper at the sight of Ethan's truck parked on the road. What in Sally Field's hair is he doing here?

Holy cow, I'm in a forced-proximity trope! Except the forced bit seems almost voluntary lately, which only makes this all the more confusing. At first, I thought Ethan and I were on the same page about sucking it up and riding this thing out for the sake of Colton and Ember. It felt like we'd made an unspoken agreement to get the renovations and wedding planning over with so we can return to mutual annoyance at best. But I think I may have legitimately upset him yesterday. I hate this ugly sting of regret. Why is he suddenly acting so broody when all we've ever done is insult one another? Our dynamic has been the same since we met, and I don't remember either of us inviting feelings into this agreement. He's supposed to help me fix the house to relieve some of his future sister-in-law's stress, and all I have to do is accept his help and put up with his grumpy disposition—absolutely no feelings necessary.

I put my car in park and release a long exhale before quickly applying some tinted lip balm, then I cringe internally when I catch myself checking my appearance in the mirror.

Why are you prettying yourself, ma'am?

But I'm not making myself look cute. This is self-care. Because my lips were dry. I remind myself of the very clear roles I just reestablished for Ethan and me.

My hand smooths over the pastel-pink bow in my hair as I take a fortifying breath. With a sense of renewed determination, I haul my giant teacher's bag over my shoulder and approach the house. The front door is closed, but I can see Ethan through the screen as I climb the steps. I trip on the last one, cursing my stupid heels.

I'd usually remove my shoes the moment I step inside, fearing I'll end up with Barbie-like calf muscles from never walking flat-footed. But today, I'm temporarily distracted by the man in my home—the tall, sweaty, muscular man. *Oh my.*

Someone pass me a hand fan, because my cheeks are feeling rather flushed. Maybe I'm getting a cold, because it certainly can't be Ethan King giving me the cold sweats, can it?

I watch as he crosses out the top line of the giant list on the wall, and I get stuck in a trance after staring at his back muscles for too long. His cap is on backward, and he sticks a strange-looking pencil behind his ear as he turns to face me.

My eyes dart over to inspect his masculine handwriting in an attempt to avoid getting caught ogling his rugged forearms. A wave of emotion hits me as I read the list, like a weight is lifted just knowing I'm not doing this alone. And the points he's already checked off make this seem a little more doable.

Fix it List:
~~Check roof for water damage~~
~~Replace door locks~~
Replace ceiling board
Check integrity of deck boards
Pull out carpets
Sand and varnish floors
New cabinets + fixtures
Replace ceiling fans
Repair holes in walls
Paint walls

"How did you get in here?"

A smirk spreads across his lightly bearded face before he turns and taps his pencil on the second crossed-out item on the wall. Then he folds his arms, like he's bracing for an argument.

"Those locks were crap, Marsh. It was a safety hazard."

"You sure are a stickler for *safety*," I add with air quotes. Although it's actually kind of sweet, I'm still annoyed he changed my locks without asking. And since I already told him the money from Gran's lawyer won't get transferred into my bank account for a few more days, he's apparently used his own money.

He turns again, showing off that chiseled back and mumbling under his breath.

"And it looks like you've got your grumpy pants on again," I remark as I pass him, stomping to the smaller bedroom I've been sleeping in. I figured I'd finish remodeling the master suite before moving my things in there.

Again, I decide to keep my shoes on, because the thought of losing the two and a half inches that they add to my height feels too vulnerable right now. I know they're that high because the length of my thumb, from knuckle to tip, is exactly one inch. I prefer measuring with thumbs and hands. Measuring tapes are not my friend; all of those tiny lines between each inch drive me crazy.

In fact, I almost refused the measuring tape Ethan handed me last week. Thankfully, he only needed an estimate for the ceiling boards, so it was easy enough to read the nearest big number.

Stepping out of my room barefoot and two-and-a-half inches shorter would feel like walking out completely naked, not to mention highlight the fact that he literally has to talk down to me.

I stall in my room, putting away my laundry and straightening my half-made bed. I release a heavy exhale once I run out of tasks before ambling back to the living area.

Ethan is returning things to his tool box when I shuffle closer, and this situation we've found ourselves in starts feeling even more awkward. We're the poster kids for things that don't mix. Yet, he's here—probably begrudgingly—as a favor to his brother and my best friend. The selflessness of his actions, him giving his time to help someone he clearly despises, is the one redeeming quality of Ethan's I've been able to acknowledge. Because I refuse to appreciate any of his physical attributes. Admitting that I like the way he looks would be like handing out an honorary doctorate to a celebrity as a reward for doing nothing more than showing an interest in something.

Ethan doesn't get a nice guy pass just because he's hot. There, I said it. Moving on.

"Good news," he turns to fold those big arms. "There's no water damage in the roof. I'll replace the ceiling boards next time I come by."

Looking uncharacteristically sheepish, he glances to the side while unclipping something from his belt.

Oh no. It's the freaking measuring tape again. I gulp, peering up at him while his mouth lifts with half a grin.

He steps closer, placing the tape in my hands as my heartbeat starts thumping in my ears. I don't have the energy to fake this right now.

"Relax," he gently reassures me. "Open it."

My eyes fall to my hands, and I turn it over, pulling out the tape that's like a mocking tongue.

But instead of only finding those tiny lines between each inch, I notice a small fraction written above each stroke. My forehead scrunches as I take in the numbers.

Ethan's raspy voice comes out with quiet tension. "It's a fraction tape measure."

When I lift my head, I find his eyes bouncing between mine, searching for my approval. It's the second show of vulnerability I've seen from him. The first was his reaction to all of my digs about him being a TV star.

Dame Judy Dench! One more mark in his favor.

I'm wincing inwardly, because this gift is both thoughtful and incredibly intuitive. My own parents still haven't recognized what he's apparently figured out in a handful of encounters.

"Thank you." The words come out scratchy. "I didn't know something like this existed."

He palms the back of his neck, eyes soft as he peers at me. "You're welcome. I didn't want to overstep. But I hope it's helpful."

This moment feels significant, like maybe we could start over with less animosity towards each other. "Ethan, I—"

I jump back at the knock on my door.

"Open up, lover! It's time to get smoochy!"

My eyes pinch closed.

Crud.

I forgot that Toby is picking me up for a movie to stage more fake-dating photos. This is going to be even more awkward than the time I asked my Uber driver about his favorite outdoor activities and he said 'hunting,' but I misheard it as 'humping.'

I force my eyes open and find myself faced with a stormy look in Ethan's. What's got his undies in a twist this time? "That's—"

"Toby," he grunts out and steps back.

My lips roll in, and I take a fortifying breath before pulling the door open.

"Hey, Bee. Ethan's here." I bug my eyes at Toby, trying to communicate that our ruse begins now.

"Oh. Hey, man." Toby offers his hand, and Ethan pauses, pushing his bottom lip over his teeth before he finally shakes Toby's hand.

Part of me wants to fake being sick so I can run and hide under my blanket, but I've created this mess. I've got to see it through.

Toby sidles closer and drapes an arm around me, then he

awkwardly repositions himself like I have a skin disease he's concerned about contracting.

Toby had thrown his arm around me before when he met Ethan in my classroom. But this moment feels different. We're both acutely aware of the need to act like this is something we do all the time.

And now we're staring at Ethan with forced smiles, the silence almost painful as we attempt to wordlessly convey the proof of our counterfeit romance.

Ethan's eyes narrow the tiniest bit, landing on the points of contact between Toby and me.

"Well, we'd better be on our way. Ethan, I'm sorry to leave like this...Actually, scratch that, since this is my house and I didn't know you'd be here...but thank you for all this." I gesture awkwardly toward the ceiling as I slowly step back toward the front door. Then I begin swaying my arms and clapping my hands, as if it'll help me look cooler. Just a totally normal interaction between adult acquaintances, right?

"Toby, shall we?" My eyes shift to the door with another quick finger point. Yes, I'm a coward.

Ethan's expression somehow grows even broodier, and a slight growl resonates in his throat before he reaches into his back pocket.

"Here's your new key, Marsh. I've gotta take some things to my truck." He glowers as he picks up his toolbox. "I'll use the spare to lock up."

"Right. Kay...bye." I wave robotically. This afternoon has gone downhill in no time. I haven't even gotten the chance to pee when I got home. With the empty state of the house, there's no way I'm going to risk having those noises echo down the hallway with Ethan around.

Toby grabs my hand, and I instinctively start to pull away but stop myself just in time. He widens his eyes, silently urging me to get it together. I mouth a "sorry" as I weave my fingers through his.

He plays his boyfriend duties well, opening the car door so I can slide in. I dare a look back in Ethan's direction once I'm buckled and find him standing beside his truck while he tugs his shirt over his head.

My jaw drops as I lean closer, my head inching towards the window until my forehead finally bumps the glass, snapping me back to reality.

"You're drooling, Vee," Toby warns me with a grin as he starts the car. He shakes his head and adds, "That guy's playing dirty. Good luck, sister."

I snap my mouth shut, scowling at all the tanned skin and muscular lines Ethan's parading around for all my neighbors to see. No one asked for this display of incredibly defined arms and the visible outline of abs over his otherwise flat stomach—certainly not me.

It still takes entirely too much effort to pull my gaze away.

"I don't know what you're talking about," I retort, brushing the hair out of my face. Toby chuckles quietly as he drives away, and I open the visor to check my appearance. And possibly to catch one more glimpse of the shirtless wonder leaning against his truck bed with a cheeky grin on his face.

Toby's shoulder's begin to shake as he snickers louder this time. "It all makes so much sense now. Your grump has a thing for you."

"He does *not*."

I may sound like a whiny teenager, but I will deny Toby's claim until my last breath. Ethan can barely stand to be around me. From what I've heard from Ember, he's a serial dater and an adventurer at heart, a free spirit that roams wherever the wind takes him. He's destined for big things. Besides the fact that we literally argue every time we're in the same room, I wouldn't open myself up to someone who can't commit and would eventually leave.

Leave the way my parents did, when they chose international aid over helping their own son and dumped Ross's problems on me. Leave the way Ross has left me in the lurch too many times to count.

No. Tolerance is the best that Ethan and I can hope for.

CHAPTER SEVENTEEN

ETHAN

I can fix a lot of things. But I'm beginning to suspect I've stumbled upon a problem I can't solve. The more I learn about Ivy, the more I want to know. It's incredibly inconvenient since I've already set us up to push each other's buttons at every opportunity. The fact that she has a boyfriend is even more problematic. Therefore, any interest in her would be wrong on multiple levels.

All that aside, I don't understand her relationship with Toby. Maybe one of them isn't into PDA, but Ivy's the kind of woman you wouldn't be able to keep your hands off of. She's the kind of woman who makes you bare your teeth when you find another man in her home instead of just smiling and shaking his hand.

There isn't much I can do but try to avoid being an ass, I suppose, and possibly a friend.

I'm afraid that won't be enough to satisfy my fascination with Ivy, though. In the short time I've known her, I've already changed so much of my routine. My Saturdays belong to Ivy now. Without her asking, here I am, parked across the street from her house, ready to do her bidding.

But before venturing back into the dragon's lair, I need to call Colton for some intel. I want to understand what she's dealing with, because the more I know about Ivy's struggles, the better I can navigate our situation and hopefully avoid angering the dragon at every turn.

Yeah, I could ask her directly, but I'm ninety-nine percent certain that would be like throwing a cat in a bathtub then attempting to hug it. I value my face too much for that.

I don't consider asking Colton about her to be an intrusion, seeing as I only want to understand her better.

Ember would admittedly be a better resource in this case, but she'd get suspicious if I showed too much interest in her best friend, and that wouldn't end well. While everyone claims *I'm* the family gossip, Ember and my mom have become their own rumor-mill headquarters.

My eyes are drawn to the front door of Ivy's house while I wait for my brother to answer the phone.

"What's wrong?" he says, a tinge of alarm in his voice.

"Real friendly greeting there, Colt."

"It's Saturday," he reminds me.

"And he's learning the days of the week too? Such a clever boy."

"You never call on a Saturday, smartass."

"And now you appreciate when I do," I reply.

"So, you're not actually dying or calling from a jail cell?"

"Who says I'd waste my one call on you?" I squint, trying to see if Ivy is moving about inside. I've hit a new low—this is definitely entering creep territory.

"Come on," Colton scoffs. "I know you're not calling our parents in this hypothetical scenario. Would you really want Mom to show up with a casserole for your cellmates?"

"Fair enough. So, um, is Ember with you?"

"Yeah, why?"

"Has she ever said anything about Ivy having some kind of learning difficulty?"

"Not that I know of. What's this about?"

Great. This probably means Ivy has been downplaying her struggles for everyone and not just her coworkers.

Except for Toby. She's clearly confided in him, seeing as she'd been seeking his help that day at school when I stepped in.

"It's nothing. I was just wondering if she knew anything about it. I gotta go though. Love you, bail bro."

"I'll answer the call, but I didn't say I'd pay your bail."

"Too bad. It's an all-or-nothing position." I hang up before he can reply.

My steps falter as I ascend Ivy's porch, my gaze drawn to a silky teal hair ribbon trapped beneath a chair leg. I stoop to free it before tucking it into my pocket. Just as I raise my hand to knock, a shriek pierces the air.

The hell?

"Ivy?"

Another shrill scream follows, and I call out again. I get no answer. Panic claws at my chest and clenches my lungs in a vice.

Stuff it—I'm going in.

My hands fumble frantically for the spare key I kept. By the time I grip the handle to insert the key, the door opens.

It's unlocked. Are you kidding me?

This woman has *zero* self-preservation.

I shove my way inside, feeling a scowl take over my face and wondering what it might take to get her to be more careful. I take three steps forward and come to an abrupt stop. Ivy is walking down the hallway, absentmindedly drying her damp hair with a towel, completely unaware of my presence.

I'd try to speak, but my tongue feels like it's been nailed to the roof of my mouth. The woman stands barefoot before me, clad only in the towel wrapped tightly around her body.

She's not tall by any means, so the towel actually covers everything from her knees to her shoulders. But it does cling to her like a second skin, drawing my attention to her curves. And...*dang*.

I'm only human, right?

She lifts her head for the first time in the ten seconds that have passed since I've been standing here, freaking out internally. This isn't helping my aspirations to be less of an ass. I raise my hands in a staying motion as she lets out another ear-splitting yelp.

"William freaking Shatner! Ethan? What the heck are you doing in here?"

She gets the fright of her life and still manages to cuss innocently enough for a toddler's ears. It's a cute little fact that I shouldn't be noting, but I do.

"You screamed, Marsh! What was I supposed to do, stand outside and wait for your murderer to finish the job?"

She scurries behind a wingback chair and holds on for support. "You couldn't have just minded your own business? And why do you always jump to such dark conclusions? What goes on in that mind of yours, anyway?" Her face scrunches with a hint of disgust. She's probably hoping I won't notice, but I observe her gradually growing taller from my vantage point. She's on tiptoes now, one hand still pressed against her chest as if she's still trying to calm her racing heart.

Nope, I'm not thinking about Ivy's body parts—organs included.

"My mind is a wonderful place right now," I reply, flashing a flirty grin.

What are you doing?

Just like pressing her buttons came so naturally in the beginning, this new flirty side seems to be springing forth of its own accord.

"Ugh," she scoffs with an eye roll. "Typical."

The floorboards creak as I step forward, and she pulls the towel in tighter around her. And to be honest, I'm growing more jealous of that damned towel by the second.

"What are you doing here?" she repeats with halfhearted scorn.

"Why did you scream?" I ignore her question and take another step closer. She doesn't back away.

"A bug?"

"Try again."

She lets out a frustrated groan. Guess I'm still coming off as an ass. Her hands fold across her chest—a classic defiant stance. My eyes are desperate to wander, but that would only amplify the steam—not in a sexy way, but to the point where it's coming out of Ivy's ears. And I'm *trying* to be a gentleman.

"The water heater isn't working, so my shower was cold. Now, tell me why you're standing in my living room at eight AM again?"

The little sprite hadn't told me the water heater was broken when I made the list of things that needed fixing.

"No reason," I retort with a shrug and my most charming smile. But I don't think she's had her coffee yet, because she's clearly interpreting it wrong—as usual. Her face scrunches up again as she throws her hands up in defeat.

"Whatever. I need to get dressed." She huffs before scurrying off to her room and slamming the door behind her.

That went well.

CHAPTER EIGHTEEN
IVY

I wasn't planning on seeing Ethan today, but that's not the reason I put a little extra effort into my appearance. I'm visiting Gran and then Opal and Gail later.

That's the reason.

The *only* reason.

I opt for denim overalls over my favorite flower patterned tank-top—nothing extravagant. My overalls are adorned with fingerprint-shaped paint smudges—clear evidence of my profession since glitter glue and poster paint find their way onto everything I wear. My teal wedges and a cherry pink hair bow complete my look.

Sometimes I entertain the idea of stepping out in flip-flops or Crocs. I admittedly find their comfort alluring. But then I'm reminded of the pizza delivery guy who mistook me for a kid who was home alone last month, or the embarrassment I feel each time I have to get a step stool just to fetch a glass from the cupboard for a guest in my own kitchen.

It's no wonder why I prioritize the added height over comfort.

"So what's the plan for today?" I call out, walking down the hallway to find the living room empty. "Ethan?"

I lift a blind open, looking up and down the street. No truck.

Rude.

My hands rest on my hips as I huff out a breath, reading over Ethan's fix-it list. My stomach cuts an annoying little flip when my eyes land on the message he must have added to the wall after I left last night.

"Your ladder is crap. Don't climb it. Will bring new one."

This man put the word *crap* on my wall. He should come with a warning: *Inclined to aggravate and cause confusion.* I don't know what to make of his grouchy protectiveness.

I decide to call Ember while I rip off wall paper in the kitchen.

"Vee! How's the reno going?"

"Meh. It's going."

"Ethan being helpful?"

I snort out a laugh. "If you call grumpy and overly protective *helpful*, then sure."

"Just to be clear, it is Ethan *King* we're talking about, right?"

"The one and only." I grunt, stepping onto a stool to start scraping the wall.

"Huh," she replies thoughtfully.

"What, *huh*?" I frown, flicking pieces of wallpaper off my shoulder.

"Nothing. It's just interesting. Ethan has always seemed so laid back. But he seems different with you."

"Yeah, apparently that's 'cause my very existence annoys him."

"Did you just roll your eyes?"

"You'll never know." I continue scraping. "Hang on," I tell

Ember when I hear a car door shut. For the second time today, I peek through my blinds, this time finding Ethan's truck backed into my driveway.

I guess the grump has decided to return after all.

"What's happening?" Ember asks.

"Ethan was here this morning. Then he wasn't. Now he's back."

"Don't overwhelm me with the details," she drawls sarcastically. "Um, Earth to Ivy," she calls out a moment later when I stop replying.

"Sorry. There's a lot unfolding."

"You're *literally* torturing me."

"Hang on, let my eyeballs catch up." I stare at the scenario playing out. "It's actually kind of delightful. Ethan is doing the 'I just walked into a spiderweb' dance next to his truck."

"Unexpected. Please continue."

"Whoa—okay. Um…his shirt just came off…"

"A show. Nice. More details?"

"He's shaking his shirt out. The shirt is being inspected like it's covered in toxic chemicals."

I'm hiding beside the window with one hand lifting a single blind, completely transfixed by Ethan's golden skin.

"Come on, I need updates!" Ember shouts, making me wince and pull the phone away from my ear.

"He's still looking for something, but the shirt has been given the all clear. Boots and ground are being investigated."

Ethan does a full body shiver, seemingly giving up on his search. "Oh my gosh! Is Ethan scared of *spiders*?" I squeal, and the grin on my face nearly touches my ears. "This is amazing," I whisper.

"I'm concerned about your level of excitement over this," Ember says in return. "Unless you're plotting ways to get him out of his shirt again?"

I scoff, dropping the blind as Ethan ends his performance and stomps toward the garage, still topless except for the tool belt he's got slung over his bare shoulder.

"It's just something to keep in my pocket, a little ammunition."

"You're starting a war."

"Ethan started this war the first day we met, and you know it." I scowl.

"Fine. What did you call about again?" she asks over a yawn.

"Just checking in. I'm doing mindless work and need the company."

"Go find the shirtless grump, and you'll have some."

I walk back to the kitchen and pick up the scraper, staring up at the faded wallpaper that's been there for decades, the one Gran probably picked out. "I'm sure he'll turn up sooner or later. He's doing something in the garage."

"That man never slows down."

I hoist myself up onto a counter, grunting out my reply. "True." Another reminder that this town won't keep him here.

"Love you, Vee. Don't murder anyone."

"But Nicolas taught me so much about how to get away with it," I joke, referring to Ember's cat and his crime show obsession. "Love you, Em. I'll see you soon."

I scrape away for the next ten minutes, peeling away the layers like old memories that have imprinted themselves into the walls.

I manage to get the majority of the wallpaper off, but there are still a few stubborn parts that will need to be sprayed. That's one thing I managed to research on my lunch break yesterday.

Dry strips of the paper rustle on the countertop as I shift

around. I probably should have covered the area before I started.

Acknowledging that I have dyslexia—if only to myself—has meant coming to terms with doing things in an order that might seem strange to others. It's all part of my life story of trial and error. Try, re-adjust. Try, re-adjust.

Sometimes it feels like pushing a wagon. For maximum efficiency, a wagon is designed to be pulled, but when my brain defaults to pushing, I have to question whether I'm approaching tasks in the most logical and energy-efficient manner.

From the looks of the mess surrounding me, there most likely *was* a more efficient way to go about this. I begin my descent, but my shoe slides over a strip of paper on the first step.

I instinctively reach out when I slip, scraping my arm against the rusty hinge I left behind after removing a cupboard door last night.

Ouch.

Slowly this time, I make it to the floor without further injury and go directly to the bathroom where I keep the first aid kit. I've done this too many times lately.

I clean the scrape below my elbow and select a Mandalorian Band-Aid. My class is on a Star Wars trend, and they love it when I jump on the bandwagon for whatever they're into.

I walk back into the kitchen and find Ethan there with his shirt back on—*whomp-whomp*. His back is turned to me and his hands rest on his hips as he surveys the mess I've created.

He peers over his shoulder when he hears me shuffling closer. Eyes with the gray of an impending storm sweep over my newest Band-Aid. His body pivots until he's facing me, his gaze tethered to my arm the whole time.

He lifts a hand with a shake of his head, as if to ask 'how.'

I roll my eyes dramatically and stick my tongue out in response. But, come on, I hang out with eight-year-olds all day. Can you blame me if my comebacks are a bit on the childish side?

"Do you walk around with your eyes closed? How are you this accident prone?" he asks, his voice deep and filled with annoyance.

"Um, *rude*. My spatial awareness may need improving, but allow me to remind you about rule number three." I step forward and poke him in the chest, my frown deepening at how un-squishy it feels. "Why are you here, anyway? I thought you left."

He turns and saunters to a cabinet, opening and closing doors. "Where are your mugs?"

When he looks my way, I unfold an arm and point to one of the lower cupboards. He opens it to find the two mugs, two glasses, and two plates that occupy the space. I can't bring myself to unpack everything, only to have to repack it all when I install new cabinets—which will hopefully be sooner than later.

Ethan picks a mug—the one with 2006 Mr. Darcy's face on it—and a grin slowly takes over his face, like we're sharing an inside joke. But I furrow my brow. No way he knows who that is.

He holds the mug under the sink and flicks the tap to fill it up, offering it to me like a proud cat that just dropped its prey onto my lap.

"What am I supposed to do with that?" I ask.

"Feel it," he says, nudging the mug closer.

I scrunch up my nose and curl a hand around the mug, then my eyes widen in surprise. "You fixed the water heater?"

"Of course I did." He beams.

"You could have just asked me to stick my hand under the faucet. This was a weird approach."

"Dang it, Ivy," he groans, setting the cup down in the sink. "Can't you just thank me? And seriously, I know I'm about to break another rule, but help me understand why you're wearing shoes like that for a job like this?" He gestures over the mess I left on the counter. I may be overly defensive at times, but he isn't putting a whole lot of effort into not being an a-hole, either.

"I'd think my reasons for wearing shoes with added height were pretty obvious."

He shakes his head like he doesn't get it. Typical.

He's unknowingly just placed the last straw on this camel's back.

"I'm *short*, okay? You think I *like* not having access to the top shelves at the grocery store? Or having people talk to me like I'm a kid? Or not having the freedom to wear a pair of those fugly Crocs? Everyone keeps saying it's like walking on air, but I'll never know, because they'd make me look even *more* like a child."

By the end of my rant, I find myself gasping for breath, realizing that perhaps the tightly sealed lid on the jar containing my feelings isn't quite as secure as I once believed.

There are people with much harder struggles than ours, Ivy, My mother would always say. With a husband so hell-bent on philanthropy, I'm sure she got plenty of practice with stuffing her own feelings into a jar. *It's never good to focus too much on our own problems,* was another phrase I regularly overheard.

As unhealthy as it is, keeping the lid on tight has just become a matter of survival.

Ethan's eyes move around the room like he's seeing things from my perspective for the first time. "Look, I'm sorry. I can't say I get it, but I can see that it must be hard for you." He looks away while one hand clenches over the knuckles of the other.

My phone vibrates in my pocket, and I groan when I pull it out and read Ross's messages.

> **ROSS**
> I'm so close to getting your money
>
> I just need $1000 and I'll be set
>
> I'll add it to what I owe you. Promise

"Everything okay?"

"Yeah. It's my brother. He's..." A heavy sigh escapes from my chest. "I dunno what he is..." I look up, mirroring the frown on Ethan's face. "Anyway, it's just not what I need right now."

"Anything I can help with?"

Why is this man so intent on helping me? He does it with such reluctance but then his actions occasionally do the opposite.

"You're already helping me, Ethan. And I am grateful."

His mouth lifts with the smallest hint of a smile, but his eyes soften, telling me how much he likes the acknowledgement and begging me to continue letting down my guard. But I've already revealed too much.

He must see a change in my expression because he purses his lips, regarding me like I'm a ticking bomb. "I'll get started on the ceiling board," he offers after a while.

"I'm heading out soon." I reply, unsure how to get the bits of vulnerability I let escape back where they belong. "Oh, the money came through from the lawyer. Can you..." I want to say give me your receipts, but it'll take me forever to figure them out. "Can you send me a CashApp request for the amount I owe you?"

"Sure," he says, his features softening while he holds my

gaze. It's a look that says he understands, and it causes a rush of warmth inside me.

"You'll lock up if I'm not back when you leave?"

He pauses to frown. "How long are you planning on being out?"

"How long are you planning on being *here*?"

"Fine. Yes, I'll lock up while you galavant," he grumbles, that frown turning into a scowl.

"Thank you."

As I walk into the living room, a pang of guilt hits me. I consider going back to apologize, but then my eyes land on the list on the wall and the note Ethan left me last night.

I grab one of his weird pencils, a crazy, scary idea forming in my head. Despite Ethan's grumpy demeanor—directed at me alone, it seems—the fact is, he's still going out of his way to help me. Maybe it's time for me to grab onto that olive branch and make this situation more pleasant for both of us.

Except the thought of accepting Ethan's olive branch makes me want to hurl.

Just do it, Ivy. It's the right thing. Who cares what he thinks, anyway?

CHAPTER NINETEEN

ETHAN

"That was perfect! You're such a natural at this," Crystal, the network's production assistant, says with a sultry smile. She brushes her shoulder against mine as we walk out to the parking lot together. We reach the sedan I rented, and I can't help but miss the beast of a truck the producers lent me for the ten-minute test episode we shot today.

"So...we should get together sometime if you end up moving here." She pauses at the car and tucks a strand of hair behind her ear.

"Sure," I say non-commitedly. Crystal seems nice, but I have no idea what the future holds, and moving to Frisco, even though it's still in Texas, isn't something I've even considered. Right now, I'm just focused on taking this renovation show one step at a time. And although we haven't discussed where the show would be based, I kind of assumed it'd be in Aster. Yeah, that's the only reason I'm turning down a date with another woman.

"Great." Crystal beams at me like I just promised her a bushel of puppies.

Yikes.

I make it back to my hotel, feeling exhausted, and flop onto the bed after showering off the dust from our staged mock demolition. I tell myself I'll just lie down for a minute before heading out to hit some golf balls, but it's not long before I can feel my eyes closing. Without my permission, an image of Ivy's house floats through my mind.

I'm half asleep but still feel the tug of my mouth as I recall the last message she left on her wall, beneath the one I started about her ladder. I'd memorized her untidy handwriting, revealing the secrets she keeps so close.

"I'll climb what I wanT. rule numbur three"

The courage it took her to write that, knowing she'd probably make spelling errors...It's enough to just about undo a man. A warmth had spread throughout my chest when my eyes first caught on the new line of words because it meant I made her feel safe. And it's a big deal, finding out that Ivy is starting to trust *me*. She sure as hell isn't letting others in. Well, besides Toby.

Toby, Toby, Toby.

I feel a little guilty despising a man that most people would find quite likable. But he's dating the woman I can't seem to get out of my mind, so who can blame me? And truly, it's a good thing she's unavailable. This show could take me places, and getting involved with Ivy would only lead to my worst fears coming true once I'd inevitably move on to the next adventure and leave her brokenhearted.

I'm drifting off again when my phone buzzes on the nightstand. I roll onto my side to reach for it, my lips parting in a grin when I see Ivy's name.

I hit play on her voice note, closing my eyes while her husky voice fills my hotel room. "Hey, um, I made brownies. Well, I microwaved brownies. The oven still doesn't work.

Anyway, just wondering if you're coming over today. Zero pressure. I just...I kinda made a mess? It's fine. But, um...I've reached the point of needing professional help I think—ouch—*dangit*! This *was* on the fixit list, so it had to happen. It just might not have happened the way it's supposed to. Anyhoo, this is officially a rambling message so I'll end it now, kay byyye!"

I plop the phone down beside me after pressing play on the message just to hear her voice again. I stare at the ceiling as I listen and try to imagine what kind of chaos she's unleashed this time.

Straightening up against the headboard, I pick up my phone and tap the video icon for a Facetime call. Her face pops up on the screen, making my mouth pull into a slow smile.

"Wow, okay, um, hi," she says awkwardly, her eyes flickering around the room.

"What's wrong?"

"Uh...nothing. It's just, you're shirtless. Didn't expect that." She clears her throat and fidgets with her collar, and my amusement grows as I reach for the shirt at the end of my bed.

"Is that your room?" she leans forward, squinting at the screen. With her face closer, I notice the red stripe above her left eyebrow.

"Marsh, tell me that's paint on your forehead."

"Yup. Sure. Let's go with that."

"Ivy," I groan, my hands itching to cup her head and inspect it.

"Stop being such a bossy pants. I can open a paint sample and swipe some on my head if it'll make you happy."

What she doesn't get—and what I can't say—is that for some unknown reason, I'll only be happy when she stops putting herself in danger.

"I left you a pair of safety goggles, but I kinda feel like you need a helmet," I say dryly.

"Safety goggles don't fit over my prescription glasses," she rolls her half-lidded eyes with a slow pivot to the camera.

But then the name *Toby* ninja kicks itself into my head, putting a damper on my Ivy appreciation. I need to remember the woman has a boyfriend, even if she doesn't act like it or talk about him.

"What's this mess you've made?" I clear my throat, redirecting the conversation to a safer topic.

Her eyes roam again while she chews on her top lip.

A noisy puff of air escapes before she looks back to the camera. "Mmm...I removed some of the cabinets. Some of them came off fine. And some of them didn't. There may be a few new holes to fill and a couple spots where the floor needs attention. I'll tell you, though, cabinets are *heavy*."

I scratch my chin while I nod, processing the two-person project this woman attempted by herself. "Cabinet removal isn't a solo job," I verbalize my thoughts, careful not to sound irritated this time.

"Hence my Bat-Signal."

I'm surprised she managed to limit herself to the one scrape on her forehead. Although, I *can* only see her from the waist up. It would be weird to ask for a slow pivot, right? Yeah. Let's not do that.

"I'm in Frisco," I admit, cringing apologetically.

"Oh, I thought your bedroom looked a bit dull. I mean... more dull than I expected of a man...such as yourself. Okay, I'll just be going now. Things to do—"

"Ivy—"

"Don't worry about me. I'll save you some brownies. Have fun in Frisco."

"Ivy!"

My chin drops to my chest. She hung up.

I open her text thread and press record to leave her a voice note.

"Ivy June, you probably won't answer if I call. If I were in town, I'd be heading over already. But I'll be back in Aster tomorrow. I'm only going into The Adventure Project office two days next week. The rest of the time, I'm yours—I mean, I'm—I can help you whenever and work on the house while you're at school."

Smooth, King. Playing it real cool right now. I roll my eyes at myself.

"Don't do anything else with the kitchen. Or anything high up...or dangerous. Just...be careful. I'll see you soon."

Way to be chill, man.

I send the message before grabbing a pillow and burying my face in it.

This woman has me turning down dates, giving up my Saturdays, and sounding like a teenager on the phone.

What will I give up next?

And what the heck have I gotten myself into?

CHAPTER TWENTY
IVY

"So you've picked a venue?" I glance at Ember before turning onto her street.

"Yeah. It's bigger than I wanted. But I'll just deal with it."

I snort out a laugh. "That's what she said."

"I walked into that one," Ember replies with an eye roll. She leans forward in her seat, scrutinizing the area ahead of us. "What are Opal and Gail doing hiding in the hedges?" She scrunches the side of her mouth as I park outside her apartment. "Are they pointing a hose at that old lady?"

My head falls onto the steering wheel with a groan. Ember doesn't look away, tapping my arm while I try to gather the energy to deal with this. "Hey, why does that look like your Gran?"

"Because it *is* my Gran." I lift my head and sigh.

"*Oh*. Well, this is about to get interesting."

"Yup."

I slink out of the car, crouch-walking to join the mischief sisters behind the hedge. They're not related, but it's the nickname they've acquired around the neighborhood.

"What are you two doing?" my voice comes out in a harsh whisper.

"Shaquile O'Neal!" Opal hisses, except she pronounces it *sha-qweel*. "Ivy June! I nearly peed myself!"

"You peed yourself when you squatted down, don't blame it on her. Hey, Ivy, dear." Gail leans forward, smiling at me like we're sitting down for tea instead of skulking behind the bushes.

"Semantics." Opal waves and re-aims her hose at Gran, who's trotting dangerously close to some begonias.

"Whatever you're about to do—as much as I know you're entitled to this—*please* don't do it. I'll explain in a minute."

"But—"

"Please?"

"Oh, *fine*," Opal grumbles, her eyes rolling skyward. "Just when the fun was about to start."

I pop out from behind the hedges, hustling to intercept Gran's pilfering little fingers.

"Gran!" I speed walk closer, pasting on a smile. "Hi! What—uh, what are you doing over here?" I'm praying she gives a perfectly innocent explanation for basically trespassing. But knowing Gran, that's not very likely.

"Oh, I'm on a walk, deciding which flower to pick today. What are *you* doing here?" Her eyes crinkle when the corners of her mouth pull up.

Opal shimmies out from behind her blind. "Hah! We have witnesses now, Agnes! You admitted to it in broad daylight!"

Ember moves to stand beside them, grimacing in silent apology.

I turn my eyes to Gran, wordlessly begging her to plead her innocence. But the woman loves a bit of drama, and I'm now fully convinced she's known what she's been doing all along.

"Did you say *Gran*?" Gail interjects.

I'm amazed I could keep this secret as long as I have. "Surprise!" I reply with a laugh that goes on a bit too long.

"Nah-uh. There's no way Ivy is related to that hussy."

"Opal!" Ember chides.

Gran's hands raise to her hips in a challenge as she spears Opal with her gaze. "It's true, and I'm only taking back what I'm owed—with interest."

"What in Shaq's shoe are you talking about, Agnes?" Opal huffs.

Gran arches a brow, her smug smile faltering ever so slightly. "I know you floozies still have it."

"Oh, for heaven's sake!" Opal folds her arms across her chest. "I told you this fifteen years ago, Agnes, and I'll tell you again. We don't have the damned thing! We bought it fair and square, and a month later, it was gone. Makes me think it was *you* who stole it from *us*."

Gran is still except for a slight narrowing of her eyes. "You really don't have it?"

"Okay, hold up!" I wave my hands at everyone. "How was I not aware you've known each other this long?"

Gran's posture is rigid as she sniffs. "Cause it's something I'd like to forget,"

"What's this all about?" Ember scratches her forehead.

"It's a misunderstanding after a bit of tipsy carelessness, really." Gail grimaces, her eyes squinting as her gaze touches each of us.

"I'm gonna need more than that, Gail," I prompt.

"Right. Well, years ago, Oliver, your Pop, had this genius idea to get rid of stuff and pretty up the place while Agnes was away for a week. There was also a community-wide rummage sale at the church that weekend. Oliver set out a bunch of knickknacks, Opal and I saw the music box in the pile, and we bought it."

"*My* music box?" I frown, turning to Gran.

She nods, a touch of sadness and nostalgia making her eyes shine. "Pop, bless his grumpy ass, had a good heart, but he had his head in the clouds sometimes."

"Ivy, love, we didn't know it was to be yours." Gail's eyebrows draw together. "Goodness, we didn't even know *you*, then. Anyway, we bought it, and a month later, we came home to find one of the back windows had been jimmied open, and the music box was gone." She turns to Gran with a small lift of her shoulders. "We would've given it back to you eventually, Agnes. We were just yanking your chain, hanging on to it."

"Well, it's hard to take the word of a couple saboteurs," Gran fires back, giving Gail the stink eye.

"That was purely accidental," Gail adds before turning to me. "I poured a failed homemade rum recipe out near the community garden one night, after a bit too much of the real stuff. You know how it goes." I don't, but I nod anyway. This is like an episode of D*esperate Geriatrics*, with all the drama of a housewives reality show, except with muumuus. "It's possible I got a bit lost," Gail continues. "And the Best Buds trophy went to someone else that year."

I bring my hand up to massage my forehead, my eyes pinching shut. "Hang on." I hold up a palm. "This competition was called *Best Buds?*"

"Told you it was a dumb name," Gail whispers to Opal, and they exchange elbow nudges before Opal looks over to me. "Can we get back to the fact that your grandmother keeps stealing our flowers?" She fists her hands on her hips as she glares at Gran. "Grow your own flowers, Agnes!"

"If you'll apologize for sabotaging my flowers," Gran adds, straightening her shoulders. "I'll refrain from decorating my home with your mediocre flora."

I let my head fall back and groan. Ember steps forward to

herd Opal and Gail together, as if they'll be easier to influence once they're contained.

"I'm sure Opal and Gail are only too happy to oblige and put this all behind us, right?" She spears them with crazy eyes.

"If it untwists Miss Hoity Toity's panties, then, fine. We're sorry for something we can't even remember doing."

Gran grunts in response, folding her arms and apparently accepting the apology.

"Great, okay." Ember smiles, ushering everyone with her hands. "Gail, I can smell cake, so I'm guessing you have something to take out of the oven? Mrs. Marsh, lovely to see you."

I wave Carl over to retrieve my mischief-making grandmother, my shoulders finally relaxing when he heads our way, throwing me a thumbs up.

"Love you, Gran! I'll visit soon."

"You'd better. And bring that boyfriend over. I need his measurements," she replies.

My jaw slackens as I turn to ask why, but Ember catches me and pulls me inside.

"You can find out what that's about later. We need tea."

Opal and Gail have shuffled into their apartment, unhappy with Ember for postponing their questions about my heritage.

"Maybe we should go over there. I feel bad about ditching them."

Ember snorts while she unlocks her door. "They have each other, and you're not ditching them. We planned to hang out just the two of us, so they're none the wiser."

"But Gail looked so sad."

"It's not sadness, it's cake anxiety. She'll be fine."

"Where's Nicolas?" I scan the room, looking for Ember's weirdo cat.

"I think he has a girlfriend." She wiggles her brows while filling the kettle.

"Aw! He's out canoodling with a lady cat?"

"That's my suspicion. Anyway, how's the house coming along? I'm sorry I've been too busy with all this wedding stuff to stop by. My mom is driving me crazy. *Ugh*! See? There I go again. Enough about me. Tell me how it's been working with Ethan."

"Oh, it's been fine." I'm trying my hardest to maintain a neutral tone, but I can already feel my cheeks heating as I recall my last conversation with a shirtless Ethan.

"*Fine*? You haven't tried to murder one other?"

"Is the tea ready?" I gesture to the stove as I walk to the kitchen. I don't quite know how to explain that I've been wanting to behead the butthead a lot less in the past few days. "He's been away, so I haven't gotten close enough to attempt homicide lately. Lucky him." I force a laugh and pour water into the two mugs Ember set out.

I lower the teabags into our cups, and when I look up, Ember's squinting at me.

"Okayyyy. And how's Toby?"

"Toby's great." I reply honestly, because he is. He's an incredibly reliable friend—one I can trust not to leave me.

And while I'm truly happy that things are happening for Ethan, Facetiming with him from a different city only served to highlight his transient soul. That's a really fun trait, but it's also one of the biggest reasons I can't allow myself to get too close to him. I've had too much experience with people letting me down or leaving, and that's exactly what I foresee happening once I get attached to Ethan and his overprotective grumpiness.

"I still can't believe you're dating him. I did not see that happening between you two." Ember walks to the sofa with her tea.

I shrug and fake a smile. And as if Ethan's giant ego could

sense I've been thinking about him, a text comes through on my phone.

> **ETHAN**
> Still got those brownies waiting for me?

No. Because I'm a chronic people pleaser, I gave yesterday's batch to Carl. I was planning to bake a fresh batch for Ethan in Ember's oven.

I respond with a GIF of Jim Halpert making an indecisive face.

> **ETHAN**
> Fine. but you created an expectation. I take my desserts very seriously.

Why is this flirty side of him bringing a goofy smile to my lips?

We just had this conversation, Ivy.

I respond with another GIF of a thumbs up. I'm usually very chatty over text, even though I get a little anxious about autocorrect not catching all my spelling errors. But the opportunity to test the extent of Ethan's patience has me holding back. I want to see if he'll work for it.

"Oh my gosh." Ember's voice brings me back. "Are you texting Toby right now? Look at your face! You look just like I did a few months ago, sitting on this couch and texting Colton while you made fun of my love eyes."

"*Love* eyes? I don't *love* him!" I blurt out, forgetting for a second that she's referring to Toby and not Ethan.

"Defensive much?" She eyes me suspiciously over the rim of her mug. I hate lying to my best friend. But this Toby thing is supposed to appear casual. No one can get too invested, friends included. If I were to tell Ember the truth, I'd open up a whole can of worms and be forced to tell her about everything else, including lying to Gran to get the house, Ross's money troubles, and my being homeless. But she doesn't need more stress. The woman gets enough of that from her mother.

I'll come clean after her wedding.

I manage to redirect the conversation to her wedding plans—an easy distraction. Planning my best friend's special day is one of my greatest delights. But I'm admittedly piling more tasks onto my growing to-do lists—both personal and professional.

Just keep that lid on tight, Ivy June.

CHAPTER TWENTY-ONE
IVY

I stretch out over my mattress, enjoying the chance to wake up without a morning alarm. Don't let anyone ever tell you teachers aren't living for the next school break. I love teaching, and I adore my class. But knowing there's a break around the corner is like food for my malnourished sanity. Even though I usually end up volunteering and putting in extra hours at school anyway, the mental break does wonders.

And I have six more *glorious* days of spring break ahead of me. My only project is coordinating the recital. Well, that and renovating an entire house. Along with my maid of honor duties...and keeping Ross out of trouble. Dang. I guess that's still a lot to squeeze into six days, but it's never stopped me before.

I fix myself a cup of coffee, making sure to avoid the lingering debris from my unfortunate cabinet demo attempts. Dust and paint flakes coat every surface, but it doesn't stop me from enjoying the silence while I sit at the kitchen table. After a while, I walk lazily into the living room and peek out the window before flopping down onto the sofa. I attempt to ignore the laptop resting beside me, but I've been feeling the urge to try again.

Just a quick little look.

I navigate to the University of St. Augustine for Health Sciences website, biting my lip as my heart pounds in my chest. I've started filling out the form to request more information at least a dozen times by now, but the memories of my struggle to complete my teaching degree keep me from following through every time. All of the stress and extra hours I put in just to get through college had taken a toll on my health, and the thought of going through that again sets off a blaring alarm in my mind.

You can't do that again.

"Ugh!" I push the computer away, deciding to do laundry instead. But a loud knock at the door stops me from loading clothes into the washer. I pause, wondering who would be at my door at 9 AM on a Tuesday. Ethan has a key—which feels way too *cohabitatey*—and he never knocks. His heavy footsteps over the front porch usually announce his presence before his voice does.

I crack the door open, peeking one eye out.

"Ross? What're you doing here?"

"Way to greet me, Vee." He smiles but the shadows beneath his eyes reveal his exhaustion.

"Sorry, I didn't expect to see you. Uh—come in." I force a smile in return and open the door wider.

"So you're fixing up Gran's old house, huh?" His lips curl as he takes in the room.

"Yeah," I say trailing behind him.

I guess we're sticking to small talk, then. It's probably better than diving into the big stuff that will inevitably upset us both. And unless Ross has miraculously started making responsible life choices, I'm not looking forward to hearing what he's been up to, especially since I'm still dealing with the consequences of his last few mistakes.

The silence hangs in the air between us as we stroll through the house. He seems wistful, his mouth tugging up when his eyes land on a few different spaces. He never spent much time here, but I suppose he has his own memories of the place.

We walk through the living room and kitchen, and he takes his time appraising the two bedrooms and glancing at the bathroom before we make it back to the front of the house without having spoken. Once again, he's leaving the hard parts to me.

"Ross. Did you decide anything about the classes I sent you? I said I'd pay, and I'd figure out a way, but you'd need to stick it out and—"

"Vee..." He lets out a heavy sigh, cursing under his breath. "I can't even think about that right now, okay. I need to get myself out of this mess first."

His thumb and index finger push into his eyes.

"Ross, I just think—"

"No, Ivy." He groans, tugging at his hair. He turns in a circle, and I feel a tight ball forming in my throat. Seeing him this unsettled twists my insides, and that tiny flicker of hope I've always nurtured begins to fade. Even though I desperately want that flame to survive this gust, I think Ross may have let in too much of the storm this time.

I never thought I could become so jaded and desensitized by his faults that I'd lose faith in him completely, but it's like, the more I try to help him by feeding that little flame, the wider he cracks the doors open, ushering in the cold and refusing to change.

His hands finally fall to his sides, the desperation in his eyes making my heart ache.

You can't lose it on him, Ivy. It'll push him away.
Keep the lid on tight.

"I need a *little* more money. Anything you can give me will help. Or maybe something valuable?" His eyes scan the room, like he's looking for expensive trinkets.

"Ross, I don't *have* any money to give you. I already gave you all my savings, which you haven't repaid."

"What about the work you're doing on the house?" He waves a hand about. "How are you paying for that?"

"That money is Gran's, and it's earmarked for renovations *only*." I frown while crossing my arms. I can feel the last of my confidence flickering as his accusatory eyes create more distance between us.

His gaze bounces around, like he's trying to formulate a plan. As much as I want to help him, I literally can't. And I hate that. I hate the look he gives me, wordlessly telling me I've let him down.

He begins pacing the room, pausing when those telltale stomps resonate from the porch. My heart beats faster as I hear the rattling of keys on the other side of the door, and then the handle turns.

"Seriously, Marsh. Unlocked again?" Ethan growls before swinging the door fully open.

He immediately straightens, a broody glower forming as he takes Ross in.

Ross ignores him and makes his way to the door. He pauses for a second on his way out, casting one last glance my way. "I'll get your money, Ivy."

"Ross—" I call as he squeezes past Ethan, but he disappears down the street. I have no idea what I'd have said if he stopped, anyway. *Don't do anything reckless? I'm sorry I can't help you?* In the back of my mind, there's always that niggling thought—

What if this is the last time I see him? What if, because I didn't do anything, something terrible happens to him?

I flinch when Ethan places a gentle hand on my elbow. "You okay?" His soft voice breaks through.

I clear my throat, tightening that lid again. "Yup."

CHAPTER TWENTY-TWO

ETHAN

I'm even more suspicious about Toby's allegiance to Ivy, because the way I felt after walking into Ivy's house and finding another man there...I mean, I'm not even dating her, but my body's reaction was borderline feral. There's no way Toby could have remained so sickeningly civil upon discovering me in Ivy's living room a while back if he really cared for her.

And hearing her call the man who just stormed out by her brother's name only slightly lowers my blood pressure. Because he's clearly upset her.

Resignation hangs over her shoulders as she gently swings the door closed.

"So. Ready to tackle that list?" She hooks a thumb over her back to gesture toward the wall. Her mouth forms a tight smile, and she stuffs her hands into her pockets.

A few weeks ago, I'd labeled this woman as "complicated" and wanted to run in the opposite direction. Now, here I am, ready to beg her to unload all of her problems on me. I don't just want to hear them, either. I want to *fix* them.

I'm equal parts attracted to and afraid of Ivy because she

makes me want to test my boundaries. But in the back of my mind, there's always a *what if*. What if I thought things would be different this time, and they weren't. What if the enticing call of adventure came along, and I couldn't resist leaving again? I'm just not sure I'm cut out for a long-term relationship, and I can't take that risk with her.

"Was that your brother?" I ask, tipping my chin to the door.

Ivy sighs, like she hoped I'd ignore the tension that's still hanging in the air. "Yeah. Nothing new. Just his usual stuff, but with bigger consequences." She stares outside the window for a few heavy seconds before her attention snaps back to me. "I have your brownies! Is it too early for brownies?"

"It's never too early for brownies," I say, grinning. "Although, I'm a little disappointed you didn't greet me in a towel this time."

"You wish," she replies with a condescending smile.

I kinda do, I think as I follow her to the kitchen. But I pull up short as soon as I walk in.

"Wow. You weren't kidding when you said you'd...uh..." I pause, nodding my head as I take in the massacred cabinets and the holes in the walls.

Ivy brings her fingers to her top lip while her own eyes survey the room. "Yeah. I did a number. They needed to come down, though, right?"

"Uh—eventually, yeah. I guess that's today's job, now."

"After brownies," she corrects me, the hint of a smile in the corners of her mouth.

We sit on the floor together, leaning against the wall while we sip coffee, and I eat way too much of the best brownies I've ever tasted.

"You make these for all your enemies?"

"I think we've progressed to frenemies by now, don't you think?" She licks a bit of chocolate off her finger, and I clear my throat and force myself to look away. But my eyes are stubborn, and I'm a glutton for punishment, so I glance back at her lips.

"Maybe we can even drop the enemies part some day," I suggest, openly staring at her now. Without thinking, I lift a hand to swipe the chocolate smudged over the corner of her mouth.

"I'd like that," she whispers, and I almost think she said *I like that,* referring to my thumb grazing her lips. Then she blinks a few times, as if she's trying to come back from a trance. "And, no. This is my Gran's recipe. I thought it was lost, but I found it stuffed in the back of one of these cabinets. I've never made them for anyone before."

Sitting next to her, our height difference doesn't feel as significant, and her face is closer than it's ever been. The green in her eyes shifts as she focuses on different parts of my face.

"You made them especially for me, then?" My voice comes out deeper and more gravelly with each bit of our back-and-forth.

"Maybe."

She has a boyfriend.

Right. I stand abruptly and offer my hand. "Well, enough lazing around, Marsh. Let's get back to work."

She takes my hand hesitantly, obviously confused by the sudden shift in my tone. But I had to do something to avoid getting drawn any farther. Gazing into her eyes while all these feelings threaten to bubble up is too confusing and complicated, especially while she's still in a relationship. I need to switch gears before I do something stupid.

I hand her the pair of gloves I bought specifically for her, and we spend the next hour picking up the remnants of her kitchen cabinets.

We return to the kitchen after hauling everything out to my truck, and Ivy begins sweeping up splinters of wood and dust. I watch her for a second before speaking. "If you're not set on custom cabinets, I think we could pick out some stock ones at a home improvement store, if you're up for it?"

"Today?" she turns to me, eyes wide and sparkling. I feel like I'm getting closer to earning another genuine smile.

"We need to get the measurements first, and they won't get delivered today, but, yeah, you could choose the ones you want."

"I'd love that," she says, the corners of her mouth lifting a little more.

Getting there.

"You're measuring," I tell her, picking up her fractional tape.

"Oh, okay."

The way she keeps nibbling on her lip is slowly becoming my undoing. With every one of these cute little things she does, it's beginning to feel more and more like she's got me under her spell.

And that doesn't bode well for my future plans, because I never counted on getting bewitched by a woman who'd capture my attention this way, especially not one who has a boyfriend.

Ivy measures the space for the cabinets, each dimension she relays contributing to the proud grin forming on her lips. And every time she flashes that smile my way, it's another jolt to my insides, my brain saying, *you're in trouble.*

"Seeing as this is your area of expertise and you know the industry, could you have a look at the budget I got from Gran's lawyer and tell me what I can afford to get done?"

"Sure." I nod over a hard swallow. She looks adorable, covered in dust and her hair bow slightly askew. I follow her to the living room, where she pulls a file from a side table and hands it to me. Then our eyes meet for an electric second when my hand makes contact with hers. *We can't have any of that,* I think, clearing my throat and gently tugging my hand back. I take out my phone to calculate some rough estimates for each task on our fixit list. Ivy watches me through the corner of her eye while she fluffs pillows and straightens things in the room.

"Okay, this is definitely doable, assuming no major issues turn up." I announce.

She moves closer to look over my shoulder at the paperwork, and it takes a surprising amount of effort to concentrate on the paper in front of me as I go over the figures and not to turn and gape at her again. Once I'm done, I slide my hands into my pockets, suddenly forgetting what it is I normally do with them. Ivy stares up at me earnestly, rambling about paint colors and fanning herself with the collar of her shirt. I respond on autopilot, my mind stalling as my fingers toy with the ribbon that's still stashed in my pocket.

It's not okay to have this kind of response to a woman who's in a relationship. *Shut it down, King.*

I suggest taking Ivy's car to the store, seeing as mine's loaded with evidence of her solo demolition. It would be better for my state of mind if we took separate cars, or better yet, if I hadn't suggested we do something together in the first place. But I can't think of a valid reason to cancel the plans I suggested without seeming a little unhinged, so I force all these weird feelings I've started having way, way down as we drive to the store. It's mostly silent in the car, and Ivy seems preoccupied with her own thoughts as we walk into the home improvement store together.

We quickly find ourselves perusing cabinets, Ivy running a hand along each surface she passes. This is followed by a small head shake or a nod of approval. And I'm like a puppy, doting on her whims.

"These are the ones I can afford?" she turns to me with a raised brow.

"Yup. So, tell me about Ross," I blurt out, opening a cupboard and swinging it shut to test its soft close features.

"Your segue game is strong, King."

"I am strong, thank you," I retort, flexing my arms.

"That's not what I—" she rolls her eyes when she catches my smug grin. "Fine. What do you want to know?"

"He's older, right?"

She's wearing those ridiculous platform shoes again, but she still stretches onto her tiptoes to reach an upper cabinet, huffing when she can't extend her hand far enough to touch the highest shelf. "Yeah, although it doesn't feel like it most of the time."

"Why not?" I prompt, grabbing a nearby step stool and placing it beside her. She pushes the corner of her glasses up, staring at me while I offer her a hand, the other behind my back like a nineteenth-century footman.

She steps up, letting go of my hand to execute a little twirl on the stool.

'Woman," I growl, my arms bracketing the space around her.

But she ignores my protest to answer my question. "Because I feel like I've always been the one having to take care of him and rescue him when he gets into trouble." She hops off the step with a bounce.

"He lands in trouble often?"

"No, well, *yes*, but he doesn't mean to. He just needs...I don't know what he needs." She sighs and shakes her head. "I don't know how to help him anymore."

I'm no expert on family dynamics, but she's clearly carrying a lot of responsibility that isn't hers to bear.

"It's not your job to save him, you know. He's a grown man."

The deep grooves between her brows tell me I've overstepped, so I deflect, choosing humor to defuse. I swing open a tall door on our side. "Should we explore this panty cupboard?"

"It's *pantry* cupboard."

"I've heard it both ways."

"You're ridiculous," she grumbles, closing the door. But her lips twitch as though she's trying to hold back a smile.

"I wouldn't say *ridiculous*...maybe an eccentric with amazing hair.' How about these?" I point to a set of white shaker cabinets with paned-glass doors on the top.

"Oh, I love them! They're so much better than the old peach ones we took out."

A store attendant wedges himself between us, making me flinch. "A great choice, ma'am, if I do say so."

"Whoa, dude. Someone was definitely named 'most likely to execute the creepiest intro' in their yearbook," I mumble as he stares at the cabinets we're all facing.

His name tag says *Farnan*, and I wonder whether that's the name he was born with or if he's one of those hippies that chose a new name as an adult.

He turns to ogle Ivy with that 'I have duct tape and a shovel in my trunk' look in his eyes, and I instinctively sidle up next to her, casually stretching an arm around her waist. Farnan must be giving her the creeps, too, because she doesn't protest when I pull her a little closer.

"You have these in stock to go, *Farnan?*" I ask, enunciating his name.

"Sure, Michelle over here can help you with the order." He directs us to a counter with a far less creepy sales associate. Once we go through the process of deciding exactly what pieces we'd like to order, Farnan thankfully moves on to his next victim.

"You're in luck, because everything seems to be in stock at our warehouse. It should be delivered tomorrow." Michelle smiles while typing on her computer. "Now, if only they magically assembled themselves, that would be amazing. But what can you do?" She laughs.

"The hokey pokey," I deadpan, furrowing my brow in mock concern. "But my friend here refuses to turn herself around. Because for her, that's *not* what it's all about."

Michelle's eyes bounce between me and Ivy with another forced laugh.

"Ignore him," Ivy says, stifling a smile as she thanks Michelle and grabs the paperwork, as well as my bicep. I flex for her again as she drags me away, and I can't resist another comedy bit when I catch her struggling to hide her grin. "See you next year, Michelle."

When we round the corner, Ivy lets out a bubble of laughter. "You've officially creeped Michelle out worse than Farnan creeped *me* out."

"You're welcome."

"You're a big goofball, Ethan King." She shakes her head with a wide smile, finally rewarding me that prize I've been coveting.

CHAPTER TWENTY-THREE

ETHAN

The snapping sound of a gloved fist hitting a punching bag fills the room.

Ooof.

"Sorry man." I lift my chin to Colton. I can't seem to find my focus this morning, and I've already taken too many hits from my big brother. And he's loving it.

He pauses, dropping his fists as we both breathe heavily from exertion.

"What's going on with you?"

"What're you talking about? I'm golden."

"Mmm, yeah, nope." He shakes his head. "You're not getting a pass on this. You were a gossiping little ass when I had that same look on my face." He aims a gloved hand at me. "I'm not letting you off the hook that easily."

"Colt, don't be the marshmallow dust at the bottom of the Lucky Charms bag. We came here to work out. Now, punch me."

"I've already punched you too many times today. Way more than usual, actually. I'd like my children to have a functioning uncle, and I'm concerned about your brain if I land any more hits in this same session."

I shake my head. "You'd have to start knocking me around a lot harder than that for it to leave any lasting damage."

He pulls his gloves off anyway, unwrapping his hands with a satisfied smirk on his face. "It's a girl, isn't it?"

I huff, unable to deny it, and his smile grows wider as he continues. "Oh, it's definitely a girl. But, who? Did Sandra finally wear you down?"

I grimace. "What? No. Definitely not." I thought Ivy was high maintenance, but she's an angel compared to Sandra. That woman's got straight up crazy eyes.

He purses his lips in deep thought while he wipes his neck with a towel. We're both zipping up our gym bags and preparing to leave when he freezes, his eyes widening as his face snaps back to mine.

Crap.

A look of elation spreads across his face. "It's Ivy."

"Hmm? I don't—"

"Of course you like her. I should have known the grumpy attitude was just a front," he says, crossing his arms and beaming at me.

I open my mouth to deny it again, but what's the use? Colton's already seen right through me. "Why do you look so happy about it?" I ask, scowling and moving toward the door. "It's kind of a problem."

"...Your voice just got real high." He says after a pause.

"Yeah. Sorry,"

"Why's it a problem?" He frowns and follows me out, sounding like a kid whose playdate just got canceled.

"Oh, I dunno, maybe cause she has a boyfriend, and it's incredibly inconvenient," I retort sarcastically.

"Which part's inconvenient, the boyfriend or your feelings?"

"Both." I sulk as we walk to our trucks.

"Okay, but the boyfriend thing—I honestly don't buy it."

"You don't?" I ask a little too eagerly.

"I've seen Ivy and Toby together, and they've obviously friend-zoned one another a long time ago. I'm just not sure why she'd go through the trouble of faking something like that." Colton unlocks his truck, tossing his bag in the back and leaning against the side. "Although, Ember says Ivy's been acting a little weird and that she suspects something's up but Ivy isn't telling her 'cause she doesn't want to stress Ember out."

She's a little bag of secrets, that one, helping everyone else and wearing herself thin by the looks of it. I smile, thinking about how cute her selflessness makes her.

"So you're admitting it? You do like her?" Colton grins and wags his eyebrows.

"What are you, twelve?" I scoff. The truth is, discussing this kind of stuff is new territory for me, even for a conversation with my brother. I've never had a problem joking about my many dates, but it's always been lighthearted. None of them ever meet my family. Casual is the name of the game.

But with Ivy, I'm starting to realize there's nothing casual about her or what I'm feeling. And I can't decide whether I want to Bubble Wrap her or act as her bodyguard, shoving anyone and everything out of her way so she can roam free.

"What are you gonna do about it?" Colton asks, bringing me back.

"Besides my extreme empathy for Ember, not much I can do about your maturity, bro."

"Your deflection is cute." He crosses his arms again, still sporting that smug look on his face.

I turn to toss my things into my truck and run my hands through my hair. "What the hell *can* I do?"

"Is Ethan King asking his big brother for advice?"

"You don't have to be an ass about it," I grumble.

"Just talk to her man," he says, still looking entirely too happy about my predicament. "Tell her how you feel...or show her what she's missing out on. Stop messing around and get serious about a future with someone."

"Yeah, okay." My voice cracks, and I clear my throat awkwardly. I'm never this awkward. What is this woman turning me into? It's not enough that I'm game for doing the whole DTR thing, but now I've got to deal with her having a boyfriend and all. Sure, I could tell her about the feelings I've developed for her, but I have no clue what her response will be. I'm still not sure she'd be willing to help me if I were on fire, instead of pulling out a bag of marshmallows.

CHAPTER TWENTY-FOUR

IVY

Ethan's latest message stares at me from the wall, a little reminder that my life is still a giant mess.

I like that you're fun-sized.

Below the message I only discovered late this afternoon is a brand new pair of lilac Crocs. I've been staring at them for the past ten minutes while they teasingly coax open that lid on my emotions. But those feelings got crammed into that jar for a reason, despite the way they're so eager to escape.

It's not like I could do anything about my growing fondness for Ethan, anyway. I'm in a fake relationship with another man, and I don't see a way out of it that would allow me to protect the sense of security I so desperately need. If Gran finds out I'm *not* dating Toby, there's a chance she'll take the house back —or in the very least be debilitatingly disappointed in me.

So I'm standing here, staring at these darn Crocs like they've got all the answers, my feet yearning to experience the comfort they promise. They *are* my favorite color, after all.

I growl as I pivot sharply toward the kitchen. The new cabinets were delivered and installed yesterday while I spent my day off at school, painstakingly organizing the recital schedule. And it would have taken even longer if Toby wasn't there to help.

You should stop saying yes to things that are out of your depth.

Yeah. I know.

The kitchen looks drastically different with the new cupboards. The wood is painted a soft white, accented with black handles and paned-glass uppers. All of this lower cabinet space has me itching to unpack the boxes that have been shoved against the wall since I moved in. I spend the next hour meticulously finding a place for every piece, desperately trying to ignore the Crocs calling me from the next room.

"Ugh!" I grunt after I realize I've been wiping the same spot on the table, and I toss the washcloth onto the floor.

Fine. But I'm only trying them on.

Standing before the alleged pillow-soft shoes, I take a deep breath and remove my platform Vans. This is like the opposite of Cinderella. I don't know how Crocs have managed to become trendy, because teenage Ivy still cringes at how uncool they once were.

I slide my feet into the Crocs and start with slow steps around the room. I'm aware of their lack of height, but *wow*. They weren't lying when they said it's like walking on a cloud.

I smile with giddiness. I definitely get the appeal now. In fact, I feel the need to apologize to every person I condescendingly questioned about their Crocs-allegiance. It's like asking why people like watching *Friends*.

I'm so enamored with my new footwear that I don't notice the footsteps treading up my porch until Ethan is swinging my door open with a "knock-knock."

His eyes drop to my shoes, and the corners of his mouth immediately curl up. I feel like I've been caught in the middle of a shameful hobby instead of trying on a popular brand of comfort shoes.

"Look away! Avert your gaze!" I shout.

"Nope. You can't be grumpy while wearing those. Those are happy shoes," he points, taking measured steps toward me.

"Don't try to convince me you own a pair of these."

"What? Of course I own a pair of Crocs. They're like therapy for your feet. I stomp around in these heavy work boots all day. My feet deserve some TLC, too."

I narrow my eyes as he steps closer.

"The difference is, you're actually wearing them." He smiles softly.

"Yeah. Thank you. It was very thoughtful. Bold, but thoughtful."

"Handsome, thoughtful, bold... Any other compliments you want to give me?"

I roll my eyes, taking a step back and putting some distance between us. I don't wear perfume or fragranced lotions because they give me a headache, but whatever subtle scent Ethan uses is like catnip. It doesn't smell like anything from an aerosol can. It's earthy and fresh, with a hint of wintergreen, and I want to get a good ol' whiff of it. And I mean the kind of whiff you only get from a creeper sniff. These shoes must be doing something to my endorphins, because I've never been so tempted to press my nose against a man's skin before.

"I never said you were handsome," I reply, clearing my throat and gesturing to our list. "What's next?"

Ethan's jaw shifts to the side, like he's formulating a plan. "Those new light fixtures get delivered?"

"Yup. And the ceiling fan for the master bedroom."

"I picked up the faucets you chose. Looks like we're doing fixtures today. If you have any old towels, you can put them in the bathroom."

"Yes, sir." I salute before making my way to the hall closet. "Stop staring at them," I throw over my shoulder, referring to my Crocs.

When I look back, Ethan's eyes are on my legs. "They're nice to look at."

Shut it down, sister.

I pull a stack of old towels out from the hallway closet, trying not to blush. "You know I have a boyfriend, right? I don't think he'd appreciate your boldness." My eyebrows raise with a stiff smile, but I'm snickering on the inside, because my fake boyfriend would be all too happy about Ethan showing an interest in me.

"About that," he begins, stalking closer.

What in the heck is happening?

It's like he's been swapped out for his flirty twin. The real Ethan is probably on a solo trip to the forest to grunt at fluffy squirrels and chop down trees with nothing but a sharp glare.

Meanwhile, this flirty Ethan is very confusing. The way he's standing there, looking so yummy in a bicep-hugging white tee—*dang it*—it threatens my resolve and my ability to keep him at a platonic distance. Who the heck wears white for a job like this anyway?

His hands graze over mine as he takes the towels from my arms. He's standing so close that, without my heels, I have to crane my neck to meet his gray eyes, the ones that are suddenly hypnotizing and making my head feel swirly.

Stop it.

"You should break up with Toby."

The nerve of this man! "Excuse me?" I squeak.

"I know you're not in love with him. Break up with him."

"*Rude.* You don't know anything about my relationship with Toby."

"Interesting that you didn't correct my accusation that

you're not in love with him." He smirks, making me want to confess the whole thing, if only to have the truth out there.

No. This man was a twerp up until a few days ago. Remain strong.

Just because he's turned on the swagger doesn't mean I'm entertaining whatever he thinks is happening here. I've worked too many late nights and need a nap. That's what's happening. I'm sleep deprived, and it's messing with my brain. I've woven an intricate web of white lies that will become infinitely more complicated if this continues.

"Who made you the relationship analyst? Also, rule number three!" I want to stick my tongue out so badly. That's the problem with hanging out with eight year olds—you pick up their mannerisms. But I can't risk anything else that would make me seem younger while I'm wearing these ridiculously comfortable shoes.

"I'll be in the master bedroom. Excuse me." I reply with a flat smile, retreating to the safety of an Ethan-free space. Because, while I know he'd do anything to prevent me from another physical injury, it's my heart that feels like it's in need of protection.

CHAPTER TWENTY-FIVE
ETHAN

So *that* went well. I watch Ivy's sassy little saunter as she stomps down the hallway. Her cut-off jeans and Crocs make her attempt at angry walking more adorable than intimidating.

I pull out my phone to text Colton an update, since I'm following his terrible advice.

ETHAN
Epic fail on talking to Ivy btw

COLTON
I'm going to need details

ETHAN
I told her to break up with her boyfriend. Then she stomped off

COLTON
🙍 You're an idiot

How have you ever gotten a date before?

> ETHAN
> *Gif of Joey Tribiani's shocked face*
> I tried to be smooth, but I fumbled, okay?

> COLTON
> Ya think?

> ETHAN
> I can't do this with you right now. I'll call you later 😌

> COLTON
> While I look forward to hearing about your attempts to come back from this, you should do something nice for her
> Show her you're not an ass

Maybe my brother's forgotten, but this all started with me doing nice things for Ivy.

Besides, it's probably a good idea to give her some space, let her cool down while the effects of my foot-in-mouth syndrome wear off.

I go on to examine the bathroom, grateful to find it doesn't need a lot of work. The shower and bathtub will eventually need to be replaced, but for now, new fixtures and fresh paint will suffice.

I grab a ladder next and follow the echoes of music to the room Ivy's retreated into, hoping for a redo on not being a jerk.

She keeps her back turned to me while she sways and bops along with the country music coming from her phone. The room is empty aside from an ornate wooden wardrobe pushed up against the wall. The entrance to the room faces three large, slightly offset windows framed by floral curtains. I quietly place the ladder in the center of the room, then lean against it as I watch Ivy dance.

"Nice moves, Marsh."

"Ethan! Gah! What is wrong with you?" She shoots me a venomous look, the tips of her fingers nudging her glasses up. "Jeez. I hope you know you're not as smooth as you think you are, leaning against your ladder with your *I'm so cool* look," she says mockingly.

"Did you just try to imitate my voice?"

She responds by sticking her tongue out, which elicits a belly laugh from me. Every one of her attempts at being feisty just makes her more adorable.

"I'm sorry." I shrug. "I figured I would've scared you either way. Whatcha scraping at there?" I frown at the seams in the wall.

"I'm not sure. There's a weird line here." She points.

I step closer, letting my fingers run along the wood, feeling for discrepancies. I've only seen something like this once before, but it would be amazing if this is what I think it is. I shove the wardrobe a foot over and marvel at the rectangular outline faintly visible along the wall. I push my fingertips against the panel, and my eyes dart to Ivy's when there's a soft click. The panel pops open, hinges squeaking as the door moves inward.

"No. Freaking. Way," Ivy says in a breathy exhale.

She steps inside the opening, and I crouch to follow her into the tiny room. It's so small that I doubt it could fit more than a twin-sized bed with little space left over. Two antique bookshelves hug the wall to our right, and a wine-colored wingback chair sits in the other corner. Ivy tiptoes further in and switches on a dim lamp tucked behind the velvet chair.

"I can't believe Gran never told me about this." She spins in a slow circle, her eyes tracing the two large paintings that face the shelves. "This must have been hidden here the whole time she was renting out the house—her trinkets have just been inside this room, gathering dust."

She delicately lifts a miniature owl statue from the shelf, a soft chuckle escaping her lips. "She used to complain endlessly about the flood of owl-themed gifts she received. She made one offhanded comment about finding them cute, and for the next thirty years, that's all people gave her. She ended up donating most of them when she moved out, but it seems she held onto this one," she muses, cradling the figurine gently in her hands.

"This room feels like a time capsule," I remark as I move closer. The door creaks behind me, and we both instinctively freeze, our eyes locked on its slow movement until it clicks shut.

"Ethan...tell me you can open that door."

I mean, being locked in here with her wouldn't be the worst thing. It's not the most romantic place, but at least she can't run away when I try to talk to her.

Okay, that sounds creepy in hindsight. Let the record show that I in no way want to keep her anywhere against her will.

I rake my fingers through my beard as I stare at the door, the one that has no handle and opens inward. I start feeling my way over the paneling again inspecting it like a caveman, tapping and knocking on different spots and pretending to know what I'm doing.

Hell, we're really stuck.

I turn to give Ivy the bad news, and maybe to capitalize on our moment alone. Hey, I'm just maximizing the opportunities as they present themselves. "It's not opening." I smile but I probably look like one of those Wallace and Gromit characters with their teeth bared.

Her breath catches, and she exhales in a series of short, panicked breaths. With every second, her eyes seem to grow bigger, and she shrinks back against the wall. She is freaking the heck *out*.

"Ivy, look at me. It's gonna be okay. I have my phone, see?" I pull it out, wiggling it in front of her. "I'll text Colton to come open the door. Everything's fine."

She shakes her head, fear sparking in her eyes. "I don't like small spaces." She runs her hands through her hair then shakes them out in front of her. She begins to pace, so I gently grasp her hands, setting them down over my chest.

"Hey. Can you look at me?" I nod reassuringly when she finally tips her head back to meet my gaze. "Good girl. Can you feel my heartbeat?"

"Mhmm."

"Can you take a slow breath with me?"

We manage five slow inhales and exhales together, and she finally begins to breathe more calmly.

"You're doing so great. I'm gonna text Colton, okay?"

"Yup," she chokes out.

I leave her hands on me while I pull out my phone, feeling a little like an ass for relishing in the fact that she's letting me help her. I hate that she's freaking out. But the feeling of her hands against my chest causes my stomach to do that same swoopy thing it does when we argue.

"What if he's busy?" She drops her hands to resume her pacing. "We could be stuck here forever."

The door isn't up to standard, and don't doubt I could break it open with a hard shove of my shoulder. But it'd require a costly repair or a custom replacement.

She continues treading back and forth, muttering to herself, but at least she's stopped hyperventilating. "I'm gonna die in here. I've never even left Texas! But I'm going to die. Single and alone."

I quirk my head as her rambling continues. "First of all, you're not going to die in here—"

"You can't be sure of that," she snaps without looking up, her brows knitted tightly.

"Mmm...pretty confident, actually. Secondly, ouch. Hi,

person who's literally stuck in here with you." I wave then gesture to myself. "So—not alone. Thirdly—and possibly most interestingly—I'll remind you that you claim *not* to be single."

"I made that up, okay! Toby's just a friend. It was a misunderstanding, and now I'm going to shrivel up from dehydration, and Gran will find me years from now, the tiny little raisin who lied to her."

There's so much in there that I want to unpack, things that make me ridiculously giddy—but her breathing is quickening again, so I put a pin in her confession.

I step in closer, cupping her face.

"Ivy June. Can you look at me?"

"Why are you being so nice to me?" She continues to ramble. "I'm struggling to match this...this new side of you with the grumpy, bossy Ethan I know." Her hand flutters, gesturing up and down my body, making me grin stupidly.

I lean a fraction closer, closing in the distance between us with a deep inhale. My brows pull together while I try and figure out a way to explain those initial reactions to her. "Think of all the times I've been grumpy, Ivy. What were you doing each of those times?"

"Breathing?"

I shake my head, hoping to convey the feelings I'm still too chicken to verbalize. "You were putting yourself in harm's way. And yeah, okay, at the restaurant I was annoyed about having to listen to you gush over another guy. But since the day I met you, seeing you in danger kind of freaks me out."

Her head rears back ever so slightly, and she frowns while her eyes bounce between mine. Her feet haven't moved, and we're still close enough that I'm mesmerized by the different shades of green surrounding her pupils.

It's like my brain and my body have taken her babbling confession a few minutes ago as a green light, and I'm involuntarily moving full-steam ahead. Other than her sort of hating me—there's nothing stopping me from pursuing her now. And I can work with that.

For years I've been worried that my fear of missing out would inevitably ruin any romantic relationship I might have. But until now, I've never experienced even a fraction of the fulfillment I get from caring about this woman, not in any of my craziest adventures. I've taken so many physical challenges and financial risks, but after experiencing the tiniest connection with Ivy, I'm finally willing to take an emotional risk. The alternative just seems soul crushing.

"But—" she begins, bringing me back from my epiphany.

"Ivy—"

"You're always growling—"

"Ivy—"

Her eyes finally trace back to mine. I'm still cupping her jaw while one hand slides to the back of her neck. Traces of confusion are etched on her face, but her gaze falls to my lips. Her palms return to my chest, and this time, her fingertips curl in to grip my shirt. When her lips part with a breath, I move closer, my mouth aching to taste hers.

Her eyes flutter closed before flinging open again, wide and startled when my phone rings and ruptures the building tension.

I cringe and bring the phone to my ear. Ivy steps away as I answer. She's got her arms folded now, defenses freshly reinforced.

I'm learning this pursuit may be a 'one step forward, two steps back' kind of thing. Not that I'm deterred, only more determined.

"Ethan, hi!" I wince at the high-pitched voice coming through the phone. "I know we planned to meet at Capelli's, but my car is acting up. Could you pick me up?"

"Sandra?" I furrow my brow in confusion.

"Of course, silly. So can you pick me up for our drink?"

Ivy's got a fresh storm brewing in her eyes. There's no doubt she can hear Sandra's squawking. I'm flipping through files in my brain, searching for any memory of committing to a date with Sandra.

It's not easy, since I'm distracted and trying to read every micro-expression flashing across Ivy's face. I'm dying to know what she's thinking and wondering whether she would have let me kiss her had we not been interrupted.

My eyes pinch closed as I realize I have a mess to clean up. I know I come across as an ass, but I can't just ditch Sandra when I apparently committed to going out with her.

"Sandra...can you give me a minute? I'll call you back."

I hang up, not overly concerned about being polite when I need to explain to Ivy that it's not what it looks like. Has any man ever made a comeback after that statement?

"Ivy—"

Our heads swing to the door as we hear the click on the other side. Colton's face is apprehensive as he pushes it open.

"Why do you look so scared?" I ask him.

"Wasn't sure what I'd find in here." He shrugs.

Ivy bolts past me, rushing out the door. "Thanks Colton, um, I've gotta go." She pauses to swap her Crocs for wedges and my gut twists when she avoids looking even remotely in my direction.

My jaw slackens, and my eyes flicker to Colton. He's standing with his lips pursed and his hands in his pockets. There's a look of brotherly empathy in his eyes, but it's like a punch to the gut, because I've only seen that look on him when I've really screwed up.

By the time I bring my gaze back to Ivy, she's throwing another "thank you" over her shoulder, and then she's gone.

I hear her as the car drives away, and my head falls back with a groan.

"I know, okay. I'll fix it."

Colton's hands lift in surrender. "Hey, I didn't say anything."

"Thanks for coming."

He nods with a thin smile. "Need any more help?"

I let out a swoosh of air. "Nah, I've got this. Thank you."

I'm actually not so sure I've got this, but I'm forming a plan. Before I can put it in place, I need to do something else unpleasant—I've got to deal with Sandra.

CHAPTER TWENTY-SIX

IVY

I don't know where I'm going. I've been driving around in circles for twenty minutes like a neighborhood creeper. At this point, I wouldn't be surprised to see flashing lights behind me. I'm sure it's safe to go back now, anyway. And if Ethan's truck is still parked outside my house when I get there, I'll just pick a new neighborhood to drive circles around.

I could visit someone, but there's a prideful gash in my ego that makes me want to lick my wounds alone, without the pressure of having to pretend everything is okay.

So Ethan has a date. Why am I so butthurt about it? I'm the one who drew the boundary lines in our relationship by keeping up the fake boyfriend ruse in front of him. Not to mention, Ethan's a well-known serial dater. I scold my heart for getting so excited and fluttery. The flirty banter and lingering looks were never meant to be taken seriously. That man has always had heartbreak written all over him—case in point.

Today should be a reminder that, ultimately, Ethan and I are enemies. That's how our relationship began, and it seems we operate best within those parameters. He growls; I do something that pisses him off. Hating him isn't as fun as liking him, but it's certainly safer for my heart. And today has proved that straying from that dynamic is too risky.

I wish I could say I had the heart of a lion, but mine's more of a chocolate covered marshmallow that I keep patching up with more chocolate. It's melting and sticky, and my insides are all warm and gooey, but I still can't help offering a piece of it to everyone. Call it my toxic trait. I'm a people pleaser.

By the time I get home, Ethan's truck is thankfully nowhere in sight, allowing me to sulk up the front porch steps. But I scrunch my forehead in confusion when I slide my key into the lock, only to find the front door open. Ethan has been nagging me to keep it locked, yet he goes and leaves it unlocked, himself? It's another strike against him. Maybe it's inconsequential, but at least it's something and right now I'm looking for any excuse to add to his *cons* list.

"Ross!" I yelp after flinging the door open and discovering my brother standing in the living room, looking awfully fidgety. "What in Bilbo's butt are you doing here?"

"Still doing that weird thing with curse words I see." He tries to smile, but he's obviously on edge.

"How did you get in here?"

"Door was unlocked." He shrugs with a jutted out lip.

Dang it. Ethan hadn't forgotten to lock the door. My dear brother just has a particular knack for getting into places he shouldn't. "Right. Well, next time, wait outside, will you?"

"Sure. Sorry. Uh...you good?"

I narrow my eyes. "Why are you being so weird?"

"Can't a guy just pop in to say hi to his favorite sister?"

I'm suddenly so angry I could scream. He's never available when I need to get hold of him, yet now he shows up out of the blue, only to gaslight me? "If this was a normal occurrence, sure, but you've been MIA for weeks, so excuse me if I find your reappearance in my home a little strange."

"Right. Sorry. I'll get out of your hair," he gestures to the door, attempting to make a quick exit.

"Oh no, you don't!" I hold up my palm, stopping him. "What's going on here?" My face is frozen in a permanent frown as I search his eyes for any semblance of the playful little boy I once knew. But right now, I can't even recall the last time Ross seemed like my older brother, the last time I felt a true connection to him.

He inhales, holding his breath while his gaze wanders to the kitchen. His eyes narrow before returning to me with an exhale.

"Look, Ivy. I know I've messed up. I'm trying to fix it, though." His face looks pained and he shakes his head remorsefully. "I've gotta go. Sorry for showing up like this."

My mouth hangs agape as he walks past me, and this time I let him go, dumbfounded wondering what in the heck he expected from me.

Ross shuts the door behind him, and I let out a heavy sigh. How am I going to shake off this poop storm of an evening, now? There's still plenty of work to be done, but I need something to cheer me up, something that'll renew my determination.

I'm too scared to explore Gran's secret room by myself, so I leave that for another time. Getting locked in that tiny space all alone would basically be my worst nightmare.

Maybe I'll ask Toby to come over and help. Ha, that would serve Ethan right!

Except Ethan already knows Toby and I aren't really dating.

Dang it.

I kick an empty box on my way to the kitchen, sending it flying down the hall.

I shouldn't be thinking of ways to make Ethan jealous, anyway. And it's a good thing I'm not jealous. Jealousy is very unbecoming on a woman. That green-eyed monster is capable of unleashing a host of uncharacteristic behaviors.

I stalk over to the master bedroom and grab the ladder. The ceiling trim and fixtures need to be removed, and I'm about to show it who's boss.

When I started this renovation fiasco, Ember very kindly discouraged me from climbing higher than three feet. And I may have a slight propensity for injury, but today's frantic need to accomplish a task overrides her warning.

However, it turns out carrying a ladder that's taller than I am isn't as easy as it seems. The walls gain a few more scuffs and my arms accrue new bruises as I drag the darn thing into the living room and stand it up.

I get some music going while I prepare by performing all the steps Ethan showed me before starting on this kind of task. Okay, first safety step—shutting off the power. These fixtures really are hideous, and while the room already looks considerably better by the time I'm done removing them, the job feels less empowering than I'd hoped. I stare at a hole in the wall as it morphs into Sandra's face. I don't even know what she looks like, but my imagination has conjured up a big-haired, over-perfumed woman that I'd kind of like to push off of a ladder.

Nope. I don't care what Ethan's date looks like or how she might be hanging all over him right now.

I need to demo something.

Smashing a wall would be ideal, since I'd get rid of some of the unfortunate rage that's started building up every time I picture Ethan flirting with his date. But I have no idea how to do that safely.

I hate how much this is affecting me. He just proved he can't be trusted by openly flirting with me and dare I say almost kissing me while he already had a date lined up for the same evening. Men like Ethan—*people* like Ethan—they always let me down. Sooner or later, they find a reason to leave or discover the next best thing. Something less complicated and less broken.

That feeling of yearning for someone to have my back is at war with my need for self-preservation. Maybe one day I'll find another Toby, one I'm actually attracted to. A guy who's stable and reliable but still makes my heart skip a beat.

That's the type of man I'm holding out for. Not an arrogant, cocky ding-dong who looks mouth-wateringly good in well-fitting jeans, a white tee, and a toolbelt.

I turn the power back on before climbing to the top step of the ladder, giving a knock and a tug on the trim around the ceiling. It's horribly outdated and should be easy enough to pull off. The pile of tools Ethan left in the corner should have something to do the trick.

I pause for a few minutes to pull up a Youtube video that explains the process simply enough to give me the confidence to tackle the job. As long as I get to use a hammer at some point, this'll be great. Climbing back up the ladder with tools in my arms proves tricky, but I manage without incident.

I'm totally killing this ladder game. Ember will be so proud.

I follow the Youtube instructions and whip out that carpet knife, wielding that bad boy to carefully slice along the molding. I switch tools, using the narrow spatula-looking one to wedge beneath the seam. Now to work out my rage with that hammer. It's not necessary to complete the job, but I wiggle the spatula just enough to loosen the trim, then move on to the hammering.

I watch as the wood falls to the ground with a satisfying

crack. Then I turn, letting out a loud shriek and throwing my hands up in shock when my eyes meet the gaze of a very angry-looking Ethan beside the ladder.

The next five seconds feel like they stretch over two hours.

Tools fall. The ladder wobbles. I think I shout out another curse—probably a celebrity name. The legends make such wonderful expletives. You want a good cuss word to shout out, try yelling *David Duchovny* or *Schwarzenegger* next time you stub your toe.

Meanwhile, I'm still falling at an unfair rate. I'm the cat who's used up her nine lives, and my slow descent forces me to face every one of the regretful decisions I've made over the last five minutes.

Ethan's deep scowl spreads into a grim line as he balances a pizza box on one arm and clenches a six pack of root beers in the other. Days from now, I'll marvel at my ability to notice these small details with such clarity, assuming I survive.

The slow-motion montage finally ends, and I force my pinched eyes open, groaning. This feels like a reenactment of Dr. Suess's *Fox In Socks* with me splayed out on top of tools, on top of a smushed pizza, on top of leaking root beer, on top of Ethan, who's spread out on his stomach, on top of an empty, overturned pizza box.

Every girl dreams of being caught while falling off a ladder, landing in the strong arms of her knight in shining armor, right? But I certainly didn't plan this, because if I had, my hero would have actually *caught* me.

And while the smell of root beer and pizza would normally elicit cheerful feelings, the bruises I can already feel forming on top of my other bruises are ruining the effect a little.

"You okay?" Ethan grunts as he pulls himself out from beneath the wreckage.

"Yup," I manage without groaning.

A burst of laughter springs forth when I notice the sauce and bits of topping smeared across his cheek, like he was slapped with a slice of pizza. I point and continue giggling deliriously.

He looks unimpressed as he wipes it off with soda-soaked napkins. I move to help him, but he stops me.

"Careful, there's glass everywhere."

"I'm fine," I say, rolling my eyes. "You broke my fall." Then I break out into another fit of uncontrollable laughter.

"You sure you're okay? Did you bump your head?" His brows knit with concern as he crouches close, his hands trembling as his eyes scan my body. My heart is still beating as if I've just hugged Jeff Goldblum. Gosh, I love that man. So classy in the weirdest way, am I right?

Maybe I did bump my head. I bring a hand up, patting my hair. Nothing feels sore.

"I don't think so. I'm okay. But you should have known I wouldn't react well to being snuck up on. Snuck upon?"

"I'm learning this," he says with another scowl.

He helps me stand, and I swipe at the remnants of the soggy pizza. He doesn't release my hand, holding it up and guiding me to safety as I tiptoe over everything. These wedges are coming in handy now, with their thick soles. I can see Ethan fighting a glower as he purses his lips, entirely unamused when his eyes track my steps. He's being forced to appreciate the very things he detests most. It almost elicits another maniacal laugh from me, but I manage to contain my evil cackle.

I feel slightly unhinged and can only think to blame it on a serious adrenaline spike.

Ethan holds up a palm, like I'm an overexcited puppy that might jump back into the mess. "Stay there."

I shoot him a dirty look, but he turns his back before it lands.

He gingerly picks up what he can, tossing the ruined pizza and larger shards of glass into a trash bag while I try to appear helpful. I fail. Every time my hand reaches for a piece of debris, he snatches it up with a wide eyed glare.

He turns to me once he's swept the last bits of the glass. "I'll mop this later. But I'm starving, and you squashed our dinner. Do you need to change before getting in the truck?"

"Oh goody. Grumpypants Ethan has returned," I say, folding my arms. "Didn't eat on your *date?*"

"No," he grunts before disappearing down the hallway. That liquid fire still burns in his eyes when he returns a minute later with my lilac Crocs in hand.

My, aren't we extra grouchy tonight...

I'm starting to wonder whether his date didn't go so well, after all. And that thought makes my mouth curl up into an involuntary smile.

"Your death traps are covered in root beer," he mutters before crouching in front of me. I'm perched on the arm of the sofa, stunned silent while he lifts each of my feet and shimmies off one wedge at a time. I can feel my cheeks heating when those callused fingers graze my ankles as he slips the Crocs on. Then, before I know it, he rises and stomps out the door. Why couldn't *that* moment happen in slow motion, too? It was delicious enough that I'd like to remember it later, maybe even recall the whole exchange in vivid detail while I fall asleep. But Ethan's heavy steps are already permeating the front porch, so it looks like I'm keeping the sticky and dusty clothes on, then.

I follow Sir Grumpylicious outside, and he silently clasps his hands around my waist and hoists me into his truck when I reach the passenger door. It really is a problem that I'm enjoying all this physical contact so much.

It must be because I've fallen...off that ladder, I mean.

CHAPTER TWENTY-SEVEN

IVY

We drive for only two blocks before Ethan abruptly slams on the brakes and pulls over beside a public park. The blues and purples of late evening cast a magical glow across the ground, but the beauty is lost on me as my mouth turns down in confusion. When I look over to ask Ethan why we've stopped, I find him glowering, his jaw clenched tightly as he stares straight ahead. His chest rises with heavy breaths, and his hands grip the steering wheel like he's trying to hold himself together.

"Are...are you okay?" I inch closer, trying to figure out if he's having a medical emergency. "Did you get hurt?"

He finally turns his head toward me, still silent, and the tension in the air sharpens. My heart races, the adrenaline from the fall still surging through me, amplifying everything around us. The sound of my pulse fills the space, merging with the steady rhythm of Ethan's breathing, making his truck feel like it's echoing with the intensity of this moment.

"Ethan...What's happening right now?"

His eyes take their time sweeping over my face, and then he's moving closer, bringing his delicious scent with him. It's his usual spicy fragrance, now intermingled with the lingering sweetness of root beer. But before my thoughts can catch up, Ethan's cupping my jaw with both hands and pressing his warm lips to mine. He backs away slightly before returning for another long kiss, except this time I involuntarily grasp at his chest, my fingers twisting into his damp T-shirt.

He pulls away from the kiss, leaning his forehead against mine, eyes closed.

Wow. That came out of nowhere. The air is still weighty, an invisible fuzziness coating our heavy breaths. It feels like he's just released a giant slingshot after it's been pulled back for so long. "I'm sorry," he whispers. His lips are still so close.

"Don't be," I tell him, unable to stop myself from smiling.

"Right."

He clears his throat as he releases me and shifts into his seat, then he steers the truck back onto the road.

The strained silence continues. I guess we're not going to talk about what just happened, then.

While the feeling of Ethan's big hands cupping my jaw and his lips caressing mine were all exceptionally nice, twisting into him just now also managed to draw my attention to a stinging in my side, one that begins to throb more painfully as his truck rumbles along.

My brows pull together, and I stifle a wince when a sharp stabbing hits me below my ribs. The spot might have only been a dull ache when I first fell, but now it's throwing a tantrum. Meanwhile, Ethan is pouting on the other side of the cab like someone's just told him tool belts are for sissies, so I withhold drawing attention to my pain.

I don't get it. One minute, the man is pulling me in and kissing me senselessly, and the next, he's back to glowering at me in silence. Then again, he did apologize, so maybe he already regrets that kiss?

"So, um...How was your date?" I squeak out when his truck hits a pothole, and I bounce around painfully in my seat.

"Didn't go on the date, Ivy."

I'd assumed that much when he showed up at my house so soon after leaving. But I needed to hear him say it. He continues to stew, glaring at the road like it's personally offended him. I turn slightly to my right, secretly lifting the hem of my oversized shirt to check the damage.

Oh. Well, crap.

"You still okay with pizza?"

"Uh...yeah. Pizza's fine. But could we stop somewhere first?"

More scowling.

"Yeah. Where do you need to go?"

"Um, just something I gotta do real quick. Take a right over here."

I inhale slowly, taking in deep, measured breaths in between giving Ethan directions. He looks puzzled when we reach our destination. "Why are we outside the hospital?"

"Okay, I'll tell you. But first, I really hope you have a good car detailing place. And also don't be mad—"

"Ivy—"

"Just, pull up outside the emergency entrance, please."

He does as I ask, but his eyes grow more frantic. "Ivy? What the hell is going on?"

"You're gonna have to help me out. It seems I've gotten some blood on your seat."

I've never seen a man move so fast. His seatbelt is barely unclipped and he's already at my door, hands hovering with uncertainty. "You're bleeding! Okay. Crap, Ivy, why didn't you say anything?"

"Don't fuss at me, okay? That's why I didn't say anything at first. Also, I just noticed."

"How did you miss this?" he shouts incredulously.

I furrow my brow. "You're the one who distracted me."

Ethan clenches his jaw, reaching up and carefully cradling my hips. I slide out of the truck and get to my feet with his help, and he curses under his breath while he searches for a shirt from behind the seat. He balls it up and gently presses it over the spot I've been covering with my hand, and we shuffle into the ER together. Convincing him to park his truck and leave me in the waiting area proves harder than getting Gail to bake something without rum. He only relents when a burly nurse hurries out with a wheelchair, both of them insisting I sit.

I'm wheeled to the check-in desk after that, where I awkwardly recount the events that led me here. I wish it were a thrilling tale, like slipping on an old dock while rescuing someone from a gator attack. But eventually I'm forced to admit that I was startled and toppled onto a box of pizza, a six pack of sodas, and an ugly light fixture. The attendant glares at me with the same skeptical look you give to someone who says they're thinking about getting a perm.

Ethan rushes back in, alarming the other patients he passes. A nurse joins us, giving Ethan a once over before ushering us both behind a screen. I've skipped the line, and as I open my mouth to protest and volunteer to wait my turn, Ethan's lips form a thin line. Before I can speak, he gives me a stern, "Don't even think about it." Apparently, having blood seeping from one's side is a big deal. I only got the one look at it, but it's not like I'm going to die from blood loss. I'm guessing the cut is a thumb and a half wide, tops.

Ethan broods silently, standing with his muscular arms folded while the nurse takes my vitals. He looks away politely when she helps me remove my bloody shirt to swap it for a scrub top. Then we're escorted to a room and the nurse leaves, telling us a doctor will be in soon.

"So, what's your more fun twin doing while you sulk it up with me?" I ask, pursing my lips to the side.

Ethan lifts his hands in frustration. "Dang it, Ivy. You put yourself in danger. *Again.* And I'm mad 'cause I'm the reason you're here."

"How do you figure that?" I lean back on the hospital bed. Ethan jumps forward when I pinch my eyes closed at the stinging on my side. I've also traded his shirt for a wad of gauze, and thankfully the bleeding seems to have slowed. Ethan still hovers close by, clearly unsure how to help.

Then I realize, this man is in a constant state of uncertainty when he's with me. But even when he's scowling at me—which is ninety-nine percent of the time—his attention is completely focused on me.

And I like it too much.

For the majority of my life, Ross and the less fortunate absorbed most of my parents' attention and efforts, while I self-sufficiently blended into the background. But somehow—no matter what I do—Ethan sees me. What he sees, though, apparently drives him mad. But he pays attention, nonetheless.

Neither of us seem to be willing to acknowledge that kiss. I'm not sure of Ethan's motivation for not bringing it up, but my rationale is back to angry-stomping its feet, demanding I pay attention.

What were my reasons for not liking Ethan again?

He's a shameless flirt.

Well...I mean, is that our only reason? 'Cause that one's actually not so bad.

Fake boyfriend.

Ah, yes. There it is.

For the first time this evening, I glance over and take him in. His hair's slightly ruffled and sticking out. His pizza-stained shirt still hugs his chest temptingly, and his tanned skin peeks out from beneath the sleeves, a pleasant contrast to the bright ribbon tied around his wrist.

Excuse me, hold the phone!

"That's my ribbon," I blurt out.

His eyes dart down to his wrist, arms still crossed. He shrugs with a lip jutting out. "Dunno what you're talking about."

"You're seriously playing that angle?"

We're interrupted by a knock and then the door opening, not that I'm convinced Ethan was going to respond to my accusation, anyway. A young, attractive man in a white lab coat flashes a bright smile before he pulls the door closed behind him. He seems vaguely familiar.

"Ivy Marsh? I'm Dr. Bryan. I hear someone got into a fight with a glass bottle?" He asks, snapping on a pair of gloves as a nurse joins our party.

I clear my throat before answering. "Sort of, but it's not what you think."

"So you weren't in a bar fight?" he asks, narrowing his eyes.

Ethan lets out a low grunt while I begin to sputter, trying to explain how the glass probably came from a crushed light fixture and get this man to understand that I'm not a senseless party animal. But then the doctor laughs, his eyes suddenly warming.

"I'm kidding, Ivy. My sister, Stef, works with you, remember?"

Ethan elicits the slightest growl, and I flash a frown at him before turning back to Dr. Bryan. That's why he looks familiar. I'd forgotten that Stef had introduced us last year.

"Oh...right. Well, this was just a home-reno accident. No alcohol involved." I laugh awkwardly, but his smile only grows. "Let's have a look, shall we? Lie back for me." He winks.

My eyes snag on Ethan's as I recline. How is it possible for him to frown deeper? Except this time his fury is directed toward the doctor who's currently lifting the hem of my shirt and prodding around.

"Not too bad." Dr. Bryan narrows his eyes while his gloved fingers inspect my side. "About an inch and a half wide and a half-inch deep. You didn't nick anything important, but we'll need to get it stitched up."

"Yay," I deadpan when Ethan growls again. This'll be fun.

CHAPTER TWENTY-EIGHT
ETHAN

Dr. McFeely continues groping Ivy's bare skin, making her giggle when he cracks a corny joke and flourishes it with another stupid wink. Isn't he breaking some ancient medical oath by flirting with a patient?

I know I've been a jerk tonight. Watching Ivy fall, knowing I couldn't catch her—it nearly gave me a heart attack. And to top it off, I was out getting a stupid pizza instead of being there for her in the first place. Then I went and kissed her. It was the hottest damn kiss I've ever experienced, and we hadn't even gotten past a PG-rating.

I don't regret kissing Ivy. I regret letting her run away again earlier this afternoon instead of coming clean about my feelings though. If I'd told her the truth, that I have absolutely no desire to go out with anyone else but her, she wouldn't be here now, getting stitched up.

Ivy suppresses a wince as Dr. Smooth numbs her skin. I'm like a lion, jumping to her side and grabbing her hand. Her eyes pop open, meeting mine in question. I squeeze her hand, reassuring her I'm here for her. I've never wanted to shove a man out the door more than I do now. In my fantasy, Ivy doesn't need her creamy skin stitched up, so hoisting this prissy intruder out the room isn't inconsiderate.

"We'll wait a few minutes for the skin to numb up," he says, reminding me that for now, he's needed.

Yeah, I'm a giant Neanderthal. I want to scoop Ivy up and growl out *mine*.

"Any inside info you can give me on Stef? I think there's a coworker she's into but she's refusing to give me anything."

Ivy looks puzzled as she pauses to think. "The only male teacher remotely her age is... Oh my gosh!" Her hand slaps over her mouth as she bugs her eyes at me. "Um...nope. I don't know anything about that." She adds, her eyes roaming over every wall in the tiny room we're in.

"Well, we'll just pretend you didn't just answer my question," He winks again as he sterilizes Ivy's skin, and I clear my throat, though it probably comes out sounding more like a snarl.

"Sorry, man. I didn't catch your name. Are you Ivy's brother?" Dr. Bryan asks, pivoting toward me on his wheely chair.

"Boyfriend." I smile flatly, giving Ivy's hand a tighter clasp and shooting her a raised eyebrow when it looks like she's about to protest. I don't bother giving my name, because all this guy needs to know is that Ivy is unavailable.

"Right." He clears his throat uncomfortably. A few minutes of awkward silence go by before dear old doc begins stitching Ivy up. She clenches my hand a little harder, sending small jolts to my stomach. I hate that she's hurt because of me. If I'd called her phone or waited for her to come down the ladder, she might not have fallen. She was asking for trouble with those freaking wedge heels she wears, but I should have known better. The woman is a walking accident waiting to happen. I purse my lips, scowling at the doctor.

"Easy tiger," he chuckles. "We're all done."

Dr. Bryan smiles once more at Ivy before leaving. I shift closer, cradling her hand more gently within mine, sending a message and secretly celebrating being close without her pulling away.

I curl an arm around her, helping her sit while the nurse relays aftercare instructions and orders Ivy to fill a prescription for antibiotics. My last few moments of pretending to be her boyfriend are waning by the second. As soon as the nurse leaves, I'm back to being a single man, brought to his knees by a woman who drives him crazy in every sense of the word.

"What the heck are you doing?" Ivy whisper shouts once we're alone. Wide, mossy-green eyes impale me while her hand whacks my arm for emphasis.

"I'm thinking you should go out with me."

"What?"

"Ivy June, can I take you out to dinner? On a date?"

"I have a boyfriend," she squeaks.

I tilt my head. "False."

"Listen here, Dwight Schrute." She points a finger while sliding off the hospital bed. "I can't date you. My life is already a mess, and Gran thinks I'm dating Toby. If she finds out that's not true, she'll be devastated. She only gave me the house because of it."

I open the door, laying a hand on her back while we slowly make our way to the exit. I'm not that easily deterred, though. There's magic between us, and I'm going to chase it. It's the first time I've ever considered changing my plans for a woman, and that's a pretty big green flag. Plus, I'm almost positive she's overthinking this thing with her Gran.

"Counteroffer," I propose, cupping her elbows as she cringes and hoists herself into my truck. "Continue fake dating Toby and have dinner with me. Just dinner."

I shut her door, leaving her with my offer as I round the truck to the driver's side.

When I climb in, she's leaning back against the headrest, her eyes closed while she talks on the phone. I gather from her side of the conversation that there's some sort of drama with Opal and Gail pulling a prank on her Gran. I slide out my phone to order a pizza delivery, because I could literally eat a horse at this point.

Ivy only hangs up once we reach her house, and she eases herself onto the sofa in the living room. I kneel in front of her, sliding her Crocs off her dainty feet. She lifts her head, eyes tracking my movements.

"This day feels like ten years," she breathes out. "And I'm starving."

"I ordered pizza," I say, taking a seat beside her and pulling her feet over my lap.

"I could kiss you," she mumbles and sighs, then her head pops up. "I mean that as a figure of speech."

"I'm game," I tell her with a shrug and a smirk.

"Ethan..." Her eyes sober as she plays with a thread of a pillow. "I'm serious about my life being a giant mess. My head feels like it's going to spin off with all the drama and white lies and withheld information. Adding this," she pauses to gesture between us, "as nice and confusing as it is, wouldn't be fair to either of us. I don't know if I could handle it once you're ready to move on. Because you *will* leave. You're meant for big things, and this town is too small for Ethan King." She smiles softly.

There's so much that I want to shoulder for her. I want to be the barrier when she feels ambushed by her struggles. I want to be the one who helps her learn the strategies that will make her life easier and to teach her that letting people in is a sign of strength. I want to know about the trouble her brother dumped in her lap and figure out how to lighten her load. I want to be someone she can rely on.

But this isn't about what I want. It's about what *she* needs. And I think she needs me to prove that I won't add more stress to her life, that I'm *not* always a giant butthead, and that she can depend on me.

A knock sounds at the door, and I gently move Ivy's feet from my lap to get the pizza. My stomach growls as the smell of cheese and pepperoni wafts into the air. I plate our food, telling Ivy to stay put. I can see how hard it is for her not to play host. She could be bleeding and on crutches and still insist on making sure everyone else is comfortable.

I hand her a plate then rummage through her medicine cabinet for some pain pills, giving her a couple with a glass of water.

"Thank you," she whispers, looking like she could pass out any minute. She gulps down the water before she speaks again. "You're not going to fight me on my refusal?"

"Nope," I answer after finishing a bite of pizza. "But I'm not that easily scared off. I'll show you that I'm here for you. And I promise not to kiss you again until you ask me."

She rolls her eyes, her mouth forming a flat line. "Unlikely."

"But not impossible."

"Thank you for dinner, Mr. King, but it's time that I retire," she adds with a perfect British accent.

"Ah, see? You've already had dinner with me. Our first date is out of the way. How about we cut to the chase and you ask me for that kiss goodnight?"

"Asking me to ask for it doesn't count," she points out, but all I do is grin at her, because she's not denying that she wants a kiss, either.

I help her stand and walk her to her bedroom, her arm

tucked in the crook of mine. When we reach her door, I turn a cheek, tapping it while I lean down.

"That counts as asking for it."

I flutter my eyes, smiling while I wait. "I said I wouldn't kiss *you* unless you asked me to. This is you kissing *me*. It's different."

"Whatever," she grumbles before laying her palms on my shoulders and planting a soft kiss on my cheek. I could get used to this. Our playful banter minus the part when her eyes threaten to dismember me is my new favorite high. Although this feels just as dangerous, because when she's not plotting to murder me, her smiles are free and lethal, wielding sharp arrows that never miss their target.

My heart is in trouble.

CHAPTER TWENTY-NINE
IVY

My lips are throwing a full on hissy fit, screaming at me as they leave Ethan's cheek. *Kiss him on the mouth, you impudent hussy!*

As tempting as that thought may be, I've drawn a line in the sand, and I'll do my best to stay on my side of it. Yet, the warmth from Ethan's body feels like an alluring wave, drawing me in until, before I know it, I'm inching closer and closer to that fragile line. And it's even more dangerous because I'm too tired to hold my ground right now.

Retreat.

I take a step back, my words tumbling out in a rush. "Okay, thanks for stopping by. Goodnight." I wave like an idiot before turning and darting into my room.

Ethan looks way too amused as he leans an arm on my doorway, his eyes sweeping over my space. He points a finger with the hand that's angled above his head. "That a blow-up mattress?"

"Yeah..."

"Great," he says as he steps inside, his manly presence

filling the room. When he'd been standing at the threshold, my plan to sleep off this bout of lowered inhibitions felt manageable. But now, that plan crumbles with every step he takes. He rolls out the folded mattress and plugs in the pump.

"Whuh...what are you doing?"

"Either I get this sucker inflated," he begins, wiggling his eyebrows, "or this becomes a one-bed trope."

"How do you know what a trope is?"

He clicks his tongue. "A man's gotta have some mystery."

"What makes you think you're staying here?"

"I'm not leaving you alone. You're exhausted, and you might need something during the night. Honestly, I don't have much confidence in your coordination, and I'm not willing to risk letting you hurt yourself further."

"I'm not a sleepwalking drunk. I plan to get in bed and stay there. Because I'll be *sleeping*."

"Perfect. You won't even notice me."

"Ethan, I don't need you to stay here. I'll be fine on my own." I yank open a drawer, pulling out my very unsexy pajamas. Maybe they'll deter him.

"Maybe *I* need *you*, hmm?" he proposes with a cocky smile. "It's the strangest thing, but I'm suddenly terribly afraid of the dark. Just developed this evening."

This man. First, I can't seem to do anything right. Now he's like a barnacle that won't let go of my rusty side. "Whatever. I'm changing in the bathroom, then I'm going to crash." I point a finger at him. "You better not snore."

I leave the room and perform my nightly routine, feeling like I could pass out right here with my face in the sink. I reach for the hem of my scrub top, letting out a hiss when the movement pulls at the stitches on my side.

I take a deep breath, trying again. The sting is just as bad.

No, no, no, no, no. This cannot be happening! I take a deep breath, exhaling with a noisy flutter of my lips. Am I really going to ask a man to help me take off my top? Completely platonically, of course—no sexy vibes here. My granny muumuu will make sure of that.

I swallow my pride—or flush it down the toilet. Either way, I'm seconds away from collapsing, and I refuse to sleep in scrubs, so I trudge back to my room, finding Ethan in a fresh shirt and—Lord, help me—gray sweatpants.

"You came prepared for a sleepover?" I muse.

"I keep a gym bag in my car." He shrugs and frowns at my top. "You *don't* look prepared for a sleepover."

Kill me now.

"About that..." I glance to the side, rolling my lips then mumble under my breath, "I need help."

"What was that?" Ethan leans a little closer, tilting an ear toward me with a cocky smile.

"I'll only say it again if you swear to uphold rule number three."

"Cross my heart."

"I can't get out of my shirt."

His eyebrows raise like I've just handed him the best ammunition ever.

"Rule number *three*," I enunciate with narrowed eyes.

He nods obediently, rubbing his hands then blowing on them. "Right. How are we doing this?"

My eyes widen as they track the eager movements of his hands. "Down boy."

He clears his throat, standing straight with his arms crossed behind his back. "Sorry. Awaiting orders, ma'am," he drawls and nods again.

His serious face has a bubble of laughter erupting from me, making me wince at the sting on my side. Ethan's hands shoot out, then he hesitates, looking so unsure of what to do.

"You okay?" he grits his teeth on my behalf.

"Yeah," I breathe, holding my side with one hand. "Lift slowly from the hem. *Slowly*. And keep your hands where I can see 'em."

"You're killing me," he groans, reaching for the bottom of the scrub top.

"Ethan."

"What? A beautiful woman just asked me to take off her shirt—my brain understands the no-groping part, but my hands can't compute."

I scoff. "Nevermind. I'll just sleep in this." I begin to turn, but he gently catches my arm.

"I'm kidding...sort of. But come on, let me help you. I'm dying to see your pajamas. This thing is coming off." He shuts his eyes, holding his hands out near his waist.

"I'm wearing a sports bra—you don't need to shut your eyes."

He mumbles something then breathes deeply, locking his eyes on mine. I lift my arms like a reluctant sloth under arrest. The last thing I see is Ethan's jaw clenching before my view is cut off when he pulls the top over my head.

"Thank you." My words come out breathy as I hug the shirt to my chest. There's heat in his eyes as that muscle in his jaw ticks again. Two dangerous words are floating around in my mind, goading me, tempting me to utter them: *kiss me*.

But then my eyes catch on the quilt that Gran gave me, and the chest of drawers that have held my clothes since childhood. There's the mirror that eight-year-old Ivy danced in front of, all of it reminding me that I have something to lose, that giving in to those delightful kisses would be playing with fire.

"There are spare sheets and a pillow in the hallway closet." I curtsy awkwardly, clutching at my side, then spin and scurry back to the bathroom.

I decide this old sports bra is due for retirement anyway, so I grab a pair of scissors and cut it off, opting for the easy way out. I manage to wrangle a waterproof bandage, shower, and dry myself off. Then, I slowly climb into the least sexy pajamas known to humankind—a white cotton nightgown with a yellow ribbon threaded through the chest seam. The long sleeves cover every inch of my skin. These are the pajamas your grandma wore, practically designed to repel any man with romance on the brain.

I enter my room to find Ethan is on the inflatable mattress he's pushed against the far wall. It's an entirely new situation for me, allowing a man to make himself comfortable in my bedroom. I thought it would feel unsettling and intrusive, yet the more I look at Ethan, the more I acclimate to his presence, the more I find it comforting. I think I might actually like having him here while my mind is so overcome with anxious thoughts and worries.

He's got an arm propped behind his head, a book resting in his hand—the one that still has one of my hair ribbons tied around it. When did he find that? I squint, trying not to alert him to my presence while I read the title of his book.

Journey To The Center Of The Earth.

Figures he'd read an adventure novel. It's another reminder that he's a wanderer at heart. I'd hold him back from that. Aster is perfectly quaint, and it's my home. I'm comfortable here, and I have no desire to leave. Sure, I'd like to travel someday, but my roots will always be here, with my Gran. She'll be buried here, anchoring me to this part of Texas forever. And since she's the only person who ever truly allowed me to be myself, I owe it to her to stick around.

Ethan turns a page, his gaze cutting to mine. Pure elation overtakes his face while his eyes consume my outfit. I hold my hands to the sides, palms out, letting him get the full effect.

"Ivy June, I did *not* expect this," he says as a snorty chuckle escapes. "I figured you'd come out in some kind of cartoon-themed pajamas, or even Star Wars. But *this*? The height of sexy-pioneer fashion?"

"It's timeless. Gail made it."

I maneuver myself into bed, feeling my cheeks heat up under Ethan's scrutiny. I can still see the amused grin plastered on his face from across the small room. He leaves to use the bathroom and climbs back onto the air mattress when he returns. Even though he's five feet away, the distance feels like it's shrinking by the second. Once he's settled, I click off the lamp and mumble a goodnight.

You can do this, Ivy. Just ignore the fact that there's a hot man in your room.

Ethan's throaty chuckle bounces my way. It's a delightful soundtrack for going to sleep. I turn onto my back, smiling as my eyelids grow heavy. Then Ethan shifts, and his mattress audibly protests. Again. And again. Every few seconds, an irritating creak or squeak rips me from slumber.

I rub my forehead, letting out a heavy sigh. "Ethan King, that thing sounds squeakier than a bed at the Playboy Mansion. For the love of all that's good in this world, get in this bed."

"Ivy Marsh, are you propositioning me?"

"This is a queen-sized bed. We're both adults and can share the space responsibly. But I will stab that mattress with a stiletto if you don't vacate the room or relocate to the space beside me."

He growls in response. "But it's really hot when you're bossy, and I'm just supposed to lie next to you and keep my hands to myself?"

"You're welcome to leave," I retort, knowing he's too much of a gentleman to oblige. I also know he's too much of a gentleman to get handsy without my permission. And it's honestly rather fun torturing him a little after all the frowning and buttheadedness I've had to put up with for the past three months.

He sighs heavily, the mattress groaning as he rises and makes his way across the room to join me. My mattress is still on the floor, too, because I didn't want to put the bed frame together only to disassemble it once I move everything into the master bedroom.

"Stay on your side. And no funny business," I order sleepily.

"So that's a no to spooning?"

"Hmm, that sounds nice. But I can't spoon with you. Too dangerous," I slur before drifting off to sleep.

CHAPTER THIRTY

IVY

I wake up to find my body curled around Ethan's from behind, clinging to him like a spider monkey on its mama's back.

Why does he smell so good? I take a deep breath, savoring his warmth. How long can I enjoy this before I'll need to extricate myself without waking him? I bet he's an early riser.

Dragging myself away from sleepy-time Ethan will feel like tearing myself away from the dessert table at a buffet. Longing and doubt begin swirling in my mind, and I haven't even left him yet. I find myself once again questioning my methods, wondering whether ignoring my growing feelings for him is really the best way to move forward or if I'm just taking the scenic route to disaster.

Yet, amidst the uncertainty, there's a blazing inferno between Ethan and me. He's unveiled this tender, caring side that has me gravitating toward him faster than most women to a shoe sale. It's like he has a secret decoder ring to my soul. In his eyes, I see recognition, understanding, acceptance—the kind of acceptance that slices through the barriers I've built around my heart. Besides Gran, and occasionally Opal, no one else has bothered to look beyond the facade I present to the world. But Ethan? He's the MVP of breaking down my walls, even though he's only a rookie.

Ember would have tried if I'd have allowed her, but I've perfected the art of the poker face with her, since she's always had her own plate full of family drama.

So here I am, stuck between a rock and a hard place, trying to figure out if I should stick to my guns or throw caution to the wind and let Ethan sweep me off my feet.

Self-preservation ultimately wins this particular battle, if not the war. I slink out of bed, grabbing my phone and some fresh clothes before tiptoeing to the bathroom. I replace the bandage on my wound after checking to make sure the area doesn't show signs of infection. After I've dressed, I find myself standing in the living room, staring at *The Wall*. I may not be jumping into Ethan's open arms, but I can at least admit I have room for growth in the area of letting people in. So in the name of personal growth, I pick up one of Ethan's pencils to scribble another message. It's a bold move on my part, but I try not to overthink it after officially deciding to not be attracted to Ethan. I'm stubborn. I can will it into reality.

Surprisingly, Ethan still hasn't risen from bed by the time I'm out the door. I wait in line at a drive-thru pharmacy to pick up my antibiotics, relieved that I still have enough time to grab a coffee before meeting Ember. I skipped making coffee at home because the thought of facing awkward small talk after waking up next to my previously sworn enemy makes me want to move to a new country. I can't shake the memory of having my hand pressed against his rigid stomach. I may be tiny, but there's no way he hadn't noticed my big-spoon impression this morning, right?

My phone rings as I pull into a Starbucks, and I'm pleasantly surprised when I read the name on my screen.

"Hey, Mom!" I answer.

"Ivy, sweetheart, I'm so glad we reached you! How are you? How's school going?"

I feel like I've been hearing these same polite, impersonal questions for the past twenty years. My reply hasn't changed either. "It's going great. Where are you guys now?"

"We're about to drive to Kathmandu, then we fly to Hyderabad tomorrow. It's so beautiful here—you won't *believe* the views! And the people are incredible. I know I keep saying they're so friendly, but they really have been treating us like family."

"That's great, Mom. Hang on a sec,"

I inch forward, covering the phone to give my coffee order. "Okay, I'm back. Is Dad still buying every souvenir he finds?"

She clicks her tongue mirthfully. "He's out of control. We had to purchase a bigger luggage bag. Be prepared for your apartment to look like a travel shop," she says with a laugh.

"Oh, I moved," I tell her while mouthing a "thank you" to the attendant handing over my coffee. It feels wrong to know every intricate detail of my parents' travels while they remain oblivious to the significant changes in my life. Although I can take some responsibility for this disconnect, it's mostly a result of keeping our conversations superficial to avoid mentioning Ross. Mom becomes emotional whenever I broach the subject, so Dad swiftly changes the topic to his favorite true crime podcast. As a result, we stick to safe, surface-level topics, never delving deeper. This pattern isn't new; I initiated it to sidestep being open about the dyslexia challenges I faced growing up.

When I was about ten years old, a neighbor, Miss Kathy, came over one evening to comfort Mom after a particularly explosive interaction with Ross. Miss Kathy had made me a sandwich while my parents had gone off to tend to Ross, getting the peanut butter-to-jelly ratio all wrong. I frowned as she slid the plate towards me, and she shook her head with a tsk. "I'm afraid they need you to be the good one, Ivy June, the kid they don't have to stress about."

I guess it stuck.

I switch the call over to speakerphone and Mom's voice fills my car. "Oh! Why'd you move?"

They're usually too busy for detailed questions, which works in my favor when I need to give a quick, drama-free recap: "Gran gave me her house; the old tenants moved out, so I'm fixing it up."

"Well, sweetheart, that's wonderful! I'm so glad you're the one restoring it. Dad sends his love, too. We've gotta go, our transport just arrived. I love you, my Ju-ju Bean."

"Love you, Mom, bye."

With every phone call that passes where we continue to ignore Ross's situation, I can't shake the haunting realization that it could have easily been the other way around. I might have been the misunderstood child struggling under their scrutiny, battling unseen demons. I could have been the one who, instead of concealing everything, turned to unhealthy coping mechanisms or cried out for attention in misguided ways.

I might have been the one to lose their confidence. Ross only has my faith left. Sure—he's acting like a big idiot—but even idiots need someone believing in them to earn redemption.

Being the pro that I am, I pack all those feelings into my trusty jar and focus on enjoying my coffee.

CHAPTER THIRTY-ONE

IVY

I drive up to Ember's apartment and find her outside, embracing her disgruntled cat, Nicolas Cage. He squirms in her arms while she presses her cheek against his fur. I continue watching as she engages in a lengthy monologue before letting him escape, and she finally makes her way to my car.

"Dress shopping day!" I clap when she shuts the passenger door.

She turns to offer me a nervous smile. "I'm excited but also dreading it."

"Don't worry. I'll be your personal bodyguard. If any oddball tries to make small talk with you, I'll just out-weird them and scare them off."

"Colton's mom will be there, so you might not want to get too weird."

"I think we've said the word 'weird' too much," I nod slowly with my mouth forming a flat line.

"Yeah," Ember agrees. "Now it really is *weird*."

What's weird is how I'm suddenly very nervous at the

thought of being around Colton's mom. Because she's also Ethan's mom. And I really want her to like me.

"Right," I muse while reversing. "Body-block the small-talkers without being weird. I could do the thing where I make crazy faces that only they can see?"

"I love that you're willing to go to such extreme levels for me, Vee, but I should probably put on my big girl panties and learn to socialize."

"Mm-kay. But if your panties start to sag, just say 'pineapple,' and I'll do my thing."

"You're too kind. But how about we just talk about something else? I need a distraction from the wedding planning for a minute. How's the house coming along? Ethan behaving?"

Oh, he's more than behaving. He's also been ridiculously kind and considerate while also making it incredibly difficult to ignore his chiseled chest and arms.

"Yup. All good."

"Ivy—"

"Hmm?"

"Never in our friendship have you answered a question without expounding with a thesis worth of words. Now, tell me the rest of the juicy information you're needlessly withholding."

I *cannot* tell her the truth. As much as I'm aching to discuss every aspect of my soap opera life, the bride-to-be deserves a drama-free, low-maintenance friendship, especially from her support team. I refuse to cause any stress for my friend when I know she'd only want to play the mother hen and insist on worrying over my current situation.

"Ethan and I have settled on a truce. He's been amiable and helpful. Sorry to disappoint you, but there's nothing juicy to report." My best bet is to divert her attention, but she'll get suspicious if I circle back to wedding talk too soon. Maybe there is some drama I can share that won't cause her any anxiety. "Oh! But get this—my Gran had this secret closet in her bedroom. It's like a monument to the seventies, Em, you have to see it! It has a secret door and everything."

I recount my discovery of Gran's hidden closet, minus the steamy bit where Ethan nearly kissed me. "I also...kinda fell yesterday," I grimace, lifting the hem of my shirt to show Ivy the bandage on my side. "Ethan had to take me to the ER for stitches. But I'm fine."

"Vee!" Her eyes widen as her hands cover her mouth. "Why do you keep climbing things in those shoes? Are you sure you're okay?"

"It's not bad, really. But I'm afraid I won't be trying on any bridesmaid's dresses, unfortunately."

"Eh, it's okay," she waves off my concern. "We'll get one eventually."

"Will your mom be joining us today?" I flinch inwardly as I pose the question. Ember's mom could make Emily Gilmore seem like a saint. She's been making an effort to tone herself down in recent months, especially after Ember opened up about her feelings and established some necessary boundaries, but the woman is still terrifying.

"Lord help me, yes. But Jeanie promised to step in if Mom crosses the line."

I let out a wistful sigh. "Jeanie's truly the best mother-in-law anyone could hope for."

"I hit the jackpot, for sure," Ember confirms, grinning fondly.

You could hit the same jackpot, too, if only...

No way. I refuse to risk ending up homeless again, all because of some foolish fantasy about inheriting an amazing mother-in-law and becoming a sister-in-law to my closest friend.

We park and walk into a bridal store that's straight out of a Hallmark movie, peering around with widened eyes.

"Your mom pick this place?" I mutter out the side of my mouth.

"Yup," Ember says, emphasizing the final 'p' with a pop of her lips.

"Good thing she's been working on lowering her expectations, huh?"

Ember snorts a chuckle, then groans as her head falls to my shoulder. "I'm seriously considering eloping."

I loop my arm through hers, pulling her inside while I whisper. "Just say the word, Em. I'll organize everything."

"That's actually very tempting," she mumbles under her breath before greeting her mother, Fretta, with a stiff hug. In contrast, Ethan's mom, Jeanie, breezes over like the ray of sunshine she is, crushing Ember and I in a loving embrace. "Ooh, I'm so excited!" she intones. "Thank you for including me in this, Ember."

I look around again while Ember and Jeanie continue talking. The store is lavishly decorated in champagne pinks and soft lighting. Every corner seems embellished with fixtures and decor that scream wealth. It's so *not* Ember. But I'm sure she'll go along with it, anyway, since she's been picking her battles when it comes to her mother's input.

A stylist glides a rolling clothing rack into view, leading it towards the dressing room to our right. Positioned in the grandest of the three dressing spaces, it features the customary pedestal where brides-to-be showcase themselves for their loved ones.

"Ember Hayes? I'm Martha Jean. You must be our beautiful bride," she greets Ember with a smile that exudes professionalism. But her eyes betray her when they flicker to Fretta, seeking her approval.

"If you'll come with me, we've preselected some gowns for you to start."

Ember cringes before she quickly recovers, her lips forming a perfect 'O' as she nods her assent, then beckons me to join her with a subtle tilt of her head. I follow, meeting her at the rack of gowns.

"On a scale of one to ten, how much are you hating this?" I whisper.

"I'm already maxed out. It's fine, though. I'll try on a few of these, and worst case scenario, I'll have two dresses." She lifts two hangers from the rail, handing them to Martha Jean.

"I could always arrange for Nicholas to suddenly develop a strong aversion to the dress your mom selects while it's 'airing out,'" I suggest in a hushed tone, emphasizing the air quotes.

"Don't tempt me." Ember's eyes widen in a playful warning before she vanishes into the dressing room. I stifle my laughter as I turn back to the mothers, who are already seated on the central sofa, each of them holding a flute of champagne, their anticipation palpable.

I delicately lift a glass from a gleaming silver tray, relishing the effervescent bubbles as they dance on my palate. Just as I begin to enjoy the sensation, a gentle ping interrupts, prompting me to reach for my phone to check the incoming text message.

> ETHAN
> Good morning, big spoon 😌

My head jerks up instinctively to ensure no one can decipher the text's contents or its sudden impact on my cheeks, which now feel like they're ablaze.

ETHAN

> Marco and I are knocking out that wall after I get back from the gym

> Make sure to pick up your antibiotics. And don't injure yourself while dress shopping, or I'm playing big spoon tonight

For a fleeting moment, I find myself lost in a daydream, imagining the cozy embrace of Ethan's arms. However, my reverie is interrupted as Jeanie pulls me closer to her on the sofa, bringing an abrupt end to my fantasy.

"So, Ember tells me you're dating someone!" She smiles giddily, and I panic, thinking she knows something about me and Ethan. But my heart rate settles once she continues. "—a coworker. So romantic!" she squeals.

"Oh! Ha-ha, yes, ma'am," I respond with a nod, bringing the glass to my lips for a long sip. My gaze flits around the room as I contemplate my next move. There's a pang of guilt as I consider deceiving Ethan's mother. Even though it's not like I'm going to allow anything to happen between Ethan and me, I'm still desperate for her approval. And for some inexplicable reason, sharing a slightly altered version of the truth feels essential.

I lean in closer, lowering my voice. "Please don't tell Ember, but I'm only going on a few platonic dates with Toby to help him out. We're actually just friends."

Jeanie leans back, her eyebrows raising. "Oh, now that sounds like an interesting story. You know, I had my own fake-dating situation when I was a young thing." She winks with a mischievous twinkle in her eye. "But what about your house? Ethan's been telling me about all the renovations he's helping you with! He says it's just darling. In fact, he couldn't stop talking about it yesterday."

My throat grows dry, and I end up choking on my spit in the world's most awkward attempt to play it cool.

Ethan is talking to his mom about me?

"Oh, sweetie, are you okay?" She pats me on the back in soothing sweeps.

"Yup," I croak. "And, yes, Ethan has been a huge help." I smile, wiping at my chin after sipping from the tiny bottle of water Jeanie thrusts in my hand, my very own real-life fairy Godmother.

I stand and excuse myself to hunt for a trash can to dispose of the empty bottle. Yet, unsurprisingly in a place like this, something as visually off-putting as a trash can is nowhere to be found. A store assistant materializes out of thin air, her smile bright as she whispers, "I'll take that for you, honey." Still perplexed, I glance back at the woman, wondering how she appeared so suddenly.

I'm turning back to continue my conversation with Jeanie when I'm caught off guard by my momentum and one foot wedges behind the other. I stumble, but Jeanie is at my side, gripping onto my arm and stopping me from hitting the floor. It dawns on me that she must have been beside me all along. Either that, or she anticipated my clumsiness and miraculously managed to save me from a side full of popped stitches and an unfortunate carpet burn on my forehead.

She chuckles softly, her shoulders trembling with amusement as she patiently waits for me to steady myself. "Ethan warned me about your tendency to find yourself in these situations."

"He did?" I gulp, trying to sound nonchalant when I'm entirely too eager for her answer.

She leads me over to the sofa, and I'm grateful once again for her steadying hand, sparing me from a potentially serious accident. The slight twinge on my side serves as a reminder that a fall in my condition might have turned this posh boutique into a horror-movie set.

"Oh, yes. It's been 'Ivy this' and 'Ivy that' ever since y'all started on that house. I've never heard him talk about a woman so much. That's why I was puzzled when Ember mentioned you having a boyfriend. But it all makes sense now." She wiggles her eyebrows suggestively, sparking my curiosity and tempting me to dig for more information, or perhaps even to confide in her. Either way, this subtle hint that she'd approve of her son dating me feels like a crack in the tight seal of my stifled-emotion jar. There's a newfound longing for someone to recognize how hard I'm working to hold all the pieces of my life together, for someone I can trust to keep my secrets and not to abandon me later.

I look up at Jeanie with a hopeful expression, but I can't bring myself to speak.

"Well, for the record, this mama would only be too happy if something *were* to happen between you two," she adds with so much genuine warmth that I'm basically a puddle in my seat.

But those old wounds are too hard to ignore, and I find my usual self-deprecating bit spilling out before I can stop myself. "That's sweet of you, but I'm a mess. And Ethan needs someone fun, someone who can roll with his sense of adventure. We wouldn't be a good fit."

Even as I say the words, they feel like a crushing betrayal of my true feelings. But they're responsible words, ones that will protect Ethan from getting caught up in my disastrous life. He's already infiltrated it too much, and I'm worried that letting him see some of the uglier parts will only trigger his genuinely good nature and throw him into fix-it mode. But my life is much more complicated than a home reno.

Martha Jean interrupts us before Jeanie can reply to inform us that Ember will be out in a few minutes. She seems to lock in on me as a potential customer once she finds out I'm an unmarried spinster, but I nearly snort in her face. I'm lightyears away from needing a wedding dress or ever being able to afford one from this store, let alone the tissue paper they use to stuff the boob areas.

She continues explaining all the benefits of investing in one of their gowns, and all I can do is nod politely. But then we reach that awkward moment when I suddenly can't decide where to direct my gaze while she speaks. It feels weird to fixate on just one eye. The forehead? No, that seems odd, too. Maybe shifting my focus to the side will reset things. I offer a bored nod accompanied by an aloof "mh-mm," then take a sip of my drink while stealing glances at the dressing rooms.

I return my gaze to Martha Jean, hoping she's gotten the hint. But the unease persists as she goes on. Should I alternate between each eye? *Just pick an eye!*

Finally, Ember's dressing room curtain opens, saving me from internally combusting because I can't remember how to look at someone. Fretta, who's been paging through a bridal catalog the entire time, finally sets it down, plastering on a proper smile. Ember gracefully steps onto the pedestal, adorned in an ivory satin empire-waisted gown. Each of us expresses our admiration of its beauty, but I can tell from the expression on my friend's face that this *isn't* the one. It's lovely, undoubtedly, but what Ember truly deserves is a dress that exudes understated brilliance, one that doesn't vie for attention with flamboyance or resemble a flashy prom dress.

We all play along, anyway, clapping excitedly and repeating the process twice more. It takes one more equally underwhelming dress from Fretta's preselected rack before I decide to intervene. "Mrs. H., Jeanie, why don't you two grab another drink. Ember and I are going to browse the gowns for a minute."

"Oh, of course." Jeanie adds a wink that tells me she knows exactly what I'm doing. "The bride should have the chance to pick out her own dresses, too."

I love her even more for having Ember's back. In truth, the bride is the only one who should be choosing the gowns she'd like to try on. But try telling that to Fretta Hayes. I return a grateful smile, leading Ember forward to sift through a rack of dresses.

Then my butt vibrates, and I pull out my phone to read another text message.

> **ETHAN**
> Woman, will you please stop wearing heels?
>
> Seriously, are you okay? Your stitches all intact?

A delightful warmth builds in my chest as I read Ethan's message, spreading like honey through my veins. It seems Jeanie has been busy giving updates. With every one of Ethan's gruff displays of concern, the struggle to ignore my feelings for him grows all the more difficult. I'm finally beginning to understand the reasons behind his bossy demeanor, to see the tender, caring soul lurking beneath the grouchy exterior. He's not grumpy. He's genuinely concerned about my safety and well-being, sort of the same way my other friends care about me. He just wants to help me, like Toby does. Except Ethan might want to kiss me, too.

I blow out a breath and slip my phone back into my pocket. "Okay, sanity check, how're we doing?" I ask Ember, yanking my thoughts back to the present.

"I mean, I expected some of this from her, so I'm doing okay. But I just want to get married. I don't care about all this stuff," she gestures around us.

"Let's pretend we're in a thrift store, and your perfect dress is hidden amongst these racks. It's preowned, pre-loved, and waiting for its second debut."

Ember's lips lift, revealing a slow smile. "Thanks for being here, Vee."

"Of course. Now enough of the morbs, we've got a dress to find."

We navigate through the racks until we finally arrive at a section boasting dresses that seem more aligned with Ember's taste. "I think I've spotted a couple of viable options," she remarks. Martha Jean, seemingly attuned to our conversation, promptly materializes at our side to swiftly whisk away the two dresses Ember indicates.

As she emerges from the dressing room, I pull the stylist aside. "Martha, the jazz music is truly delightful, but this isn't my girl's vibe. Considering we're the only ones here, do you think we could switch it up to something a little different? Something a little more upbeat for our bride?" I gently suggest, and a spark of enthusiasm flickers in her eyes at the prospect.

Taking my place between the mothers, I applaud eagerly as the lively beats of Shania Twain's "Man! I Feel Like a Woman" fill the air, courtesy of the store's speakers.

"Oh, Ivy," Fretta remarks, rolling her eyes. But there's a hint of amusement in her exasperated sigh. It seems the ice queen is beginning to thaw, after all. While I've never been her favorite person and thus managed to keep my distance, Ember's mom has admittedly shown a newfound effort to be more cordial, maybe even friendly, over the past few months.

Ember reemerges from the dressing room just then, a whole new expression lighting up her face. Fretta and Jeanie share in the palpable shift, and together we release a soft, synchronized "ooh."

She bops along to Shania as she steps onto the pedestal. This time, genuine joy dances in her eyes.

"This one is definitely more you," Jeanie gushes, taking in the details of the gown with its delicate cap sleeves.

Fretta concedes with a slight nod, but there's a softness in her eyes as she smiles at her daughter. "You look beautiful, dear."

Ember grins and slips away into the dressing room, hinting that the next one will be even more amazing. We're eagerly awaiting her return when Jeanie surprises me by leaning in once again, her voice a comforting whisper. "I didn't get to say this earlier, but I want you to know that Ethan would be lucky to have someone like you, hun. Don't doubt yourself just because your life's been rough." Her expression comforts me in that familiar parental way, nudging me gently towards self-assurance. I gulp down the lump in my throat, fighting back the tears itching to break free.

Fretta angles herself to face me on the other side, offering a surprisingly tender pat on my knee. "She's right, Ivy. Any man would be fortunate to have you."

"You...you heard all of that?" I sputter.

She laughs daintily. "Sweetheart, my age may be showing, but my ears work just fine."

"Please don't tell Ember," I implore, sniffing as I search my pockets for a tissue. Ever the fairy godmother, Jeanie holds out a tissue of her own. I take it and dab at my nose in the most ladylike fashion I can manage. "It's a long story that Ember doesn't need to stress over."

Fretta mimes zipping her lips, and Jeanie envelops me in a side hug.

"What did I miss?"

We look up to find Ember back on the pedestal, her brow furrowed with concern. Fretta, Jeanie, and I collectively gasp, struck by the breathtaking vision in front of us.

"Oh, Em!" The slow leak of tears before have started

flowing freely as I take in my friend and her glowing smile. The A-line gown cascades gracefully over her hips, elegantly accentuating her curves. Delicate lace covers the bodice, creating a subtle sparkle under the soft glow of light, and the skirt's airy layers of flowing tulle sweep the floor in a way that make it look like she's floating.

Jeanie offers more tissues to Fretta and me without turning away from Ember, and we both take them gratefully.

"I think this is the one," Ember gushes breathlessly, her face splitting into a wide grin. She steps off the pedestal and performs a graceful twirl. "Oh! And the best part—" She sticks her hands into the sides of the gown and wiggles them. "It has pockets!"

I squeal in delight, and we all surround her for a group hug. It's about as awkward as you'd imagine until we end it with a few pats to the back.

Ember reluctantly returns to change back into her clothes while Fretta settles paying for her daughter's gown, and I'm so grateful this ended well. Three months ago, Ember would have *never* willingly invited her mother anywhere out of her fear of being constantly berated. But Colton helping her find her voice has truly been the best thing for her whole family.

Another message vibrates on my phone.

ETHAN
I'm taking your walls down today, Ivy June

My breath catches in my throat as a wave of anticipation and a hint of apprehension wash over me. The weight of his words, both literal and metaphorical, settles in my stomach. I honestly don't think I have what it takes to keep those walls up for much longer, anyway.

CHAPTER THIRTY-TWO

ETHAN

Marco keeps snickering and shaking his head every time we pass the wall—the one with the list and the notes Ivy and I have been exchanging. Her latest addition feels like warm, gooey chocolate sauce poured over ice cream.

You're realy good at what yuo do.

What is it about Ivy's compliments that make my insides turn to mush?

"Would you hurry your ass up?" I grumble halfheartedly. "This mess needs to be cleaned before Ivy gets home."

"Man," he shakes his head teasingly, "you *are* whipped." His shoulders shake as he continues on, hefting bits of drywall into the trailer hitched to the back of my truck.

"Dude, don't be the exclamation in *Panic! At The Disco*. Ivy has a boyfriend. We're barely friends. I'm just helping her 'cause Colton asked me to." We lift the wheelbarrow together and empty its contents into the trailer. I pull off my gloves and use my arm to wipe the sweat off my forehead. Marco clears his throat, nudging me with an elbow.

My stomach drops when I turn, finding Ivy's slitted eyes laser-focused on me and her hands fisted at her waist. How did I miss her arrival? There's no doubt she heard my words—their effect is currently evident in her face. But I only said them for Ivy's sake, to get Marco off my back and protect her fake relationship. If it were up to me, I'd happily admit to Marco that I'm beyond whipped, but I'm just hoping for a pity date. Although going *out* would probably have to be dinner *in* so long as she's continuing her ruse with Toby. And to keep up that nauseating facade, we couldn't allow word to get out that we're dating. But *hopefully* we're dating...or will be soon.

In other words, regardless of Ivy's feelings for me, it's official. I'm whipped. Not mad about it, either.

My mouth involuntarily curls up into a smirk as I stare back at the feisty little thing trying to fry my brain with her eyes.

Marco's gaze bounces between us while he slowly lifts a finger to point inside. "I...need to go...sweep things."

I continue smiling at Ivy while Marco speedwalks away from the tension forming across the driveway. "How was dress shopping?" I call out. "You ignored my text. Your stitches okay?"

She folds her arms, lips pursing while she gazes down the street. "We're barely friends. I don't see how that's information you'd need to know."

"Ivy June," I begin, softening my tone. "You know how I feel about you. I only told him that to throw him off, for your sake, not mine."

Her shoulders relax the slightest bit while she moves hair out of her face, still seemingly captivated by her neighbors' front lawn. With deliberate steps, I close the gap between us, gently taking hold of her hand. She doesn't protest as I lead her to the side of the house, where we're hidden from the road. With my back propped against the siding, I pull her in closer, leaving a bit of space so she doesn't feel caged-in.

"I missed you today," I whisper, my voice barely audible, yet my grin betrays the joy within. I'm captivated by her presence, unable to tear my gaze away. Each freckle, curve, and crease on her face forms a mesmerizing tapestry that I could study forever.

"Is that why you used your mom to spy on me?" she asks, her tone soft yet guarded, maintaining the invisible barriers between us. Though she allows me to draw her near, her arms remain crossed over her body, a silent reminder of the boundaries she's set.

"Maybe," I admit. "But besides your latest brush with danger, how was your day?"

"Dress shopping was fun. A little rocky at the start, but...it ended well," she says, shaking her head contemplatively.

"Good. And your stitches?"

"A little achy, but fine."

I nod. "Ready to see your brand new open-living space?" I ask, resisting the urge to yank her in even closer, yearning to wrap my arms around her and bury my face in the warmth of her neck.

A bright smile overtakes her face "I'm dying to."

She lets me take her hand until we round the corner of the house before she slips her small palm from mine, leaving me feeling robbed. I'm praying that one day I'll have the right to hold her hand proudly for everyone to see.

Ivy gasps as we step inside, her hands flying up to cover her mouth. "Oh! It looks amazing! There's so much more space in here. Thank you!" I stay close as she slowly spins around the room, ready to catch her if she trips.

Marco continues sweeping up the last bit of debris, though he's grinning proudly now, eating up Ivy's praise. "Thanks, man. I'll take it from here," I tell him, acknowledging his hard work as I reach for the broom.

Ivy thanks him with a warm smile before he leaves, and I pick up the pencil near our list, holding it out to her.

"I feel like you should do it," she says, eyeing the pencil like it's a piece of candy she wants to grab, "seeing as you did all the work."

"You're practically salivating over it, Marsh. Take it." I chuckle when she bites her lip before finally snatching the pencil and slowly drawing a line through the words on our list.

"The carpets will need to come out next, but the wood floors underneath should be good. Hopefully, all they'll need is a good sanding and refinishing."

Her eyes light up again. "I can't wait. I've been chomping at the bit to rip them out. Can we do it tomorrow?"

"I've gotta go to the office tomorrow, and you've got school, Miss Marsh. You also *will not* be ripping anything out until your stitches are healed."

She pouts adorably, straightening the bow on her hair. "I guess that's wise."

My hands slide into my pockets as I step closer, my eyes locked onto hers. "How about this: I'll bring dinner tomorrow night, and after our date, you can watch me rip out the carpets. I'll even take my shirt off halfway through the job, just for you."

Her jaw slackens before she shuts it with a swallow. "I told you, we can't...I...Gran thinks..."

"You sound real convincing." I smirk, standing an inch away from her pretty green eyes. I can feel her warm breath on my neck as she stares up at me, fighting an internal battle. I don't think it'd take much to change her mind. But I want her fully invested when she finally agrees. I don't care if she has to fake date Toby for a little while. Okay, I do care—I'm jealous, and it pisses me off...a lot. But I'd deal with it if it meant having her.

"We can't," she repeats with barely a whisper. I lean a fraction closer, watching her eyes flutter closed. Her lips part ever so slightly, and I nearly groan at the temptation. But I'm playing the long game now.

"This may be the hardest thing I've ever done. But I said I wouldn't kiss you till you asked, Marsh." And with that, I straighten and take a few steps back. Her eyes shoot open, that jaw that I'm dying to pepper with kisses once again hanging loose. "I'll see you later," I say, winking and turning to pick up my tool belt.

She follows me to the door, pausing at the threshold while she watches me walk to my truck. "I'm not going to ask you. It could never work between us, Ethan," she calls out to my retreating back. "You may as well quit wasting your time and move on to the next woman."

Her words carry the palpable weight of her regret, as if she's grappling with her own emotions and trying to persuade herself as much as she's trying to convince me.

As I glance back at her, a hint of sadness touches my smile. I just want her to let me help. I wish she'd get it—that it would be my greatest joy to ease some of her burdens.

"I fixed the secret door in the master bedroom. It has a handle on the inside and a door wedge to prop it open," I tell her, ignoring her last protest.

"Thank you," she murmurs, her expression etched with desolation.

It's agonizing, getting in my truck and driving away when my heart is demanding I run back and scoop her into my arms. But I can't force her into this. I have to let her meet me in the middle, or at least some of the way. I just pray she'll do it willingly—and soon. Because If I have to walk around with this feeling churning in my gut for too long, I'm one-hundred-percent certain it'll break something inside of me that will never be repaired.

CHAPTER THIRTY-THREE

IVY

It's rare for me to leave school before three in the afternoon, but today I had an appointment to get my stitches removed, so I had to get a sub to cover my class. I'm very grateful to have the stitches out, because my kids are huggers, and hugs around my middle have been a little uncomfortable with all the poky bits pulling at my skin.

Now I'm heading home earlier than usual, excited and nervous about what I might find when I get there. I haven't seen Ethan since our awkward encounter last week. A gut-twisting uncertainty swirls in my stomach—the fear of not knowing which version of Ethan will be there to greet me. Is he still going to be the flirtatious guy who loves pushing my buttons, the overprotective grump, or the sullen, painfully platonic acquaintance? And the worst part is that I'm not even sure which one I'm dreading—or hoping for—more.

I'm also dying to explore Gran's hidden closet again, but I haven't dared to go in alone. Which means I'll either have to wait for Toby or Ember to join me, or I'll have to do the scary thing and ask Ethan to accompany me, like I'm a Regency damsel who can't go anywhere alone.

The twang of country music floats through the screen door, greeting me as I walk up the porch steps. My lips tug up at the door that no longer whines when I push it open.

I stop mid-stride, narrowly avoiding a tumble as I trip over the threshold. My fingers cover my parted lips as I take in the newly exposed wood floors that flow seamlessly across the open floor plan and into the kitchen. For just a split second, I seriously reconsider everything I've told Ethan, because as I take in the form of the man currently wielding an industrial sander like a renovation god, I can't help going all gooey inside.

Let's be real, the man is beyond easy on the eyes. But he's so much more than that. He's still here, even after I've all but chased him away and told him to go on and date other women. He's *here*...when he could literally be anywhere else.

Snap out of it, Marsh!

Right. Stick to the plan.

The buzzing of the sander slows as Ethan turns it off, smiling at me like I've just delivered his favorite meal. When in reality, all I've brought with me is my usual drama and chaos. I'm the ammunitions delivery to a war zone—highly volatile. I still can't figure out why he'd even *want* to be here. But seeing as he is, I may as well ask for the favor I need, because I'm aching to explore the secret closet.

"Hey." The gray in his eyes swirls and twinkles as he grins at me. "How was your day?" he drawls. So, it seems Adorably Chipper Ethan is here. I hadn't expected that one.

"It was good..." I pause as the smell of warm, freshly sanded wood fills the air. "The floors look amazing."

"Yeah." His eyes sweep over the fruit of his labor. "They were in better condition than I thought they'd be." A chuckle rumbles out of him, the sound luring me in while my insides are at war over whether I want a flirty comment to fall from his lips. He gives me nothing but a crinkly eyed smile before turning to continue sanding.

I disappear to my room, bunching up scattered items of clothing with my fists. They're thrown into the wash basket with more force than necessary, but I don't dare open my mouth or stomp a foot in frustration. I won't allow myself to be that sulky brat who throws a tantrum because she's getting what she asked for.

My room is cleaner than it's ever been by the time Ethan taps on the open door.

"Hey, need anything else before I head out?"

Go on. Ask him.

I pinch my eyes closed, rubbing a hand over them. The poor man is about to think I'm an absolute whack job, demanding space then asking him to stay close.

"Uh...yeah. Could you hang around for a few minutes? I want to explore the hidden closet, but..." My eyes roam the room as I try to come up with a legitimate-sounding excuse. I'm drawing a blank, though. Seriously, nothing. Of all the times for my brain to space out on me!

"You don't wanna go in alone," Ethan finally finishes for me.

Dang it, why is he so intuitive? It's incredibly inconvenient and wildly swoon-worthy. A small groan escapes as I roll my lips in with a nod. He steps back, motioning with his hand for me to lead the way.

I release a slow, controlled breath as Ethan follows me down the hall to the master bedroom. *I can do this. Remain strong.*

Ethan opens the door, propping it open with the cutest hedgehog doorstop.

I turn to him with wide eyes and a smile that's desperate to break loose. "Where did you get this?"

"I have no idea what you're talking about. That was always here." He sniffs, a tiny dent on his brows as he scans the room. He walks past me, and I pick up the little hedgehog, turning it over to find a fresh price tag stuck to the underside of its cute little butt.

This man is killing me.

"I can't believe your Gran kept all this stuff hidden in here," he remarks from inside, thankfully stopping me from turning into a pile of goo. I join him in the small room, and there's an air of wonder as we inspect the shelves. For the second time, I take in all the trinkets on display.

"What's this?" Ethan asks, sliding a box out from the corner.

I shrug. I hadn't noticed it the last time we were here. He places it in the middle of the small room, and I slowly lift the floral-print lid.

My breath catches as I take in what's nestled inside.

"No way!"

"What is it?"

"It's a music box. My Gran's been looking for it."

"It looks...fancy." Ethan frowns.

"It's called the *Pièce À Oiseau Chantant*. It means 'piece with a singing bird,' " I explain. I sink to my knees as I tell Ethan the story of how Gran's Swiss grandmother gifted her with the music box on her eighth birthday. Ethan's brow furrows before he pulls out his phone. A wave of nostalgia washes over me, bringing a slow smile to my lips as I lift the lid reverently and wind it up. An enchanting melody fills the air, and the tiny mechanical bird nestled in intricate foliage comes to life, flapping and twirling its wings to the music.

"Uh...Marsh." Ethan stares at his screen, nodding. "Do you know how much that thing is worth?"

I shrug a shoulder, making an I-dunno face.

"Somewhere in the ballpark of sixty-four-thousand dollars."

"Shut the front door!" I gasp, my hand flying to cover my mouth as my eyes widen. Suddenly, it all makes sense, especially the part where Ross has been so eager to get his hands on it. My eyes fall back to the music box playing the same tune I remember from all those years ago.

"No wonder Ross is looking for it," I tell him and hastily nestle the music box back into its hiding place. Then I rush out of the closet with Ethan right behind me. "Can you help me push the wardrobe?"

"Ivy, hang on. What's happening right now?"

"I have to keep the closet hidden in case Ross comes back to look for the music box. I can't let him find it."

Ethan is frozen in place while his mind apparently pieces things together, unintentionally leaving me to push the wardrobe alone. My back is against its side while I attempt to scoot the monstrous thing back in place. It goes nowhere. "Uh, a little help here?"

"Crap. Sorry. You shouldn't be doing this anyway."

"It's fine." I grunt. "I got my stitches out today, and I'm mostly healed up."

He perks up and grabs my arm to stop me. "Who took them out? Was it that same creep from the ER?"

"It was a nurse," I say, rolling my eyes and stifling a smile. "A female nurse."

"Oh, okay," he mutters quietly before sliding the wardrobe into place with minimal effort. "You gonna tell your Gran you found the music box?"

"I think I want to surprise her with it when I'm done fixing up the house. But I do owe her a visit. Maybe I can sniff out whether she had any clue what Pop was up to when he hid it back here."

"You want me to come with?"

There's so much hope swelling in his eyes as I watch him struggle to appear casual. Eventually, he'll get bored of me, and he won't look so dejected each time I have to put more distance between us.

That distance doesn't have to be there.

Shut it, you. My subconscious clearly has no problem drowning in drama.

"Thanks," I give him a soft smile, sliding my denim jacket on. "But I should go alone."

"Right," he says, pressing his lips into a fake smile.

He follows me out the front door. I wave goodbye as he climbs in his truck and drives away, praying that same excuse doesn't become the story of my life. Because I don't want to go alone for very much longer. But it's the fear of being hurt that's keeping me from saying yes.

CHAPTER THIRTY-FOUR

IVY

I make my way across town to my grandmother's retirement home. By the time I'm standing in front of Gran's door, there's only one question looping through my mind: *How does Ross know how valuable the box is?*

"Ivy! This is a lovely surprise!" Gran beams, her eyes crinkling as she swings the door open. I gape at the view behind her. Gail, Opal, and Nicolas the cat are seated around a poker table.

I feel like I've walked into the craziest cheese-dream ever. "When did this happen?" My voice squeaks while I wave a finger between the three of them. Nicolas is a whole other story, I'm sure, but this revelation is mind-blowing. All along, I thought the three ladies in front of me were just neighborly rivals. But their history obviously runs much deeper, and I can't help but feel like the world needs to brace itself for the effects of their reconciliation. "Opal...is...is that a *cigar*?"

"What?" She shrugs, pointing her cigar at Gail and Gran. "I gave these two first choice between the cigarette, cigar, and pipe. They declined. And Nicolas doesn't quite have the dexterity of the canines in the painting." She tsks, as if she's highly disappointed by this shortcoming.

"Like the *Poker Game* painting? What's that got to do with what I just walked into?"

"It'd take too long to explain. Tea, dear?" Gran smiles.

"What's Gail drinking?" I plop down onto the open seat beside Nicolas, who's wearing a bowtie and a hat. I gesture toward him, looking up at Gran questioningly.

Is someone secretly spiking the AC air in my car with hallucinogens? Or maybe I'm actually passed out on the floor of Gran's hidden closet, my mind tripping on the old lead paint fumes. What I'm witnessing right now is like diving headfirst into a Salvador Dahli painting—a whole new level of surrealism unfolding before me.

"Gail has a mojito with white rum. Oh, doesn't Nicolas look darling, though? He's such a good boy," Gran answers, reaching out to stroke him.

Nicolas glares at her, like he's plotting the murder of everyone at the table. He could also be the mastermind behind this whole thing, though.

"I'll have what Gail's having. Maybe it'll bring me back to reality."

"Oh, nothing to it, sweetheart," Gail smiles while expertly shuffling a deck of cards. "We've agreed to put the past behind us."

Gran returns with a mojito adorned with all the trimmings. I lean back to peer behind her. "Are you hiding a mixologist back there? How did you learn to do this?" I ask, tugging on the springy coil of lime hugging the sugar-crystallized rim.

"I'm a woman of many talents."

"Apparently." I continue to frown over a sip.

"How's the house coming along? I can't wait to see it," she says, her face lighting up with a sunny smile.

"It's going fine. A lot of work, but I'm making progress."

"Doesn't hurt that you've got a sexy man helping, either." Opal smirks under her breath. I bug my eyes, signaling for her to shut it.

"The renters were good people," Gran muses.

"Those *good people* made a giant hole in the living room ceiling."

"Eh, they told me about that. Something about removing one of those dancing poles when they left," she says with an amused head shake.

"Gran...has Ross asked or said anything more about the music box?"

Her head lifts sharply as her eyes narrow. "He's asked you about it, hasn't he?"

"No, but he's getting desperate. I was just wondering if he's been bugging you about it." I love Ross, but I don't want him peppering Gran and finding out Opal and Gail took it. They don't need to be bothered over something they haven't seen or thought about in years.

"You find it—you tell me. *Don't* tell Ross," she orders, pointing a finger at me. "I know you think you can save him, but he's gotta get there himself."

My shoulders fall as the bitter truth in her words settles in my stomach. "Yeah."

Opal taps the cigar that she hasn't once lifted to her mouth, eyes narrowing in her usual discerning way. "Might be wise to be extra vigilant for a while."

"Ross would never do anything to hurt me," I say defensively. For the first time I'm starting to feel the effects—the bone weary fatigue of constantly fighting for someone who doesn't seem to want my help.

"Not physically, and not intentionally. But the people he's

involved with won't feel the same, sugar," Gail adds with her gentle wisdom.

"Yeah. Okay. Does anyone else think Nicolas looks depressed?" I ask, shamelessly deflecting.

Opal waves a hand dismissively. "He's just mopy because his girlfriend's at the vet."

"That makes so much sense." I nod, not understanding anything. It's getting late, and I'm dead on my feet.

"I'm gonna go home and...sleep this off." I stand, gesturing around the room. "Chin up, Nicolas." I croon into his grumpy face, then hug the flock of eccentric geriatrics goodbye.

"Stay safe!" Gran calls out before I walk toward my car, grateful I'm no longer sleeping in it. Ross's asshat decisions have already landed me in enough messes. I just hope it doesn't happen again.

CHAPTER THIRTY-FIVE
ETHAN

Did I purposely wear my favorite pair of jeans and that blue button down shirt that makes my eyes pop for a cake tasting with my brother and his bride? You bet I did. I'm not usually one to fuss over my outfit, but I know when I look good. And today I'm using every bit of ammunition I've got to show Ivy what she's missing.

Slightly juvenile? Maybe. But it's just a small step in my game plan to win the fair lady over. And let's be real, these jeans? They've earned me the seal of approval from Opal and Gail. I get catcalls and whistles every time I wear them.

I haven't seen Ivy in four days. She's been busy with school things in the evenings, making me wonder how she's coping. Is she taking care of herself? Is Ross causing any more trouble over the music box? I know she's a grown woman, but it's not easy to turn off the need to protect someone when you care about them this way. And we've been no better than ships crossing in the night, passing with nothing more than a few notes written on the wall.

Those notes feel like tiny drops of sustenance to a starving man.

She says her life is too complicated right now, but I'm about to show her how much better it is with me in it. I tried playing it cool and keeping it in the friend zone for a whole day, but the electricity between us was off the charts, and I officially can't let this go. I've never experienced this before—this yearning to know everything about someone and the unquenchable desire to be a part of her future. I've never felt this drawn to anyone before Ivy. And I think I owe it to her and to myself to see this through.

I walk through the doors of the hotel and into the restaurant where Ivy, Ember, and Colton are already seated at a large, white table next to the kitchen.

"You're late." Colton frowns as I approach them.

"*Brodo*, don't be the dude who has to blur out the bits on *Naked and Afraid*. It's only five past two. Hey, Flames," I say, greeting Ember before venturing a look at the woman who always manages to rile up the butterflies in my stomach. I swallow, suddenly feeling awkward. I'm desperate to touch her in some way, but that fluttering morphs into an ache, because I have no right to reach out to her.

She's not mine.

"Ivy," I manage to croak out, taking a seat opposite those eyes that drive me wild when they're lit up. The same eyes that are currently cataloging every inch of me.

My mouth turns up in a smirk. I knew these jeans were magical.

"I hope you came hungry," Ember says, raising her eyebrows. "You're about to consume more cake than you've ever eaten in your life."

"Doubt it," Colton and I say in unison. The ladies roll their eyes in response as a server steps near.

"Hi! I'm Jesycca, with a *y.*" She giggles, curling her hair behind her ear. "Is this your whole party?"

"It is. We're ready to be stuffed. I mean, not in a taxidermy way. That would be weird. Just the regular way, when your tummy wants to be happy and full. I'm rambling. Um...feed us cake, please," Ember waffles while Colton morphs into the heart-eyed emoji beside her.

"Perfect! Get ready to embark on a flavor adventure. Pace yourself, though—we've got five mouthwatering creations lined up for you. Our opener is a real head-turner. Picture this," she gestures enthusiastically with her hands, "a bourbon-vanilla sponge cake, oozing with mango cream filling and topped with a mango drizzle that's got a bit of a kick. Trust me, it's a real flavor bomb. It's also my absolute favorite, 'cause it's got that spicy twist that keeps you coming back for more," she says, tossing a playful wink my way.

I can't help but chuckle under my breath when I catch Ivy aiming her icy glare across the room toward Jesycca's oblivious backside.

Well, well, well. Looks like things just got a tad more interesting around here. Ivy avoids looking at me while her dainty hand pushes the rim of her glasses.

Jesycca glides back to our table, carefully balancing a tray laden with four plates. She places a generous slice of goodness before each of us. I flash her my warmest smile, and the corners of her cheeks flush pink as she invites us to savor the first bite.

"The rest of the flavors are pretty standard," Ember assures us. "But I wanted to try something a little out of the box." She flashes a giant grin at Colton, who's smiling proudly.

"It's definitely unusual." I eye the cake, cutting a piece with the side of my fork.

"Hmm, it's...interesting." Ember hums, her eyes narrowing

while she swirls a bite in her mouth. "I don't hate it. But I'm not sure I'd want it for a wedding cake. What do you think, Vee?"

"I don't think I'm adventurous enough for a flavor like this." Ivy mumbles, her eyes flashing to mine for a second before returning to the piece of cake she's shifting around on her plate.

Another soft chuckle escapes me, and I shake my head. Her words echo our last few conversations, when she fed me all kinds of excuses about not wanting to clip my wings and me being destined for more adventurous things. Little does she know, I'm more than eager to embark on the grandest adventure of my life, and I want her right there beside me. I realize blurting that out would make me seem like a total weirdo right now. But I can't ignore this feeling in my gut that's telling me she's the one I want to share every twist and turn with. So here I am, seated across from her, pining over her and watching helplessly as she repeatedly takes out her frustration on a poor piece of cake.

Although, I did come here with the intention of getting a rise out of her. So if she's going to pretend I'm invisible or sit there sulking while she attempts to convince herself we're still not a good idea, then I'm going back to the basics, back to where it all started between us—I'm going to push her buttons. And she's revealed some new ones in the last few minutes that my fingers are just itching to press.

Jesycca returns, smiling sweetly while she expertly whisks away our plates, replacing them with new slices of heaven. She explains the flavor, a chocolate one, thank God, because *I'm* not adventurous enough for that mango concoction.

"Thanks, Jess," I smile as she sets a plate down in front of me.

Ember and Colton are holed up in their own cozy bubble, huddled together on one side of the table. Ivy and I sit across from them, the silence almost palpable and threatening to make the moment awkward. But Jesycca, oh Jesycca, seems utterly content to flirt with me throughout the next couple of courses. I'm barely even making an effort to flirt back at this point, but Jessyca's attention is clearly having an effect on Ivy. We're on our third slice of cake now, and she's only gotten grumpier, glaring at her plate, exhaling short, humorless chuckles each time Jesycca's hand grazes my shoulder.

Ember finally pulls herself from her bubble long enough to notice little miss sulky-pants huffing and mumbling under her breath, and she calls Ivy over to the side. Then Colton becomes aware of his surroundings again, giving me the 'What's going on?' head shake. I return one with a smile, but I'm fighting so hard to hide the laugh that's bursting to escape.

Time to hit that last button. I'm hoping it'll finally prompt Ivy to stomp away, giving me the chance to nab a moment alone with her. Over in the corner, Ember and Ivy are locked in some kind of whispered exchange—mostly Ivy's attempts to reassure her friend that everything's fine, from the looks of it. I lean back in my chair, idly toying with the napkin holder.

Ivy and Ember return to their seats, and Ivy stares at her plate, curling her lips in before lifting her head and frowning at something behind me.

Ivy

I roll my eyes, slouching back against my chair, sulking and digging my hands into my pockets. My hand latches onto something in my pocket, feeling its shape to determine what it is when a delightful giddiness begins to bloom inside me. It's the fake spider I confiscated from one of my students last week. I kept it, remembering Ethan's spider aversion and saving it for the perfect time. Oh man, this is brilliant.

Sir Flirts a Lot thinks he's so smooth. While, yes, he does look torturously good in those jeans, his pompous head needs to be yanked back down to earth. There's a ball of frustration in the pit of my stomach, one he and Miss 'Jessyca with a Y' have stirred up. No—not jealousy. It's more like nausea or a fit of rage, but I can't stop to process that response. I so badly want to throw a shoe at his head. However, that would require removing a shoe, and we know how I feel about that.

Preparing to enact my revenge, I point behind him, squinting my eyes in thought. "That wall over there, it's rather minimalist. You seem to be interested in simple things, tonight, Ethan. Can you expound on that?"

He frowns, doing a slow turn to peer over his shoulder, and that's when I slip the fake spider out of my pocket and slide it under the rim of his plate. Colton narrows his eyes at the wall, trying to force some meaning out of my awkward segue, but Ember tracks my move, bugging her eyes in question. I give her the death stare, silently commanding her to *zip it*. I deserve this.

Then Ethan turns back to the table, frowning like I've gone crazy, and I plaster on my most innocent smile, blinking like I'm eager for his reply.

"It's a wall," he replies dryly.

"Oh. Well, that proves my point then. Isn't this cake divine?" I smile sweetly at Colton and Ember, picking up my fork.

Ethan's eyes ping around the table, trying to figure out what he's missing. Colton gives him a shoulder lift before eating another bite of cake. Ember, bless her heart, is biting the corner of her lip while her gaze bounces between Ethan and me. The delicious silence grows while we all chew, and I fight to suppress an evil cackle when Jessyca struts over. Of course she goes to Ethan's side first, batting her fake eyelashes as she lifts his plate.

She continues to flirt with him as she walks around the table, collecting the empty dishes. Ember's eyes are saucers as they dart down to my little prop in front of Ethan. Somehow they get even wider as she glares back at me. It's all I can manage to stop myself from giggling.

Jessyca walks away, leaving the table empty, aside from my unfinished slice of cake, and Colton finally notices what's in front of his brother.

"Uh...Eth..." He arches his brows with a grimace at the spider. Ethan looks down, prompting a moment I wish I could replay in slow motion.

He yelps, and within two seconds, he's standing ten feet away from the table, jerkily rubbing a hand back and forth over his hair. He's panting like he's just finished a sprint, while Ember and I double over, laughing so hard we're wiping tears. Colton's shoulders shake as he attempts to stifle his own laughter. He picks up the rubber spider and throws it at Ethan, who dodges it with a few extra flinches, like there are bugs crawling all over him.

Jessyca comes trotting out of the kitchen, concern on her brow. "Is everything okay? I heard a child scream." She pouts, scanning the room.

Ethan picks up the fake spider, his head falling back as he runs his tongue over his teeth. I watch his chest rise with a deep inhale before he clears his throat, sauntering over to Jessyca with that charming smile.

They share a hushed conversation, the sound of Jessyca's giggles scratching my skin as it floats over to our table.

Ugh. Well that blip of joy was rather brief. I shove my seat forward, my lips forming a flat line as I resume stabbing the cake with my fork.

Ethan

Well played, Ivy June. Well played.

The little minx somehow knew my weakness. Yeah, I'm not a fan of spiders. I wouldn't say it's a phobia, rather an extreme desire to avoid occupying the same space as one. Tiny ones I'll squish or spray, but the chunky, hairy black ones—they make me want to hurl.

Arachnid Avoidance Syndrome aside, I kind of love that she had the guts to pull off something like that. To think she had that little fake spider in her pocket this whole time, planning her attack. It's actually kind of adorable. If she'd seemed unphased by Jessyca's flirting or sat here happy as a clam, that would have been the real downer. But this just adds fuel to the fire.

Time to press the last button. I just hope this doesn't backfire.

"Easy there, Marsh—looks like steam's about to start whistling out of those pretty little ears of yours again." I flash a smile as I casually scan her face.

She ignores me, pressing her lips together while her chin juts forward. Just as I'd hoped, she scoots her chair back, plopping her napkin beside her plate with a forced smile for her friend.

"Excuse me for a minute. I'm going to the ladies' room."

Anxiety swirls in my stomach as I stand a few seconds after her, ignoring Colton's reprimand. This could go very poorly if I push her too soon. But I can't waste my one chance, either.

I find her scowling at the wall, arms folded as she waits in the hall outside the restrooms. I push aside my nerves, determined to get through to her. But first, I need to poke the bear a little more.

"Ivy Marsh. This is one of the most delightful days one can have, eating plate after plate of delicious cake, and you just pulled off one hell of a prank." I purse my lips in thought. "I know you've got the grumps because you haven't been waking up next to me, but that's an easy fix."

"Why are you here?"

"For the cake," I retort with a shrug.

"You know what I mean," she growls. "Why are you *here*, right now? If you need to pee, the men's restroom looks open. Or better yet, if you're looking for a bed to warm, you should find *Jess*. The two of you seem to be hitting it off. Just keep it PG-thirteen for now, since this is a public place."

There's so much fire bubbling inside, she's like a volcano ready to blow, yet I'm still desperate to look inside. "For someone who told me to move on to other women, you seem pretty upset about Jesycca flirting with me." I step closer, peering down at her eyes as they dart around nervously, like she's been caught out. "Why does that bother you?"

"It doesn't." She gulps.

"Ivy," I swallow hard, too. "Tell me you feel something here?" I'm nearly pleading for her to make the first move, to ask me to press my lips to hers.

She ignores my question, ducking under me and she begins pacing. "Oh! And why does everyone else get a nickname? Even Jesycca with a Y gets one," she adds, her nostrils flaring. But I get the feeling she's rallying her anger so she doesn't let the more vulnerable feelings show.

I gently lay my hands on her shoulders, turning her to face me. Once she finally lifts those crystal green eyes, I bring my hands to her jaw, making sure I have her attention.

"You wanna know why I haven't given you a nickname, Ivy?"

"Yes," she lets the word scrape out.

"Because I wanted you to know that I see you. I see *you*, Ivy June Marsh. I see the show you put on to keep anyone from noticing when you struggle. I see the walls you put up to protect yourself. I see how hard you fight and how fiercely you love. And I want to be your champion, I want to support you, to defend you, to brag on you, if you'll give me a chance. But you gotta give me a chance, baby."

Her eyes leave mine, and I can see the second she starts making up reasons why this won't work. "Take a chance with me, Ivy," I beg as I await her response. This is it. If she refortifies those walls right now, her heart will be so bricked up, it'll take forever to get her to this precipice again.

But I'd do it. I'd fight for her, again and again.

"Let me support you. Share the load," I plead one more time.

"Did you just quote Samwise Gamgee to me?" she blinks. I shrug as I watch her eyes bounce around my face, her thoughts warring with her heart. And then, like the dramatic ending of a song, everything goes quiet, and I can see when she's made up her mind. Peace washes over her face as she allows the slightest curl of her mouth.

"Kiss me," she demands.

My lips crash to hers in one sharp inhale, my hands cradling her head as she rises to her toes. I don't know how she manages while wearing those damned wedges, but I can't pull her in close enough. I'm lost within seconds, savoring the taste of her lips until I'm yanked from my euphoria when she suddenly pulls away.

Her eyelashes flutter as she blinks and brings her fingers to her lips.

"Don't you dare tell me that was a mistake," I rasp, trying to catch my breath.

"I couldn't. Not after *that* kiss," she concedes, shaking her head. "I just can't believe you're a fan of *The Lord Of The Rings*..."Then a frown etches between her brows once again as she looks up at me. "Okay."

"Okay?" I grin. Does this mean what I think it means?

"Yes. But this has to stay a secret, at least for a little while."

Hell, I'm so elated that she's not brushing me off, I'd agree to almost anything. However, I reserve the right to be salty about the last part, since I know it technically involves her allegiance to another man. "Fine. But you make up for it with kisses when we're alone."

"Deal. Also, I will rip Jesycca's eyes out if she touches you again." She squints and pokes me in my chest. Then she spins and trots back to the table, a whole lot less explosive than when she marched over here. I'm a hell of a lot more smug than before, too. Just call me the bomb defuser.

I give it a minute before sauntering over to my seat, just as everyone digs into their fourth slice of cake. Ivy's piece is spared the fate of her previous three as she happily eats the one in front of her, a hint of a smile never leaving her lips. The ones I just kissed the heck out of. And, man, what I wouldn't give to kiss her right now and taste the cake she's devouring...

"What's going on with you two?" Colton points his fork between us, bringing me back from a trance. My gaze darts down to my plate and away from Ivy's lips, at least for the moment.

"Is he being a tool about renovation stuff?" Ember adds, narrowing her eyes.

"I'm being a perfect gentleman," I announce.

If by "gentleman" you mean daydreaming about making out with my secret girlfriend, then I'd give that Mr. Darcy punk a run for his money.

Ivy clears her throat. "We had a disagreement, but we've sorted it out. This strawberry cake is definitely my favorite, by the way," she says, expertly redirecting the conversation the way she always does. But as it turns out, I still love pushing her buttons.

"Yeah, we kissed and made up. No more fighting, so you can relax," I mutter dryly before finishing the last bite of cake.

Colton and Ember are oblivious to the double meaning of my words.

Unfortunately, my chance to relish that last bite is interrupted as Ivy delivers a swift kick to my shin beneath the table, causing me to inhale a chunk of cake. Cue two minutes of me hacking up a lung while everyone at the table and a few onlookers stare helplessly. Ember tries to assist with pitying pats on the back. Meanwhile, my coughing fit has summoned Jesycca, who saunters over to offer assistance in the most impractical way imaginable. I'm gulping down water, still trying to breathe normally while her hand rubs my shoulder. Ivy stares murderously while flinging napkins in my general direction.

"Thank y-you...Jesycca. I'm good," I sputter, leaning forward so her hand falls away. I'm just trying to spare her eyes from being removed with the spoon Ivy is currently trying to bend with her fists.

"Right. Well, that was sufficiently awkward, so thanks, Eth," Colton says with a fake smile and sarcastic sway of his eyes. Then he turns to his fiancée. "Which flavor is it, Em? We could do two if you want. We can have *all* of them if you can't decide, although that mango one should be kept to itself."

Ember lets out a snort, hugging Colton's bicep. "I'm happy with the strawberry shortcake, if you're okay with that one."

"Perfect." He leans in, planting a tender kiss on her temple, igniting a spark of anticipation within me. I can't wait until I can freely express my affection for Ivy in public. I turn my eyes to hers, conveying my thoughts with a tilt of my lips, and she smiles back.

CHAPTER THIRTY-SIX

IVY

"So you haven't seen it anywhere in the house?" Ross inquires with an air of urgency through the phone while I walk to my car. No 'hello,' 'hi,' or even a 'hey, how are you, Ivy?' I answer the phone to nothing more than an impatient interrogation about Gran's music box. Which is now *my* music box.

"No, Ross." My tired response drags out while I walk to my car. "Why do you suddenly care about that old music box, anyway?"

Of course, I'm well aware of his motives, but for once I want some honesty from him. *Any* redemptive act would alleviate the sting from the slashes he continues to inflict on my heart.

"You wouldn't understand, Vee. Look, I gotta go, but if you find it, let me know. It would save both our asses."

And then he hangs up, leaving me growling loudly at the empty parking lot. Everyone else left hours ago, but it took me longer than I thought to organize the information the parents have been sending through for the school production volunteer signup. So long, in fact, that I had to cancel my plans to get a drink with Stef.

I shift my hefty tote bag onto my shoulder, its weight tugging at my muscles, and reach for the handle of my car door. A flicker of annoyance crosses my mind as I realize the interior lights aren't illuminating as they usually do. The sun will soon bid farewell, darkness enveloping everything, save for the lone floodlight I carelessly parked away from.

I twist the key in the ignition, a futile attempt to start my car's stubborn engine. This feels like the beginning of every horror movie. The thought makes me shiver as I reach for the door locks. A pang of uncertainty hits me as I secure the doors, and I offer a silent prayer that this simple mechanism isn't as defunct as the rest of the car's powerless features.

The locks thankfully engage, but I still tug on the handle to make sure. I slide my phone out of my pocket, staring at it, hoping for a solution to magically appear. I consider calling Toby, but he'd be useless in this situation. I doubt he knows anything about car mechanics. With a heavy sigh, I tap Ethan's name.

"Hey," he answers with a smile in his voice. "I was about to call you. Did you have fun with Stef?"

"I, uh, actually didn't end up going. I wasn't done with this schedule thing." My eyes pan the empty parking lot while I muster up the balls to confess my current situation.

"You're still at school?"

"Yeah. About that...I was going to leave, but my car won't start. I think my battery's dead or something."

"Marsh, are you currently alone in an empty parking lot?" There's a gravelly tone to his voice that causes another shiver to run down my back.

"That would be correct."

Then he growls as I hear his signal light ticking. "Stay in the car. Lock the doors."

"Yes, sir."

"There's no security guard on duty?"

"Gus goes home at five." I answer.

"Right. Stay on the line. I'm only a couple minutes away."

A delicious warmth melts over me. I'm not used to being taken care of like this. Ethan may be a grump when he's being protective, but being important enough to him to warrant his concern in this way—it's invigorating and encouraging, all at once. I was never neglected, but I worked hard to blend into the walls and not to cause a fuss. Yet Ethan seems to have made a hobby out of fussing over me whenever he can.

I hang up the phone as the welcoming beams from his truck pierce the incoming darkness. Relief loosens my muscles, prompting a long exhale. Ethan pulls up beside me, sporting a furrowed brow as he steps out of his vehicle. His expression darkens when he surveys the dimly lit surroundings of the parking lot.

I slide out of my car, tilting my head up and batting my eyelashes playfully when he and his scowl approach. "I already know what you're going to say, so just save it and kiss me instead," I offer.

His mouth tilts up on one side, and he hooks an arm around my waist, pulling me close while he plants a kiss on my lips. Although, he pulls away a little sooner than I prefer to deliver his lecture, anyway.

"I'm talking to CJ on Monday about putting up more lights. Also, call me next time you plan on working till you're the only one here," he adds, frowning again.

"CJ'll do anything for you. But don't mention your reasoning for the lights. We're still a secret, remember?"

"I guess I can be your hot secret for a little while longer."

He smirks then leans down, placing a kiss on my neck this time and lingering afterward with a deep inhale.

"Did you just sniff me?"

"I've wanted to do that for so long," he mumbles against my skin, causing my toes to curl. That's it. I've died and gone to sexy boyfriend heaven.

He straightens with a short grunt, shaking his head like he's emerging from a trance. I place a hand on the side of my car, steadying myself before my knees buckle due to swooniness exposure.

He presses a kiss to the back of my hand before walking to the front of my car. "Let's see what's going on under here."

We go through the motions of Ethan jump-starting my car before he follows me home. As soon as I park, he's already rushing out of his truck to open my door for me. "What time do you need to be at school tomorrow?" he asks.

"Seven-thirty," I say as he takes my hand, like I'm emerging from a chariot. There's a very addictive boyish glint in his smiling eyes.

"If I promise to have you there on time, are you up for an adventure?"

A spike of fear pierces my chest, as I wonder if this beautiful yearning in him will be our downfall, if his desire to see the world will outlast his desire for me. But I shove those thoughts away for now, choosing to embrace the delight I see on his face.

"I'm in," I say with a smile.

An eye-crinkling grin shines back at me. "Good. Wear something warm. And pack whatever you'll need for the night."

Ten minutes later, I'm sitting cross-legged in Ethan's truck, enjoying the view as street lights wash over his rugged profile.

"How was your day?" I ask after a warm stretch of silence.

"Good. The usual stuff at the office. I had another phone

meeting with The Home Network. They liked the pilot episode. It was mainly feedback of what they think worked and how they'd spin the show to make it unique."

He glances at me for a second while he drives, an excited curl to his mouth. I plaster on the most genuine smile I can. I never want him to think I'm not incredibly proud and overjoyed for him. That little niggle of doubt pokes its head up again, but I whack-a-mole the rabid thought away. There's no use borrowing worries. We'll take it as it comes. Ethan asked me to trust him with my heart, so that's what I'm doing.

"Then I went to your place," he continues. "Marco and I patched up the remaining walls. We should be able to paint soon."

I let out a squeal, clapping my hands. "Thank you, Eth. I wouldn't have been able to do this without you."

"You would've figured it out." He lays a palm on my leg, eliciting a yelp when he squeezes the spot above my knee. "You're capable of more than you think."

"Maybe," I whisper while peering out the window.

The roads have turned to gravel as we continue driving toward the outskirts of town. We're only ten minutes out, but the properties begin to stretch farther apart, as if they need more room to breathe out here.

"Your house is so beautiful," I sigh as the wheels crunch onto Ethan's road. Soft lights illuminate the brick-paved driveway, and the whole house seems to glow invitingly among the dark surroundings.

"You've been here?" he asks, slightly confused.

Crap. I forgot Ethan doesn't know about Ember and I sneaking into his Halloween party last year dressed like a pair of psychotic ninjas so no one could tell who we were. We had to be incognito so that Ember could spy on Colton and figure out whether he was in a relationship with a coworker. Turns out, said coworker had made the whole thing up, and the rest is history.

"Oh, um. I just figured this is your house." I reply vaguely.

He pulls his truck into a double garage, grinning over at me. "Yeah. I've been working on this one for about a year."

I want to ask what he means by *this one,* but he jumps out, running around to open my door before I can. And then his hands are on my hips as he turns me to face him. We're eye to eye, giving me a whole new perspective of his handsome face and his eyes that seem to swallow me up. Even through the thick hoodie I'm wearing, his hands on my sides send a wave of heat all the way up to my cheeks.

"Your shoes are pretty cool," he remarks, giving a playful wiggle of his eyebrows. I glance down at my purple Croc-covered feet and feel a surge of pride at how far I've come. Ever since hitting thirteen and realizing just how much my peers were towering over me, I've been too self-conscious to wear anything other than heels or platforms in public. But it's another fear Ethan's been determined to help me tackle.

"Fishing for compliments, Mr. King?"

"Never. The way you're looking at me is compliment enough," he jokes, giving me a quick kiss before sliding me out of his truck. "You hungry?"

I refrain from giving him the satisfaction of knowing just how correct he is.

"I could eat."

"How does steak salad sound?" he asks, leading me through the garage into the kitchen.

"Amazing. I haven't eaten since lunch. Okay if I use the restroom first?"

"Sure, it's just down the hall. Last door on the left."

"Thanks." I smile, doing my best to hide the fact that I already know where the restroom is. I head back after freshening up, but a slightly ajar door catches my eye, making me pause. I push it open a little wider with my finger, and the sight inside makes my jaw drop. Without thinking, my feet carry me farther into the room, and I do a slow spin, taking it all in. Both walls are lined with floor-to-ceiling shelves and filled with books, framed maps, and photos. Ethan is a total closet book nerd! The discovery makes me grin with delight. I hear his footsteps just before he appears in the doorway, leaning casually against the frame, looking irresistibly handsome, as always.

"I see you found my secret project," he says, tucking his hands into his pockets. His eyes soften, a hint of pride dancing in them as they sweep across the room before settling back on me.

"Are you kidding me? I'm having a total *Beauty and the Beast* moment here. All you need is the rolling ladder! This room is amazing!"

He pushes off the doorway, still wearing that irresistibly warm smile, and takes my hand. For the next twenty minutes, he guides me around the room, pointing out his favorite books, sharing where he found them, and telling stories about the photos and maps on display. They're an ode to his adventurous spirit, a constant reminder—like an echo drifting over a chasm—that this man wasn't meant to be tied down. I both love and hate that fact. Shame swirls within me at the selfishness of the thought, but I swallow it down and push it away. I refuse to resent this beautiful quality in him.

Back in the kitchen, Ethan busies himself, washing his hands and taking steaks out of the fridge while I appreciate all the work he's done since the last time I was in here. Of course, I can't tell him that.

During my last visit, the kitchen was nothing but bare bones, but now it radiates modern colonial charm with its wooden panels and exposed brick. A stunning smeared-stone backsplash perfectly complements the house's country setting, while the navy blue cabinets are straight out of a dream.

I'm perched at the massive island, its surface reminiscent of an old dining table, but this one seems sturdy and custom built, and it commands attention. Across from me, Ethan bustles about, sprinkling salt and pepper onto the meat.

"Why were you stuck at school so late?" His expression knits with concern. I find my hands suddenly restless, hesitant to delve into the embarrassing reasons behind my regular prolonged stay in the classroom.

"Just class prep, student work to check. Administrative things to get done." I shrug.

That frown is still hovering on his face when he flips the steaks, seasoning the other side. He washes his hands and pauses, seeming unsure. "Is it...typical to spend that long on those tasks?"

His sweet hesitancy to offend me brings a smile to my face. "No," I admit, letting out a self-deprecating laugh. How does this man keep pulling secrets out of me that I'd normally fight to the death to hide? He makes me want to verbalize my struggles, for the first time ever. The gentle way his eyes sweep over me is so encouraging, I might just be brave enough to do it.

"I have a form of dyslexia called dyscalculia. I struggle with math calculation skills and understanding numbers and math facts. It takes me a lot longer to figure out some things which most people breeze through. Plus, I have some of the typical dyslexic struggles, as well."

He releases a weighty sigh then rounds the island, bringing his large form near. He turns my legs to face him, stepping in closer, and he closes his eyes as he leans his forehead against mine. "I'm sorry you've had to struggle with that."

His words gently twist open that lid, causing a tear to spill over my lashes without permission. No one has ever acknowledged how hard it's been for me.

I pull away and choke out a laugh, determined to have a fun evening. "Are those steaks gonna cook themselves?" I joke, sniffling.

He doesn't say anything, but one of his hands palms my neck and holds me still while he kisses my temple. Then he steps back, allowing me to change the subject while he fills the kitchen with the sounds and aroma of sizzling steak.

I devour my food, still amazed that he had a salad in his fridge like a responsible grown-up.

We wash up as I continue to ask him about the houses he's flipped and what he's hoping for with the show.

The Show. He's unsure what the network is thinking, location wise, and I push down the anxiety that starts to rise at the thought of him relocating. There's an ugly feeling of guilt as I despise my desire to keep him tethered to this town.

"What now?" I ask, swinging my arms awkwardly after we finish the dishes.

"We gather supplies," he answers cryptically.

He plops a chunky blanket in my arms, instructing me to wait while he continues gathering things which he won't give me any answers about.

He's determined to be mysterious, and I kind of love it. It's like an adventure within the safest boundaries ever, because I've learned he's constantly considering how something might affect me.

With a lantern, some chocolate, another blanket, two water bottles, and a smirk, Ethan finally gives me the signal to follow him outside.

He leads me past the pool that was sporting floating Halloween decor the last time I'd seen it. We round a hedge that I assumed lined the end of his property, and I pull up short, my mouth agape at the sudden change in scenery. Wide-open fields that roll into low mountains are dimly lit by an unobstructed full moon. Oak trees sprinkle the wild grassy land. A wooden platform deck fills the space between two mighty oaks, creating a peaceful little oasis amidst the natural beauty. Fairy lights strung high throughout the branches create an inviting glow.

"Ethan...this is breathtaking," I whisper in awe.

"It's even better at sunset. But at least we've got the stars on display." He grins.

I stroll onto the deck as he carefully arranges the cozy blankets inside a hammock suspended between the two sturdy trees, perfectly positioned over the center of the deck. It's the fanciest hammock I've ever seen. It's wide, with a sleek mosquito net hanging beside it.

"This isn't your average hammock," I remark, watching it swing after I nudge it with a finger. Ethan huffs out a chuckle. "Yeah. I'm not exactly short, so I got the deluxe edition."

"Why's this all hidden back here?" I frown, gesturing to the openness around us.

Ethan straightens, the shadows on his chiseled jaw distracting me in the moonlight. "The hedges were here when I bought the place. I just need to rent a machine to pull them out. It's on my list." He says with a curl of his mouth.

"You have *another* list? How dare you. My list will be jealous."

"I'd burn my list in a heartbeat if it meant sharing your list."

"Did *list* just become a euphemism for something else..." I snort.

Ethan grabs me around the waist, pulling me closer. His voice is muffled as he laughs into my neck. "The point is I like you, Marsh. And you're my priority."

My face is leaking again. I wipe a stray tear with my hand

that's wrapped around his back. "Okay. What's the plan here? I'm ready to get cozy."

He draws in a deep breath against the curve of my skin, the bristle of his short beard grazing my neck. He steps back and arranges our supplies on the hammock, then sweeps his hand theatrically. "After you, m'lady."

Like a newborn fawn finding its footing, I gingerly make my way up. "Try not to ogle my butt while I struggle."

"Too late," he says, joining me in the swaying embrace of the hammock.

He uses his phone to switch off the fairy lights, and it takes a few moments of awkward shifting and shared laughter before we settle into a comfortable position, nestled together beneath the expanse of twinkling stars.

"This is beautiful, Eth."

"Thank you," he replies, his smile radiant in the moonlight, though his jest earns him a playful swat on the chest from me.

I rest my head on his shoulder as the breeze and crickets create a soundtrack around us. "Babe?" he begins, running a hand up and down my arm.

"You've gotta come up with a better nickname than that." I poke him in the side. He grabs my wandering hand, bringing it to his lips for a kiss.

"Venusaur."

"Ethan King, did you just call me a Pokemon?"

"Ivysaur evolves into Venusaur." He flutters his eyes dramatically.

"Don't you dare make this a thing," I point a threatening finger his way. "I will not be nicknamed after a Pokemon!"

"Noted." He laughs, pulling me back down beside him. After another stretch of silence, he clears his throat before speaking. "Can I ask you something about your dyslexia?"

"You're the only person I don't mind asking about it."

"Have you told anyone at school?"

I turn to the stars, a heavy sigh leaving me as I gather my thoughts. "No. I kind of just get on with it. Toby's probably figured it out. But I think I've been scared that my teaching abilities will be questioned if I admit to how much extra effort I have to put in just to keep up."

This is the first time I've verbally processed that fear. It's been a tormenting motivator in the back of my mind for the past few years. Saying it out loud is like dropping some of the weight of that burden.

"I hate seeing you struggle more than you need to. I'm trying to learn everything I can about it, but I know it's nothing to be ashamed of. And CJ would be devastated to know you've been hiding this and how big of a hurdle it is for you."

"Yeah," I breathe, not fully convinced of CJ's understanding. I respect her and love her, but she's got board members and parents to answer to. I'm sure there'd need to be some kind of official investigation of my abilities and techniques if this big secret got out. The thought of that kind of scrutiny makes me want to hurl.

He turns his head, pressing a warm kiss to my temple. "Would you consider talking to her?"

Considering something and planning to do something are two different things. I nod yes, because considering something is non-threatening. It only happens in my head.

"Feed me chocolate while we stare at the stars?"

"Can I do this first, though?" He shifts, cupping my jaw with a hand as he brings his mouth to mine. Never in a million years would I have thought I'd be making out with my hot boyfriend in a hammock at ten PM on a school night.

But here we are, wrapped up in each other's arms while I get thoroughly kissed. Eventually, we come up to somewhat untangle ourselves. I fall asleep, gazing up at the stars, feeling lighter than I have in a long time.

CHAPTER THIRTY-SEVEN

ETHAN

I'm in heaven—total bliss.

Enveloped in the comforting embrace of sleep beside the woman who's come to embody my deepest desires. Yet that euphoria begins to fade as I'm awakened by movement, and I crack my eyes open, witnessing said woman's discreet departure from the warmth of our shared cocoon. The one we created within the plush confines of the hammock I purchased with the hopes of this very moment, minus the woman sneaking away.

"Ivysaur, where ya goin'?" my voice rumbles, disturbing the dark night.

A sudden thud resonates, followed by the muttered names of former presidents.

"I need to pee. And I refuse to respond to that name." She whisper shouts into the darkness.

"Hang on, I'll walk you to the house."

"I'll be fine. I didn't mean to wake you."

I release a throaty chuckle. "If you think I'm letting my coordinately challenged girlfriend navigate her way past a swimming pool in the dead of night, you're very mistaken, Marsh."

A few seconds pass as she seems to contemplate the accuracy of my words. "I concede. Lead the way."

I grab her hand before walking her inside and making a mental note to put in some small solar lights for a pathway to the house once the hedge is down.

Once Ivy is done, we amble our way back to the hammock, and I pull her close, covering us in the warmth of the blankets. It doesn't take long before we're both asleep again. This really is the stuff of dreams. I know without a doubt I'm currently living in *the good old days*. I'll look back on this night with vivid clarity, grateful that I had the common sense to know a good thing when it was in my arms. And hopefully, she'll still be in my arms in the years to come.

But when morning arrives, I still don't get the slow, sleep drunk cuddles I desperately want with this pixie I'm falling for. Instead, I'm startled awake by a whack on my chest.

"Ethan! Wake up! I'm gonna be late for school!"

I grasp her gently around the waist, burrowing into my favorite spot in the crook of her neck. "Just one more minute."

"Ethan!" she squeaks, giggling but wriggling out of my grasp to climb over me and once again escape.

"Fine," I grumble with fake annoyance. "I'll drive you to your place then drop you at school?"

She's speed walking ahead of me, shuffling in her purple crocs, teal sweatpants, and matching hoodie, making her look like a pastel dessert. Her blonde bed hair catches the first rays of sun, and I smile at her lopsided hair bow.

"Uh...about that..." She gazes back at me, while grabbing her bag from the sofa. "I think it's better if Toby picks me up for school."

"Why?" I frown, not liking this development at all. Not one bit.

"Cause this is a small town, and rolling up at school in Ethan King's truck will get tongues wagging faster than a church scandal."

I purse my lips, fighting hard to remind the part of me that wants to argue about this that I need to pick my battles, especially when it took so much convincing to get her to give me a chance. "Right."

We drive to Ivy's house, talking about the final few stages of her renovations. My eyes are on the road, but I catch her gaze flickering my way every few seconds while her hand nervously folds pleats in the hem of her hoodie. "You know Toby is like a brother to me, right? He's more of a brother than my *actual* brother."

I grab her hand, lacing our fingers together. "I know. I'm just anxious to show the world that I'm yours." I add with a wink, even though there's a small part of me that still wants to punch Toby for being so handsy with my girl before she was my girl. The logic isn't there, I know.

I putter around the house when we arrive, trying my best to ignore the sound of the shower going and the images that arise with it. After snuggling next to Ivy all night, I'm already struggling to keep my thoughts somewhat gentlemanly. I've messed up in the past, but Ivy makes me want to do things differently—to prove that I'm laying a lasting foundation instead of simply seeking momentary gratification.

She's still getting ready when there's an eager knock. The scowl on my face forms unconsciously as I stomp over to open the front door. I nod at Toby, with his checkered sweater vest over his button up. My arms fold while I lean against the frame, making him have to hunch his shoulders to get inside.

He doesn't look the least bit perturbed, which annoys me even more.

"Hi." He grins, wagging his eyebrows like we share some kind of secret.

"What's happening to your face right now?"

"Nothing. Have a nice evening?"

"What's it to you?" I bite out a little defensively. Ivy chooses this moment to flutter into the room, catching my death glare aimed at her dearest Toby.

She clears her throat with a reprimanding tone, her gaze unwavering as she extends a pointed finger toward the list. "Rule. Number. Three."

I purse my lips and summon a forced smile, shifting my attention to Toby. "Thanks for escorting Ivy to school."

"Anytime," the little twerp chirps, draping an arm affectionately over Ivy's shoulder. She responds by rolling her eyes, deftly sidestepping his embrace. And because I'll probably always break rule number three, I meet her in the middle of the room. With tenderness, I cup her face in my hands and plant a fervent kiss on her slightly pink lips.

"Have a good day." I wink, then smile triumphantly at Toby who's awkwardly looking at his feet. Ivy's cheeks flush adorably while she pushes her glasses up her nose, squeaking out a "You, too" before following Toby out to his car.

I blow a kiss as she peers back at me through the car window, chuckling when she waves robotically in response.

I reluctantly drag myself to the office for my other job, the one that's started to seem less and less fulfilling. That familiar itch tingles up my spine. It's like restlessness, except this time, it's a feeling of not being where I want to be. This feeling usually has me eager to jump into the unknown, sailing or hiking off into a remote adventure. But now, the only place I'm yearning to be is beside Ivy.

Man, I have fallen far and fast. If Colton caught wind of this, he'd swear I was an alien who'd invaded his brother's body.

Just when I'm starting to make a dent in the work piled up on my desk, my phone buzzes loudly over the wooden surface.

I answer, making it through a few minutes of small talk with Crystal from the Home Network. There's excitement in her voice as she continues. "This is incredibly unusual, since things never move this quickly. But congratulations, Ethan, your pilot has officially been green-lit! We'll send the paperwork for you to look over. Your show is gonna be a hit, I just know it!"

"Wow..." I lean back, running a hand through my hair. "That's—"

Colton and Ember breeze their happy, soon-to-be-married faces into my office.

"That's exciting. Thanks, Crystal."

"I look forward to working with you, Ethan."

My brother and his fiancée exchange amused glances, their faces contorting into cringe-worthy expressions with each awkward sentence that slips from my lips until I end the conversation with Crystal. While I'm genuinely thrilled for Colton's newfound happiness, there's no denying the smugness that seems to have settled over him since popping the question. Normally, I'm the one teasing him relentlessly, but lately, it feels like the tables have turned, and I'm not quite on board with this new shift in our dynamic.

"Struggling with the ladies?" Colton remarks with a sympathetic click of his tongue. If Ember weren't here, he'd be nursing a dead arm right now.

"Colton, don't be the things that look like Steve Harvey's mustache. I've never had that problem in my life."

"You sure? Haven't seen you on a date in a while." He juts his chin forward, looking entirely too self-satisfied. I know he hasn't told Ember about my feelings for Ivy, otherwise I'd already have endured an interrogation that would make James Bond cry. But he's loving this opportunity to torture me with the information.

"I'd be very concerned if you had a habit of watching me on my dates, big bro."

"Mm-kay, I'm going to interject before I pass out from rolling my eyes so much," Ember adds with a raised finger. "We're having an impromptu *pre-rehearsal dinner* tomorrow night. Can you make it?" She smiles sweetly.

"Oh, he'll make it," Colton smirks. "Tell him who else will be there, babe."

"It's basically just the wedding party and one or two others. Opal and Gail. Jed and his wife. Ivy and Toby, and the three of us, assuming you can make it."

Toby.

That's why my brother looks like he's talking to someone who's had a unibrow drawn on their face while they were sleeping. Because he knows I'll be seething while the woman I like is sitting across the table with another man. What he doesn't know is I'm currently dating said woman and will have to watch her fake date another man. Only slightly less agonizing than the first scenario.

CHAPTER THIRTY-EIGHT
IVY

"You didn't have to come, you know," I whisper through the side of my mouth to Toby.

"Ember invited me, how could I miss this?" He aims a giant smile at Opal and Gail. We're all seated at a long table at Capelli's, the Italian restaurant Ember and Colton both love. Well, not *all* of us. Ethan still hasn't arrived.

I joked with him earlier about how hilarious it would be to end up seated between him and Toby. I also assured him I'd come up with an excuse as to why Toby couldn't make it tonight. Jokes on me! Ember took it upon herself to personally invite my fake boyfriend, and soon I'll be sandwiched between him and my real, but also secret and slightly jealous boyfriend. It's my own personal hell.

And Toby seems to find it all hilarious, while I squirm uncomfortably as Opal and Gail impale the two of us with suspicious glares.

I've made a giant mess of things, but I'm in too deep. This fake relationship needs to fizzle out, and soon. I wasn't made for the double life. I'm constantly on the verge of needing smelling salts with all the stress of keeping up the multi-faceted charade. Can I add circus master to my resume?

The small talk around the table continues, my face aching from forcing myself not to frown too much. Who knew it took so much effort to appear casual. Ember is chatting excitedly with Jed's wife, Rachelle, while Colton and Jed trade short sentences about sports. A server bustles around the room that's softly lit with a warm glow over the rustic wooden tables and chairs. Exposed brick walls adorned with vintage photographs transport patrons into the charm of Italy's countryside.

I catch a whiff of garlic and herbs as our server places a basket of heaven on the table, the warm rolls practically steaming. The soulful Italian ballad that plays over the speakers seems to come to a record-scratching halt as Ethan enters the room, and the vibe shifts immediately.

Holy cow—the man looks *good* in a sports coat.

Toby coughs under his breath beside me, hiding a smirk while he slides a napkin into my hand. "For the drool."

I can't help it. For so long I fought the urge to acknowledge my attraction to Ethan. But now that I'm dating him, it makes it hard not to appreciate how *fine* he looks. It's actually rather sad that I still need to hide my feelings and blatant googly eyes for him.

For the briefest second, his eyes meet mine, flashing a deeper blue that threatens to float me out of my seat and into his lap. Thankfully he greets everyone else before he takes his seat beside me. "Ivy. Toby." He practically growls when his eyes flicker to the point of contact between Toby's shoulder and mine. There's enough chatter in the busy restaurant that nobody notices Ethan's sudden surliness, but I bug my eyes at him for a second, reminding him to behave.

I need these two men in my life to get along, and as hot as

the jealous growls may be, I really want Toby and Ethan to be friends.

"Oh, Ethan, you do clean up nice," Gail gushes from across the table. "It's a pity you're sitting on that side, seeing as you're the only single man and there's two perfectly delightful ladies across from you."

Ethan flashes his devastatingly handsome smile at her, doing that thing where he feigns a bashful glance down, then lifts his head ever so slightly, flashing his pearly whites as his cheeks rise with a face-splitting grin. It's enough to make me hum audibly. Toby elbows me, bringing me back to the unfortunate reality where he and I need to appear to be an item.

Ethan proceeds to shamelessly flirt with the seventy-year-olds across from him, and I shake my head in an attempt to remember the goal.

Fake it with Toby for a little longer. Try not to look absolutely enamored with Ethan.

Easier said than done.

Ethan leans away from the table, a hand casually resting on the back of my chair. I'm still cozied up to Toby, feeling more awkward than ever. Meanwhile, no one can see Ethan's hand behind me in the dimly lit room, but it's certainly there emitting an inordinate level of heat. The thin straps of my sundress leave most of my upper back exposed, causing me to flinch when Ethan's thumb grazes my skin, tracing soft circles over my back. He pauses long enough to tug lightly on my ponytail, a silent admonishment to sit still and not give anything away. It's remarkable how the man can carry on a conversation while my brain is practically short circuiting due to his subtle contact.

I suppress a shiver when he slides his thumb under the strap of my dress. Who would have guessed the skin just beside my armpit would be so sensitive?

Ooh, he's playing dirty right now, punishing me for bringing my fake boyfriend tonight. Toby snickers beside me as he tries to stifle his obvious amusement at my reaction to Ethan's touch.

I turn my head to whisper in Toby's ear, but not enough to put any space between myself and Ethan's hand. Because I'm a glutton for punishment. "You're not helping."

"You've gotta admit, it's pretty funny. I've never seen your brain overheat like this 'cause of a man." He smiles then moves a piece of hair out of my face. The action clearly pushes Ethan's buttons, which was undoubtedly Toby's intention. Ethan has moved on to a different conversation while his hand tugs gently on my dress strap, pulling me ever so slightly away from Toby.

"You could stop antagonizing my actual boyfriend, though," I whisper back. To anyone else it must appear as if we're in our own little whispery, mushy love-bubble. Which doesn't help my plan to bow out of this faux-lationship any time soon.

"I'm sorry." He smiles. "I'll make it up to you. But only after I get the chance to gloat and say I told you so." And then he pulls out his phone, frowning at it before leaning closer. "I'll see you at school. Don't look too upset when I leave. It'll help sell our conscious uncoupling soon." He winks at me after kissing my cheek.

"But..."

"Vee, we'll figure everything out. But I don't know how much longer you can convince your friends that you're not hopelessly gone for the man sitting beside you, and I'm not going to keep standing in the way of your happiness."

A deep frown etches onto my forehead and my jaw slackens.

"That'll do it." He grins, then stands and politely excuses

himself due to a fake family emergency, thanking Ember and Colton for inviting him.

I push my chair in, smiling at Gail's attempts to comfort me after my 'boyfriend' had to leave. Opal only sips her drink, eyes narrowing in their knowing way. I haven't given anything away, have I? Ethan and I have barely acknowledged one other. And there's no way she saw his hand on my back.

No, everything is fine. I'm just worrying over Toby's words and about ending our mutual fake relationship.

I mean, I said it myself. I need this thing to fizzle out, but I haven't thought about what I'll say to Gran. If the relationship that spurred her generosity suddenly ends, will she see me as just as fickle as Ross? I know she wouldn't kick me out onto the streets, but she may ask me to leave, without knowing I have no place and no money to fall back on. I naively gave it all to Ross, and if she finds *that* out, it would only further prove how irresponsible I am. Just like Ross. Everyone has written him off. And I suddenly don't feel very far off from that same fate.

The hand that's rubbing at my temple stills when I feel Ethan's palm slide over my thigh in a comforting grip. My eyes bounce to his for a second, catching the concern in his expression. But there's also so much steadiness cemented there. I don't let my gaze linger, as much as I desperately want to swim in his baby blues. Opal is already watching me with too much suspicion.

Ethan's hand on my leg helps to ground me, and I manage to calm my thoughts and remain present for the rest of the evening. I'm not even sure why we're having this get together, but I assume the mothers, particularly Ember's, are getting to be a bit much as the big day gets nearer, and this is Colton's way of reminding Ember that she has people in her corner.

An hour later, our bellies are full of the best Italian food I've ever eaten, and I'm about ready to slip into a food coma.

Opal shimmies into the open seat beside me on the way back from the restrooms.

"A lot of interesting developments happening this evening." There's that glint in her eye, telling me this is the setup to whatever she's about to say next.

"Really?" I squeak.

"Fascinating how Ethan ate his entire meal with his left hand. Like the right one just took the night off."

I gulp. "Hmm. That is interesting. He should see a doctor about that."

"Strange how his mood seemed to perk up after your Toby left."

"Maybe he bumped his head. You should ask him about that. He really listens to you and Gail. Um, excuse me, gotta run to the whiz palace." And like the coward I am, I speed walk to the safety of the restroom, lingering until everyone is putting on their coats and getting ready to leave.

Ethan winks at me as I rejoin our group, and I catch myself as I'm about to smile in return. Opal's eyes are also zeroed in on my face, but with much less affection. She means well, but sometimes she's too inquisitive for her own good. She and Gail have a new-found chumminess with Gran, and I don't need them spilling any secrets that I'd rather keep to myself.

She's staring at me like she's charting all my reactions, trying to find clues in each one.

Ember loops her arm through mine as we walk through the bustling restaurant to the exit.

"You okay? You seemed a bit distracted. It's not Ross, is it?"

For once it's not my wayward brother causing my stomach to swirl. But I can't tell Ember that I'm malfunctioning because her future brother-in-law is too sexy for my own good.

"I'm fine. Ross is Ross," I say with a sardonic laugh. "Did you enjoy tonight?"

"It was the perfect wedding de-stressor." She sighs.

"Is wedding planning supposed to be so stressful?" I cringe, hoping this isn't a 'that's just how it is' scenario. I'm nowhere near this phase of life, but I hope my future holds the type of wedding bells that someone else will organize on my behalf.

"I'm not sure. I can't imagine everyone has such an opinionated mother," she says over my shoulder, wrapping me up in a hug when we reach my car.

"What can I do to help?"

"You mean, on top of all the Maid of Honor stuff you've already done?"

"Of course. If I can buffer some of that stress, then you bet your butt I'm gonna do what I can." We shout our goodbyes in unison to Opal and Gail as they wave and pull out of the parking lot.

"Thanks, Vee, but you're doing enough already." Ember holds my door open while I climb in. Ethan is chatting with Colton and Jed while Rachelle talks on the phone. It sounds like she's reassuring their babysitter that they'll be home soon. Before Ethan slides into his truck, he catches my gaze, lifting his phone with a tiny wiggle. I roll my lips in to hide the grin that wants to overtake my face. With a small dip of my chin I let him know I understand.

"Love you, Em. Give Nicolas a squish from me."

Colton joins Ember, curling his arms around her from behind. "I'll try." Ember laughs as her fiancé kisses her neck. "I'm sorry Toby had to leave. Ooh, we should do a game night or something with the four of us."

Colton's eyes jump to Ethan, who's standing outside his truck with the driver's side door open. It makes me think Colton knows more than he's letting on. Although, he apparently hasn't divulged any of it to Ember, which is commendable.

But I've got to backpedal on this happily ever after I can already see forming in Ember's eyes. Now that she's found her soulmate, she desperately wants that for everyone else.

I will not, however, be finding it with Toby.

"Oh, um...I'll let you know. He's not really a game person. Hates them actually. Total weirdo. Kay, love you, bye!"

I drive away, leaving behind Ethan's amused grin and Ember's slightly confused frown. Nothing like an awkward exit to end the evening.

I put my phone on speaker, calling Ethan once I reach the first traffic light.

"Opal knows something," I blurt out after he picks up.

"I wouldn't doubt it." He laughs. "Especially after you gave me heart eyes the whole night."

"Did not," I whine.

"I'm not complaining," he drawls, and I can hear the smile in his voice. "You want me to come over?"

"You know I want nothing more than an evening of snuggling with you, but I can't do another late night, King. I'm already a zombie."

"I'll make sure you go to bed early. I won't stay long." I can practically hear him pouting.

"Nah-uh. That's what you said last time, and then we stayed up talking till two in the morning."

There's an exaggerated sigh before he changes the subject, keeping me company until I arrive home.

"I'll say goodbye after you get inside and lock the door." Again with the assertive tone that I find problematically attractive.

I lock my car, stifling a squeal as I notice Ross hulking near my front door. I mime a shush motion to him, pointing to the phone while I let us inside. Ethan's assertive tone will increase a few defcon levels if he finds out my brother is visiting. Thankfully Ross nods, seeming to understand my instructions and the stern frown.

I make sure to hold the phone near the lock mechanism as I turn it. "There. Door's locked."

Ethan chuckles, and I can picture him shaking his head. "Sleep well, Ivy June."

"Night."

My arms instinctively cross over my middle as I hang up and turn to face Ross, who's jittery energy immediately puts me on edge. His eyes shift constantly—cataloging, watching—like he expects someone to jump out from around a corner.

"What do you want, Ross?"

"Vee...I need the music box."

I throw my hands up, half-turning before looking back at my ghost of a brother. "This again? I'm starting to think you'd sell this house out from under me if you could. When does it end?"

He chews on his lip, the ball of his foot bouncing nervously. "Are you saying you don't have it?"

"I'm saying you can't have it."

He presses his palms into his eye sockets, then slides his hands up to clench his hair. With a resigned sigh, he nods and walks away.

I march after him only to be met by the reverberating slam of the front door. I engage the locks for the second time, banging my palm against the wood before turning to slide down to the floor. Why can't anything ever be normal with us? This habit from the past keeps ringing in my ears, nagging me to give in and fix everything. But I know I can't anymore. I'm Bilbo Baggins, feeling like butter scraped over too much bread, and not even the good butter. I'm the generic, store-bought kind that's been surreptitiously swapped, wrapped, and slotted into a box of the fancy stuff. I feel like a fraud, walking around pretending that everything is fine. I'm fine. I'm thriving.

Except I'm not.

And that's when I know Ethan is right, and I have to talk to C.J. There's still the fear that once she sees my struggles, she'll declare she hates the generic, store-bought stuff and I've repulsed her with my duplicity.

But I guess there's only one way to find out.

CHAPTER THIRTY-NINE

ETHAN

There's a buzzing sound that keeps pulling me in. No...not pulling me in—pulling me out. Out of this blissful, deep sleep. My hand shoots out, swatting at my bedside table in search of the source of the noise.

Something crashes to the ground, yanking me awake.

It's my phone. One hand rubs at my eyes while the other reaches down to pat the floor until I grab the offending device, which has started buzzing again.

"Hello?" I croak, not awake enough to bother checking to see who's calling.

"Babe. Put some pants on. We're going on a mission."

"Wh—how do you...Ivy—" I pull the phone away, squinting at the offensively bright screen to read the time. "It's one AM."

"Correct. I'm on my way to you. I'll explain when I get there. Dress in dark clothing. Oh, can you pick a lock?"

I sit up, rubbing a hand down my face. There's never a dull moment with this woman. "Uh...Colton and I practiced a few times as kids. But I haven't done it in a while. It's kinda frowned upon."

"Well, it's a green flag for me. Splash some water on your face. I'm almost at your place."

Three minutes later, I've done as instructed in addition to swishing some toothpaste around in my mouth. I'm guessing middle-of-the-night breath is the same as morning breath. Ivy pulls into my driveway, looking way too alert for this time of the morning. But she's also ridiculously stunning. She's like a fairy or an elf...something magical and too beautiful to be human. There isn't much light besides the ones on my front porch, but it all seems to glint off her hair, making her glow.

I slide into the passenger seat, flashing her a sleepy smile and pulling off my baseball cap. "If we're going to be sneaking around, you'll need to cover up your golden locks." I tighten the strap and slip the hat onto her head. "Now, tell me whose body we're burying."

"That's tomorrow. Tonight, we're thieves." She wags her eyebrows as she drives.

"Explain."

She sighs. "Something isn't sitting well. Like, how does Ross know about the music box? There's no way he figured it out on his own. Plus, he was in my house a few weeks ago when I came home—"

I choke. "Wait—hold up. He was in your house! How'd he get in?"

"He also practiced some of these skills as a kid." She quirks the side of her mouth. "Anyway, he was acting weird—fidgety. Almost guilty. I know that look. But it didn't click until the other day, when a kid in my class had the same look. He'd done something he shouldn't have. And I realized Ross did something that day, or maybe he took something. And if he found something, then it has to be with him."

"That's quite a leap, though."

"I know Ross." She glances at me before setting her eyes

back on the road. The way she gestures with her hands as she drives, so passionate and fired up... Gah, I just want to pull her in and kiss the heck out of her.

"He's always kept a small box taped under the seat of his car," she continues, and I do my best to focus on what she's saying. "When we were kids, he'd tape it under his bed, so you couldn't see it unless you got *really* low. But he hasn't lived in one place long enough to do it. I'm telling you, whatever he's found, it's in his car."

"So, we're breaking into his car? How do you know where it is?"

"*You're* breaking into his car. I'm just an accomplice. And I don't know where he is. We need to drive around a bit. There are a few spots he usually crashes at."

"Okay...next question. Why the middle of the night? You're going to be a zombie tomorrow."

"I know," she groans. "But I couldn't sleep. And then the idea just came to me, so I went with it. In hindsight, I probably could have waited. Sorry." She flashes her teeth in a cheesy smile, eliciting a chuckle from me.

"Never apologize for involving me in your life, Ivy June. Especially when it involves a clandestine adventure."

Her smile morphs into something more genuine.

Twenty minutes and three locations later, we finally spot Ross's car. Ivy parks, reaching behind her seat and lifting up a wire coat hanger while she smiles triumphantly.

"What the heck is that for?"

Her eyes sweep the space between us. "To get into his car. Isn't this what you need?"

"The last time I broke into a car, I used something a little different. You know, the tools for us auto-thieves have really come a long way over the years."

"Really?" she tilts her head and her shoulders drop.

"No."

She snorts, swatting my arm with the back of her hand. "Stop! Should we watch a Youtube video?" She starts pulling her phone out, and I snatch the coat hanger from her hand.

"Woman. Give me that." I untwist the hanger, straightening one side of it as much as I can.

"Yes, sir," she mutters, and I can't help the smug smile that forms on my face when I notice her watching my movements appreciatively.

We climb out, each of us scoping out the area. It's not the best neighborhood, but there doesn't seem to be anyone watching us. We meander over to Ross's car, and I throw an arm around Ivy to appear as casual as possible.

"Here, I'll lean against the car, and you lean over me like we're gonna make out," she says.

I growl. "I'd much rather just do that."

"Focus, King. This is your chance to impress your girlfriend. We'll make out later." She bats her eyelashes while pulling me closer. It's quite scary how far I'd go for her. This isn't considered a crime, is it? Just taking back what's hers?

I pull the coat hanger out of my jacket, squinting at the windows of the apartments surrounding us. "I'm pretty sure I just saw someone peep through their blinds," I whisper.

"Then hurry up so we can get this over with."

"What if the car has an alarm?" I grunt, fighting to get the wire into the window. It's not an easy maneuver with Ivy in front of me and one of my arms slung around her.

"It's an old car. There's no alarm," she swats at the air, as if that's the most ridiculous thought in the world. Finally, the wire slides into place, and I manage to get it down to the button inside the door. I hear a click as the locks unlatch, surprised it actually worked. Ivy lets out a squeal, which I quickly shush, but she hops around excitedly on her toes.

"You did it!"

She opens the passenger door, and the most obnoxiously loud car alarm begins blaring, announcing our illicit activity for the whole block.

I turn to her, my lips pursed. "No alarm, hmm?"

"Gloating isn't a good look on you," she says, shaking her head before ducking down. But hiding is pointless, because this thing is loud enough to be heard within a two-mile radius. I pull her away, crouch-walking behind the next car as two men approach from the shadows. I'm grateful I wore a clean shirt for my inevitable mugshot. I try to position my body in front of Ivy, but we're sitting ducks. If we run, we leave ourselves exposed. This is my worst nightmare—wanting to keep the woman beside me safe but feeling utterly powerless to do so.

"Ivy?"

She stands suddenly, too quickly for me to pull her back down. My only option is to stand with her, shielding her as we wait for this to play out. The blaring car alarm finally stops when one of the men presses a button on his keys.

"Hi, Ross."

"Ivy? Whatcha doin over there, sis?"

"Oh, well, we heard this was a great spot for stargazing," she says, gesturing with a circular motion to the dimly lit parking lot where we're loitering. "You wouldn't think so with all the light pollution, but word is, this is the place to be. Yup." She swings her arms awkwardly while her eyes survey the area.

Ross's friend gives him a head tilt to the car, seemingly in a hurry to get somewhere. "We gotta go."

Ivy's brother climbs into the passenger seat and tosses me the bent piece of wire. He tries to appear casual, but his body is rigid with tension. Forcing a chuckle, he shakes his head. "Whatever you think I have, it's not here. I don't stash things in my car anymore, Vee."

She jumps forward, her hand reaching out as the car starts, urgency in her voice. "But you found something that day you were in my house. What was it?"

He rolls the window down, his voice stretching over the breeze as the car pulls away. "Pop had hiding places, too."

"Well, that was unhelpful," she whines as she watches the retreating vehicle.

"Come on, Nancy Drew," I begin, sliding my arm around her waist again and leaning down to kiss the top of her head. "It's time to go home."

As I drive us to Ivy's place, I can't shake the awareness of how differently things could have turned out. My heart slowly settles into a steadier rhythm, but Ivy's mind is still racing as she rattles off every possible meaning behind Ross's cryptic words.

I park her car and she runs into her house, opening drawers and searching desperately. "It has to be here somewhere!"

"Hey, look at me for a second, will you?" I smile, turning her shoulders toward me. "It's almost three in the morning. You need sleep. And whatever Ross found, it's hidden well enough that your Gran and her tenants probably haven't found it, even after all these years. Go to bed. We'll look for it tomorrow."

Her eyes finally rest on mine as she rubs her forehead. "You're right. Okay. Sleep. I need sleep."

I kiss her goodnight and collapse onto her uncomfortable sofa. I could ask to use the spare inflatable mattress, but even walking into her room feels like too much temptation right now. My control and logic are already hanging by a thread. I must have been out of my mind to let her rope me into this with so little questioning.

But I'm realizing there is very little I wouldn't do for her.

CHAPTER FORTY
IVY

You know what's worse than back sweat? Boob sweat—because there's no way to dab anything away without drawing attention to the location of the unfortunate perspiration. And I currently can't seem to calm my nervous system enough to stop this humiliating response, not only because I'm sitting in C.J.'s office, but also because I'm about to rip off a very big Band-Aid.

Mother of pearl, I think I just audibly gulped.

Calm the heck down, Marsh.

"What did you wanna talk about, honey?" C.J. asks, placing a large stack of papers and a coffee cup on her desk as she takes a seat.

I nearly melt every time she talks to me in that matronly tone. I know it's just who she is, but I tell myself it's because I'm her favorite. It's all part of my little make-believe world, one I'm praying I won't be setting up in flames in the next two minutes.

Here goes nothin'.

"C.J...I need to tell you something. I probably should've told you before you hired me..."

"Go on," she says encouragingly. "But if you murdered someone...at least tell me they deserved it."

I sigh. "No murders...yet."

"Dang it. I've always wanted to be an accomplice in burying a body. Oh well, out with it, then."

"Okay..." I take another shaky breath before I word vomit my lifelong struggles to C.J. I tell her about everything—hiding my learning disabilities from my parents, overcompensating to be the uncomplicated child, putting in extra hours of work just to get by. She doesn't fidget or show any emotion in her face as I continue, which only seems to fuel me on. My words begin falling out haphazardly, like a bag of scrabble letters being turned upside down. I can't bring myself to make eye contact, instead focusing on various objects around her office as I continue rambling. I'm barely coherent by the time I conclude, at least managing to throw in a disclaimer at the end. "I'm sorry I didn't tell you during my interview. And I understand if—if you need to reevaluate my position here."

When I finally meet her eyes, I see a familiar warmth. Her face softens with kindness, calming my stampeding heart.

"Ivy June, how long has this been twistin' you up inside?"

"Since you hired me. Well, technically, most of my life, but..."

"Sweetheart, I'm sorry you've had to struggle with this. Does it in any way affect your students ability to learn?"

"No ma'am." I force down the lump threatening to clog my throat. "I make sure of it."

"I'm sure you do. But are there things we can do to make it easier for you?"

This question may be the tipping point. Little puddles gather in my eyes, and I blink rapidly, attempting to will them away. But my heart has been aching to hear those words for so many years that it feels like a million clamps are loosening around my chest.

"I think so...yeah." Another audible gulp. I'm basically a cartoon character with the way my tears are spouting out. C.J. rises from her seat, rounding her desk to perch on the arm of my chair and offering me a tissue and a tight squeeze.

"Well, then, we'll figure it out," she says, resting her chin on my head while I make very unladylike noises into a tissue. She releases me, but her regal, motherly hand still rubs circles on my back. "Your students thrive, Ivy. And my guess is your struggles have forced you to teach them in more hands-on ways, which is how kids learn best. Did you know Benjamin Franklin had dyscalculia?"

"I didn't," I say, feeling my brows pull together as the knot in my stomach relaxes. "Thank you, C.J."

I stand, sniffling into my tissue. When I look up, C.J.'s hazel eyes are still regarding me with unexpected affection. "You're not broken, Ivy. In fact, you have a strength that's fierce and unique. Don't hide it."

Right for the jugular. I croak out another thank you, hugging her one more time and scurrying off to my classroom before I blubber all over her neatly pressed blouse.

C.J.'s words are important, I realize, ones I should declare every day. Learning to be kind to myself isn't easy, but I'm starting to understand that I must fully love who I am before I can truly love someone else. And since I'm already well on my way to falling in love with a certain someone, I need to get this self-love stuff right, too.

When I reach my classroom, I find Toby waiting for me with his brow furrowed. He rubs a thumb under his lip, his focus consumed by what he's reading on his phone, like he's trying to piece things together.

"Hey, Bee," I greet him, giving my nose one last wipe. He

lifts his head, smiling for a second before fading back into a frown.

"What's wrong?"

I gurgle a laugh, waving his words away. "I just told C.J. about my *problem*. You know. The dyslexia thing." I add, realizing I've never actually told Toby about it either. He's just supportively pieced things together over the last year and a bit.

"Oh! Wow. She didn't take it well?" he asks as he moves to stand.

"She was amazing. These are happy tears."

"Oh...Okay. Good...Well, done, Vee. I'm glad you told her."

"So, why are *you* so frowny?" I ask, gesturing to his phone.

His brows raise as he inhales slowly. "This is gonna sound crazy, but I'm worried about you. And I'd rather be safe than sorry."

"What are you talking about?"

"After you told me about the music box and how much it's worth, I set up some bots to flag any internet searches for it. A few have been popping up in this area. Unfortunately, it looks like someone caught the search I did."

I glare at him with one eyebrow cocked. "You're looking at me like I should know what that means."

"It means whoever's searching for the music box probably knows you have it. It's a stretch, but if I were this other person also looking for it, I'd follow this lead. I mean, why would anyone else be looking for the exact same insanely valuable yet rare antique music box that you just found in your Gran's house?"

My eyes begin shifting aimlessly over the desks in front of me as I process what Toby is insinuating. "So I need to...what, watch my back in case any goons are after some treasure?" I ask over a laugh. "This is ridiculous. I'm sure it's all in our heads."

"Vee, I'm a math teacher, I don't believe in coincidence or

operate 'in my head.' Come on, you *know* I wouldn't make a big deal about this if it was nothing. Just be careful, 'kay?"

"Yes, sir." I respond, rolling my eyes before sobering with a serious look and pointed finger. "But *don't* tell Ethan. The man will put up burglar bars on every window."

"I think he should know, Ivy."

"He's supposed to go away for his show soon, and he won't leave if he thinks I'm in danger. You can stay over while he's gone. Please, Bee? I don't want him to turn down an opportunity this big because of me."

"Fine." He grunts and crosses his arms.

"And play nice when you come over later."

He narrows his eyes at me. "You put your bossy pants on this morning?"

"And don't mention my pants. Ethan probably won't like that either." I smile as he stands and shakes his head, even though there's an eerie feeling lingering in my gut. I still haven't found whatever Ross stumbled upon, and it's driving me crazy. It's got to be the missing piece of this puzzle. But I can't ask Gran about it, because I'm ninety-nine-percent sure she has no idea the secret closet even exists, and I can't bring myself to rope her into whatever drama Ross has created.

CHAPTER FORTY-ONE

ETHAN

"Write this down real quick?"

"Write *what* down?" Ivy frowns her green eyes down at me.

"I'm 'bout to tell you, Marsh. Ready?"

"What about me looks ready to write something?"

"Ivy, if I keep crouching like this, I'm gonna end up with a back like Quasimodo. Grab the pencil." I motion with my eyebrows and nod to the spot where my construction pencil has been lying since I first marked the wall.

"I don't have paper," she grumbles, pouting those kissable lips.

"Write it on the wall."

"But—"

"Quasimodo," I grunt.

"Okay, okay!" She rushes to retrieve the pencil, turning the flat line of her mouth toward me while I rattle off a series of numbers and species of wood.

"Why did you need the different kinds of wood written down?"

"I didn't," I respond with a real grunt this time as I stand.

She huffs loudly, whipping that hair around as she turns to scowl. "Then wh—"

"To show you that you can do it. And that I don't care how you write."

"*I* care," she says, dropping the pencil and walking into the kitchen.

I stroll up behind her, slowly curling my arms around her waist and resting my chin on her shoulder. "Baby, I think you're the only one that does. You are not your struggle."

She releases a deep breath, leaning back against my chest. "You're right."

"I'm proud of you, you know, for telling C.J., for putting yourself out there and learning to let the rest of us make life easier for you."

She turns in my arms, snuggling closer and making me wish I weren't covered in sweat and dust. "I feel like a kid, learning all these strategies and skills I probably should have been taught a long time ago."

"Hmm. You feel like a woman to me." I lean into her neck while my hands prove my point.

"Smooth," she says, laughing softly. "What's next once we get the floors done?"

"Spackling."

"Is that what the kids call it these days?" She grins, lifting her chin and wiggling her eyebrows.

"You work with kids, you tell me."

"I work with eight-year-olds, they call it 'mom and dad wrestling with their shirts off.'"

"Sounds fun," I say, my smile growing as I peer down at her and move a piece of hair away from her face. "I got you something."

"Ooh! Is it cake?" she asks, her face lighting up. She's

ridiculously easy to please, which makes spoiling her so much more fun.

"No," I snort, letting her go to pull a crudely wrapped box from my toolbox on the floor. I suppose having a girlfriend makes you realize you suddenly need things like nice wrapping paper and stationery.

Her eyes meet mine as she gently brushes a bit of dust from the brown paper wrapping. A slow smile spreads across her face as she turns it over, carefully peeling away the tape. She inspects the Kindle e-reader, a questioning slant on her brows.

I clear my throat before speaking. "It has a dyslexia-friendly font on it. I've already set it all up..." I swallow, hoping she doesn't hate it.

"C.J. told me about this..." Her lip trembles before her face splits in a wide grin. "It's perfect. Thank you." She throws her arms around me, and I pull her close, holding her tight. "You're such a book nerd," she teases, her voice filled with affection.

"Guilty."

She steps out of my arms to open the Kindle, her eyes absorbing the titles I downloaded.

"*The Hobbit?*" She says with a lift of her brow.

"That one, we'll read together. You can't fully appreciate the movies without reading the books."

"Deal." She rises on her toes to plant a kiss on my cheek, but I can't resist slipping an arm around her and pulling her closer. "You need a shower," she murmurs, a teasing smile on her lips. "Toby will be here soon."

"Way to kill the mood," I groan, planting a kiss below her ear.

"Rule number three, King. Toby's important to me."

My hands move to my sides as I take a step back. "I'll be nice, I promise. But I'd feel a lot better if he had a girlfriend, or if he at least stopped touching you. I just don't get how the guy *isn't* into you. I mean...*look* at you. And you're like walking sunshine—once you stop murdering people with your eyes, that is."

"*You* weren't into me in the beginning."

"Oh, I was. I was just an ass about it," I say and she responds with an eye roll. "If he had a girlfriend and she had a male best friend, maybe he'd understand. I actually kinda hope that happens to him. Turn the tables a bit, so he knows how I feel."

Her smile fades, her face clouding over with thought. "Turn the tables..." she whispers, repeating the phrase as her gaze drifts across the kitchen surfaces. I trail behind her as she mutters to herself, lost in concentration. Suddenly, she stops beside the coffee table in the living room, her eyes widening as she looks up at me. "That's it! I can't believe we missed it before..."

She drops to her knees beside the small table and flips it over. "Pop loved making these weird hiding places for things. Look!" She traces a seam along the wood, then turns the table back over and begins feeling around blindly.

A soft click sounds, and a small drawer slides open, tilting down just an inch. A spontaneous laugh escapes her lips. "I can't believe it...This has to be it!" Her eyes widen as she pulls out a small envelope.

"Your Pop was quite the secretive man." I chuckle, wishing I could have met him.

"He was so much fun," she says softly, scooting beside me. We read over the letter in silence, and Ivy's hand flies to her mouth.

"You going to show this to your Gran?" I nod toward the letter in her hands.

"I think I want to surprise her with it when the house is

done." She turns a soft smile to her hands. "So this is how Ross found out. Thank goodness it didn't lead him to the closet."

"Next time you feel the need to go on nighttime adventures, though, at least bring me coffee."

She lets out a husky laugh that wraps around my whole body. Every time I hear it, I find myself questioning what I'm doing with my life. Nothing else matters besides this woman. It's like I'm finally at peace in her presence, as if all my questions and uncertainties have settled, either fading into insignificance or finding their answers. Because *she* is the answer. She's the thrill my heart has been searching for. But I can't tell her all that just yet.

"I'm excited to meet your Gran," I say instead.

"Eth...I'm sorry about this whole hiding-our-relationship thing. I promise I'll fix it soon."

I pull her closer, cupping her jaw with my hands. "As long as I get to do this..." I tell her, leaning down to press my mouth against hers for a lingering kiss. "Then there's no rush on my side. Remember, I just want be the guy who gets to support you."

"Thank you." She sighs, resting her head on my chest. "You go shower. I'll start the food."

"So, no wrestling with our shirts off?"

"Nice try," I hear as she heads to the kitchen. "As my students will tell you, that's for moms and dad's who are married."

Working on it.

CHAPTER FORTY-TWO

IVY

Ethan bringing a duffel bag over and showering at my house feels so domestic that I'm beating the crap out of this pizza dough to distract myself from freaking out. Things are moving so fast. I think that's why I keep finding things to keep us busy, because if we're still too long, then the real, raw parts of our relationship are brought to the surface. And it scares me. We haven't exactly had a long time to establish roots. Heck, I only moved out of the *despising him* phase a few months ago. Is that even long enough to build a foundation strong enough to keep him from inevitably jetting off?

My sticky hands continue kneading, transferring all my frustrations into the dough. Hopefully this isn't like talking to plants, and the food won't taste bitter and gross because of the energy I'm massaging into the gluten.

I attempt to move my hair out of my face with a heavy exhale, switching to the crook of my elbow when it falls back in front of my eyes.

Then my head pops up at a sudden knocking on the door, and I lean back to hear if Ethan is still in the shower.

The knocking picks up, increasing in urgency. With a huff, I grab a dish towel, wiping my hands as I rush to the door and swing it open. "Jeez, Toby, keep your pants—*Ross*. What're you doing here?"

"Hey, Vee. Can I come in?"

With my hand on the door I turn, biting my lip as I glance behind me. "I'm actually in the middle of something."

"Can I just talk to you for two minutes? I swear Ivy, I'm trying—" He begins pacing the porch, hands gesturing haphazardly. When he pivots sharply, looking into my eyes for the first time—that's when I know. I know what he's here for. I only just manage to stop myself from groaning out loud, because the cycle of hope and disappointment has drained every last bit of energy from my bones. It's like the stain on a shirt that you love. You treat it, throw it in the wash, only for it to come out flaunting the ghost of an oil mark. So you try again, rubbing in a bit of Dawn, because hey, if it can save the penguins, why can't it save my shirt from the curry I had last week? But then it emerges, stain firmly in place. Sometimes you just have to accept it's no longer the fancy going-out top you thought it would be. Now it's just a yard work shirt, and you'd be less disappointed if you changed your expectations of it.

"Ross—" I croak out, my voice laced with sadness. We're still standing in the doorway, but the space between us feels like the Grand Canyon. I keep wishing he'll make a choice that will bridge the chasm that's been growing for the past twenty years, because it's not a gap I can mend on my own.

I'm about to continue when we're both startled by Toby's car door slamming shut. A storm cloud follows him as he marches up my driveway to stand beside me, his eyes locked on Ross. "Everything okay?"

My brother releases a heavy sigh, ignoring Toby's presence as he resumes his pacing. He doesn't give me a chance to answer as he pivots back to me. "Ivy, just tell me if you've found it."

"You can't have it, Ross," my voice comes out in a strained whisper.

"What's going on?"

Perfect.

Ethan steps outside and joins my bodyguard detail, adopting a posture that mirrors Toby's. Ross finally notices the two men beside me, crossing their arms and puffing their chests.

"I don't know who you are, but this is between me and my sister."

Ethan looks down at him like a kid who just tried to punch The Rock but broke his hand instead. "Wrong."

Ross ignores him again, his eyes darting back to me, but I interject before he can say anything. "No."

It only serves to dial up his agitation, and he speaks through clenched teeth now. "You don't *get it*, Vee—"

"Stop, Ross! I'm done being told I don't *get things,* or that I don't understand. You don't get to use that card this time. No matter how differently I see things, it doesn't change the fact that I can't keep rescuing you."

He presses a palm into his bloodshot eye before lacing his fingers behind his neck. The dark circles create a ghostly look, and the man before me is hardly recognizable as he paces, each step crushing the last pieces of hope I've been holding onto.

"You have it, Ivy, and I know you don't understand it, but I *need* it." He pauses to shoot me one more beseeching look. Toby and Ethan sense the tension, both of them angling their bodies in front of me.

My lips tremble as I shake my head. Ross doesn't understand that saying no to him is one of the hardest things I've ever done. Harder than giving him all my savings, harder than living out of my car and lying to my friends about it. A war rages on inside my head, as part of me still wants to give in, desperately thinking this could be the last time.

But we've had too many last times, and I know it'd never end.

My brother finally sees the resolution in my stare and turns with a curse, shoving his hands against the flimsy porch railing. At the sound of the wood cracking, Toby takes hold of my wrist, placing himself squarely in front of me while Ethan rushes for Ross.

It's like someone turned the volume down in my head as I watch him march Ross off the porch.

"It's time for you to leave," Ethan's stern voice growls out.

Ross shoves him away, and I'm numb as I watch him climb into a car I've never seen before. He drives off, while Ethan's rigid form stands sentry, making sure he disappears. It's only a minute, but it feels like hours pass before Ethan walks back up the porch.

What if...did I just sign my brother's death sentence by withholding something that I don't even need?

As Ethan approaches, his warm hands envelop my arms, drawing attention to the fact that I've been hugging myself, trying to ward off the chill that settled in as the sun dipped below the horizon.

My eyes slowly reach his, wide with growing panic. "What...what if I made a mistake? What if something happens to him? Maybe he was serious—"

"Vee," I hear Toby from behind as Ethan's face floods with sympathy. "It's not your responsibility."

"Yeah...okay. You're right." I hear myself say, but I'm not fully convinced.

Ethan places a kiss on my forehead before lifting a chin toward the door. "Let's head inside."

As I enter the kitchen, Ethan's phone buzzes insistently on

the counter, displaying the name *Crystal* on the screen. He ignores it and strides over to the fridge to grab a water bottle. I inadvertently catch a glimpse of the text that pops up a second later.

> **CRYSTAL**
> Give me a call when you can. We can't wait to have you in Frisco!

Ethan twists the lid from a bottle, handing it to me while I hover, unsure where to stand or what to think. I bring the bottle to my lips, sipping robotically while Toby and Ethan stare at me like they're worried I might break.

"I need to think...I just need some space." I nod while my brows crease. I'm just going along with the words that are spilling out of my mouth. The frowny twins in front of me seem to have bonded in their mutual overprotection. They share a concerned look, then it's back to silently eyeing me.

"You need to eat," Ethan finally lets out.

I shake my head and begin tossing items into my purse, while Ethan and Toby seem on the verge of short-circuiting from what appears to be a case of 'unsure of female hormones.' "I'm fine. I'm going to Opal and Gail—I'll eat there. Promise."

Everything feels like it's unraveling. I'm peeved at these two for their overbearing ways. Who knows what would've happened if they hadn't told Ross to leave, but I would have liked the opportunity to stand up for myself. And now the anxiety over what might actually happen to my brother begins ramping up. Then, there's Ethan and the fact that adventure is literally calling at this very moment.

After giving Toby a quick hug, I turn to Ethan, my palm resting against his cheek as I rise on my toes to kiss him. "I'll call you later."

My chin quivers as I turn and walk out the door. I have to

be okay with letting Ethan go, if that's what he wants. He's an adventurer at heart, and I won't hold him back. This thing between us always had an end date, anyway.

"Let me get this straight," Opal frowns, waving a wrinkled hand while leaning over the arm of her wrought iron chair. "You're upset 'cause two men—the man you love, plus another man-friend—chased your brother away when he got violent?"

"He wasn't *violent!*" I scowl back at her after an eye roll. I also don't mention that she's probably casting the other two male roles backwards in this story.

"Honey, if someone breaks something when they're mad—it's violent," Gail adds.

"Fine. Then, yes, that's the gist of it."

"Well, goodness, how terrible it must be for you to have a couple of strapping, young men coming to your defense. And without your permission? That's just...despicable," Opal quips, glaring at me from under her lowered brow. The sarcasm is strong with this one.

I stab a fork into the pasta bowl cradled in my lap. Of course, I'm not just sulking over Toby's and Ethan's overprotective tendencies. The truth is, I hate how much I've come to care for Ethan in such a short time. And just as soon as I allowed him to sneak past my defenses, I'm reminded that he's going to take my heart with him when he jets off into the sunset. Maybe being able to process this with someone would help, but I'm still stuck in my web of lies and struggling to remember which degree of the truth I'm supposed to be admitting right now.

Opal narrows her eyes, locking her gaze on me like she's trying to extract more of my secrets with her stare. She purses her lips in thought. "How'd that sexy boyfriend of yours handle you running away?"

"Fine," I add hesitantly.

She knows. She knows it's Ethan we're talking about and not Toby, and she's waiting for me to come out with it. But I've got to hold onto this secret a little longer. She's too close to Gran. I need to figure out how to tell my grandmother the truth in the least detrimental way before divulging this mess to anyone else.

Opal and Gail allow me to continue brooding over the meal they lovingly made when I showed up at their door, heavy-shouldered and grouchy.

I hug them goodbye, letting out a loud growl when I shuffle into my car and Dwight Schrute repeating the word 'idiot' blares from my phone. The ringtone I assigned to Ross's contact still hasn't stopped me from making stupid decisions in regard to him, or in life in general, for that matter.

"Ross, I swear if you're—"

"I thought about what you said, Vee..."

My shoulders instantly straighten as I look ahead through the windshield. "Yeah?"

"I need to get my life on track. I'll sort this stuff out, and then I'll look into those classes you mentioned."

I pull the phone away from my ear, double-checking the name on the screen. For what seems like my whole life, I've been waiting for my brother to have this kind of life-changing epiphany. In high school, we all hoped he'd grow out of his rebellious phase, but it only got worse. And he's never gone long without needing rescuing, bailing out, or saving since then. I'm ashamed to admit that I'd finally given up hope of ever hearing these words from him, but it's finally happening.

"Vee...you there?" I hear him ask while my jaw hangs open.

"Yes. Yeah, I'm here. I'm just...I didn't expect this. Especially after today."

"I read through everything you sent me. I think I could be good at the electrician stuff. I need to work with my hands, so it's a good fit. Can we talk about it tomorrow? Maybe meet for coffee somewhere, my treat?"

My eyes bounce over the dashboard as I continue to process his words. "Okay, yeah. Sure."

"Can you meet me at the Starbucks on Market Street tomorrow at ten?"

I nod as I stare out the window, rolling my lips in before answering. "I hope you know what you're doing Ross. I'll see you tomorrow."

CHAPTER FORTY-THREE

IVY

> **ETHAN**
> You up yet, princess?

I had been lying awake for hours, staring up at the ceiling and looking for shapes in the once uneven surface, but smoothing out the old popcorn texture left behind a sleek, white finish. Now I'm watching my favorite part of *The Lord Of The Rings*, and Aragorn is just about to push those huge double doors open... It's a lovely distraction from reality.

> **ETHAN**
> If you're still sleeping when I get there, I'm getting into bed with you. I hope you know that

> **IVY**
> No! I'm up. Very much awake. I'm watching LOTR

> **ETHAN**
> Which one?

> **IVY**
> Two Towers. Aragorn is about to make his earth-shattering grand entrance

> **ETHAN**
> I think I'm a little jealous of a fictional character right now…

> **IVY**
> *tsk* He's created a very high standard for entering a room, I'm afraid. For men in general

> **ETHAN**
> Just say the word, and I'm ready to crush those standards. ;)

> **IVY**
> I still need some thinking space today…

> **ETHAN**
> Ivy June
>
> Please don't shut me out

> **IVY**
> I'm not…

I am, but I'm claiming one more day to sulk before talking to him again. Seeing his sexy face in person will confuse me, and I'll forget all the reasons why I need to let him go. Keeping some space between us lets me hold onto this little fantasy for a tiny bit longer. It's pitiful, I know.

Besides, I need to sort out this Ross situation first. My brain can't handle this much stress at one time, and this is my weird way of compartmentalizing and keeping myself from cracking under the pressure.

> **ETHAN**
> It's Saturday

> My Saturday's are yours now. I don't know what to do if you're not on my Saturday agenda

I whine aloud. The man is going to make me disappear right here into the cracks of my newly polished floors after melting into a puddle.

IVY
> I just need more time to process
>
> Can we hang out tomorrow?

ETHAN
> You sure I can't just stare at you while you process? I'll be quiet. Real creepy like, but I won't make a sound

IVY
> 😊 Go bother Colton

> Ethan: Fine. I'll see you tomorrow, Ivy June. Let me know if you change your mind.

I'm smiling like a smitten little idiot. I can't even pretend to stop myself from falling in love with him. I've already fallen. I'm deep at the bottom of the well, staring up at the cruel blue sky that led me here under pretenses of a happily ever after. But there's no escaping this reality. Ethan will jet off on exciting adventures any day now, and I'll never find another man who makes my knees go weak or cares for me the way he does.

My morbid thoughts are interrupted by light footsteps on the porch, followed by a knock on the door. "Vee! I have donuts and mimosas. Open up!"

Crap.

I love my best friend, but her arrival just made things all the more complicated. I'm at least grateful for the tarp I nailed on the wall the other day, covering *The List* and the little messages Ethan and I have been exchanging. It's become something intimate, and I didn't want it out in the open for just anyone to see.

"Em?" I unlock the door to find my frazzled friend staring at me. "You okay?"

Her lip wobbles and she nods, shuffling inside with a box of donuts balanced on one hand and a grocery bag in the other.

"Don't ever plan a wedding, Vee." She sniffs while opening and closing cupboards until she finds champagne glasses. "Marry rich so you can get someone else to organize the whole thing."

"Em...you *are* marrying rich. And you *can* get someone else to do it," I remind her as she hands me a bottle of orange juice, silently tasking me with pouring while she struggles to open the champagne bottle.

She lets out a noisy exhale, pausing after the cork pops. "Yeah. I guess you know that's not the real problem."

"Is that part of the problem at all?"

"Of course not. Colton keeps offering to up the budget." She pauses and sighs again. "It's my mother. She's out of control! I've gotten more attention from her in the last three months than I have in my entire life. She questions *every* decision I make, but in a super nice way, making me doubt what I actually like in the first darn place!" she rambles as she pours champagne.

I carry our glasses and the box of donuts back to the living room before we sink into the sofa together. Ember lifts the lid and picks out a chocolate donut while I glance at the time on my watch, my eyes flicking to the door.

It's almost time.

"I'm sorry, Em. What can I help with? I'll intervene. I can

come along the next time you meet with her. We actually kind of bonded the last time I saw her, anyway. Maybe she'll listen to me."

"And by *bonded*, you mean she said something half-decent and didn't shred you to pieces with just a stare?"

"Yup."

"Ugh, I just hate how much energy it takes to be around her. She's a nicer person after everything that happened last year, but every interaction still leaves me drained. Where's your car, by the way? I didn't see it out front."

"Oh, I uh...had to move it for renovation stuff." I circle a hand around the room. Ember nods and I continue. "I'm sure things with your mom will get better after the wedding, though, right? I mean, you're on the right track, at least."

"I hope so," she mumbles over a huge bite of her donut. I take a sip of mimosa before pulling out my phone to read the text that just came through.

> ROSS
> Stopping for gas. See you soon

Our eyes both fly to the door when the handle begins to jiggle. Ember frowns at me questioningly while she continues to chew.

"Um...so can you be real quiet for a minute, and whatever happens next, just follow my lead?"

She shifts on the sofa, bringing her feet under her while her back straightens. "I know you're hiding something, Ivy June." She whispers. "Don't think I haven't noticed just 'cause I've got my own drama right now. You've got some explaining to do," she scolds me, wagging a finger in my direction. But both of us turn our attention to the door handle as it continues to rattle ominously.

Well...this'll be interesting.

The knob is silent as it turns, but the door hasn't been oiled, and it moans as it slowly creaks open, just wide enough for a body to slink through.

Ross freezes when he notices us. I lean forward, one leg crossed over the other. I gently swish my champagne glass while my arms casually rest on my thigh, working hard to lift one brow.

"Lost, dearest brother? This ain't the gas station." I'm trying to appear super confident when internally I'm like a blob of Jell-o sitting on a dryer running a tumble cycle.

"Ivy—" He laughs without humor in his voice. "You're home."

"Surprise."

"Hi, Ross." Ember waves, taking a sip from her glass. "Long time. Nice lock-picking skills."

"Ember... Wow. You look...amazing! H-how are you?"

"She's engaged, Ross, so you can wipe the Joey Tribbiani look off your face."

"This looks bad, but I swear I can explain—"

"I think you've done enough explaining." I scowl at him.

"This isn't just about me anymore, Vee. Some bad people know about the music box. And they know it's here."

Ember does a spit-take. "Say *what* now?" she demands, mimosa dripping down her chin.

I roll my eyes, since I'm already accustomed to my brother's routine of embellishing a story to get what he wants. "Ross, I'm not giving it to you, and I'm not leaving my house 'cause some 'bad guys' know where I live," I tell him, making quotation marks with my fingers. "We're kinda busy here, so I think you should leave. Lock the door on your way out, will you?"

I had a hunch Ross wouldn't show up for coffee this morning. His offer felt too desperate, like he was saying exactly what he knew I wanted to hear. But it was his line about reading through everything I sent him that tipped me off. I'm ninety-nine-percent sure Ross has dyslexia, too, and that's why he's acted out his whole life. It was that and his offer to pay for coffee. He's always been the one mooching off me. Even as a tween, Ross would beg me to borrow my hard-earned babysitting money and conveniently forget to pay me back.

He lets out a growl before roughly dragging a hand down his face. "I'm trying to do the right thing here, Ivy. You don't understand—"

"No, Ross, *you* don't understand! Maybe I see things differently, but that doesn't mean I'm stupid. You can't play that card with me anymore, because I've finally realized that my struggles are also my greatest advantage—I know how to push through when something is hard. I'm guessing you probably faced the same obstacles. The difference is that I've learned to overcome my hurdles instead of just blaming others for them."

I may have hid my struggles in the past, but I'm determined to be kinder to myself. And although I'm finally learning to love myself, I can't make my brother do the same. He has to take responsibility for his life.

Ross breathes heavily, his brows forming a sharp V as he stares at me.

Ember's eyes ping-pong between us. "I don't know what the heck is going on right now," she says, breaking the silence. "But can we get back to the part about the possible bad guys? Like, what kinda bad guys are we talking here? Run 'o the mill, low IQ? Kevlar vest-wearing with bald heads? 'Cause I'm thinking that information could be useful right now."

"I haven't seen them," he grunts, walking laps around the coffee table. He stops and throws his head back, growling out before swinging his head to me. "Please, just tell me if you have it?"

"Ross—" I pause when my phone starts ringing.

Frik. It's Ethan. And despite the way I've been trying to put space between us until I can figure things out in my head, just seeing his name on the screen makes me wish he were here so I could run into the safety and security of his arms.

Make up your mind, Ivy. Either chase that hunk of a man away or stop letting fear tell you what to do, I scold myself as my eyes flicker back to my phone. Answering at least buys me time while I dodge Ross's question.

"Hey," I say into the phone, bugging my eyes out at Ember and hoping she'll get the hint and keep her mouth shut about our little situation.

"Ivy June," Ethan drawls, and I can hear the smile in his voice. "How's your thinking time going? You missin' me yet?"

"It's fine. Yup, I sure am."

Gah! How am I supposed to let this man go? Just hearing his voice has me questioning if I'm doing the right thing, because all I want to do now is snuggle him like a baby koala.

Ross stares at me, making a 'wind it up' signal with his hand. I roll my eyes in response, turning my back to him. Ember steps closer to me, utterly unashamed in her attempts to eavesdrop.

"Is that *Ethan?*" she mouths.

"You get today, and that's it, Ivy. Then I'm smothering you in hugs and kisses, kay?"

"Noted," I say, laughing while my heart breaks a little more. I don't think I can let him go. Ending things because I'm afraid of being hurt won't save me from anything. It'll just hurt either way, right?

I bring the phone away from my ear, covering the speaker, although I'm not entirely sure where that is on an iPhone, if I'm being honest. "I'll explain later," I whisper harshly to Ember.

"I'm on my way to the airport," Ethan continues. "I got a call from the network because the meeting they scheduled for next week got bumped up to tomorrow. Otherwise, they'll have to push it out a month. You gonna be okay today?"

"Mh-mm. All good."

"Ivy June. What's going on?"

"She's not okay!" Ember shouts from beside me, making me jump. "Ross told some bad people where she lives! And they might be on their way!"

I shoot her a death glare while Ethan fires a million overprotective questions my way. Ross growls and starts tapping his wrist, whispering, "We need to leave!"

"I'm sorry, Ethan, I've gotta go. Ember's just exaggerating. Talk to you later, kay? Good luck at your meeting. Love you, bye!" I hang up and toss the phone onto the couch, and my hands fly up to cover my mouth. Ember's gaze snaps to me, her eyes wide with shock at the declaration that just slipped out of my mouth.

Dang it! I'm supposed to be putting space between us, not professing my feelings! This can't be good, my subconscious has managed to overpower my extremely stubborn will. But maybe my subconscious knows what's best? I don't feel like I want to take the words back, so that's a good sign, right?

Oh, what the hell. My life is already so insane that I might as well lay my heart on the chopping block while I'm at it.

"I just told him I love him."

And I do. *I love Ethan King.*

Ember begins to laugh, her shoulders shaking as she speaks. "You just told *Ethan* you love him! Oooh, you have *so* much explaining to do!"

My phone starts buzzing again but I ignore it.

I'm saved from responding when a rustling outside the window has all three of us freezing, our eyes darting to one another as we wait, questions hanging heavily in the air.

"What the heck was that?" Ember wimpers.

Eliza Doolittle's hat! This isn't good.

The three of us wince when we hear it again, then Ember gasps as two dark forms creep past the window.

Ross looks at me with a slow turn of his head, his lips pinched. "Told you so."

CHAPTER FORTY-FOUR

IVY

"You guys saw that, right?" Ember mumbles from behind her hands.

The hairs on my nape and arms lift as I grab hold of her arm. "Should we call the police?"

"We're not calling the cops," Ross hisses.

"We need weapons," Ember says with one single nod. She unplugs a lamp and hands it to me before lifting the small coffee table it was sitting on and turning it upside down. "How attached are you to this table?"

"Minimally," I frown, my eyes darting back to the windows at the sound of another shuffling noise. Ember swiftly kicks off two of the table legs, tossing one to Ross. My jaw drops as I watch her wield the makeshift weapon like a baseball bat. "Who the heck are you?"

"Nicolas has prepared me for this," she deadpans.

Footsteps echo on the porch, prompting a curse from each of us before Ross urgently whispers for us to hide.

"Uh... Ross, any chance you remembered to lock the door after you picked it open?" I ask, trying to keep my voice steady.

Before he can answer, we watch the handle twist for a second time. Ember and I hide behind the sofa, ducking when the door creaks open.

My body trembles uncontrollably while my heart pounds in my chest.

Could we have picked a worse place to hide?

I pull out my phone, and Ember gasps as she jabs me with her elbow. "Holy cow, are you checking your email right now?"

"I get productive when I'm nervous," I whisper with a grimace.

"Shhh! What if someone's home?" We hear the intruder mutter in a hushed tone.

"No one's parked outside. It's fine. If we're caught, just pretend you're lost."

"Ow! For the love, woman, would you mind your bony elbows!"

Ember tilts her head to the side, pursing her lips and I pop my head out from behind my lame hiding spot. "Opal? Gail?"

"Ivy?" Gail responds, narrowing her eyes. Ember shifts onto her knees as she makes herself known. Someone better pinch me and wake me from this dream or quit slipping shrooms into my food, because I can't take any of this craziness anymore.

Ross fights his way out from behind a curtain, then wanders a short distance away before turning back. "Wait, you all know each other?"

"Yup. Pretty well, actually."

"What are you two doing here? And why are you dressed like that?" I question, gesturing a palm to the all-black outfits and rocky headbands they're sporting.

Opal eyes Ross, her mouth twisting to the side. "We got a tip-off that the music box was here. Why're *you* two here?"

"I live here."

Ross's head falls back as he breathes a heavy sigh before looking at my geriatric friends. *"You're* after the music box?"

Before they can answer, the door handle begins to jiggle for the third freaking time today. "You've got to be kidding me."

We watch, each of us frozen in place, except for Ember who raises her table leg up to her shoulder.

"It's unlocked," our newest intruder whispers as the door squeaks open again.

"Carl?" My lip curls up on one side, causing my glasses to slide down the bridge of my nose.

"Hi, dear," Gran chirps, suddenly appearing from behind Carl.

Aaaand, I've officially lost it. Reality has completely slipped away. It must be those fumes someone keeps spiking my car with. I drove recently, right? That has to be it. None of this is real.

"Can someone explain what is going on?" I demand a bit too loudly, then clear my throat.

"Carl gave us an address where he believed we'd find the music box," Gail says, pointing at Carl, whose cheeks flush as he tugs at his collar. "We knew he was helping Agnes investigate its whereabouts."

"They tricked me. With *cake,*" Carl adds in his defense, crossing his arms. "Told ya that's how they get you, Miss Ivy," he continues, shaking his head with a creased chin.

"Why are *you* here, Gran?"

"Well, Carl here didn't tell me the address we were headed to, just that he had a lead. I followed along and figured I'd see how this plays out once I realized where we were. Love what you've done with the place, by the way," she adds as her eyes track the changes in the newly opened space.

Thank goodness Ethan knocked out some walls in here, or

the seven of us would be pretty cramped. How has this escalated to DEFCON 1 in a mere ten minutes?

I hear my name being shouted just before Toby and Stef burst through the door.

Make that nine people. At least we were spared from watching the door handle turn spookily again.

"Ivy! You okay?" he huffs, breathing heavily with his hands on his hips.

"The boyfriend?" I hear Gran ask Opal with a stage whisper while she gives Stef the stink eye.

Opal bobs her head to the side. "Well...yes and no."

"Everything's just peachy. How'd you get roped into this? Wait...Is...is something finally going on here?" I wag my finger, motioning between Toby and Stef.

"I'll explain later," Toby waves his hand, still panting. "And Ember texted,"

"In my defense," Ember grimaces, "I thought he was still your boyfriend."

"*Was?*" I hear Gran squeak.

"Um..." I exhale, letting my lips flap noisily while I decide on my next move. I push my glasses up, settling on dodging the question.

"Where'd Ross go?" I shift to peer behind each person in the room.

Freaking monkey nuts!

I race down the passage, silently chanting "please let me be wrong" over and over in my head. Six sets of hurried footsteps echo behind me. Then I come to an abrupt stop, nearly causing a pile up when the others don't react in time.

"I don't think he got to it, but I need to check. Toby, will you help me?"

"So my granddaughter isn't good enough for you, hmm,

Toby?" Gran decides to start an interrogation while Toby and I heave the wardrobe away.

"Gran, I'll explain later. I promise. But Toby is innocent in all of this." I smirk at Stef, who shares a small smile with me. I'm glad the two of them seem to have connected. Carl steps in, insisting he take my place to shift the closet, revealing the hidden door.

Gran gasps. "I thought Oliver had sealed this up…" There's a wistful tone to her voice, and she inhales sharply when I slide the door open. "It was just an unfinished storage room when we bought the house, so we boarded it up and shoved a wardrobe in front of it. Oliver always said he'd spruce it up some day…"

"He redid the whole thing for you. He wanted to surprise you with it. But he passed away before he could," I tell her. The dim light in the room glints off the tears pooling in her eyes as a shaky hand raises to her mouth. I grab Pop's letter from the shelf, handing it to her. She reads it silently while everyone else squishes into the tiny space.

"Oh, for goodness sake, Agnes," Opal sighs heavily. "We don't have long to live. Would you read the darn thing before I die?"

"Speak for yourself. I plan to live to a ripe old age." Gail smiles.

Opal rolls her eyes Gail's way. "Check the mirror, you're already overripe"

Gran clears her throat, waiting with heavy-lidded eyes for Opal and Gail to pipe down.

"My dearest Agnes… You always said this room was a waste of space. I finally got rid of all my junk. I'm sorry I sold your music box, but I got it back for you. Got to live out my spy dreams doing it. Good thing we never told anyone what it's worth. Thank you for putting up with my grumpy old ass. Love, your Oliver."

"So he's the one who stole it from us," Opal grumbles.

"And that's how Ross found out about its value when he found Pop's letter," I say aloud. "Thank goodness Pop didn't mention the actual location of the closet."

Gran sniffs, dabbing at her eyes with a tissue before turning to me. "Is it here?"

"It is." I beam, turning to where I left the box. "Well...it *was* here..."

CHAPTER FORTY-FIVE

ETHAN

"None of them are picking up?" Colton asks, his brows pinching as he glances at me for a second before continuing to race toward Ivy's house.

"No," I breathe out after a long exhale. I'm trying to stay calm. But this woman has a propensity to put herself in danger with little thought of the consequences. Who knows what the hell she's doing right now. I only hope that she and Ember have managed to get the upper hand in whatever situation they've found themselves in this time.

"Ember know any self defense moves?" I ask.

"Nope. Not unless you count what she's learned from weird true crime shows. Ivy?"

My hand covers my mouth as I try to wipe away the smile that breaks free but a chuckle escapes without permission. "I caught her judo chopping a mosquito once..."

Without warning Colton punches me in the arm.

"Ow! What the heck was that for?"

"I figured this would happen, but I hadn't expected this day to arrive so soon. I'm so happy for you little brother."

I click my tongue as I scrunch up my face. "Colt, don't be Bono's accent from *Sing* 2. I'm not discussing this stuff with you until I've spoken to Ivy."

"*Fine*," he retorts with an eye roll as he swerves into Ivy's driveway. "This it?"

"Yeah," I barely get out, unfastening my seatbelt and bolting out before the truck has come to a complete stop.

"Why are you so calm? Ember could be in danger, too," I demand when he jogs up behind me. "What if they aren't here?" I scowl, annoyed to find the front door unlocked.

"Nah, I tracked her location on her phone. They're in the house."

"That's a little creepy."

"She knows about it." He shrugs as we step inside.

"Ivy? Ember?" I call out, feeling like my throat is in my stomach when there's no answer. My heavy boots thud on the newly varnished floors as I hurry to the master bedroom. My heart rate settles a fraction when I hear voices as we near.

"Ivy?"

I get to the room and find the closet door open, and Colton and I walk nearer.

"Ethan? What are you doing here?" Ivy emerges, pushing through the small crowd to get to me.

"You okay?" I whisper, finally feeling my jaw relax now that I can see she's in one piece.

She hooks her pinky around mine as a slow smile overtakes her face. "Yeah."

Colton finds Ember and wraps his arms around her, placing a kiss on her head, and the rest of the closet attendees shuffle out, surrounding us.

"Did you mean it?" I ask, bringing my palm to her waist and ignoring everyone else in the room. I'll implode if I have to wait for a private moment to find out if the words that slipped out earlier were true.

I watch as the slightest crease flickers on her brow before she speaks. "What if I did?"

"Then I'd tell you that I'm sorry," I reply, and her brows pull together behind her glasses. She lifts a hand to nudge the corner of the frame up.

"What?"

"I'd tell you I'm sorry for breaking rule number four," I say quietly, but the gathering of people around us are standing so close, there's no doubt they're still hearing every word.

Ivy's eyes ping between mine as the curve of her mouth slowly grows into a face-splitting grin, and then she leaps on me. I wrap my arms around her, lifting her feet higher off the ground and burying my own cheesy smile in the crook of her neck.

In my peripheral, I catch whom I presume to be Ivy's grandmother elbowing Toby. "You okay with another man *literally* sweeping your woman off her feet?" She scowls at him with a narrowed side-eye.

"Agnes, for Pete's sake, Ivy was never dating Toby," Opal groans.

"Well, why not? Look at her! She's the whole package!"

"What's rule number four?" Gail asks.

"Rule number four was that I couldn't fall in love with her. But I'm a rule breaker," I turn back to the woman of my dreams. "I love you, Ivy June" I whisper into her ear while the group releases a collective "Awe,". I hear her inhale and let out a little groan, like she's disappointed we aren't alone right now. I lower her to the ground, keeping my arm curled around her waist as I lean forward, holding out my hand to her grandmother. "Mrs. Marsh, I'm Ethan, Ivy's real boyfriend."

Agnes shakes my hand, narrowing her eyes at Ivy. "You've

got some explaining to do, young lady." Then her face softens and she cups Ivy's face, smushing a kiss to her cheek. "But I'm still so happy for you."

I didn't know how badly I wanted to be able to love Ivy freely, but making this declaration in front of all these people who mean so much to her, it feels redemptive. A little awkward —yeah—but worth the chance to finally let her and everyone else know that she means the world to me.

"So...why's everyone in here again?" I ask, nodding my chin toward the closet.

"Oh my gosh! I nearly forgot!" Ivy turns to me, wrinkling her brow. "The music box is gone," she adds, her shoulders sinking with a pained, watery gaze.

Agnes shakes her head, crossing her arms with a deep sigh. "I knew that brother of yours was up to no good."

"Ross didn't take it," I say, gently laying my hand on Ivy's back. "I did."

Opal gasps while everyone else remains silent. "Saboteur," she accuses me, stretching the word in a low voice.

"What?" Ivy squeaks.

"Don't worry, I was only having the bird's wing repaired," I explain with a chuckle, thoroughly enjoying being a presumed thief. "It's at Colton's office. I had someone come there to work on it. It felt like a safe, neutral location."

"He's got muscles *and* he's noble." Gail sighs wistfully before turning to Ivy. "I get it now. I mean...look at the man. No offense, Toby."

Toby scrunches his face, his chin tilting to the side. "Some taken?"

"Who's the big guy?" I lean over and whisper to Ivy.

"Oh, that's Carl. He's Gran's accomplice and the security guard where she lives. He's also Gail and Opal's informant, with a weakness for cake. And he helped me move all my stuff."

"Carl," I say, leaning forward again from within our circle to shake his hand. "Thank you for helping...I think. What exactly led to this little gathering?"

Carl clears his throat and puffs out his chest, hiking his pants a bit higher. "My grandson is a computer science major," he begins. "He helped pinpoint the location of the music box when Agnes approached me. Gail and Opal tried to get it back, too. This Ross character was after it as well, and that's how we all ended up here.".

"Ross was here?" I ask, turning to Ivy. She releases a long heavy sigh, then lifts regretful eyes to her Gran.

"Yeah, up until a few minutes ago, but he bolted. I'm assuming he thought he had a buyer for the music box."

"That would be me," Carl interjects. "All fake, of course. It was just a ruse to locate the box. I may have embellished the threats a little too much, but I was only trying to put pressure on him and confirm he had the box in his possession. I guess he got antsy."

Ivy nods as she puts the pieces together. "So he thinks you —aka the buyer—has tracked him down, which is why he tried to break in and look for it this morning. Turns out the *bad people* he thought were after it were Opal and Gail...and Gran." She rubs her forehead, pacing the very small space in the middle of our increasingly stifling circle. "But he still owes people money."

Agnes shuffles close, her mouth downturned as she rubs a hand on Ivy's back. "That's not your responsibility, sweetheart. It's his mess to clean up."

Opal clears her throat and begins fanning her face with her hand. "Y'all, not to be a party pooper, but can we wrap this up with a 'hands in' and a cheer or something? This muggy huddle is getting to me."

Gail nods, flapping the front of her blouse. "I dunno about

anyone else, but I'm fixin' to sweat through my favorite brassiere if we don't get out of here soon. And there's a reason you don't hear about wet T-shirt competitions for women our age."

"Careful, your overripeness is showing," Agnes snorts.

"Touché," Opal nods, herding everyone out of the room. "Ivy, honey, you got any sweet tea? Nevermind. I'll make some if you don't. We'll give you two a moment."

Ivy and I are finally left alone in the room, and I waste no time in tilting her chin up with my finger and pressing my lips to hers. I can't hold her close enough as relief floods my veins, and our kiss deepens until Ivy pulls away with a gasp. "Wait, why aren't you on your way to Frisco?"

"Something more important came up."

"Ethan, I can't keep you from your dreams. I'd never want to stand in the way of your heart feeling fulfilled or you getting to enjoy all the adventures you crave. You'll only resent me later," she says, taking a tiny step back.

"Nuh-uh," I grin. "We're not doing that. We're skipping that whole bit where you push me away, and we're both sad. I've found the most fulfilling, enticing, exasperating, adorable adventure I'll ever encounter. And there's no way in hell you can keep me from this one."

"But what if you have to move?" she frowns.

I bring one of her hands to my lips, placing a soft kiss on her knuckles. "When I started doing all these things for the show, I just kinda went with the flow. I didn't think too much about the location. But that's only 'cause there's no question where it'll need to happen. I told them today, we either do it here, or they do it without me."

"Ethan. Are you sure about this?" She squints an eye, one side of her mouth lifting skeptically.

"You trying to talk me out of loving you, woman?"

"I'm trying to save you from feeling weighed down by a girl who doesn't want to leave this town. And I'm trying to save myself from heartache..." She pauses, closing her eyes before mumbling, "but I think it's too late for that."

My stomach swirls with nausea, the feeling of failing her hitting me like a freight truck. I promised her I'd be the one drama-free part of her life, and she's been freaking out over me breaking her heart this whole time. "Baby, I'm so sorry for not making sure you knew without a shred of doubt that I'm all in. I didn't wanna scare you away—"

"Ethan, no. This isn't on you. This is my fear, and you're not responsible for that. I'm—I choose to trust you," she says, rising on her toes to place a kiss on my jaw. When she lowers, a slow grin spreads across her face. "But I still wanna hear you say it again."

"I love you, Ivy. *You* are my greatest adventure."

"Okay," she nods with watery eyes, her smile giving me the rush of a lifetime. "I love you, too."

CHAPTER FORTY-SIX

IVY

The top of my thighs tingle as the sun continues to warm them through the glass wall. Gran's chair squeaks beside me while we rock our wicker chairs in the solarium.

"I'm so glad you redid this little room. It's everything I always dreamed it could be," she says, smiling softly at the little additions and updates.

My eyes sweep over the thrifted Persian rug and the abundance of potted plants, the latter all gifted from Gail and Opal. Each plant is carefully positioned for optimal happiness. A smile spreads across my face as I glance at the chandelier hanging above us—the one Ethan wouldn't let me hang, even though I tried to do it myself, anyway. At least there were no major injuries, and now it's up and shining beautifully.

The low bookshelves lining two of the walls have a small growing collection of books. In the past I mostly listened to audiobooks, but I find myself liking the real thing better now that Ethan is around to read to me. "It's my favorite room," I sigh, closing my eyes and leaning back, lulled by the motion of my chair.

The room is filled with the melodic chirping of birds and the gentle creaking of our chairs as we relax, soaking in the serene afternoon.

"Now, tell me about this Toby business, honey. You were never dating?" Gran raises one eyebrow, straightening to sip her sweet tea.

A snort escapes before I sit up and explain how my small, fake-dating fib ended up spiraling out of control. By the time I'm done, Gran shoulder's are shaking at how I let things get carried away in my mind. "Toby actually just started dating another teacher at our school," I add. "I'm sorry I didn't tell you the truth, though. I should have trusted you."

"I forgive you, Ivy June. But I think there's something else we should discuss, too," she says, leaning over to grab my hand. "You've been holding yourself back 'cause of your struggles. But now that everything's out in the open, are you finally ready to take the plunge and go after your dreams?"

A crease forms between my brows as I struggle to speak. My lips move, attempting to form words, but the exposure sends a swarm of anxiety through my stomach, stealing my voice.

"I've seen your interest over the years, sweetheart. How you can't ask the occupational therapist at the retirement village enough questions. I remember the college applications you'd spend hours staring at in your senior year of high school. And I'll bet you're still curious about studying O.T." She lets out a short chuckle as her kind eyes roam my face. "You're a lot like your Pop, you know that? He struggled with dyslexia, although it didn't have a name back then. But I knew his mind worked differently."

"I...I didn't know that," I breathe.

"I didn't realize it was something a person could get help for till much later. I should have spoken to your parents about it when you were a child. The problem with this family is we don't talk about things enough. But I'm not too old to change that, starting now." Warm wrinkled hands grasp mine lovingly. Gran shifts so she's facing me, her crystal blue eyes moving closer. "As long as you promise to look your fears in the face and figure out how to make your dream come true, despite your challenges."

For the first time, the idea she's nudging me toward doesn't feel like something insurmountable. It's still daunting as hell, but the past few months have helped me shed some of the misconceptions I've held about my abilities and self-worth, and I've learned to truly love myself. I glance down at my feet to admire the Crocs I now wear comfortably and confidently. These purple monstrosities are just a small symbol of how I've become more confident in my skin. I actually believe that I *can* pursue these scary things now, despite knowing it'll still be difficult. But I know there's help out there, and I'm not afraid of accepting it anymore.

I dab at the tear that rolls down my cheek, giving Gran a watery smile. "Yeah. I think I'm gonna do it."

"I'm so proud of you," she whispers into my hair as she wraps me up in a tight hug. Then she pulls away and cups my face with her hands. "You're so brave," she adds, smiling warmly. "Now. Tell me about Ethan before he gets back. That man is smitten with you, by the way. He looks at you the way my Oliver looked at me."

"I wish they could've met." I sigh, leaning back in my chair. "Ethan is amazing. But believe it or not, we couldn't stand each other in the beginning," I say over a bubble of laughter.

Gran nods, pointing a finger my way. "That's how you know you'll always have passion in your relationship. Did you know your Pop and I were engaged a week after we met? A month later we eloped. Best decision I ever made," she tells me, her tone wistful.

"No way! I didn't know that."

"Yeah, I knew right away that he was one of the good ones. Ethan is, too. Now come on, I wanna know how he swept you off your feet."

The sun continues to move slowly across my thighs, the ice in our teas melting as I recap how Ethan and I got to where we are now.

"I wonder where he is," I lift my wrist, checking the time. "He wouldn't tell me what he was up to today. Just said if it went well, he'd have a surprise for us."

"*Us?*" She lifts a brow. "Well, now I'm intrigued."

"Hey, Vee."

"Ross?" I gasp, turning to find Ethan and my brother filling the doorway of the sun room.

"Ethan...Wh—what are...uh...what's going on?" I stammer, getting out of my chair.

"Hey, babe, let's sit." He smiles, placing a kiss on my cheek before ushering us to the kitchen table. Ross rubs the back of his neck, avoiding eye contact as we take our seats. Gran carries our empty glasses to the counter before pulling two more from the shelf.

Ethan sits next to me, scooting his chair closer before propping one foot on his knee. He interlaces our fingers over the table, a hint of pride in his expression as he nods toward Ross.

Ross clears his throat, finally lifting his eyes to meet mine. "Vee, I know words aren't enough right now, that I'll need to back them up with my actions. But I want to say I'm sorry for taking advantage of our relationship for so long."

My heart thuds in my chest, eyes bouncing to everyone in the room. Gran places a fresh glass of tea in front of each of us and rests a palm on Ross's shoulder, giving him a squeeze and a pat as she passes him. She finally takes a seat, and Ross continues.

"Ethan has paid off my debts—"

My jaw lowers, and my brows pull together as I glance between Ethan and Ross. My first instinct is to apologize to Ethan for having fallen for Ross's sob story and giving him a reason to get dragged into this mess in the first place. But Ethan made the decision to help Ross on his own, so all I can do is trust him and allow my brother the opportunity to earn back some of my faith in him.

Ethan squeezes my hand before picking up where Ross left off. "I'd like to think of it as more of a loan, since my help includes a few conditions. Ross has agreed to get help for his gambling and also get assessed for dyslexia. He's also going to work for me so he can pay back some of his debt while he gets back on his feet, at least until he decides what he wants to do with his life."

"And 'till I can figure that out," Ross continues with a soft smile toward Ethan, "I'll be staying busy, using my hands, and making an honest living." He clears his throat, his brows creasing as he lifts his eyes back to Ethan. "Thank you, man, for giving me a chance to fix my mess. I dunno where I'd be right now if you hadn't helped me." His fingers sweep under his eyes, and he clears his throat again as he pushes back tears. "You saved my life, Ethan."

Ethan's lips curl into a slight smile as he nods in response. Gran and I join in, our sniffles mingling with the sounds of our watery laughter. I take a moment to really look at the my brother. The tension that once weighed heavily on Ross's soul and casted shadows over his eyes has lifted. Although I know he still has a long journey ahead of him, I feel my own burdens easing and being replaced by a renewed hope in my brother's future.

"All right, enough blubbering," Gran swats with her hand.

"Wait, I have something else for you ladies," Ethan announces, walking to the living room. Gran gasps loudly, her hands covering her mouth when he returns with the music box in his hands. He gently places it on the table in front of her, and a soft "oh" escapes her lips.

Ross and I huddle behind Gran, sharing a smile as she opens the lid, her hands hovering reverently over the delicate flowers and little bird.

She cranks the handle, clapping when the bird begins to sing and flap its wings.

"Thank you," I mouth to Ethan, and he returns a wink and a flash of his incredibly sexy grin. And suddenly, my biggest problem is having a boyfriend I find utterly irresistible. Well, that in addition to the fact that he knows it.

CHAPTER FORTY-SEVEN

ETHAN

"I'm actually kinda sad about saying goodbye to this." Ivy pouts, a paint roller hanging from one hand as we stare at our wall. Painting over our list is the final task before we can officially say we've completed this renovation. It's crazy how quickly I've shifted into 'we' statements and an even bigger miracle that I can say them without Ivy freaking out.

"It'll always be here." I smile, contentment in my voice. I wrap an arm around her, breathing her in. She doesn't wear perfume, yet the scent of *her* has an astounding effect on my brain. I clear my throat before speaking again. "A coat of paint over it doesn't take away its part in our story."

"You're right," she agrees with a sigh and digs her phone out from the pocket of her overalls. Then she steps back to frame the shot before taking a series of photos to document our messages.

Dang. Now I'm gonna miss this thing, too.

But we'll always have the memory of it. There's no point leaving it up, even if we covered it with a mirror or a painting. Once we eventually get married, I'd like Ivy to move into my house and make it *our* home. This place is cute. But it's also very...*cute*, AKA too small for more than two people. However, I haven't mentioned any of this yet, because I'm pretty sure I'm a few steps ahead of Ivy in our relationship and being very careful not to freak her out.

We release a collective sigh, neither of us making a move as we continue staring.

"Ready?"

"Can I use the ladder?" she asks, causing my brows to lower. I've still got PTSD from the last time.

"What for?"

Her eyes move around the room like she's looking for a good enough reason. " 'Cause it's fun?"

"Not for me," I grunt, moving a strand of hair from behind her glasses. "Besides, we've got the rollers with the long attachments. No ladders required."

"Boring."

I grab her around the waist, making her squeal while I dip her back, letting my lips graze the side of her neck. "We could always leave it like this. I'm sure I can think of a few other things we could do with our time..."

She giggles, halfheartedly pushing me away while hooking an arm around my neck. "Tempting...but..." She pauses when I begin to pepper her collar bone with soft kisses. " We've got to finish this last thing. I'll reward you later with kisses...after we're done."

"Counter offer," I begin, straightening to place another kiss on her shoulder. "I get a kiss after we tape the sides, after the first coat, and after the second coat."

Her throat clears before she pushes me away, shaking my hand. "Deal."

"Now, who says painting is boring?"

She responds by sticking her tongue out. "That only makes me wanna kiss you again."

We get to taping the ceiling and walls, and a little over an hour later, Ivy's managed two coats of paint on the wall and I've managed to turn a couple kisses into a makeout session. I wrap up the paint rollers before chucking them into the back of my truck to throw away later. Then I walk back into the house and find Ivy glaring at a corner of the wall with her fists planted on her hips. "We missed a spot," she says without turning around.

"What?" I squint, stepping closer to inspect the spot she's pointing at. "Huh... Look at that. I blame the kisses—they scrambled my brain."

"Ladder?" she asks hopefully, her eyebrows raising with a giant smile.

"Nice try." I grab one of the smaller, unused brushes and dip it into the paint, holding it out to her. "Hop onto my shoulders."

"Do I look like a goat?"

"You're a fox, baby, now get on." I smile, crouching after turning my back toward her.

She steps closer with a grunt. "Nice save. How is this safer than a ladder?"

" 'Cause I've got my hands on you." I grin, standing as she grips my hair.

"Ethan!" she shouts as she wobbles slightly. "Do *not* drop me!"

"Relax. I've got you," I reassure her with a tap on her thigh. "Get 'er done, cupcake."

She stretches and uses the paintbrush to fill in the spot we both somehow missed. "*Now* I get a nickname? Do explain."

"I kinda just want my lips on you all the time... Same as how I want a cupcake all the time."

"Hmmm," she hums, and I can hear the mischief in her voice. "Even when I do this?" She reaches down and paints a dot on my cheek. "And this?" Another splotch on my forehead.

She's got me. I'm so tempted to give her leg a pinch, but we both know my greatest fear is this woman injuring herself, so I'm stuck, my grip on her thighs tightening as she happily brushes a streak of paint down my nose. I walk her to the sofa, and she belts out a terror-filled giggle when I dip to the side, catching her behind the back as she topples from my shoulders.

"You're playing with fire, Ivy June."

"Does that make you the fire?" She arches a brow in question. Now that she's not in danger of falling from my shoulders, I walk us to the nearest wall before lowering her feet to the ground, freeing one arm as the other holds her close.

"Well, I *have* been called hot before, so..."

"Cocky much?" She laughs, swatting my arm, and I use the moment to try to snatch the brush from her hand. I pin her free wrist above her head, and we end up scuffling playfully and spreading paint all over our hands before the brush falls to the floor. I couldn't care less about the time it's going to take to clean this mess, not when Ivy is biting her lip and staring up at me with those half-lidded eyes. I drop her wrist and lift her up against the wall as my free hand tilts her jaw up. Then I press my lips against hers, and it's like finding the missing piece of a puzzle. It all just feels so...*right*.

We finally come up for air many minutes later, and Ivy has paint smeared over her cheeks, down her arms, and across her butt and thighs. She throws her head back, laughing at the handprints plastered over my arms and neck. I suspect I'll find some paint in my hair later, too.

"This stuff doesn't come off easily, does it?" she ventures, wiping at her cheek.

"Nope. Totally worth it, though," I add, wiggling my eyebrows.

I lower her back to the ground, and she turns shining eyes up at me. I catch a tremble in her lips.

"Ethan, thank you for what you did for Ross. It means the world to me."

"Told you, I'm here to be your rock. I'll always have your back."

"Just 'cause you're my rock, doesn't mean you have to be strong all the time, though. You can show me your softer side, too."

"You have all of me, Ivy. And, you've already seen my softer side—every time I have a run-in with a spider. You'll need to be the one dealing with all the eight-legged creatures in this relationship."

"Deal." She nods and walks to the fridge to pull out two glass bottles filled with root beer. She pops the lids off, handing one over as she nudges me onto the sofa, then turns her back to snuggle against my chest.

"It's a good thing we put an old sheet on this couch." I sigh, pulling her close.

She hums, taking a long sip before sobering. "So... I know you've only known me while my life has been in turmoil. And I'm hoping things calm down a little on that front." She pauses, playing with my fingers before inhaling a deep breath. "But things may still be a little chaotic for a while longer. I wanna go back to school... To study O.T."

"I'll one-hundred-percent support you in your endeavor to become an outdoor tickler."

She snorts out a laugh before turning to me with narrowed eyes. "You don't know what O.T. stands for, do you?"

"Pfff, of course I do—ostrich therapist is a noble profession. Some might say, unnecessary? But I'd disagree."

Her lips roll in as she stifles a laugh. "Occupational therapist."

"I've heard it both ways."

"You're ridiculous."

"Maybe, but you love me." I grin against her cheek.

She takes both our bottles, placing them on the floor before pushing my shoulders so I'm forced to lie back on the sofa. Although, technically, my legs are mostly hanging off the edge, because as I said—this place and its furniture are *tiny*. Ivy squeezes in beside me, gripping the front of my shirt as she pulls me closer. "I do love you," she says on an exhale. Her fist tightens again as she yanks me in and presses her mouth to mine. I relax into the kiss, feeling utterly content in her arms, but it isn't long before I'm overcome with the need for more... more of her...more of us. I want more of these moments for the rest of my life, but only with her.

Things continue heating up until we can't get close enough to one another. Just as my brain threatens to relinquish all control, both of our phones begin vibrating on the kitchen counter.

We break apart, our eyes still locked and Ivy's hands resting on my chest as we pant for air.

"We should...probably get that," she says, breathlessly.

"Yup. G—uh...good idea," I stammer. Jeez, this woman scrambles my brain in the best way. She hops off of me, straightening her clothes as I follow her into the kitchen.

"It's Ember," she announces, looking at her phone.

"Colton," I confirm as we both frown before answering. Ivy glances at me while she listens to Ember, then walks to the living room.

"Colt?"

"Eth. You and Ivy busy?"

My frown deepens as I feel my ears heating. I squint into

the living room, trying to make out any silhouetted shapes through the window. I worry for a second that he and Ember have witnessed our hot and heavy make out session. My cheeks lift as my eyes stray to the white handprints on her butt. How caveman is it of me to love the sight of that so much?

"Earth to Ethan..."

"Sorry, nope. Not busy."

"Good." The sounds of cabinets opening and closing sift through the phone. "Pack a bag. Meet us at the airport."

"If you're escaping a felony, they'll find you there."

"You're hilarious. We're eloping."

"What?!" Ivy and I both shout at the same time, our gazes meeting with hanging jaws. Ember must have just dropped the same bomb.

"It's what Ember wants, so it's what I want. The stress was getting to be too much, what with the wedding planning and our mothers having morphed the whole event into something completely different from what we pictured in the first place. And I figure this is an 'easier to ask for forgiveness' sort of thing."

"Wow." My brows raise but I can't help grinning again when I catch Ivy's face lighting up with elation. I know she's dropped a few hints to Ember about being game for an impromptu elopement. "You're sure this is what you wanna do?" I ask my brother.

"I'm sure. Will you be there for us, Eth?"

"Of course, I'm not letting this once-in-a-lifetime opportunity go by. Do you really think I'd give up years worth of getting to make fun of you for letting Elvis officiate your wedding? And being able to remind Mom of it any time I want? This pretty much guarantees me favorite-son status for *at least* five years."

"Except you'll be all but forgotten when we give Mom a grandchild first. So suck it, bro."

My lips roll in as my nose scrunches up. Dang it. I forgot that 'after marriage comes the baby carriage' part, even though I'd technically been thinking about those activities in a different context a few minutes ago. But Colton's right. He'll definitely reclaim the top spot in the family hierarchy once that happens. I should clarify that our mom has no idea we play this game. She'd never actually have a favorite...is what she'd tell Colton if we asked.

"*You* suck it."

"Are you coming or what?"

"*Maaan*, you know we're coming."

"Thanks, bro." He chuckles before giving me the details of our flights. After we hang up, I find myself staring at an exuberant Ivy, clapping her hands and wearing a giant smile on her beautiful face.

"This is gonna be so fun!" she exclaims, bounding over and planting a kiss on my cheek.

"Everything with you is fun, Ivy June."

CHAPTER FORTY-EIGHT

IVY

The whir inside the airplane's cabin creates a cushion of white noise around Ember and me as we huddle together—or at least as much as our business class seats will allow.

"I can't believe people travel like this. Look at all the storage nooks in this thing!" I lift open every flap I can find. It will be hard to return to economy class after this.

"It feels like a waste to use these seats for such a short flight." Ember leans down the aisle to glance at economy class. I snort out a suppressed laugh, because only she would worry about something like that.

"Em, your fiancé wanted to spoil you. Just accept it. Look at him," I nudge her with an elbow. "He'd do anything to make you happy."

She straightens, blushing slightly when Colton winks at her. And then she whips her head around and pouts while her eyes get all Disney-princess big. "Your man seems quite taken, too. Look at that smirk...and those love-sick puppy eyes he's giving *you*? I mean, who is that guy and what have you done with Ethan King?"

I lean forward and stick my tongue out at Ethan before turning my attention back to my friend. "Yeah, he's a total sap. What can I say? Now, back to the plan." I blink dramatically, trying to draw her attention away from the subject of Ethan and me. I love him, but I still get a bit squirmy when talking about our relationship in front of Ember, mostly because I feel guilty for hiding it from her. I stir my plastic cup of root beer with the tiny straw, making the ice clink. "How are we doing this? Do you have a dress?"

"I packed the white sundress I planned to change into for the reception, but I guess now it's getting upgraded to the main event." She wags her eyebrows over the rim of her glass.

"What are those two wearing? Wait," I hold up a palm, rolling my lips in. "Don't tell me. They own their own tuxes, don't they?"

"See, you're already fitting into this family so well." Ember smiles in return. "You're really happy with him," she says matter of factly, her eyes softening as her hand squeezes mine. "Have you told your parents?"

I inhale deeply when I remember I need to update them. I've been avoiding a conversation with them, mostly because Ross's name would eventually come up at some point. And even though he finally seems to be making better choices, I'm not sure I'm prepared for my defense of him to fall on deaf ears. Not to mention, I'm still a bit resentful. There are also so many questions I have about our dyslexia, like how a doctor and his wife could remain in denial of their own children's struggles while going out of their way to help others.

It's tough admitting that I feel let down by them, even though I have a better understanding of why they tried to set boundaries with Ross. But how could they miss such a huge deficit? Why couldn't they tell we needed help? Just thinking about it is so upsetting that I've put off having any sort of conversation with them besides the usual surface-level texts. It's always been easier to pretend I'm just peachy and allow them to assume my life is drama-free. But I'm learning that my needs are important, and I have the right to demand those answers from them. It's past time I brought this up.

I blink away my thoughts, looking up at Ember. "They're supposed to be back in Texas next week. I'll introduce them to Ethan then." I smirk. "What will you tell *your* parents when you return home as Mrs. Ember King?"

"Wow. That sounds so nice," she gushes. "I dunno. I'll figure that out tomorrow. Right now, this is what we want. If I have to endure one more of my mother's opinions on bouquets, I'm afraid I'll throw one at her."

"How very unladylike of you," I tease, sticking my pinky out with another sip.

"She'd love that," Ember says with a laugh.

"Excuse me ladies," Ethan announces, his face sporting a sheepish grin as he nods at Ember. "My brother has informed me that he's sick of looking at my face and would prefer to see yours, Flames."

"Or maybe you just wanna make out with your girlfriend." Ember smirks as she lifts herself out of her seat.

He slides into the empty space beside me, his delicious scent washing over me in an instant. "Always," he rasps, flashing a wink and his most devilish grin.

Contrary to Ember's accusation, we actually spend the rest of our short flight Googling things to do tomorrow. Colton and Ember will spend one more night in Vegas before flying home, but Ethan and I will have a good few hours to kill before catching our return flight tomorrow afternoon.

By the time we make it through the airport and to the hotel, it's already seven o'clock.

"You ladies have a room to yourselves. Eth and I will get

ready next door." Colton smiles after tapping a key card to our door and walking in. He does a quick survey of the room before placing a kiss on Ember's lips. "Pick you up in forty-five minutes?"

"I'll be waiting." She beams, radiating the gooey kind of love that makes your eyes constantly misty from all the undiluted happiness.

Once the guys leave, I tell Ember she can have first dibs on the shower. I plop myself onto the end of the bed, staring blankly at the phone in my hands. I inhale, feeling a tightness in my chest as I navigate to my mom's contact. My eyes pinch closed as I press call.

"Hi, sweetheart!"

"Hey, Mom. How are you and Dad? Are you on your way home?"

"We're tired, but ready to be home. We're in Dubai. Our flight leaves in a few hours, but... Oh, Ivy, this trip was phenomenal! I can't wait to come back here. I could eat this food every day. So many cultures merged together. It's the most beautifully diverse community," she rambles.

"That sounds amazing." I smile, happy to hear the joy in her voice.

"How's the house coming along? The photos look stunning. I'm so impressed with what you've done."

"Thanks. It's actually all finished, thanks to some help. Ember's soon-to-be brother-in-law, Ethan, is a contractor, and we've been working together..." Now I'm the one rambling as I spew out little updates while trying not to blurt out the fact that said contractor is also my boyfriend. "He's actually given Ross a job, too..." I add, feeling my heart drumming in my chest. This is my segue into that taboo topic that usually gets shut down within seconds.

"Oh, honey..."

My stomach dips at the sympathy coating her words. Like she pities me for falling for another one of Ross's empty promises.

"Mom, just listen, okay. I know Ross has let you guys down...a lot. But I promise, he's actually taking responsibility this time. He's open to getting help..."

"Ivy...he does this—"

"No. He *did* this. *We* did this, trying to deal with something we weren't equipped to deal with on our own."

"What are you talking about, sweetheart?"

"Mom...did you know that Ross and I have dyslexia?" I'm staring across the room as a thundering tightness hammers in my chest. This is the most confrontational I've ever been with her. It feels like kicking up dust and not knowing what I'll find when it settles. I'm just waiting to see whether she'll lump me in with Ross and label me the same way they did him for so many years or if she's finally willing to look at things a little differently and take up some of this responsibility.

There's a pause before her whispered reply comes through. "What?"

I go on to explain my coping mechanisms and how I hid it growing up, trying my best to help her see how Ross's behavior was related to his low self-esteem and his struggles with school. She asks questions every now and again, and by the end I can hear the sniffle in her voice.

"Ivy. I...I don't know what to say. We knew Ross had some behavioral issues...but we never suspected it was because of a learning difficulty. I don't know how we missed something like this...I'm just—I'm so sorry."

"It's okay," I croak. "But will you please give Ross a chance? He's really trying."

"Yes. Of course, honey. I'll...we'll call him when we land. I need to fill your Dad in on all of this. I love you, sweetheart."

"I love you, too, Mom."

I hung up with my heart beating wildly in my chest. We still have a few more difficult conversations before we can process this as a family, but it feels like crawling out of the end of a long tunnel. Now I just need to break the news about having a boyfriend, and we're all set. Right?

Ember finishes in the shower and I gather my things to take my turn getting ready. I walk out of the bathroom, pulling up short, my breath hitching at the sight of my best friend in her timelessly chic little white dress. The classic silhouette suits her perfectly, and the sleek boat neck is balanced with a playful A-line skirt. Plus, she's absolutely glowing.

My hands fly up to my face as I simper and fan my eyes with my hands so my makeup doesn't run. "Em..." I sniffle, taking her in. She turns to me as she fastens an earring, pouting when she sees my watery eyes.

"None of that, missy. Save the crying for after the photos. Seriously, Vee...stop, or I'll cry, too. Ooh! Look!" She straightens, shoving her hands into the hidden pockets in the dress.

"Of course it has pockets," I croak over a huge grin, already walking toward her. "I'm so happy for you," I manage to get out after wrapping her up in a tight hug.

"Likewise. You know this makes us sisters, soon."

"Pshhh, stop. That's a long way off. I doubt Ethan will be ready to tie the knot any time soon, if ever." I wave my hand dismissively before taking a seat at the vanity table.

"I dunno..." Ember sings while stepping into her white heels. "He looks pretty ready to me."

"Okay, that's enough of that," I reply with an eye roll. The man's barely over his two-date rule. Not to mention, I don't want to jinx our future by focusing too far ahead. He hasn't even met my parents, for goodness sake!

One step at a time.

I shake off those thoughts as I apply soft makeup to match the dusty pink color of my wrap-front mini-dress. I straighten my hair, adding one of my favorite bows in the back. When I stand and strap on my heels—yes, I still like to wear them when the occasion calls for it—a knock at the door has Ember and I releasing simultaneous breaths.

"Ready?" I ask, holding my hand out as I stand beside her.

"Yup." She winks. *"Let's go girls..."*

CHAPTER FORTY-NINE

ETHAN

"It says here you were supposed to fill out a pre-application." I turn to Colton. "Did you do that?"

"Are *you* seriously asking *me* if I've done the admin part of getting married?" He snorts.

I roll my eyes. "Just doing my best-man duties."

"Yes, I filled out the form. But even if I hadn't, it's a quick online application. The Marriage License Bureau just wants as much of the info ahead of time as possible to make things go quicker."

"Then why are we here?" I grimace.

"Eth, can't you give me a whitty pep talk or something? What's with all the questions? We're here to pick up the actual marriage license before going to the chapel."

"Right." I nod, pursing my lips as my eyes scan the halls. A rogue idea has been creeping in and stealing my attention all afternoon. And I just need to know if it's even viable.

It's too soon. Focus on your duty. You're the best man. Do something best-manish.

I don't even know what my best-man duties are, anyway.

Do I need to prepare a toast? That would be weird with just four of us, right? Colton and I stand in the small foyer inside the Clark County Marriage License Bureau, waiting for Ember and Ivy to return from the ladies' room. They'd made a dash over to powder their noses as soon as we'd arrived.

Colton paces before he pivots and abruptly shifts my way. "Did Ember seem okay when we got here?"

"You're asking *me* if *your* fiancée seemed okay?"

"Fine. Nevermind."

"What's going on?"

"Nothing. It's just...she got a text in the car and seemed a little quiet after that. Then there was the rushing off to the restrooms..." He gestures in the direction in which our dearly beloveds disappeared to.

Dearly beloved? We only have two of those here, and that's Ember and Colton.

Unless...

The restroom doors swing open, and a watery-eyed Ember emerges while Ivy and her furrowed brow follow close behind. Colton bolts forward, glaring behind Ember, probably looking for someone to punch for upsetting his fiancée. "Hey, what happened?"

Ember sniffs and begins chewing on her top lip before she finally raises her eyes to Colton's. She steps into his arms, and they have some sort of silent exchange in which something important dawns on Colton. I watch as he relaxes his jaw and his expression softens. "You want our family with us," he says knowingly.

"I do," Ember admits with a wobbly chin. "I thought this was what I wanted. But then your mom texted about these adorable flowers she found for the centerpieces, and the guilt hit me like a ton of bricks. She's so excited. And so is my mom. I can't do this without them or Opal and Gail... I'm so sor—"

"Hey, Em, it's okay. If that's what you want—then that's what we'll do."

"But what do *you* want?" She sniffs into the tissue Ivy hands her.

Colton smiles and brings his hands up to cup Ember's face. "I want to make you happy," he whispers, and Ivy sidles up beside me, hooking her pinky around mine. She looks so beautiful in her dress, and I remind myself to tell her so again later.

Colton leans down to plant a kiss on Ember's lips, then he turns to us, still looking insanely happy. "Might as well make this trip count. Where's the best place to have dinner?"

Colton and Ember link arms and begin walking toward the exit, but my heart is suddenly on board with a certain rogue idea that's been swimming around in my head that my feet have become sluggish.

I glance down at Ivy, and she looks deep in thought, her steps slowing.

Man up and just ask her!

I drop my eyes to my feet, willing them forward again. This is crazy, right? It's too soon. She'll never agree to it. It'll freak her out.... I'll scare her away.

By the time I look up again, Ivy's stopped moving, and Ember and Colton have turned to look at us questioningly. Ivy's brows crease as her eyes fall to my wrist. She glances at me for a brief second before returning her gaze to my arm, reaching out to lift the sleeve over my left wrist. Her small smile grows into an ear-splitting grin as her thumb grazes the ribbon tied around my wrist. "You still have this..."

"Yup." I swallow.

Do it.

Okay. If she thinks I'm crazy, we'll laugh it off. But I'm going for it.

Ember is waving us over and smiling at us, probably

wondering why we've stopped. I take a deep, fortifying breath, and just as I open my mouth to blurt out my question, Ivy beats me to it.

"Ethan, let's get married!"

My jaw hangs open as I stare at the beautiful lips that just stole the words right out of my own mouth. Her eyes bounce between mine, and my face breaks out into an ear-to-ear smile.

"I know it seems soon," she continues as Ember and Colton take tentative steps closer, "but I love you, Ethan King. And I kinda wanna spend forever together." She pauses again, nudging her glasses up. "Don't freak out," she adds quietly.

I grab her hand in mine before I answer her. "Ivy June Marsh, since the minute I laid eyes on you, you've been driving me wild. You're like springtime, a burst of life wherever you go. Maybe we haven't been together for long, but I already know that *you* are my greatest adventure. And I kinda wanna spend forever with you, too." Her eyes begin to water as I continue staring at her. "I can't promise to make an earth-shattering entrance into every room, but I can promise to spend my life loving you and to never stop trying to sweep you off your feet for the rest of our lives." I step back to get down on one knee. Because if I'm going to have to retell this story to my mama, she's going to whack me in the back of my head if she hears I didn't kneel before asking Ivy to be my wife. I clear the emotion from my throat before I go on. "Ivy, will you marry me, right now?"

"This doesn't get you out of a few decades of stories about how *I* proposed to *you*."

"Will you just say yes and kiss me, already, woman!"

"Rule number three." She smirks, folding her arms.

"Ivy..."

"Yes! Of course I'll marry you," she says before bursting out in laughter. I stand and catch her around the waist, kissing her deeply. When I lower her to the ground, I take hold of her hand and she does a full spin, making her dress and her hair ribbon flare out with her three-sixty twirl. I pull her close, curling my hands around her.

"Rosie Cotton dancing.... She had ribbons in her hair," I say, pausing in awe of her beauty and strength. "If ever I were to marry someone, it would have been her."

"More Samwise quotes, King? You do know how to woo a girl."

"Maybe I'll start calling you Rosie," I mumble through my grin, nuzzling my nose against her neck and making her giggle.

When we finally pull apart, Ember and Colton begin to holler as the four of us garner a small applause from the handful of others in the room.

"You're not worried about Mom?" Colton questions.

"Nah. She'll forgive me. I'm the favorite, remember?"

Colton barks out a laugh. "You sure about that?"

"If she gets upset, I'll just make it up to her the same way you mentioned before on the plane," I tell him, winking at Ivy and making my brother chuckle loudly.

We get through the paperwork, and an hour later, Ivy and I are standing in front of Elvis and professing our love for one another, and then he pronounces us husband and wife.

I have a wife.

Out of all the risky ventures I've ever embarked upon, in all the exciting excursions I've taken, every challenge I've faced, nothing has ever scared me more or made me as unfathomably happy as the woman in my arms. Getting to love her and watch her become the beautiful force of nature that she is, all while cheering her on and supporting her—it's the greatest privilege of my existence, loving Ivy King.

EPILOGUE
IVY

Hot Jean-Claude Van Damme, my husband is fine. I've got quite a lovely view from my perch on the front-porch swing. Ethan has his hat turned backward as he packs his tools into his truck. The man sure can rock a tool belt.

After we got back from Vegas and broke the news to our families, who were incredibly happy for us, we spent two days hibernating before the real world called us back. With the school year still going and Ethan's job, we can't take a honeymoon just yet. But I'm so grateful for Ethan's parents' response to the news of our elopement. I think on some level they expected something like this from him. Not that he ever took risks in relationships before, but he's always been pretty spontaneous. I'm just so glad he picked me to test his courage in the long-term relationships department. I truly lucked out. We didn't say a word about the original plan being for Ember and Colton to tie the knot. I think that might have broken Jeanie's heart. In the end, Ember made the right decision. Her wedding is just another opportunity for her to practice her communication skills and setting boundaries with her mom, and she gets the big, family wedding she really wanted. And Colton gets a happy wife and a mother who won't disown him. My parents took a bit more convincing when we broke the news to them over a Facetime call. But I opened with telling them how Ethan has helped Ross, so it set him up well, and I know they'll grow to trust him more over time as they see how he loves me.

Ethan does his usual stomping up the steps, catching me staring at the ring that glitters obscenely on my finger. We bought them just before heading to the chapel in Vegas. The pink morganite stone is framed by a tiny row of diamonds on a yellow gold band. When we walked into the jewelry store, I told Ethan I wanted him to pick the ring for me. It only took him two minutes of perusing before he pointed to this beauty.

"Got something for you," he announces as he sits beside me, pulling my legs over his lap.

"Wh—what? Why? I didn't get you anything. Is this a married people tradition I've screwed up?"

He throws his head back, cackling at my expense. This man. "Relax, Mrs. King. It's a just-because gift."

"Oh."

"I plan to shower you with plenty more of these, too. But I never want this to turn into a competition or for us to start keeping score. I love you, and I want to show it in every possible way, for the rest of our lives. You don't have to earn my love. I've chosen you, and I'll keep choosing you every day."

My heart is a puddle while an even soppier pool forms in my eyes. How is he real? And how has he chosen *me*? For as much growth as I've had when it comes to my own self-worth, it still amazes me that this book-loving, sexy-as-fudge man wants to love me for the rest of our lives.

"I don't know what to say to that." I gulp. I'm a newlywed, okay, and my husband still makes me weak in the knees. And I think he will until we're both old and wrinkly and have no filters like Opal and Gail.

"You don't have to say anything. But I'll take a kiss." He lifts one side of his mouth in that cocky way that once drove me nuts when we first met. Except now it drives me wild in a different way...although, now that I think about it, it probably drove me wild for the same reason, but now I'm choosing to embrace the fact that his smirk makes me want to kiss him.

Yup, definitely not mad about that anymore, I think as I lean forward with my own smug little smile, only too happy to oblige.

Our kiss heats up quickly, and if we weren't currently on the front porch giving the neighbors a show they hadn't bought tickets to see, it might have progressed to another level. But thankfully, Ethan has the presence of mind to calm things down before we make any old ladies faint or clutch their pearls. When I reluctantly pull back, he's holding a small, flat box in his hand.

"What is this?" I ask as he places the box in my palm.

"Open it," he grins.

The little box snaps open, revealing a delicate gold chain attached to the sides of a small, diamond-studded wreath. The elegance of its simple design is enhanced by the tiny light that shines on it from the roof of the box.

"Eth..." My voice comes out breathy as I stare at the necklace in awe. "It's so beautiful."

"In ancient Greece, newlyweds wore ivy wreaths to show their loyalty and devotion to one another." He says as his eyes sweep over my face, a gentle smile on his lips.

My mouth splits into an elated grin at the information. "I love it! Will you fasten it?" I hand him the box, turning to lift my hair out of the way. He removes the necklace and drapes it in front of me before fastening the clasp, and then I feel a gentle kiss being pressed right below my hairline, sending a shiver down to my toes. I'm so glad this man is my husband.

"Where's your wreath? If newlyweds both wore them, shouldn't you have one, too?" I ask, dropping my hair and turning around to find a heated look smoldering in Ethan's eyes.

"Well...that scratch I told you I got yesterday when Marco and I were moving your things...It's not really a scratch." He grins cheekily as he begins to lift the bandage on the inside of his forearm.

"Oh, " I gasp, covering my mouth with my hands. My eyes bounce back and forth between his arm and his stormy gray eyes. On the area between his wrist and the crease of his elbow is the most beautiful ivy vine tattoo. It's simple and masculine, and I can't believe this man got a tattoo because of *me*. "okay, that is ridiculously cool," I sigh, grabbing his shirt to pull him closer for another brain-fogging kiss.

Before Ethan came into my life, I never thought I'd find someone who could love me through all my chaos and mess. But the real difference now is that I've learned to love myself, and now I know I'm worthy of being loved so wildly and freely. The adventure I once feared would take him away from me has only brought us closer, because he's chosen me to share his adventures with—and I've realized I quite like the idea of being spontaneous and adventurous with Ethan.

THE END

ACKNOWLEDGMENTS

Katie—Ethan and Ivy wouldn't be who they are without you. Thank you for diving deep into their minds, for all the brainstorming, alpha reading, and countless hours of editing. I love you and am so grateful for your friendship.

Lisa, Libby, and Louise—you make me feel so celebrated. Thank you for loving me and cheering on every milestone in this writing journey. I love you all!

India, Stef, M.J, Grayson, and Jessee—thank you for being my safe space every week. You're the best writing group a girl could ask for.

Dean, thank you for always supporting me in everything I do. I love you so much!

ALSO BY CINDY RAS

Change Of Plans

ABOUT THE AUTHOR

Cindy Ras is a South African living in Northern California with her husband and three sons. She's survived motherhood without any caffeine and much prefers a good cup of tea. This is Cindy's second and she plans to write more when she isn't homeschooling her kids or drawing covers for other amazing authors. You can connect with her on Instagram @cindyras_author or check out her cover art @cindyras_draws

Thank you for reading and reviewing! Reviews are incredibly helpful to indie authors and yours would be very much appreciated.

Made in United States
Troutdale, OR
04/29/2025